"Don't look at me like that."

Grace's soft demand didn't hold any kind of conviction, even to her own ears. Cade hadn't touched her and yet she tingled from her toes up, her towel chafing her.

"Look at you like what, Gracie? Like you've been *it* for me since the second you walked into my life? Why? So you can keep denying the truth? We're good together. Always have been and always will be."

He wasn't wrong, and, God help her, she didn't want to deny it either. Right then, her next breath wasn't as important as kissing him. She leaned closer, sliding her hand into his hair.

Cade stopped her. "I told you before, I want—"

"*Yes.*"

Holding Fire

"Passionate chemistry and nonstop drama drive Hunt's second book in the adrenaline-charged Alpha Security series."

—*Publishers Weekly*

"4 stars! The suspense is ever-present...and the heat between the hero and heroine is intense."

—*RT Book Reviews*

"April Hunt has me hooked!"

—HerdingCats-BurningSoup.com

"April Hunt has quickly become one of my one-click authors. Her daring heroes are so damn charming. And with sassy, take-charge women by their sides, it makes for one hell of a ride."

—NallaReads.com

Heated Pursuit

"Smartly balances slow-burning passion and explosive high-stakes danger. This book kicks off an adventure-packed romance series, and readers will eagerly anticipate the next installment."

—*Publishers Weekly*

"4 stars! Fast paced and intriguing."

—*RT Book Reviews*

"Fun and sexy."

—SmexyBooks.com

LETHAL
REDEMPTION

ALSO BY APRIL HUNT

Heated Pursuit

Holding Fire

Hard Justice

Hot Target (novella)

Deadly Obsession

LETHAL REDEMPTION

APRIL HUNT

FOREVER
New York Boston

Forever
Hachette Book Group
1290 Avenue of the Americas, New York, NY 10104
read-forever.com
twitter.com/readforeverpub

First Edition: April 2019

Forever is an imprint of Grand Central Publishing. The Forever name and logo are trademarks of Hachette Book Group, Inc.

The publisher is not responsible for websites (or their content) that are not owned by the publisher.

The Hachette Speakers Bureau provides a wide range of authors for speaking events. To find out more, go to www.hachettespeakersbureau.com or call (866) 376-6591.

ISBNs: 978-1-5387-6338-4 (mass market), 978-1-5387-6336-0 (ebook)

Printed in the United States of America

OPM

10 9 8 7 6 5 4 3 2 1

To my second mom and dad...
"Love recognizes no barriers. It jumps
hurdles, leaps fences, penetrates walls to
arrive at its destination full of hope."

—Maya Angelou

ACKNOWLEDGMENTS

They say it takes a village to raise a child, and the same could be said for writing a book. None of this could be possible without my family. A and N, you guys keep me humble and make me laugh when I need it most, and M, your encouragement means everything. To my mom, who always told me that I could do anything I put my mind to, THANK YOU! I'm the person I am today because of you. And to my second mom and dad—one of these days I'm going to buy the both of you pom-poms, because your cheerleading has kept me going on more than one occasion.

Sarah E. Younger...mentioning you in acknowledgments doesn't begin to express how thankful I am to have you in my corner. I truly did win the agent jackpot with you, and I wear my #TeamSarah pin proudly.

Madeleine Colavita...THANK YOU for helping me bring my stories to the page and making them more than I could've possibly done on my own. P.S.: Don't be surprised if I name a future heroine after you...And to everyone at Forever, it's been such a pleasure to bring every book into the world with your team standing at my side. THANK YOU.

And to my #GirlsWriteNight crew—Tif Marcelo, Rachel Lacey, Annie Rains, and Sidney Halston. You are the four best sounding boards a girl could ask for, and I ask myself every day how I hit the lottery being able to call you friends.

And to my readers—I'm so appreciative of each and every one of you. I'm able to do what I love *because of you*. THANK YOU!

CHAPTER ONE

From the back seat of her Lyft, FBI profiler Grace Steele eyed the old Kline Textile factory. It was one of the many abandoned riverside structures she saw daily during her New York City commute, and had never once given the building a second thought.

She gave it that second thought now. And a third. And as trash skidded across the potholed utility road like urban tumbleweed, she gave it a fourth.

Windows not boarded up gaped open, their glass long since fallen victim to a game of handball or a good rock toss, and less than six feet away, the only somewhat-working streetlamp flickered ominously. It was as if the horror movie she'd watched last week had come to life.

"You sure about this, lady?" Her Lyft driver pulled the car to a slow stop. "My ma always claimed I couldn't spot a bad idea if it stared me dead in the eye, but I can see that isn't a place you should walk in daylight, much less after the sun goes down. I can take you back—no charge."

Grace read her boss's text message for the third time in as many minutes: *321 Pier Six. Nine o'clock. Be there.*

Correct address. Correct time. And loaded with an

invisible warning that to defy the FBI director would mean severe consequences. Disobeying orders had never been so tempting—except when Aunt Cindy forbade Grace from buying a prom dress she considered "light-years too short."

Thwarting Aunt Cindy had gotten her a month on laundry duty, which was no small punishment living with four overgrown male cousins. But disregarding Director Vance would get her fired.

She was already on her boss's shit list and couldn't afford a second ding. Not that the first one was her fault. If given a do-over, she'd still tell her former regional supervisor where he could stuff his sexist comments. Except, maybe, with more explicit detail.

But Grace's notorious Steele temper flare-up last month was the reason she couldn't disobey orders now. Karma had a wicked sense of humor.

"Thanks for the offer, but I'll be fine. I already put in a request for a ride back." She tucked her phone into her back pocket as she climbed out of the car.

"It's your life, lady. Hope I don't see you on the morning news."

Grace did too.

If it wasn't December, and if the text hadn't come from Vance herself, she'd think this was an April Fool's prank hatched by one of her colleagues—maybe Toby for the wasabi toast incident.

But the director didn't joke, or smile, or make second requests, which meant Grace had ten minutes to get her ass inside.

She tugged her coat collar up to protect her from the

chill wind whipping in from the Hudson and headed to the rusted iron door. She kept her head on a swivel and surveyed her surroundings, something she'd done even before entering the FBI, thanks to her four military-trained cousins.

This far down the river, there were no tourists soaking in the sights, and any dockworkers who frequented the place during the day were long gone, their statuesque cranes sitting unused.

But Grace wasn't alone.

She'd sensed the telltale shiver slide down her spine the second she'd stepped out of the car. It was the same one a woman felt while being eye-fucked on a nightclub dance floor or when the creepy man from the produce section miraculously appeared in front of the milk, then again by the bakery, and ended up behind you at checkout.

Every woman everywhere knew how to pinpoint The Source, and Grace wasn't any different. Beneath her jacket, Magdalena's weight warmed her right side, her trusted Magnum .22-caliber handgun reminding her in its own way that it had her back.

One man—no, two—stood on different sides of the factory's front door. She came to a stop six feet away and unzipped her coat to give them ample time to identify themselves.

"I'm going to throw out a warning because I'm feeling magnanimous tonight. I *really* hate being cold. It's a fact. I'm a perpetual bitch from the months of December to March—give or take an early spring. Just in case you lost track of time, it's December and we're supposedly in the crosshairs of an arctic blast. Do with that information what you want." Grace paused and waited for acknowledgment.

The one on the left stepped forward, leaving his partner in position.

Clean-shaven with close-cropped hair and a fit, lean physique, the man couldn't have been much older than she was. Maybe early thirties. His long, confident stride and the cocky glint in his eyes gave him away as law enforcement. "Special Agent Steele. It's good to see your reputation wasn't exaggerated."

"You'll have to excuse me for not returning that sentiment—at least until you tell me who you are." Grace's eyes flickered to the pin attached to his suit's left lapel, and she swallowed a curse.

"Agent Jake Corelli, ma'am. Secret Service." He flashed a set of credentials. "Are you carrying a weapon?"

"Yeah, I have my service weapon, like I do any time I'm called to the field."

"You'll need to relinquish it to me before you go inside." Corelli held out his hand expectantly.

Grace laughed . . . and realized she was the only one. "Oh, wait. You're serious? Yeah, sorry, but that's not happening."

"Sorry, ma'am, but it is."

Again with the ma'am *crap.*

Releasing a heavy sigh, she carefully reached beneath her jacket and handed over Magdalena. "Only God can help you if something happens to her. You hear me?"

The Secret Service agent's lips twitched. "Loud and

clear, ma'am. I'll take good care of her while she's in my custody."

"You better. And while you're at it, you can stop the *ma'am*."

"Noted...*Special Agent Steele*." He smirked, the move showcasing an impressive set of dimples.

Once upon a time, the handsome, self-assured type had been her catnip. Oh, it was fun at first. Exciting. But reality always rushed back, and it usually did so with a harsh metaphorical smack on the face. Or the ass. Thankfully, Grace learned early on that the only way to ensure a happily-ever-after was to make it yourself.

Knights on white steeds need not apply.

Agent Corelli tapped the communication device hooked around his left ear. "Special Agent Steele has arrived and is on her way inside."

The door behind him opened with a heavy *thunk*.

"And where exactly am I going once I'm inside?" Grace asked.

"You'll see."

"Oh goodie. I love surprises that lurk in dark warehouses," Grace muttered, her sarcasm earning her a small chuckle from the agent.

Truth was that she hated surprises with a passion, nearly as much as cliffhangers in books. Unanswered *anything* practically gave her hives, which was one reason why profiling suited her perfectly...and why her boss's severely-lacking-in-details text was driving her up the wall.

She gave Magdalena one last, longing look and

stepped through the doorway, where she was instantly greeted by two more Secret Service agents, one of whom had traded her own weapon in for a metal detector baton.

"Arms and legs out, ma'am."

Grace bit her tongue at being called ma'am *again* and waited as the agent ran the baton over her body. Once satisfied, she nodded to her cohort. "All clear."

"You can go inside." The second agent opened the next set of double doors, and Grace stepped into the large, and obviously unused, old factory.

When Kline Textiles had declared bankruptcy a million years ago, they hadn't bothered taking all their belongings. Stacked three high, old, mildewed boxes took up the far left corner, and on Grace's right, at least a dozen cobwebbed sewing machines had been lined up in two rows. The place was an industrial wasteland, but she didn't spare any of it a second glance, because her gaze locked on the lone table in the center of the room...and the man standing next to it.

Grace's earlier curiosity weighted her stomach to her feet.

Pierce Brandt.

Vice president of the United States.

Deemed too pretty for government work while on the campaign trail, the former Army General sported a full head of salt-and-pepper hair and broad shoulders. Both his smile and his youthful appearance had been media fodder before he'd taken office, but neither was in the room with them.

Dark circles framed his once brilliant green eyes,

and his well-known smile had been replaced by a tight-lipped grimace. This Brandt looked a far cry and a few decades away from the man on the news who effortlessly charmed foreign dignitaries.

This *so* wasn't her typical office appointment with an FBI colleague or a direct superior. Agents at her level did *not* get private audiences with the second most powerful person in the country.

It made her all the more wary.

"Special Agent Grace Steele. Finally, we meet." He held out a hand in greeting. "I've heard many great things about you from Director Vance, and I can see that my presence is a shock, which means the director didn't tell you about this meeting."

"Not a thing, sir."

"Good. I'm sorry for all the secrecy, but it was a necessary evil. This conversation needs to remain private."

Grace barely withheld a snort. "Because the White House isn't secure, sir?"

He chuckled at her sarcasm. "Secure? Most definitely. Private? No. I've asked you here as a personal favor because, for a litany of reasons, I can't involve local law enforcement or federal resources."

And the surprises keep coming.

Secret meetings and personal favors didn't ease Grace's mind one bit. Nothing good ever came from them, especially when they involved politicians.

She chose her words carefully so as not to offend him. "You do realize that I'm a *federal* agent, right?"

He smiled, but the act never reached his eyes. "I know many things about you, Special Agent Steele. I know that you graduated at the top of your class at Quantico. I know that you could've written your own ticket to any high-valued branch of the Bureau you wanted, and yet you chose criminal profiling."

Grace shrugged. "I've never been a glory seeker. I'm more than happy to work behind the scenes and let others get their time in the spotlight."

Brandt leaned against the table, crossing his arms over his chest. "And from what I understand, you also work well with a team."

Grace's internal warning light blinked to life.

Criminal profiling was a solitary job. She dissected people—*psychologically*. She picked away at their thought processes, examined their motives, what made them tick, and why they did the things they did, with the hope of stopping them before they did it again.

Though trained like any field agent, most of her time was spent behind a desk or across an interview table...which made her even more suspicious about the vice president's comment.

There was only one time in her eight years of service that she'd worked with a *team*.

"Sir," Grace treaded carefully, "I don't mean any disrespect, but this cloak-and-dagger business isn't my thing. Director Vance summoned me down here in the middle of the night for a reason, and I'd really like to know what that reason is."

"I like your no-nonsense attitude, Special Agent Steele. And you're right. You were asked here because I've hired Steele Ops to help me deal with my personal matter."

And there it was.

Steele Ops. Her four overgrown cousins who'd made laundry punishment hell on earth.

"I believe that you worked with the private security firm in the recent past."

"I was actually consulting with the DCPD on the Beltway Cupid Killer case, but you didn't ask me here about the BCK. Are you looking for a personal recommendation? I may be a bit biased, but you're in good hands with my cousins. Failure isn't in their vocabulary."

"Which is exactly why I hired them... and why Steele Ops has requested the use of your expertise." Pierce Brandt's gaze slid over her left shoulder. "Isn't that correct, Mr. Wright?"

Grace froze.

Wright.

A common name. Thousands of people had it in New York alone, but only one possessed the power to raise her body temperature a good few hundred degrees. Right now, she was dangerously close to finding out how hot a human had to be before bursting into flames.

It didn't make sense. This was New York, not DC, where her cousins had been deep in the throes of wooing *him* into the family business.

Steeling her spine, Grace turned and came face-to-face with the last man on which she ever wanted to lay eyes—or anything except a strong right hook.

Cade Wright leaned against the far wall, looking better than he had any right to in worn blue jeans and a long-sleeved Henley. The shirt molded to his upper body and didn't leave much to the imagination as to what was under it—a rock-hard chest and eight pairs of abs, the last time she'd counted.

Grace forced her gaze off his body and up to his eyes.

Big freakin' mistake. More times than she could count, those cobalt-blue eyes had been her undoing. Lord knew they'd been a key factor in gifting him her virginity a million years ago. And when she'd been in DC for the Cupid Killer case, those eyes—and an ample amount of Jack Daniel's—were directly responsible for her sexual relapse.

Grace fisted her hands at her side, barely resisting the urge to throw the nearest object at his overinflated head. Probably a good thing, since that thing happened to be the vice president. "What the hell are you doing here?"

"It's good to see you too, Grace." Cade smirked, the move showcasing the old scar on his chin. His few days' worth of dark blond stubble nearly covered it, but she knew it was there.

She'd been the one to give it to him during her one and only motorcycle lesson.

Not a day went by that she didn't wonder how her sweet best friend, Zoey, shared an entire gene pool with the cocky ass. Cade Wright made her cousins seem humble, and that was saying a lot, since each of their pictures could have been published in a visual dictionary under the term *smug*.

Granted they had the right.

Roman's Special Forces career wasn't exactly spent behind a desk. No one knew what he actually did in SF, but considering his perpetual grumpiness, it wasn't hunting for leprechauns at the end of rainbow. And Ryder and Liam, a Marine and a Navy intelligence officer, saw more action than a movie director. Cade, like her oldest cousin, Knox, had spent his service years in the 75th Ranger Regiment—high demand, high stakes, and high bragging rights.

Cade Wright and all of her cousins were heroes without the glittery capes and skin-hugging tights.

Grace ripped her gaze away from her ex and turned to Brandt. "I'm sorry, sir, but I'm going to have to politely decline Steele Ops's *request*. I can't help you."

Brandt's eyebrows rose into his hairline. "I haven't even told you what the job entails."

"You obviously need a criminal profiler, right? I'll happily give you the names of a few colleagues who would do a fantastic job."

"I'm afraid you don't understand. *Your* name is the one that's been recommended—not only by Steele Ops, but by the director herself." The vice president's tone didn't leave room for debate. "I'm not taking any chances with my daughter's life, Special Agent Steele."

Grace didn't read social magazines, and when the news programs ventured into gossip territory, she turned them off. But she would have heard about a threat against the politician's daughter. "Isn't your daughter studying art abroad? In Europe?"

"That's the public excuse we gave to explain her absence."

"Absence? If she's not in DC and she's not in Europe, then where is she?"

"With a group I believe that you're familiar with."

Brandt squared his shoulders and looked her dead in the eye. "The Order of the New Dawn."

Grace's blood froze.

Making a living diving into the disturbed minds of criminals, her shock factor was practically zilch. But that name. *That group.*

No wonder the vice president wanted her working alongside Steele Ops. No one knew the OND like she did, but she hadn't studied them at Quantico or used them as her dissertation topic.

Grace knew the organization intimately because from the age of five to thirteen, Grace Steele had been considered a Child of the New Dawn.

She'd spent most of her childhood in a cult.

* * *

No matter how badly Cade wanted to intervene, he couldn't for two reasons—and they stood less than six feet away in an epic stare-down. They were both confident, both stubborn. Brandt, a former Army General, had been trained never to retreat, and yet if Cade had to bet money on who the winner would be, he'd choose Grace.

Hands down.

Grace was a Steele, through and through, and like her cousins—his best friends—no one could talk her into something she didn't want to do. And there wasn't a doubt in his mind that she didn't want to do this.

It was why he'd been volunteered to represent Steele Ops at this meeting. Grace already hated him, and his presence kept her cousins in her somewhat amiable good graces.

She straightened her spine. "Mr. Vice President... sir. I'm sorry about your daughter, but—"

"Then help me. You know New Dawn better than anyone. Steele Ops has been working tirelessly to get into Teague Rossbach's inner circle, but it's proven more difficult than expected. *You're* the missing link. Both your training and your history with the group could help bring my daughter home."

Jake Corelli stepped up to Brandt, clearing his throat. "Sir, we need to be moving along."

The vice president locked Grace in his sights. "I'm not going to lie, Special Agent Steele. My daughter isn't perfect. She's made some personal choices in her life that I don't particularly care for, but until now, they've been *her* choices. And like any self-respecting parent, I want to support her. New Dawn wasn't a choice. They preyed on her weakness and used it to their advantage."

"I'm flattered that you and my cousins have so much faith in me, sir, but it's been seventeen years since I've lived with the OND. There's no way that they're the same organization I remember."

"You're right. They've had time to grow, to damage more lives." He gestured to a manila envelope on the table. "That's everything we have on Sarah's activities leading up to her disappearance, including intelligence on the man we believed recruited her. All I'm asking is that you try."

Grace remained statue-still. Hell, even Cade temporarily stopped breathing, waiting for her response.

As close as they'd gotten after she'd come to live with her father's family, Grace still hadn't told Cade everything about her time in New Dawn. He'd respected that privacy. Taking the little snippets she did share, he'd listened and hadn't pushed.

Much.

But *I'm fine* had been her mantra, and the only way he'd been able to tell if it was true or an automatic response reserved for her family was by looking into her eyes.

That was the real reason he'd agreed to trek to New York.

He needed to look her in her pretty golden-brown eyes and make sure she was okay with what they were asking her to do.

Grace picked up the file, her fingers slightly trembling. "I'll do my best, sir."

"Thank you. From both myself and my wife." Brandt shook her hand before doing the same to Cade. "I trust you'll keep me updated?"

"Yes, sir."

When Cade looked back to Grace, she'd already retrieved her firearm from Corelli and snapped it back into her holster. He waited until Brandt and his security detail left and braced for impact. "Grace—"

"Not. One. Word." She tucked the manila folder under her arm and stalked angrily toward the exit.

Cade followed from a distance, although judging by her silence, he wasn't sure if the next county would be far enough to be considered safe. Quiet Grace was more dangerous than her fly-off-the-handles counterpart. Quiet Grace meant time to dwell and stew. Quiet

Grace plotted retributions that made grown men cry and call out for their mamas.

They'd barely cleared the front door when Grace whirled around, no longer quiet. "*An ambush*, Cade? Seriously?"

"*Ambush* is going a little too far, don't you think?"

"No, I don't. DC is the capital of the free world. They don't have working telephones? Or hell, email? You let me walk into this freakin' blind!"

Cade's hackles rose. He crossed his arms over his chest, going on the defensive. "It's not like we didn't try to get hold of you. Knox, Roman, *and* Ryder. Liam was five seconds away from attempting carrier pigeon. We even roped Zoey into the coordinated effort, but surprise, surprise, all voice mails, texts, and emails went unreturned."

"If I didn't get back to you, then there was a good reason. Oh, say, my *job*!"

"That's your go-to excuse these days, isn't it?"

"What the hell's that supposed to mean?"

"Pretty sure I meant it how it sounded. You don't exactly make regular appearances home. You probably wouldn't have come to town six months ago if the Bureau hadn't sent you there for the BCK case."

"I'd *really* like to not discuss six months ago with you." With a low growl, she stalked away, even the clack of her heels telling him to fuck himself.

Cade couldn't help but watch. Tall and curvy, she filled out her suit in a way that was meant to be business-smart, but instead fueled every naughty-librarian fantasy he'd had as a horny teenager.

Hell, he didn't need the suit to fire up a Grace-inspired fantasy reel. He needed the woman herself—

which was exactly what had happened earlier that year. Stress and a little Jack had lowered their inhibitions, and they'd fallen back on old habits.

Sex—the one thing during their nine years together that they never once argued about—except when he'd told her that he wasn't taking her virginity after her senior prom. Hell had no fury like Grace Steele being cock-blocked.

The flash of headlights ripped his attention away from Grace's ass and onto the approaching sedan. She flagged it down, and it slowed.

"Where are you going?" he asked.

"Home. Which is where you should go."

Cade spotted the Lyft sticker on the car window. "There's no reason for you to pay for a ride. I'm parked around the corner."

Grace stopped cold, aiming her glare his way. "Why would you think that I'd get in a car with *you*?"

"Because I'm your ticket to the Steele Ops jet. Or has your love of commercial flying changed? I bet on this short of notice, there's a nice middle seat within toilet-sniffing distance. Or we can drive down to DC. Five long hours. You and me. Side by side."

Her nose wrinkled as if smelling something bad, but he wasn't sure if it was at the mention of commercial seating or close quarters with him.

"*Or*"—Grace smiled sweetly and opened the Lyft door—"I can drive my own damn self. See you in DC."

Without another glance, she slipped into the back seat of the waiting car, leaving him to stare after her like some kind of abandoned lover…which, coincidentally, was pretty damn close to what he'd done to her nine years earlier.

CHAPTER
TWO

Nestled in the heart of Old Town Alexandria, the once notorious Keaton Jailhouse loomed over the Potomac riverside, its four castle-like turrets giving it a gothic feel. The Steele brothers had bought it almost a year ago and poured a hell of a lot of blood, sweat, and money into its renovation so it would serve their needs—and the needs of their two businesses.

Iron Bars Distillery and Beer Garden, located on the three aboveground levels, had quickly become a riverside hotspot. They hosted community events and company functions. Last week, they'd held their first wedding reception and were written up in some kind of event magazine.

But tucked deep in the underbelly, beneath the unsuspecting feet of the Iron Bar patrons, Steele Ops ran its operations, doing what the government couldn't do thanks to red tape and bureaucracy. It sure as hell wasn't for the faint of heart, but despite Cade's original uncertainty about leaving the DCPD Special Crimes Task Force, he knew he'd made the right decision in teaming up with his best friends.

Not only did he get to keep his family and country safe, but he did it using the skills he'd acquired during his time with the 75th Ranger Regiment. And yeah, there were additional perks, like individual living quarters for times they had to work round-the-clock and a training facility that made his community center's gym look like a high school locker room. And Liam had outfitted their ops center with all the latest tech, which he boasted would make NASA cry.

Going topside wasn't necessary unless they chose to be around people—which the man currently boring annoyed holes into Cade seldom did.

Roman Steele, one quarter of the Steele brother quartet, kicked his boots up on the desk and followed Cade's trek around ops with a critical eye. "You're making me motion-sick. Either sit and wait, or go punch the hell out of the sparring bag until they get here, but if you don't pick one, I'm diving into Ryder's medic kit and dosing your ass with a sedative."

Cade stopped pacing and threw his friend a glare. The former Special Forces soldier didn't flinch...or bluff. Not before the IED explosion that took the lower third of his left leg, and not now, years later.

Disgusted with himself, Cade tossed his now ice-cold coffee in the trash. "I should've made her come with me on the jet. I don't know what the hell I was thinking."

"That you valued your life." Roman stood, stretching his back and then his legs. He winced, but erased the grimace as quickly as it had appeared. "The only reason she would've agreed to go with you was so she could toss your ass out the emergency exit the second you reached thirty thousand feet. Count yourself lucky."

"If I had any kind of luck we wouldn't be talking

about New-fucking-Dawn." He scraped his palm over his face. "Sarah Brandt couldn't go and pick those nature worshipers out in California? It *had* to be the OND?"

"I don't like this any more than you do, but I wouldn't have agreed with Knox to bring Grace in if I didn't think she could handle it."

"Just because she handles shit well doesn't mean she should have to."

Grace was one of the strongest women he knew, right up with his mom and his sister, Zoey. She dealt with things head-on regardless if it was the easy route or not. Hell, he remembered clear as day the morning a thirteen-year-old Grace Steele showed up on the Steeles' front porch.

He and Knox had been sucked into whatever video game had just come out when the doorbell rang. Thinking Liam was fucking with them again, Cade had flung the door open in full tirade mode, and by the time he'd realized it wasn't the youngest Steele brother on the front stoop, it was too late. He'd already cussed out the rail-thin young girl in front of him.

She'd beaten him to an apology when she'd thrown his attitude right back in his face, not the least deterred by his extra seventy pounds and twelve or more inches.

That spunk had served her well through the years, so Cade got why Roman wasn't more worried. Sometimes even he forgot that the strong woman she'd become was also the one who he'd held through countless night terrors.

Roman and the others hadn't seen *that* side of Grace.

She wouldn't let them. She'd barely let *him*, and they'd been inseparable as teenagers. But now, after years clawing her way out from that darkness, they all expected her to dive right back in.

"Grace will be behind the scenes," Roman said, as if reading his thoughts. "We just need her to make Tank and Jaz's backgrounds look attractive to the New Dawn recruiters. Once they get their invite into the Order, her part's over. Relax. Decaffeinate. Grace'll be here. She'll be fine. And things will run as smooth as they always do."

"You didn't see her face after meeting Brandt. If looks could kill, the NYPD would be fishing my dead body out of the Hudson River right now."

"Like I said, things will be back to normal." Roman's lips twitched. "Look, I'm not saying she'll be all smiles when she shows. I gave some serious thought to breaking out a pair of flak jackets from the pen."

"Where are you going with this?"

"We both know that the second she left your ass on that dock, she called Zoey, and your sister talked her out of doing anything to spite your dumb ass."

"That's how you know she'll be here, huh?"

Roman flashed his cell phone. "That, and Ryder just texted to say she's upstairs."

The words no sooner left Roman's mouth than Grace's voice echoed through the compound.

The sound of her throaty chuckle twisted his stomach into knots. Once upon a time, he'd been able to coax that laugh from her better than anyone. They'd spend entire weekends of his R and R holed up in her dorm room doing nothing but talking and stripping each other's clothes off. On the rare occasion they ventured outside to do something in the real world, they'd always ended up rushing back to get naked—again.

These days all Cade got out of Grace were insults, snide comments, and eat-shit-and-die glares.

Grace stepped into the room.

In well-worn blue jeans and heeled knee-high boots, she looked more like the young woman he'd once pictured himself spending the rest of his life with than the federal agent who'd gladly use him for target practice.

Her dark hair, which complemented her red sweater, fell over her shoulders in soft waves, and her golden-brown eyes damn near twinkled even under Steele Ops's fluorescent lighting.

FBI Special Agent Grace Steele revved up his libido, but this laid-back version burst it into flames.

Sending a mental scolding to Little Cade for his inopportune half salute, Cade stuffed his hands into his pockets and waited for Grace's inevitable glare. The second her eyes locked on him, her smile vanished.

"Guess you decided to walk back to DC rather than take that solo drive." Cade internally groaned the second he heard his own voice.

Everyone froze. Ryder and Knox, standing on either side of Grace, looked prepped to move if she leaped for him. Roman shook his head, muttering something unflattering under his breath about Cade's intelligence.

At this point, Cade was ready to agree with him. He wasn't sure why he'd said what he did, which seemed to be his new modus operandi when it came to Grace. Foot in mouth. Perpetually.

But it put him in her crosshairs.

It might be sadistic on his part, but he preferred her I'm-going-to-skewer-you-alive-with-the-power-of-my-glare to being ignored completely. The little electrical charge that whipped through him each time almost mimicked their good-natured barbs back in the day.

A smile way too sweet to be real formed on Grace's pink-glossed lips. "Considering I wasn't given a length of time for my services, I needed to make sure that I brought enough clothes."

"Because there aren't washing machines in the world."

"Pushing it," Roman mumbled.

Grace's smile remained despite the ocular javelin spear she heaved his way. "You never told me where we'd be going, so I had to pack for all contingencies. For all I knew, we were headed to a Nepali hilltop—with no washing machines. You shouldn't be complaining. If it had been Ryder, you'd be twiddling your thumbs for another three hours while he ironed his jeans. And that's a safe estimate."

Ryder, former Marine and peacekeeper of Steele Ops, laughed. He took a seat at the conference table and lifted his boots onto the shiny wood surface. "Leave me and my creaseless jeans alone, haters. Just because you lot don't care about looking like slobs doesn't mean that the rest of us have to do the same."

Knox, the oldest of the Steele brothers, glared. "Boots. Off. Now."

"Come on, man. Seriously?"

"Do I come to your place and shit in your bed?"

"No. You shit in my latrine, and then I have to light those damn scented candles just so I can take a piss afterward."

Knox's continued scowl dropped Ryder's feet to the ground. "Hard-ass."

"Lightweight." His one-word reminder of Ryder's recent failed attempt to outdrink Jaz, Steele Ops's resident sniper, broke the two brothers out into near matching grins.

Knox nodded for everyone to take a seat. "Let's get this show on the road."

"And not on I-95 during rush hour," Ryder joked.

Everyone groaned, and Roman threw his empty coffee cup at his younger brother's head. "What did I tell you about those lame-ass jokes?"

"Oh, come on. That was funny," Ryder protested.

Grace patted his hand and took a seat; the one as far from Cade as possible. "It really wasn't, honey. If those are the kind of jokes you dole out during happy hour, no wonder you're still single."

"I think I like it better when you ride Cade's ass. Dude, switch seats with me." He lifted his ass off his chair as if to get up and got yanked back—hard—by Grace.

"I think you guys need to start talking." She glanced around the room. "But aren't we missing someone? I seem to be one cousin short."

Knox nodded. "Liam's going over the logistics of the New Dawn op with Tank and Jaz."

Ryder chuckled. "And probably regretting his chosen

occupation as the Steele Ops smart-ass. You and Cade are cuddly kittens compared to those two."

Grace arched a delicately curved eyebrow. "And you paired the two of them together?"

"You'll understand when you see them interact," Cade interjected. "But we're also running low on options. We've used undercovers, both ours and local law enforcement, and haven't gotten much more than a nibble. For a cult, New Dawn is pretty damn particular."

"And let me guess, when you got a nibble, it didn't go anywhere."

"Exactly."

Grace pulled a stack of files from her bag and spread them out on the table in front of them. "Because they weren't the right *fit*. Even though Teague Rossbach's a sociopath, he isn't stupid. The Seekers—or recruiters—that he sends out into the general population are little more than sheep. He gives them *just* enough information for them to do their job."

"So even if they had nibbled..."

"They wouldn't have been able to give you a damn thing, or at least anything that we're looking for. Anyone who knows anything of use is going to be in his tight circle—his *Council*. And they're going to be on the Order compound—which is where Brandt's intel states that Sarah's been since leaving DC."

"So then why the hell are we bothering with winning over these *Seekers*?" Cade's question earned him everyone's attentions. "Sarah Brandt's on the OND compound, right? Then we perform an old-school recovery. In and out. Everyone's happy."

Grace rolled her pretty eyes at him. "That's not going to work."

"Why not?"

"Because in order to *raid* the compound, you'd need to *find* it. It's not like it's on a map, and I highly doubt even the Seekers know the exact location."

Roman scratched his scruffy beard, deep in thought. "Then how do they get new members there? If they do most of their brainwashing at the compound, then they have to transport them somehow."

"Members of the Council. I vaguely remember that there'd be times when a few of them disappeared for a day, sometimes two, and when they returned, our little 'flock' had grown."

"Flock?" Roman lifted a dark eyebrow. "What the hell did he see his followers as? Geese?"

"Please don't get me started on Rossbach's twisted dictionary of words. I could spend weeks talking about the psychology behind it all."

From the file, Cade pulled the surveillance images of Bethany and Thomas Williams, the New Dawn couple they'd been tailing for the last few weeks. Fairly recent transplants in DC, they both worked steady jobs at one of the private schools across town. Teachers, for God's sake.

A realization nearly smacked Cade in the face.

Teachers. "Most school systems don't exactly dish out a lot of personal time. These recruiters aren't going to be able to drop everything to play escort to new members very often."

"You're right," Grace admitted. "I think I remember

it being about once a month, and it wasn't as if they brought a busload. It was maybe two or three people at a time. At the most, four. Rossbach's selective. He's only going to pick people who he thinks he can do his mind-meld thing with."

Ryder snorted. "So basically the chances of getting recruited are the same as someone's chances of being drafted by the NHL. Nice."

Grace eyed the photos in Cade's hands. "If you've been tailing those recruiters for weeks and haven't seen anything suspicious, it probably means they haven't transported any new members recently."

Cade's eyes snapped up to hers. "Their flock's overdue for a population increase."

"Exactly what I was thinking. If we move on this quickly, your operatives can be first-round draft picks." Grace grinned at Cade, nearly making him fall off his damn chair.

Fuck. That smile. At the sight of it, his body never ceased to come alive. There'd been times when they were teenagers that he'd do something purposefully stupid to see her flash one his way. It was more addictive than caffeine.

As if suddenly realizing who'd she'd been smiling at, Grace's grin melted away, and the loss of it was a like a sucker punch to his gut.

She leaned back in her chair and tucked her hands on her lap, turning toward her cousins. "I'm going to make sure your people get on the inside, but there's one thing you may have to prepare yourself for that I haven't heard anyone mention."

"What's that?" Knox asked.

"What are you going to do if Sarah Brandt doesn't want to leave?"

* * *

No one moved. No one took so much as a shallow breath or blinked. It was more than a little eerie.

Grace hated being the bearer of bad news, and judging by the looks on her cousins' faces as well as Cade's, it was probably one of the worst she could have delivered. But they had brought her here to do a job, and that was what she needed to do even if it meant dropping a metaphorical monsoon on their parade.

"Didn't think of that, did you?" Grace asked.

Knox opened and closed his mouth, unable to form words. Ryder and Roman both looked horrified at the concept.

Cade looked her dead in the eye, the first to speak. "You seriously think that could be the case?"

"I would be surprised if it wasn't." Having prepared to drop reality into the situation, Grace popped open three files and slid them down the table. "The People's Temple in Jonestown. Heaven's Gate in California. The Branch Davidians in Waco. All with very different belief systems. But one thing they have in common is the followers follow blindly. They stay because they want to."

"You didn't."

Grace forced herself to meet Cade's eyes.

As a general rule, she didn't talk about the OND. It wasn't the healthiest coping strategy, and as her old therapist had told her with routine frequency, it would come back to bite her on the ass one day.

That was why she'd opened up to Cade all those years ago. Not *wide* open. A girl had to keep up some protective walls in this day and age, but she'd given him enough glimpses for him to know what getting involved with her meant.

For him. For her. For *them*.

She'd expected him to run away screaming, but instead he'd held on tighter...until her college graduation, when he'd let go completely and re-upped his service with the Army.

Grace pulled her head out of the past before it swallowed her whole. "My issues with the OND weren't exactly *typical*. I'm pretty sure that I'm the reason Rossbach even designed the Reconditioning Center."

Roman winced. "Is that as bad as it sounds?"

"If it sounds like manual labor mixed in with solitary confinement and a lot of *self-reflection*, then yes."

Her cousin's dark eyes narrowed. "And where was your mom during all this?"

"*Mother Dearest*? Rossbach's fiercest cheerleader and mega-groupie?" Grace let out a humorless snort. The idea of Rebecca Steele giving a damn about her daughter, other than how Grace's disobedience made her look to others, was laughable. "She probably would've been thrilled if he'd kept me in the Rec full-time. But we're getting off topic. We need to focus on Sarah Brandt, not me."

Knox leaned his arms on the table. "So you're saying that we're looking at two scenarios: the vice president's daughter either being a permanent resident of the Reconditioning Center or someone who leads the freakin' evening blessing."

"That's pretty much what I'm saying."

Cade glared at Rossbach's picture on the wall-mounted computer screen, which Grace had been careful to avoid looking at until now.

His broad forehead looked wider due to a receding hairline, and his rounded face was devoid of any angles except for the slight crook of his nose. Unassuming. Unthreatening. And unremarkable. Most people passing him on the street wouldn't give him a second glance.

Grace, on the other hand, would sprint through a busy intersection to get away from those eerie mud-green eyes.

Cade still stared at Rossbach's picture, shaking his head. "Why the hell do people follow him so blindly? And why the hell hasn't anyone stopped him before he put a mysterious compound in the middle of nowhere?"

Grace forced her stomach to stop rolling. "Because like most cult leaders, he's charismatic, and on paper, he's a law-abiding citizen. He pays taxes, obeys the law—even if that's only a public façade. Cults like the Order of the New Dawn don't want to give the government any reason to infiltrate their space. They don't want another Waco."

"So you're telling me that he's a simple, hardworking couples therapist?"

"No. He's a narcissistic megalomaniac with psychopathic tendencies and delusions of grandeur. But on paper? Yes. He's a certified family counselor."

"Scary-ass shit if you ask me," Roman muttered.

"Not going to disagree with you."

"I'm sorry, G," Knox said. "We tried keeping you out of this, but when Brandt did his own digging and found out about your connection he was a man on a mission. Are you sure you're going to be okay working on this?"

She waved off her cousin's apology. "For eight years, my mother and Rossbach tried erasing every aspect of myself that made me *me*. If there's even a chance that they're doing that to Sarah Brandt, or anyone else, I'm going to do what I need to do."

"That doesn't really answer the question."

It didn't, but that was the only answer she had to give him, because the truth was that she didn't know. For seventeen years, she's shoved her New Dawn memories into an airtight vault, and now she had to jimmy it back open.

But she'd meant what she said. She'd do whatever was necessary to get Sarah Brandt home—and then she'd hope like hell all of her shit fit back in its box.

CHAPTER
THREE

If Grace had spent one more hour with her cousins and Cade at the Steele Ops headquarters her head would have exploded.

She needed a hot shower. Chocolate. And her best friend. Not necessarily in that order.

Zoey stood at her apartment door when Grace came up the steps and pulled her into a tight hug. "Look what the cat dragged in."

"Speaking of cats…where's Mr. Evil?" Grace warily looked for Snuggles, an oxymoron-of-a-name for her best friend's twenty-pound behemoth. The last time she'd visited, the admittedly beautiful hairball hocked an *actual* hairball on her five-hundred-dollar Jimmy Choos and then pissed on her backup Louboutins.

Zoey chuckled, obviously remembering that fated day. "I think he's hiding. I told him you were coming, and he zoomed right underneath the bed."

"Lying in wait's probably more accurate, but fool on him because I'm not planning on taking my shoes off this time."

Zo's eyes flickered down to her feet. "You're going to sleep in boots?"

"And shower," Grace joked, tossing her things on the kitchen table. "And speaking of hot water..."

"Towels are already in there."

"Bless you, my child." Grace planted an obnoxious kiss on her cheek and hightailed it to the bathroom. Forty minutes later, she donned her fuzzy flannels—and boots—and found Zoey on the sofa with two mugs of hot chocolate, already sufficiently marshmallowed.

"You're an angel." Grace took the cocoa and spotted the heating pad on the empty couch cushion. She sunk on top of it with a groan. "Strike that. You're a goddess. I worship you."

Zoey chuckled. "Worship me so much that you used up all my hot water?"

"I spent half the day in a car and the rest of it dealing with my cousins. Trust me, I *earned* that shower."

"So it wasn't to avoid my probing questions about my brother?"

Grace threw her hand to her chest, feigning shock. "You? My longest friend on record? Probe for information? That never once entered my mind."

"You're a freakin' liar, but I love you anyway. But seriously, on a scale of one to ten, how tempted were you to throw Cade in the Hudson last night?"

"The scale only goes to ten?"

Zoey snort-laughed. "If I didn't love my job in crime scene so much, I could quit and become a self-made millionaire by selling tickets to the 'Grace and Cade Show.'"

Oglers do love watching a good train wreck.

Grace couldn't fault her best friend for her curiosity. To everyone around them, they'd once been a solid, unwavering couple. Cade had joined the Army under a four-year term while she finished up her last two years of high school and then ventured off to NYU.

Between the two of them, they'd clocked about a million hours' worth of air miles traveling back and forth on weekends, and added even more during her last two years of college, when they took advantage of every scheduled R and R and family holiday that they could.

They'd had a plan.

FBI Academy for her. College on the GI Bill for him.

And then he'd enlisted *again,* and all those plans went up in a plume of smoke. Or more accurately, with the fumes of Cade's Boeing as it left Andrews Air Force Base.

Happy graduation to her.

Before her sour mood transferred to her best friend, Grace changed the subject. "So now that I can see your face and tell if you're lying...how have you been doing? *Really*. My cousin's been treating you right? Everything's back online with that stinker-of-a-ticker?"

A pink blush rose to Zoey's creamy cheeks. "Knox is great, and the replaced heart valve is doing exactly what it's supposed to do. I've actually been downgraded from monthly cardiac appointments to quarterly."

"Which is no doubt driving Knox bonkers."

"And by extension, me." Zoey's fingers played with the blanket over her lap, a ghost of a smile on her lips. "But we're good. We're...great. So great, actually, that I sometimes wait for the other shoe to drop. Do you know what I mean?"

She did. Completely. But she wasn't about to say it

to her best friend, not with everything Zoey had gone through this past year. If anyone deserved a shit-ton of worriless happiness, it was her best friend.

Grace squeezed Zoey's hand. "You have paid your dues, lady, and then some. It's time for you to bask in the sun...and in Knox. But it should be pretty easy to do both since you're living on the *Angel Eyes* now."

Behind black-rimmed glasses, Zoey's eyes went a little too wide and a lot too innocent. "I don't know what you're talking about. We're sitting in my apartment right now."

Grace smirked over the rim of her mug. "You're really forcing me to break out my powers of observation? Fine. Your bathroom toiletries are all new, and I'm talking just-cracked-open-the-seal new. When I first turned the faucet on, the water was brown-tinged like it had been sitting in the pipes for a while. And then there's your toilet."

"What's wrong with my toilet? And you looked inside? Ew!"

"A girl has to pee. And there's nothing wrong with it...other than having that orange stagnant-water line. Which, as you know, Miss Crime Scene Investigator, means that it hasn't been used, probably in weeks. There's also the distinct lack of the freesia odor stuff you spray to mask His Evilness's litter bombs. Either Snugs isn't here, or you toilet trained him. And we know that's not the case because *water line...*"

Zoey's cheeks went from pink to fuchsia.

"Oh, so nothing to say, huh?" Grace teased.

"Knox said you'd notice."

"And he was right. You didn't need to do this. I could've gotten a hotel room or stayed with Aunt Cindy."

"Or you could've asked one of your adoring cousins."

Grace's mouth dropped, openly horrified. "I swear it's like you don't know me at all! I served my time living with those barbarians. *Never. Again.*"

Tears of laughter rolled down Zoey's cheeks. "No more talk about a hotel, and if you really want to stay with Cindy and be coerced to go man-hunting with her and my mother, I'm not going to stop you. But I'd love for you to stay here. Even if I'm on the boat with Knox, I want you to act like this place is yours. For however long you need."

"Judging by tonight's events, I'm going to be here a lot longer than I want to be." Catching Zoey's concerned look, she added, "You know I love everyone here—well, except Cade. It's just..."

"New Dawn."

Grace dropped her head to the back of the couch. She wished she could rewind time and pretend she hadn't seen Director Vance's text. "I've spent the last seventeen years trying put it all behind me."

"So tell Knox that you can't do it. He'll understand."

"That's just it. I *can* do it. I just don't want to have to, and I know that makes me the worst kind of person."

"Grace Ann Steele," Zoey said sternly. "You are not a bad person. You took a horrible experience and used it as motivation to do something good. You've *saved* people. You've brought closure to loved ones who without you, probably never would've gotten it. You—"

"Down, girl." Grace bumped her shoulder gently. "I'm not the First Evil. I get it."

"You're using Buffy references on me now? Did we swap lives?"

"No, because you're with Knox and that would just be *ew*." She shrugged, smirking. "I just figured it would get me extra bonus points."

And the change of subject she desperately needed.

A half dozen of her old professors condemned the act, not to mention every therapist she'd seen since the age of thirteen. But words could be weaponized.

Rossbach's teachings spurred his followers into action. Rebecca Steele verbally denouncing Grace as a daughter killed a young girl's dream of motherly affection. And sharing bits of her past with Cade all those years ago resulted in the crushing blow of watching him walk away.

Grace needed to get her cousins into the OND, and then she needed to get the hell out of Dodge before her life imploded in front of her eyes.

* * *

There were a lot of things Cade didn't look forward to. Dentist visits. The time when he needed to go to the gastroenterologist and get a camera shoved up his ass. Now, he could tack on summoning the vice president of the United States to the list, especially since this one involved a Grace-grilling.

And it would be a grilling.

She'd stormed into Steele Ops bright and early that

morning, a color-coded timeline clenched in her slender but capable hands. Thanks to the ridiculous hour and his bad idea to sleep in the barracks, he'd been the only one subjected to her tirade—twice, the first time without coffee.

After two cups of stark black down his hatch, he'd finally connected the dots. But not without a lot of hand-holding on Grace's part and a sarcastic offer of an illustrated storyboard to help him keep up.

Cade now nursed his third cup of coffee and waited in the deserted restaurant section of Iron Bars. After fifteen minutes of peace and quiet, the distinct clack of Grace's footsteps turned the corner.

She only wore sneakers under duress or if placed in situations where there was chance her footwear wouldn't come out intact. For example, his boot camp graduation.

According to Liam, she'd complained for days leading up to the ceremony, obsessively watching the weather forecast, and privately cursing his commanding officer for not moving the graduation indoors. Cade had loved every second of that ceremony, and it had little to do with the start of his military career and everything to do with the hot—although soaked to the bone—brunette in the slinky red dress...and his old shit-kicker boots.

"Why are you here?" File folder tucked against her chest, Grace glided over to the table.

"I work here. Cutting it a little close to the meeting time, aren't you? Or do you really have no clue what it means to summon the vice president and then keep him waiting?"

Grace muttered under her breath and took a seat, her unusual acquiescence making him grin. Any time she didn't tell him to go to hell put him one step closer to getting that second chance with her. Considering where they'd started off a few days ago, he'd take every inch she gave him.

When he signed that four-year extension with his Ranger Regiment, he'd hurt her. Hell, he'd hurt himself, because despite loving that he got to protect his country and the men he served with, he'd loved Grace more. That was the *real* reason he'd re-upped for another tour. He'd just never found a way to tell her that didn't make him sound like a pathetic ass.

Grace sat and drummed her fingers against the table. "You know, if Brandt hadn't wanted to be summoned again so soon, then maybe he shouldn't have doctored the intelligence reports he handed over."

Cade scrubbed his hand over his face. Three cups of coffee wasn't enough for this. "Are you absolutely sure it wasn't an oversight? I mean, I get where you're coming from. I do. But it could've been overlooked, right? Or have a simple explanation? Hell, when I first glanced through it, it looked like everything was in order."

"Because you're not a profiler. You're a...*you*."

He chuckled. "Somehow I don't think that was meant as a compliment."

"Then you thought right. Why are you here, Cade? And I don't mean *in the building*. I mean here...in this room...with minutes to spare before I meet with Brandt."

She studied him from across the table before sucking

in a sharp breath. "You're here to babysit me, aren't you? Which cousin made the directive? Was it Knox? I'll *kill* him—although it might hurt my friendship with Zoey. Oh, well. I'll help her get over him by introducing her to a few hot FBI agents. I definitely know enough of them."

An unfamiliar emotion twisted Cade's insides. *Jealousy?*

It wasn't as if he'd deluded himself into thinking that he'd been Grace's one-and-only. After their split, he'd done his own sulking in the cleavages of various blondes and redheads—never a brunette, because he couldn't tolerate the memories of the one he really wanted.

But sitting across from Grace and hearing her talk about the men she knew chafed him raw. She hadn't even said she'd slept with them, or dated them, and it shouldn't matter to him if she had.

But it did. Way too damn much. "Knox suggested it, but he didn't call it babysitting."

"What did he call it?"

"Lion taming." Cade smirked.

Grace pinched her lips closed before breaking out into a belly laugh. "I hated it when they called me Gracie the Lion."

"That's why they did it—along with your tendency to bite heads off first and *then* ask for an explanation."

She shrugged, still grinning. "I didn't need to ask for an explanation because nine times out of ten they were guilty as hell. Remember the time Liam raided my closet for that stupid varsity football hazing and ruined my favorite sweater? You guys thought I was nuts for thinking he'd taken it—but I was right."

Cade chuckled, remembering that afternoon with perfect clarity. "Couldn't exactly picture Liam wearing powder blue angora, but you proved us wrong when you got your hands on those pictures."

They exchanged knowing smiles. For a quick moment, it was like old times. Except nine years ago, he would've reached across the table, kissed the hell out of her, and watched that sweet smile turn to a heated look of lust.

Her gaze dropped to his mouth and back as if thinking the same thing.

"Are we interrupting anything?" A deep voice disrupted the moment.

"Yes," Cade answered.

"No," Grace replied in unison. She threw Cade a warning look and got to her feet. "Hello, Agent Corelli."

Corelli nodded for his agents to spread out and check the grounds. "Twice in three days, Special Agent Steele. Is this going to become a habit?"

"You wish," Cade muttered under his breath.

Grace flashed the vice president's protective detail a thousand-watt smile. "No offense, but I hope not. Am I going to get to keep Magdalena this time around?"

Corelli chuckled. "Yeah, we're good this time."

An agent nodded to the VP's detail head. "All clear, sir."

"Send in Papa Bear."

"Papa Bear?" Grace chuckled.

"The vice president loved reading the Berenstain Bears to his daughter when she was little."

Pierce Brandt walked into the room. "Corelli, outside the door, please. Everyone else stays farther out."

"Will do, sir." Corelli flashed Grace a wink before walking out.

"Special Agent Steele and Mr. Wright. I have to admit, I wasn't expecting to see the two of you this soon."

Grace grimaced. "Sorry, sir. I would've come to you but—"

"Not possible." He nodded toward the table where Cade stood. "I'm gathering you have some additional questions?"

"First, let me begin by apologizing," Grace preempted as they all sat.

"For what? What did you do?"

"It's not what I did but what I'm about to do. I know your daughter means a lot to you, sir. Your first instinct is always going to be to protect her. But in this instance, that protective streak is doing more harm than good."

Fuck. *Right out of the damn gate.*

"Grace," Cade warned.

She ignored him. "The files on Sarah and her boyfriend are extremely lacking. There are gaps. One I probably could've overlooked. Maybe even two, because things happen. But this many? These aren't accidents. They're deliberate."

"I'm not certain I know what you mean." Brandt's suddenly cool tone indicated he knew exactly what Grace meant.

She had him.

She'd been right.

She opened the file in front of her and slid a set of printed images toward the VP. "Ten months ago, Sarah posted on social media an average of four times a day. Art. Fashion. Food. Books."

"That sounds about right. She was very passionate about all of it."

Grace replaced the older examples with new pictures. "And then eight months ago, after meeting Simon Reynolds, her posts changed. It makes sense. New love has a way of dominating the life of a young woman. These posts focused more on travel. Date nights. Philosophical quotes and existential questions looking for life meaning."

Cade couldn't tear his gaze away from Grace as she worked her magic. She knew her shit, and she didn't pull any punches. It made him awfully glad she was on the good side.

Brandt shifted in his seat, a faint dew forming on his forehead. "I'm the one that gave you all those posts from her social media, Special Agent Steele. You're not telling me anything that I haven't already looked at."

"You're right. Which means you know that seven months ago, all her accounts go dormant. There's nothing. Not a post, retweet, share, or like."

"Reynolds monopolized all her time...and not to mention brain-wiped her into joining the OND. I doubt they'd let her continue on with her life as she once did."

"Oh, you're right. They totally cut you off from everyone and everything that you care about. There's no question about that, sir. But you told me that Sarah disappeared with Reynolds six months ago." Grace tapped on the timeline spread out in front of them. "That meant she'd gone dark an entire month before she left for the Order compound—and for someone who's a religious poster, that's highly unlikely."

She didn't say any more. Hell, she didn't have to. Pierce Brandt had been on two campaign trails as vice president alone, been grilled at debates, questioned by hungry journalists. Through it all, the man didn't once squirm.

He squirmed now.

He cleared his throat and casually loosened his tie. "What exactly are you accusing me of, Special Agent Steele?"

"Caring about your daughter, sir...and deleting posts that you know wouldn't have painted her in the best patriotic light." Grace handed him the last meme quote. "Divided We Stand, United We Fall."

Pierce's face lost what little color it had left. "How did you get that?"

"You can delete Sarah's accounts, sir, but nothing's lost forever. When the vice president's daughter posts government distrust quotes and retweets resistance videos, people take notice. They talk. They screen-shot. They *blog*."

"Reynolds is the one who filled her head with that nonsense. The longer she stayed mixed up with him, the more the daughter I knew melted away. Before she left, my wife and I barely recognized her anymore."

"She wasn't happy with the things happening around her."

"She wasn't happy about *anything*...except *him*, but I blame myself for not seeing it sooner. I thought it was a phase that she'd get over, and by the time I realized it wasn't, it was too late." Tears formed in the older man's eyes as he relived the past few months. "The way she looked at me before she left? With pure, unfiltered hatred? It still keeps me awake at night. It's why..."

"It's why what, sir?"

"I hired someone to follow her prior to her disappearance." Brandt's gaze flickered to the closed door and back. "Her mood shifts. Her rants. I needed to be able to stop her before she did something she couldn't take back."

Cade's internal alarm system fired up. "You believed your daughter might hurt someone?"

"Not directly. But you hear about eco-demonstrators all around the world, ready to prove their points to anyone who'll listen. Even if they don't intend on people getting caught in the crosshairs, it almost always happens. I didn't want Sarah to get mixed up in something like that."

"What happened to the PI following her?"

"He lost her...which is why I'm here."

Grace slipped out of her badass FBI profiler persona and put her hand over Brandt's. The vulnerability in her eyes as she looked at the vice president took Cade's breath away, because she didn't let it out easily.

Or often.

"None of this is your fault, sir, and Sarah may be very misguided, but it's not directly her fault either," Grace assured the country's second-in-command.

"There's nothing that either of you could've done differently. Once New Dawn gets into a person's head, it's nearly impossible to get them out. Trust me, I know. It's been seventeen years since I left, and sometimes I still catch myself falling back on old habits."

Brandt cleared his throat, fighting back more emotion. "Thank you, Special Agent Steele. For saying that. And I'm sorry about the deleted posts. I gather that they'll help you get closer to my daughter?"

"They will. Immensely."

"Then I'll get them to you by the end of the day." A lot more somber than he'd been when he arrived, Vice President Brandt stood and shook their hands before taking his entourage out of Iron Bars.

Grace collected her intel on Sarah Brandt and kept her back toward Cade. There wasn't a doubt in his mind that it wasn't intentional.

He spotted the tremble in her hand. "Grace—"

"This changes things." She spun toward him, her jaw angled in determination.

"What does?"

"Sarah Brandt went into New Dawn angry at the world. There's no way they're not going to use that anger and her position as the vice president's daughter to their advantage. This entire situation is sitting on a land mine."

"That's why we brought you on board. We just needed a little bit of your magic to get us on the inside."

"We need more than magic, Cade. And more than my thirteen-year-old self's memory."

"If you have any other ideas, we'll take them, because we're a little short on supply ourselves."

Grace swallowed audibly. "I have one, but it's not going to be well received."

"By who? Your cousins?"

She nodded. "Yeah, them too. But I was mostly thinking of the man we need to talk to. As far as I know, Rhett Winston's the only person who hates New Dawn as much as I do."

That name sounded way too familiar for Cade not to know who the hell she was talking about.

And then it hit him.

All the times he'd held her through a nightmare. All the times he'd kissed away the tears and soothed her through the quiet sobs afterward. And all the times he cursed the faceless bastard haunting Grace even when she slept.

The name she'd woken up screaming would always echo inside his head.

Rhett.

CHAPTER FOUR

Although not eager to traipse around a booby-trapped mountain in the middle of the night, Grace couldn't wait to get out of Cade's truck. He'd gone from sweetly supportive to quietly livid in a snap of fingers... and Rhett's name.

She'd known the news wouldn't go over well, but it didn't change the fact that to get to Sarah Brandt before it was too late, she had to do what she promised Rhett she'd never do.

Find him.

Technically, she knew where he was. Nondescript postcards, written in a Caesar shift cipher, came in the mail twice a year. Always short, sweet, and to the point, they let her know that he remained far off the grid and that their agreement still held.

She'd broken that agreement five years ago, afraid for the older man when he'd missed a check-in, and she'd been glad she had. He'd been sick and nearly comatose, septic from a scratch, of all things. She hadn't helped him escape seventeen years ago so he could die alone on a damn mountain.

Rhett, as someone who'd once been in Teague Rossbach's inner circle, could shed some clarity on Grace's fuzzy teenage memories. Talking with him could mean the difference between bringing Sarah Brandt home or losing her for good, and the vice president didn't seem the type to accept the latter scenario.

Grace glanced down at the handheld GPS. "We're almost to the point where we need to park and hike. There should be a turnoff about a half mile up the road, but it's not going to be obvious."

"Of course it isn't. Just makes it fit in with all the other surprises piling up today," Cade muttered.

Grace sighed. "You can stop huffing about this any time."

Cade shot her a glare. "I'm not huffing. I'm pissed. How many times did I hear you scream this guy's name and get told after the fact that—"

"Rhett's story isn't mine to tell . . . and it's still not."

"Except it obviously involves you in some way."

"Still doesn't mean that you need to know." Grace folded her arms and stared out the side window as they bounced down an unused service road.

Through the years, she'd told Cade snippets of her life in New Dawn. The structure. The expectations. The ridiculous idea that in order to get to your happy place—or New Dawn—you needed to deal with your personal Obstacles.

But she'd never been able to tell him about the night she decided to leave—the night Todd Winston, her only true friend in the Order, came within minutes of taking another life. To be more accurate, his father's.

Rhett's.

Sometimes the mind blocks out traumatic life events.

It was a coping mechanism to help a person put one step in front of the other. But Grace couldn't forget any part of that night. Until a few short years ago, it had been cemented into her memory vault and opened every time she closed her eyes.

The hatred that had poured from Todd still left her cold. Her once mild-mannered friend had had every intention of ending his father's life—but not before putting him through physical hell first. She'd begged Todd to reconsider. She'd used their friendship as a bargaining chip.

None of it had worked—and she'd seen in Todd's eyes that nothing would.

If she wanted him to stop, she had to be the one to make him. And she did, which was no small feat considering he'd been double her size. Todd hadn't seen her betrayal, or the broken chair leg, coming until she'd knocked him to the ground, unconscious—and then she did everything she could to right his wrong.

Rossbach's once second-in-command had begged her to leave with him, but she couldn't...not until *after* she'd told the Council what Todd had nearly done. Imagine her shock when they announced that they already knew—and that by aiding Rhett's escape, she'd violated Rossbach's most cardinal rule: *Never deny someone their New Dawn.*

Twenty-four hours later, Rhett Winston had snuck back onto the Order compound and broken her out of the Reconditioning Center. She'd saved his life and he'd returned the favor—and she hadn't looked back since.

Outside, the wind howled, slamming into Cade's truck and jolting Grace from the past.

Cade brought the vehicle to a stop and frowned at the virtual nothingness outside the window. "This guy couldn't hole up on a beach somewhere near the equator?"

"Rhett was a loner even before he got involved with New Dawn. I can't really see him sitting back and sipping mai tais at some tourist resort." Grace pulled Magdalena out from her holster and checked the clip before stuffing it back under her side. At Cade's curious look, she shrugged. "A girl can never be too careful. And speaking of careful, you can't go charging up that mountain like a bulldozer. Stay behind me so I can get us past Winston's alarm system."

"He has Safe-house all the way out here?"

"No. He has punji pits and explosions that could create an avalanche and bury us alive if they don't blow us to bits first. Do you have any other smart comments? Get them out of the way now because when we get to Rhett's place, you're going to want to curb your asshattedness."

Cade snorted on a chuckle. "Now you're making words up."

"Excuse me? Who was trained on personal traits? Asshattedness is totally a word and you don't need to look it up. Just look in the mirror. The definition will literally stare you in the face."

Cade laughed, signaling, more than likely, a very temporary truce. But she'd take it. At least long enough to get them up and down that mountain in one piece.

It wasn't an easy hike during daylight hours, much less at night with the threat of snow about to fall down on their heads. Brandt's worry about his daughter fueled Grace's motivation to get her cousins the inside edge they needed to bring her home. Unfortunately that meant every minute counted—and every available recourse mattered.

Their boots crunched through the already fallen snow as they squeezed through foliage and stepped over rocky outcroppings. Grace's breath swirled around her head as she panted, working up a sweat only fifteen minutes into the hike.

"Do you want to tell me again how this guy fits in to Rossbach's little world?" Cade asked from behind her. "Or is that not your story to tell either?"

She let the comment slide. "He was his second-in-command. He gave instructions from time to time, doled out punishments if Rossbach wasn't available to pass judgment."

"And he woke up one morning and suddenly said, 'To hell with all this, I'm going rogue'?"

"More like Rossbach woke up one morning and said, 'I don't need a second.'"

Cade grabbed her hand and gently tugged her to a stop. "Explain."

"I've told you about the concept of New Dawn."

"It's basically everyone's individual little heaven on earth, right?"

She nodded. "But to get there, you need to let go of the past, dole out forgiveness so you can move forward."

"Sounds simple enough. A lot of faiths teach the same thing."

"It wasn't forgiveness that Rossbach was encouraging the night I left...the night Rhett and I both Defected."

"What did he want?"

Grace's throat dried as she remembered her once best friend moments away from becoming a killer, and the pure disappointment in Rossbach's face at hearing she'd stopped it from happening. "Revenge. But I don't know if it was Rossbach trying to punish Rhett or if it was a—"

"Permanent detour in his peace, love, and harmony shtick."

"Exactly. And considering Sarah Brandt's views about her father before she left, I'm afraid it's the latter. Which makes getting on the inside a little trickier."

A branch cracked less than six feet away. Grace and Cade turned at the same time, their guns pointed toward the direction it came from.

Moonlight glinted off the rifle barrel Rhett Winston pointed in their direction. The older man stepped out of the shadows, his face hard as stone. "Tell me who the fuck you are before I blow holes in both your heads."

Grace re-sheathed her gun and whipped her knit hat off her head. "Put that damn thing away. It's me."

"What the hell are you doing here, girl? I thought I told you that I didn't want to see you back on this damn mountain ever again."

"And I told you I wouldn't be unless it was a matter of life and death—or unless I just wanted to see your happy, smiling face." Grace nudged her chin toward his still aimed rifle. "Now can you put away the gun?"

* * *

"I'll put mine down if your friend there puts his down."
Rhett Winston glared past Grace and straight at Cade.

Cade didn't budge. He aimed his Glock at the man
in front of him and eased in front of Grace, keeping
himself solidly between her and Winston. She may trust
him, but he sure as hell didn't. Defected New Dawner
or not, he'd still been Rossbach's right hand.

"Oh, for God's sake." Grace stepped around him
and simultaneously shoved both guns toward the
ground. "Keep the testosterone and the guns tucked
away or I'll be forced to shoot you both in the ass
myself."

Rhett Winston growled, his gaze flickering toward
Grace. "You're still a pain in the ass."

"Life would be boring if I wasn't." She cocked a
dark eyebrow and waited for them to put their weapons
away. When they reluctantly complied, she nodded.
"There. That's better. Now can we get out of the freezing cold?"

"*You and I* can..." Winston shot Cade a distrustful
look.

"Seriously, Rhett. I really don't have time for your
Oscar the Grouch routine. This is Cade. Cade, this is
Rhett."

"*Cade*?" Winston shot a curious glance to Grace,
and the two exchanged a look.

"Yes, *Cade*." Grace sighed. "Now...*heat*? *Please*?"

The former New Dawn councilman didn't look any
less thrilled, but he nodded. "This better be important."

"I wouldn't be here if it weren't."

"Keep up and don't go wandering off unless you want an unpleasant surprise." He grunted and stomped away through the six inches of snow, expecting them to keep up.

Cade shook his head. "You failed to tell me how charming he was."

"Like you're Mr. Charisma." Grace stuffed her hat back on her head and quickly hustled after Winston. "Rhett's heart's in the right place. He just likes doing things his own way. *Alone.*"

"And with explosives."

Grace shrugged, and they quietly followed the older man off the beaten path. Cade wasn't sure how they would've found the place if Winston hadn't found them first.

Tucked beneath a thick tree canopy of trees sat a small hunting cabin. If it weren't for the faint plume of smoke rising from the stone chimney, anyone passing would have thought the place abandoned.

Winston notably skipped the third step leading up to the porch and gestured for them to do the same. "Unless you're feeling lucky today."

Cade didn't even want to know.

He and Grace followed Rhett into the cabin. The inside looked as worn as the outside, except for six computers lined up along the kitchen table. Their screens displayed surveillance footage from the surrounding woods.

"Interesting setup you got here." Cade's gaze slid back to the wall nearly entirely filled with handguns and assault weapons. "A lot of firepower for one man."

"Don't like surprises." He gave Grace a pointed look and bent down to drop a few logs into the fireplace.

"I need your help." Grace sat on the threadbare couch, looking totally at ease.

"Figured as much. With what?"

"I need to get inside New Dawn."

"Are you asking for trouble, kid?" Winston let out a curse even more inventive than Roman's and shot Cade an accusing glare. "This your stupid idea? Because I sure as hell know she wouldn't have come up with it on her own."

"I'm working a case," Grace intervened on Cade's behalf. "I need to get two members of Cade's team into the Order."

"It's suicide." The older man was shaking his head.

"It's important. We need to get someone out."

"Who?" At her silence, he added, "You want help. I want details."

Cade scoffed. "And how do we know you can actually help us? Grace seems to think you can, but I'm not sure how a man who doesn't leave this mountain is going to tell us something about New Dawn that we don't already know. You've both been out seventeen years, right?"

"You came trespassing up my mountain and now you're going to insult me?" He glanced at Grace. "Way to pick a winner, kiddo. I thought you learned your lesson after the Army Asshole left you high and dry."

Cade blinked, digesting the fact that this guy even knew about their past. "I *am* the Army Asshole."

"I know."

Getting to her feet, Grace shot annoyed daggers at them both. "Enough. None of this gets us any closer to what we need. We need to get the vice president's daughter away from New Dawn, and the sooner we do it, the better."

Winston turned his back and tossed another log onto the fire.

"You *know*." Grace's mouth fell open, and she skirted around him tugging his arm so he looked her in the eye. "You know she's there. How?"

"Maybe my son told me when he called for our weekly check-in."

"Not funny."

"It kind of was." Winston glanced at Cade, immediately noting his confusion. "She didn't tell you about how I came to live on this mountain, did she?"

Cade cleared his throat. "Said it wasn't her story."

Appreciation flickered in the older man's eyes as he glanced toward Grace.

Not having his own dad around, Cade had never really experienced fatherly affection, but he saw it now as Winston nodded for Grace to take a seat. "My story's going to directly affect what you guys have to do, so take a load off."

Grace snuck Cade a glance and nervously shifted toward the couch. "You don't have to go through this again, Rhett. You can just give us the highlights that'll help us do our job."

"Giving highlights screws up a mission just as much as they fuck up relationships. Sit and listen before I change my mind about helping you."

Cade wasn't sure if that was a dig on him and Grace or not. He was too preoccupied with the realization that after years of wishing he'd known about the night Grace left New Dawn, he was finally about to hear what happened.

He wasn't sure he was ready, but he *knew* he'd rather it be her decision.

He sat next to Grace and felt her go stiff. "If you don't want me to be around for this, I can go outside while you get the information we need."

She folded her hands in her lap and refused to meet his gaze.

"Gracie?"

"I'm fine. It's fine."

It wasn't fine. Cade could tell not only by the way she avoided looking his way, but in the tightness in her voice.

He stood to leave, but her hand snaked out and grabbed his. Her golden-brown eyes peered up at him through her dark lashes, the nervousness in them nearly bringing him to his knees as much as the truth. "I'm okay with you staying. Sit. Please."

It was damn hard not reading into her words, or that look. He'd spent the better part of the last nine years wishing that he could earn her trust back, that she'd let him inside that gorgeous head of hers, even a little bit.

Hearing her ask him to stay, and meaning it, mattered more to him than he could ever put into words. "If you're sure..."

She nodded, but worried her bottom lip between her teeth. "Just...don't think bad of me."

"That would never happen, sweetheart." He squeezed her fingers to emphasize his point, and at the clearing of Winston's throat, the spell was broken.

"We ready now?" the old man asked without holding back any snark.

"We're ready." Grace nodded for her friend to continue.

"First thing you should know is that I didn't join New Dawn as a fluke, or stumble into it like Grace's mother. I was *sent* in to get close to Rossbach."

"By who?" Cade asked.

"The CIA."

Cade did a double take. Okay, so maybe there were a few things out there that could still surprise him. "You're saying that you're CIA?"

"Former. *Now*. But twenty years ago, there'd been chatter about the self-help therapist from Georgia. My superiors wanted to make sure he was as harmless as they'd been told, and at first, he was. He was a weird little shit, but he brought people inside who had issues to work through. And hell, a lot of the stuff he talked about made sense. Who didn't want to live peacefully without the shadows of the past following your every move?"

"You agreed with him," Cade realized.

"I had a job that took me away from home and left my ex-wife and kid alone more often than I was with them. So, yeah, I wanted to feel as guilt-free as possible. I stayed about four months and was prepping to leave and report back to my superiors when Seekers brought a van of new members. My teenage son was one of them."

Cade's brows lifted. "He followed you to the Order?"

Winston shook his head. "While I'd been on assignment, my ex was killed by a drunk driver on her way to pick him up from soccer practice. It wasn't long after her death that Seekers recruited him."

"On purpose? Because I have a hard time believing that it was a coincidence."

Grace leaned heavily on her knees and answered, "We're not one hundred percent sure, but if I was forced to make a guess, I'd say that it was all planned out."

Winston agreed with a nod. "We don't know whether Rossbach did it because he knew I was CIA and he wanted leverage over me, or if it was done in some misguided attempt to bring my family together. Whichever reason he had, I had no choice but to stay with Todd."

The more he heard about Teague Rossbach, the more Cade wished for a little time alone with him in a locked room. "And I'm guessing your employer didn't like it much."

Winston scoffed. "Not in the least. They wrote me off, but at the time, I didn't care. I had my son, and Todd made friends with Grace"—he sent her a small smile—"and so I worried a little less about him—until Rossbach's teachings shifted from peace, love, and harmony to retribution and retaliation. Rossbach preyed on my son's anger at me for leaving him and his mother."

Leaning back into the couch, Cade saw exactly where this was going. "He painted you as your son's Obstacle. Is that the right term?"

"Yep," Grace confirmed softly. "Anything that

Rossbach believed kept you from reaching your New Dawn was called your Obstacle. Getting rid of it was the only way you could find your true path in life."

Winston nodded. "Between Rossbach's ever-growing nonsense and my son's inherited ability to run a good con, I didn't even see it coming. Before I knew what happened, I was knocked unconscious and tied up like a Thanksgiving Day turkey in some off-the-beaten-path cabin. The only reason my son didn't put that bullet in my head is the brave girl sitting next to you."

Grace was already shaking her head, and her voice wavered. "It never should've gotten that far, Rhett. I'm sorry."

"The blame isn't on you, girl. You hear me?"

Grace didn't look convinced, refusing to meet Cade's eyes. "I'd considered Todd a friend, and I knew he had a problem with Rhett. I thought he just wanted to get him alone so he could vent his issues, tell him how much it had hurt that he'd abandoned him and his mother. Todd never told me about the gun or what he planned to do with it. But that doesn't excuse my part in it."

Winston scoffed. "It sure as hell does. You'd been subjected to Rossbach's teachings for how many years at that point? Nine? And you still knew the difference between right and wrong."

"You got him out?" Cade asked Grace gently.

Winston snortled and answered for her, "Swung a chair at Todd's head and knocked him out cold."

She'd risked her friend's wrath to help an innocent man escape. It wasn't the brave act that surprised Cade. It was his need to hear the answer to his next question: "Why didn't you go with him when he left?"

Grace hesitantly met his curious gaze. "Because in my naïve mind, I didn't think there was any way Rossbach would've approved of what Todd had planned. I went back to report it, and not only found out it had been given his golden seal of approval, but I got sentenced to the Reconditioning Center for 'withholding someone from their New Dawn.'"

White-hot rage burned through Cade's veins.

He jumped up and was in the former CIA operative's face before anyone else could move. "And you fucking left her there? After she saved your ass, you left a thirteen-year-old girl with those fucking bastards?"

"Cade! Stop!" Grace jimmied her way between them, her hands prying him away. *"Stop!"*

"Who the fuck do you think found her father's family and dropped her off on their doorstep?" Winston glared back, not in the least bit threatened by his anger. "Grace was *five* when that bitch of a mother took her away from them. You think she knew their names, much less their address? Hell, she barely remembered that there *might* be someone out there who cared about her other than me. Unlike another person in this room, I don't run away at the first sign of a challenge."

Winston meant him. There wasn't a doubt in Cade's mind.

Before he said something he couldn't take back, Cade grabbed his coat and stormed out into the freezing cold.

Grace had been a huge part of his world for seventeen years, and she'd been the other half of his heart for nine of them, yet she'd never trusted him as much as she seemed to trust Winston.

How the fuck could he fix *that*?

Cade's previous jealousy over Grace's nonexistent relationships with other FBI agents had nothing on the raw resentment that ate away at him now.

Inside the cabin, Grace bellowed at Winston in typical Steele fashion, but the tongue-lashing didn't bring Cade any joy. He stayed far away from the ominous third step and leaned heavily on the porch's railing, the wood biting into his bare palms. Fuck, he couldn't feel it anyway, the freezing cold numbing his skin.

An undeterminable amount of time later, Grace stepped outside. Her gaze settled on him like an anvil before her hesitant steps scraped against the porch. "He shouldn't have said that about you. I'm sorry."

"It's nothing I haven't berated myself for a million times in the last nine years," Cade said truthfully.

He mentally prepped himself to confront the judgment in her eyes, or the anger, but when he turned toward her, he saw neither. She'd folded her arms protectively over her chest and stared into the woods.

"Why didn't you tell me any of that?" Cade wasn't sure he was ready to hear the answer, but he asked anyway. "About the night you left? How many times did I hold you through those nightmares, and you never once said anything more than 'it's over now.' Did you not trust me even back then?"

"It had nothing to do with not trusting you and everything to do with not trusting *me*," Grace said softly. She turned, leaning her butt on the railing, and met his questioning look with a shrug. "Cults like the OND use the knowledge that you, the good little flock member, gave them, and they turn it into a weapon. They use it to control you, sometimes so effortlessly that you don't even realize it's happening until it's too late to take it back."

That wasn't what he wanted to hear.

He clenched his teeth until his jaw ached. "And you thought that's what I'd do to you? That I'd use it to bend you to my will or something?"

"You were the *last* person who'd do that...but letting my guard down with you made it easier for others to piggyback in too. Trust makes a person vulnerable, Cade, and I wasn't about to risk trusting the wrong people again. Look what almost happened to Rhett when I did."

"You can't blame yourself for the actions of someone else. Todd never should've roped you into his issues, and I'm pretty sure we all agree that Rossbach promoting that kind of violence is all sorts of fucked up. And don't get me started on your mother."

Grace emitted a humorless snort. "Thank God I take after my father, right?"

"Did she really drag you to the Reconditioning Center?"

"I had the bald patches to prove it. And you should've seen her face when I begged her to leave with me. You'd think I'd asked her to cut her still-beating heart from her chest."

Cade cursed. "Your mother doesn't have a heart."

"You won't hear me say anything different." She cleared her throat, glancing back toward the cabin. "After talking to Rhett, I think I can come up with a plan of attack for getting Tank and Jaz accepted by the recruiters. It's not perfect. We don't know if Rossbach's looking for the same thing he was when Sarah Brandt joined, but it's more than we had before. And now we have this... for when we do get our official invite."

Grace held up a thin piece of plastic. It looked like a nondescript credit card, blank except for a thin white stripe.

Cade took it and examined it front and back. "What's this?"

"Something that might open a few doors for us while on the compound. Rhett swiped it from Rossbach's office before Todd duped him into going to that cabin. We just have to hope that Rossbach's as allergic to technology as he was seventeen years ago and things haven't been updated too much."

"So we have some kind of access card that may or may not work and a plan to paint Tank and Jaz as people with an axe to grind?"

Grace nodded. "Or electric power saws. The time for subtlety is over."

CHAPTER FIVE

Ten minutes into the staged protest and Hunter "Tank" Dawson and former Marine sniper Jaz Curva had already worked up a good crowd. Passing tourists stopped and watched, and a few hopped into the chant of "People Before Politics" with little urging from Jaz up on the makeshift stage.

Watching the camera feeds on Tank's and Jaz's persons, Grace nodded, impressed. "They're good."

Sitting next to her in the back of the surveillance van, Roman grunted. "That's why we hired them. When they stop trying to purposefully piss each other off, they work well together."

Liam messed with the video controls and zoomed the cameras a little closer in to the action. "Sounds a lot like two other people we know. What are their names again? Blade and Trace? Or something like that."

Grace stopped her finger tapping and shot him a glare. "That wasn't exactly subtle, Liam."

"Good. Then I'm not losing my touch. And I'm not wrong."

He wasn't. Which was why she clamped her mouth shut.

On the way to Rhett's mountain, she'd been nervous

about Rhett and Cade meeting. She'd worked hard making sure her past never collided with her present. No one knew every sordid detail about her history with New Dawn except her therapist, and only after Grace found one she knew wouldn't give her sympathy or, worse, *pity*.

Cade now knew about the night she'd escaped, and the sky hadn't fallen down on her head, and not only that, he hadn't looked at her any differently. A small weight had been lifted off her shoulders, one she hadn't known was there until it suddenly felt easier to breathe, even during their close-quarters drive back to DC.

She wasn't sure how long the temporary truce would last, but she hoped it was a lot longer than their last few.

"So where did this down-with-the-patriarchy approach come from?" Liam asked, turning back to the monitors. "I mean it's good, but we wouldn't have thought of this on our own."

"I wouldn't have either if it weren't for Sarah's deleted social media posts. Once Brandt handed over the missing pieces, it was pretty easy to see which direction we needed to go."

"That's it? No other epiphany-inducing activities? Mental exercises? Or...physical ones?"

Grace slowly spun in her chair, and as expected, her cousin was struggling to swallow his laughter. "What exactly are you asking?"

"You to obviously kick his ass," Roman answered for him. "Man, leave it alone."

Liam chuckled. "Where's the fun in that? But since you asked, dear cousin, I was referring to the fact that you and Cade went off all night last night and only resurfaced this morning. And with a brand new plan of attack. Coincidence? I don't think so."

"Roman's right. You *do* want a swift kick in the ass. Get your mind out of the gutter."

The van's back door opened, and Cade climbed inside. "Tell me you guys see something that I don't out there. It's been two hours, and the recruiters haven't moved more than three feet."

Grace reached for the bottle of aspirin, a headache forming behind her eyes. "This isn't working. They're not making an approach. It isn't enough."

Liam shook his head. "What more can Jaz and Tank do?"

"Nothing. They're doing everything that I asked. It's just not what Rossbach wants."

"Then what *does* he want?"

Grace rubbed her temples. He wanted power. He wanted influence. He wanted the kind of influence that gave him power over others. The answer suddenly kicked her in her own ass.

"He wants to win."

"Like what? A fucking card game?"

"The adoration of others. Of *everyone*." Grace shoved down nerves that rose the second she realized what had to happen. She slowly stood and prepared herself for the arguments she was about to get. "Especially of the one that got away...the one he couldn't win over."

Silence took over the back of the van for three entire seconds as her words sunk in.

"No way," Liam broke it.

"There's got to be another option," Roman added.

"Not a chance in fucking hell," Cade growled.

"If I don't show myself, then we *don't* have a chance in fucking hell." Grace took her time staring both cousins dead in the eye before turning to a red-faced Cade. "Teague Rossbach's an opportunist, but lucky for us, he's also a narcissist. Failure isn't an option for him because it makes him look bad in front of his adoring followers. And how does a cult leader fail?"

"He loses one of his flock."

"Exactly. With me coming back, he'd seem even more powerful, both to himself and to his people." Grace tugged on her coat to give her hands something to do.

Roman scrubbed a hand over his face and cursed. "I don't like it. At all."

"You don't have to like it for it to be the only logical solution."

Lord knew she didn't.

Seventeen years of freedom, of living life on her own terms, was about to end. Even if her stint in the OND was temporary, there wasn't a doubt in her mind that the repercussions would be lasting.

She couldn't let that stop her. If she did, she'd not only be failing Sarah Brandt but herself. She'd be giving Rossbach and New Dawn power over her all over again.

No. Way. In. Freaking. Hell.

"You guys brought me here to help you find a way to get on the inside. This is it. We can't let this chance pass us by." She put Liam in her crosshairs, and her cousin flinched.

"Shit. I don't like it when you look at me like that. What do you need me to do?"

"Alter my background. Keep things as close to the truth as possible."

"That's not a problem, but what do you want to do with your service record? I can't make your years with the FBI disappear."

"Saddle me with a disciplinary action or two." A small smile slid to her face. "There's probably already one or two there to work with. And we'll bring Director Vance in and see if she has any additional ideas."

"Okay. Sure. I'll get on it."

Cade shifted his body in front of the exit. "Can we think about this for one extra minute?"

Grace shrugged. "I already thought about it last night and this morning. It was always one of the fall-backs in case things didn't go the way we hoped. And newsflash, that's exactly the point we're at right now."

"Good of you to clue us the hell in, but you even said it a few seconds ago...*we* brought you in. That doesn't mean you suddenly get to change the rules on the fly."

She tilted the badge on her hip for him to see. "This right here says that I can. Where's yours? Oh, that's right. You don't have one anymore."

They stared each other down, neither one willing to break first.

Cade cursed and turned to Liam. "Fudge up my background to go along with hers."

Grace's eyes widened. "What? Why?"

"Because when you designed this operation, you made it a two-person undercover-lover assignment."

Shit. She did. Being a dark op meant no comms and no link to the outside. It was too dangerous for a single operative, which meant—

A slow smile spread on Cade's face, telling her he realized what she did.

"That's right, Special Agent Steele. Tank's out of the running because he's already been seen with Jaz, so unless you're willing to give the term kissing cousins a new definition, I'm the only available choice to be your second."

Liam coughed. "I think I threw up in my mouth a little."

"Shut up, Liam," Grace and Cade said simultaneously.

Grace sighed. She hadn't thought that far ahead, but backtracking wasn't an option. As much as she hated the idea of flaunting herself in front of New Dawn, it needed to happen. And it needed to happen with Cade by her side.

Literally.

"Fine," she said reluctantly. "We're a couple. But bring your lips within an inch of mine, and I won't hesitate to bite them off your face."

A mischievous glint flickered in Cade's gaze as it dropped to her mouth and back. "I'm not opposed to a little biting, if you remember. I know *I* remember you being pretty fond of my lips . . . among a certain few other attributes."

Roman cursed. "Now *I* threw up in *my* mouth."

Grace ignored them all and, after tossing Roman her badge, reached for the door. "Call your contact at

DCPD and have them come in and break up the protest in about fifteen minutes. In the meantime, we need to go out there and literally show my face."

"You think they'll recognize you?" Roman asked.

"I think that I resemble my mother enough that they'll be encouraged to make an approach. Once they do, I'll hit them with the name." For the first time in her life, being Rebecca Steele's daughter was going to get Grace what she wanted.

Cade muttered under his breath. "I can't believe I'm letting this happen."

"It's cute that you think you have any say in it." Grace ignored the hand he offered and hopped out of the van. "Fifteen minutes," she reminded her cousins. "Give Cade and me enough time to poke our noses around the protest."

"Got it." Roman was already dialing his cell and gave them a quick look. "But I'm putting in my formal Not It when it comes to telling Knox about this hare-brained idea."

Cade closed the van, and then the two of them crossed the street toward George Washington Park. Twenty yards away, Tank and Jaz were still going strong, and the New Dawn Seekers loitered around the outskirts. *Watching*.

Despite the quickly dropping temps, people filled the park, some walking, some bundled up and playing on the grassy knoll. It wouldn't be much longer until the area would be hit with their first snowstorm or, worse, ice.

Nothing brought the nation's capital to a standstill more than slick roadways.

"Over there." Grace veered left toward the mobile coffee truck that would put them in direct sightline of the Seekers.

Not even chocolate would chase away the sudden angry mob of butterflies in her stomach, but it was worth a try. She waited for her turn, and when it came, Cade's arm handed the barista a twenty from over her shoulder. "Two large hot chocolates. Extra whip."

Grace tossed him a glare before turning back to the teen. "And *I'll* take a large coffee—on him. Black. No sugar."

The girl's attention bounced between them. "So two large hot chocolates with cream and a naked black coffee?"

Cade shook his head, amused. "I guess make it one hot chocolate."

"Got it."

"I thought—and I'm pretty sure this is a direct quote—'black coffee is just another name for battery acid.' Since when do you do coffee?"

Grace's chin lifted in defiance. "Since I decided I wanted a coffee and not a hot chocolate."

After graciously thanking the young woman, she locked her eyes on him from over the rim of her hot cup and took her first sip. Battery acid would have been an improvement, but she forced herself to swallow, nearly gagging.

Cade smirked knowingly. "Good?"

"Mmm. Just what I needed." She stepped closer to the iron railing separating the park from the river.

"Sure you don't want to switch?" He offered her his foam-laden hot chocolate, and her mouth salivated.

Was that cinnamon? "I'm good."

A swift breeze blew in off the Potomac River. Grace tugged her hat further over her head, but hair escaped the knit cap and swirled around her shoulders. Before she could corral it, Cade's hand caught the loose strand and slowly tucked it behind her ear.

His fingers, gloveless, stroked along her cheek a little longer than necessary, and his gaze strayed down to her mouth. She licked it on reflex and heard him suck in a soft breath. "You're killing me here, Gracie."

She pretended she didn't hear him. That was all she could do, because if she let herself fall into that conversation, she'd end up with her lips fused to his. If what happened six months ago proved anything, it was that her brain wasn't attached to her body.

Logically, she'd known that falling back on old habits—and naked fun-time with Cade—was a horrible idea. But she also knew from experience how that horrible idea never failed to make her eyes roll back in her head and her body scream for more.

For her and Cade, sex had never been a problem, except for the months he'd been deployed. But then on his first weekend back, they'd always made up for lost time. There was one distinct R and R where her cousins drew straws to see who had to show up at her dorm to make sure they were still alive.

Liam still claimed the image of Cade's naked ass was burned onto his retinas.

Cade's arm snaked around her waist, taking her off guard nearly as much as the shiver that slid through her body.

"What are you doing?" Voice breathless, Grace dropped her free hand onto his firm chest.

He lowered his mouth to her ear in a move that to anyone watching would look like two lovers sneaking in a snuggle. "We have some admirers, Special Agent Steele."

"Already?"

"You sound surprised. This was your idea."

"I know. I just..." *Didn't expect it to work so fast.* "We're going to have to set some ground rules."

"Setting rules doesn't always seem to go well for us, in case you don't remember."

"It will *this* time," she snapped, narrowing her eyes on him, "because we're both in agreement that what happened six months ago was an after-effect of prolonged stress levels and way too much alcohol. So unless the barista spiked our drinks, we'll be fine."

His mouth twitched. "If that's what you choose to believe, sweetheart, who am I to stop you?"

"Do you really think that you're so damn irresistible that I won't be able to help ripping off your clothes if you get within three feet of me?"

"Three feet? Nah. More like six."

She growled, her frustration growing because he was dangerously close to being right. Physical boundaries had never been their thing. "You're forgetting one important factor."

"And what's that?"

"I resisted the temptation of your body for nine long years."

"Pretty easy to resist temptation when that temptation is conveniently hundreds of miles away."

She knew exactly how far away he'd been.

The nights she'd spent alone in her dorm, wrapped up in one of his old T-shirts, were too many to count. And with each one, she'd felt Cade drift further and further from her life, and the pain got worse, not better. It had gotten so bad that she'd forbade her cousins and Zoey from mentioning his name, but it hadn't made the pain go away. It had just made it barely tolerable.

All that pain now rushed to the surface in one overwhelming flood. "Any distance between the two of us wasn't created by me. *I* wasn't the one who got on a plane and flew across an entire ocean."

"How long are you going to punish me for serving my country?" Cade gritted his teeth, the muscle in his jaw ticking wildly. *Good.*

"*That's* what you think I'm doing?" They both needed a hefty dose of reality, and Grace was more than happy to give it to him. Hell, she needed to hear it too. "I was sitting in the front row at your boot camp graduation ceremony. *And* your induction into the 75th Regiment. I drove you to the base before every deployment, and I stood on that tarmac holding a sign every time you came back. I supported you through all of it because it's what *you* wanted to do. *You're* the one who punished us when you re-enlisted without giving me so much as a 'hey, I've been thinking about signing my life away for another four years.'"

On Grace's left, the New Dawn Seekers shifted from

the position they'd held for the last two hours. Heads bowed, they occasionally glimpsed in their direction.

They were prepping to move.

Grace took a deep breath in an attempt to get her head off her sad love life and back on the operation. "Rehashing the past isn't going to get us anywhere but at each other's throats. The bottom line is that I learn from my mistakes, and you were one of my biggest."

Cade flinched as if she'd struck him.

Grace cringed inwardly at her lie. They hadn't been a mistake. Fifteen-year-old Cade had given her thirteen-year-old self what she'd needed most— friendship, a steady shoulder to cry on, or to vent to because she didn't often do tears. When they were older, he'd given her a hell of a lot more. As bad as things ended between them, she was glad that they'd had that time together.

The good definitely far outweighed anything else— but focusing too much on the good made her Cade-blind to those dark days right after the split.

Grace opened her mouth to apologize, but Cade beat her to it.

"You're right." His playful side was replaced by the all-business Ranger she used to know. "We were a short moment of time. I got it."

Movement on Grace's left caught her eye. "They're headed this way."

"You ready for this?"

No. Her worst fear—or one of them—was about to come to fruition. The other had been watching the man she loved—and trusted—walk away and out of her life.

Now she stood with that same man, contemplating the second.

"Just try not to get too chatty, and follow my lead," Grace said.

Linking their fingers, she turned toward the river and leaned on the railing. Cade's chest warmed her back as his other hand slid around her waist. He settled in like it was the most natural thing in the world. And for a moment, it was. Her body melted into his, and the moment his mouth brushed the rim of her ear, her knees buckled. Grace closed her eyes and took a breath, thankful he couldn't see the effect he had on her.

Still.

Neither time, nor distance, nor dating other people dampened it. She'd broken things off with a gorgeous pediatrician whose hobby was donating his time to underdeveloped countries because she hadn't felt *it* after six dates. And here she stood, in Cade's arms for less than ten seconds, and *it* was all she could feel.

Damn traitorous body.

The entire situation would backfire if she wasn't careful.

But she was a federal agent.

She'd been trained to create designated—and controlled—outcomes.

Dealing with a handsy ex and a growing erection nestled into the small of her back was child's play.

The New Dawn couple stopped three feet away, their attention sliding from the river to them and back.

"It's a chilly, but pretty day, isn't it?" The woman, dark-haired and slender, slid a quick glance Grace and

Cade's way. "I'm glad there are other people who are content to stand around and enjoy the scenery. It's rare to find with everyone rushing all over the place, focused on time and to-do lists."

Grace pushed a smile to her face. "Especially in this city."

The pretty woman laughed, her dark hair tossed back over her shoulder. "Very, very true. We've only lived here about two months, and it's something we've already noticed. That, and it's hard to make friends around here."

"Then let us be your first." Grace held out a hand in greeting. "I'm Grace. Steele. And this is—"

"Cade Wright. Future husband," Cade announced.

Grace studied the other couple carefully. She hadn't counted to two when she saw it. The couple shared small, knowing smiles that nearly flipped Grace's stomach.

Bingo. Reel cast and bait gobbled up.

"And you two are...?"

The woman laughed, leaning in to the man beside her. "Bethany Williams, and this is my husband, Thomas. I'm sorry, you just look *so* familiar."

"I get that a lot. I guess I have one of those faces."

"Cade and Grace. That sounds beautiful together. And congratulations." Bethany's gaze dropped to Grace's bare ring finger. "Is it pretty recent?"

"Practically feels like a second ago," Grace quipped.

"It was long overdue." Cade pulled her tighter to his side. "I should've asked her a million years ago, but instead, I was a total bonehead and let her get away. Not letting that happen again."

Bethany smiled. "So you were—"

"High school sweethearts," Grace explained with a strained smile. "Life—and egos—kind of got in the way—*his* ego. Mine was perfectly rational."

"At least you know where things went wrong." Bethany smirked. "Were you guys here as part of the protest? We'd seen it from a ways off and ended up checking it out, but I guess we caught it at the tail end."

"We saw it from a distance too. If we'd known about it ahead of time we would've been here holding our own set of signs."

Thomas grinned. "Rule breakers?"

"Hater of double standards is probably closer to the truth," Cade added. The hand banded around her waist flexed. "Sorry. This probably isn't the type of discussion to have when you first meet people, right? Isn't it a faux pas or something?"

"Normally"—Bethany took her husband's hand—"but it just so happens that we feel the same away. It's tragic to be standing here in our nation's capital and feel so..."

"Dirty?" Grace added.

"Exactly. You guys get it too."

"Definitely."

Thomas wrapped his arm around his wife's shoulder. "I have a great idea. Why don't we invite Grace and Cade to New Beginnings? We can get to know them better and introduce them to the others."

Bethany clapped, bouncing on her toes. "That's a great idea!"

"New Beginnings?"

"We're renovating an old bar and turning it into a community space for adults. We were so out of sorts when we moved here, and I'm not going to lie, we were at a crossroads in our lives." Bethany gave her husband an adoring look. "But now we're on the same path, and thanks to New Beginnings, we're able to help others find theirs."

Grace wanted to vomit at the mention of *paths*. She'd fought for years to break herself from New Dawn's terminology, and here she was prepped to jump right back in. "I think that sounds great...but are you sure you want to invite strangers that you met right off the street?"

Thomas laughed. "Please, Bethany hasn't met a stranger that she hasn't turned into a friend within ten seconds."

Cade's hand slid up Grace's spine and gently cupped the back of her neck. His fingers deftly massaged the knot that had been growing by the second. "New Beginnings sounds like perfect way to spend a Friday night. Tell us where and when, and we'll be there."

Bethany squealed. "I was hoping that you'd say that."

Grace didn't doubt that one bit.

CHAPTER
SIX

Cade paced, his boots scuffing up the floor of the Steele Ops command center. He couldn't help it. He needed to do *something*.

"You're making me motion sick, man, and that's saying something because I was in the Navy." Liam sat hunched over his computer, Grace at his side.

"It's been two hours since we left the park, Liam."

"Dude, I know. You can't rush art, okay?"

"Well, you better rush, Michelangelo, because if New Dawn goes searching for our backgrounds before you have our new ones in place, then we're screwed."

Actually, if any number of things happened they were fucked, and his gut, usually a strong guide, stood solidly on Shit Creek's stony banks.

"Voilà." Liam leaned back in his chair and grinned like a kid in a candy store with an unlimited gift card. "All right, lady and gents. Come. Gather around and bask in the power of my awesomeness."

He pushed a button, and two official documents, one branded with a US Army insignia and the other from the DCPD, slid off his laptop and popped up on the large wall-mounted screen. "You, Cade Wallace Wright, narrowly missed a dishonorable discharge for failure to comply with direct orders. And coincidently, it was the straw that broke the Ranger's back. Turns out, you were never fond of taking orders from people so far removed from the action."

Knox snort-chuckled. "Not so far from the truth except for the dishonorable discharge."

"On your return to civilian life, you went into the police academy and quickly advanced to detective, where you were primary lead on the Cupid Killer Task Force. And although the case brought two former lovebirds together again"—Liam smirked at both Cade and Grace—"it proved too much. You blame—once again—the out-of-touch hierarchy for nearly losing your baby sister."

Liam brought another form onto the jumbo screen. "You gave one hell of an exit interview stating all the fallbacks of the system. I mean check this out. You—I mean *I*—should write fiction."

Cade nodded, impressed. "That definitely paints a 'screw authority' picture of me."

"Which is what we want New Dawn to believe." Liam shifted things around on his screen. "Since Grace is practically a New Dawn celebrity, I didn't have the luxury of manufacturing a background from the ground up. I had to work with what I got—and with what the FBI director gave me. And can I say that that lady is *not* a breath of fresh air."

"You should meet her in person," Grace said.

"I'll pass. Thanks. But she's smart." Liam brought up Grace's fudged-up background. "She didn't think it would be a good idea to keep you listed as a criminal profiler. Why give New Dawn ammunition to question you with?"

"So what am I?" Grace leaned closer to the screen. "*Special Crimes Department*?"

"Vance's idea, not mine. She said you profiled those cases all the time so you'd have enough knowledge about them if questioned, and it's not audacious enough to be a threat to New Dawn. Hell, it could help them out if they're collecting skill sets like Pez dispensers."

Cade asked, "So why did she leave?"

Liam flipped up the next report. "Best part. I took an already filed suspension, altered the date, the jargon, and the outcome…and boom. Suspension turned permanent dismissal. Sweet cousin of mine, I'm *shocked* at the language in this report. What would my ma say if she read this?"

"She wouldn't…because she doesn't have the clearance needed." Grace's mouth twitched with a smirk.

Cade blinked as he read the monitor and chuckled. "She called her supervisor a misogynistic ass? Where the hell did you come up with that?"

Liam smirked. "Oh, I didn't come up with that bit. That was already there."

Cade glanced to an eerily quiet Grace.

Stone-faced, she folded her arms across her chest. "What? I don't regret a damn thing. The jerk proclaimed that female profilers didn't have the genetic makeup to get *down and gritty* into a killer's psyche. But the real breaking point was him waiting a single beat before offering to give me private mentoring so I could play with the *big boys*."

Liam whistled. "Damn. He's lucky all you did was call him an ass."

"How do you know that's all I did?" Grace's eyes glinted mischievously. "Men haven't changed so much since the beginning of time that they like admitting they got their ass handed to them by a woman."

An odd mixture of anger and pride swelled through Cade. He wanted to beat her former supervisor to a bloody pulp, not just for being an ass, but for being a slime ball on top of it all.

"Glad to see you haven't changed much." Cade fought the urge to pull her into a proud hug.

"Actually, I've changed a lot, because he was still somewhat upright when I left the room." She nodded toward Liam's computer. "So we're a rule-breaking Ranger and ex-cop, and a pissed-off former FBI agent with an attitude problem. I can work with that."

"Good." Liam handed Grace physical copies of their new files. "And your apartment in New York is officially on the market."

Grace looked a second away from throttling Liam. "*Are you kidding me*? Do you know how long it took me to find that place?"

"Relax, it's not really. If your old friends are as thorough as we think they'll be, keeping your apartment in a city where you're not currently living would raise red flags. And speaking of living arrangements, Jaz is hauling your things to Cade's place as we speak."

"Excuse me?" Cade and Grace asked in unison.

"You guys are engaged, right? Grace can't exactly show up with a suitcase in tow *now*. Don't worry. It'll be discreet." Liam cleared his throat and turned, but not before Cade got a glimpse of the smirk.

"What did you do, Liam?"

"Nothing. I did absolutely nothing."

"Fine, then what did you tell *Jaz* to do?"

"She's just making it look a little more...co-habited."

"What the fuck's that supposed to mean?"

Grace tried and failed to withhold her laughter. "I think what he's saying is that Jaz is making it look less like the headquarters for every fraternity in the United States."

Cade scoffed, offended. "My place does not look like a frat house."

"Seriously? All it's missing is the dogs playing poker picture and a fishnet-stocking leg lamp."

"Nothing wrong with a little decoration."

Grace rolled her pretty brown eyes. "At least tell me that you finally got a couch. If not, you better dust off that sleeping bag, because it's the floor for you. I'm commandeering your room."

Liam's attention bounced back and forth between them. "Wait. How did you know Cade didn't have a couch? You've been to his new place?"

Cocking a single eyebrow, Cade turned to Grace and swallowed a chuckle. A pink hue rose high on her cheeks as she mentally backed herself out of the corner she stepped into.

"Yeah, Grace," he goaded, smirking. "How *did* you know that I didn't have a couch until recently?"

With a throaty growl that made Cade half hard,

Grace stalked out of command ops, the heavy iron door slamming shut behind her.

Liam chuckled. "You, my friend, are *so* fucked."

Cade couldn't disagree.

He was screwed . . . and not in the sweaty, naked, fun kind of way.

* * *

As an FBI profiler, Grace traveled. She visited crime scenes and interviewed witnesses. If she'd been sent as damage control, sometimes she had a face-to-face with the perpetrator as she'd done with a serial killer case last year.

She spent more time in hotels than she did her own apartment, and she'd never once had trouble falling asleep. But she'd been staring at the same spot on the wall for the last two hours and hadn't come close to drifting off.

She couldn't blame Cade's snoring, because with him sleeping on the couch, she didn't hear him. Nope. It was all her and her racing thoughts that wouldn't turn off.

A second before she was about to give up and go in search of something hot and sweet, the bedroom door opened. Careful not to give herself away, Grace eased her hand between the mattress and box spring until her fingers brushed against Magdalena.

So she'd been a little on edge. That was to be expected. The fact she and Cade had been tailed from Iron Bars out to his place in Foggy Bottom didn't help much. They'd known that New Dawn would be keeping tabs on them, she just hadn't expected it right out of the gate.

Or for them to commit a break-in.

Grace's heart beat in her chest as a tall shadow darkened the wall. She slowed her breathing and counted as it closed the distance. When it reached the corner of the bed, she whipped her arm out, and with it, her Mag. "Move closer and see what happens."

"Shit! Put that away!" Cade cursed, bumping into the end table and cursed again. "You sleep with your fucking gun?"

"Wasn't exactly sleeping." She leaned forward and tucked Magdalena into the nightstand.

"You and me both. Our friends outside just left. Guess they figured we were a boring ol' about-to-be married couple so they didn't need to stare into our windows any more tonight."

"Thanks for telling me."

Cade didn't move.

"That was a hint for you to leave."

"Yeah, about that...I figured out why someone put my couch on the corner to be taken away. It has a million broken springs."

"Sorry to hear that." She fluffed the pillow and tucked her hands beneath it for extra poof factor. "Your bed's pretty comfortable."

Cade grumbled and walked away. The second Grace thought he'd left, the other side of the bed dipped. She flipped over in time to see him, clad only in those damn sexy boxer briefs, slide into bed. "What the hell are you doing?"

"Sleeping. In *my* bed."

"We're not sharing this bed, Cade."

"Then feel free to go sleep on the couch. Watch out for the spring in the top right corner. It partially impaled me." He rolled over, giving her his back, and released a loud, obnoxious yawn and burrowed into the mattress.

"You're seriously making me sleep out there? What happened to chivalry?"

"It died about two liters of blood ago. And no one's forcing you. Unlike you, I'm capable of sharing."

Grace lifted her pillow to smack him.

One second she was poised over his head, and in the next, she was flat on her back. Cade hovered over her, his chest the only part of his body not in contact with hers. "Assault with a fluffy pillow, Special Agent Steele?"

"Would you rather I used Magdalena?" Grace twined her leg around Cade's and shoved him right while she rolled left, quickly swapping their positions. "Give me that pillow back."

"No way in hell. All weapons need to be registered with the proper district, and you, Miss FBI lady, haven't done so. It's all mine." He lifted his head and tucked it beneath him.

"Oh, really?"

"Yep. You're going to have to take it by excessive force if you want it back." Grinning, Cade casually propped his arms behind his head while he waited for her to make the next move.

That freakin' smirk.

Grace's stomach flipped. Suddenly hyperaware of their intimate positioning, she glanced down at her thin yoga tank top and purple panties.

Cade seemed to realize it too because his gaze darkened, and the smirk on his face melted away. Bracing her palms flat on his bare chest, Grace slid her legs to either side of his waist and leaned.

"What are you doing?" His voice dropped to a lusty bass.

"I should think it's pretty damn obvious. Or maybe I'm doing it wrong."

Inch by slow inch, she ran her hands up the contour of his torso. The man made body hair work, and her fingers brushed through the dark blond hair covering his chest.

Beneath her palms, his muscles flexed. "You're playing with fire, sweetheart."

Grace ran her nose along the curve of his jaw and barely skimmed her mouth over his cheek. "No I'm not. I'm playing with *my pillow*."

She ripped it from beneath his head, and his body dropped with a loud *umph*. Tears sprung to her eyes as she laughed, blinding her to the coming attack. Cade gripped her hips and flung her sideways, and then she was back on the bottom, his weight pinning her down.

"You play dirty." His chest rumbled with laughter.

"What can I say? I like playing dirty when it comes down to you, babe."

Cade gently pinned her wrists above her head and leaned his mouth to her ear. "You're not the only one."

She knew that look and laughed, squirming to get

out of the hold. He didn't even have to touch her because just the thought of being tickled made her laugh, and he knew it.

"Stop squirming, Grace." Cade's voice dropped to a low rumble.

She giggled. "Then don't—oh."

Trapped between their bodies, Cade's growing erection made its presence known. Now that they were in this situation, Grace wasn't sure what to do about it. He stared down at her, his lust making her body come alive.

Every inch of her skin became hypersensitive to his. His bare legs shifted against hers, making her suck down a groan.

Cade released his hold on her hands and climbed out of the bed. "Take the bed. I'll deal with the springs."

"*Cade*," Grace called after him. He stopped by the door but didn't turn to look at her.

She knew it was a bad idea. Down to her core. And yet she padded barefoot across the room.

His body tensed as she closed the distance. "If you know what's good for you, you'll turn around and get back under those covers. I mean it. I'm trying to do the right thing here."

Funny how at that very moment, she didn't want to do the right thing. Grace laid her palm on the center of his back and slowly trailed her mouth up his spine, occasionally flicking her tongue out for a small taste. "And I'm trying to do what's going to feel good for both of us."

"So you can go back to hating me in the morning? Been there, done that, have the T-shirt."

Grace stepped around him and slipped her fingers through his hair, ready to tug him down to her waiting lips. He gripped her hips, stopping her.

"What's wrong?" She searched his face for the answer, but all she saw was the same desire she knew was written all over her own. It was palpable and right there for anyone to see.

"Not this time, Gracie. Not now. Not when I know things are going to go back to the way they were the second the clothes go back on. I want...more."

She laughed before realizing she was the only one, and quickly sobered. "More? You want what? You want love ballads and sonnets? A picket fence and two-point-oh children?"

"Years down the line? Maybe. But for now I'd settle for a clean slate and an honest-to-God stab at a second chance."

He couldn't have cleared her head more if he'd doused her with ice water.

Grace pulled away. "I don't think you know what you're asking."

"Yeah, actually, I think I do. I know I fucked up nine years ago. I own it, and as much as I wish things had played out differently, I can't go back and change any of it."

"Well, gee. I guess I should be thankful that you know that you derailed both our lives. Actually, I guess just mine, right? You went on as if nothing ever happened." Emotions clogged her throat. She turned around, eager to be anywhere but near him. She didn't do emotion easily, and as good as she was as hiding it,

Cade could always see right through her. "You want the couch? Go for it. I'll be right here if you change your mind."

Cade paused at the door and slid a tense, pain-filled look over his shoulder. "Just so you know, I didn't disappear entirely that day. When I stepped on that plane, I left a piece of myself right on your doorstep...my heart."

The second he closed the door behind him, Grace's emotions broke through her carefully built barriers. She flopped on the bed and buried her face in the pillow, her hot tears wetting it within seconds.

It could have been the stress of the long day or the fact her past was about to smack her between the eyes. But in reality Grace knew it was because while Cade had left his heart stateside nine years ago, she'd most definitely sent hers on that plane with him.

CHAPTER
SEVEN

Cade's knuckles screamed from each impact with the heavy bag, but he ignored the pain, hitting it harder and throwing in an occasional roundhouse kick for good measure. He'd woken up to a note from Grace saying that their stalker friends from the night before were across the street again, and she was taking them shopping for the day with her and Zoey.

That was it.

No mention of what almost happened last night, or what he'd stupidly admitted. Fuck, he couldn't even blame Iron Bars's good tequila on the slipup. He'd done it stone cold sober, and with one hell of a hard-on. His dick had expressed its displeasure with his decision to keep his hands off her with a serious case of blue balls.

But damn it, he'd meant every word. He didn't want to be the bad decision or the next morning's regret. At thirty-two, he wanted the same thing he did when he was fifteen.

Her. Her heart. Her *trust*. All the physical stuff didn't mean shit if every time she looked at him, she did it expecting him to fuck up again.

Cade growled and released a series of left and right hooks that had the sparring bag swinging wildly.

"You're attacking that heavy bag like it insulted your sister," Roman chided. "Seriously, man. If you'd wailed on me like you're doing right now you could've won that MMA tourney years ago."

Roman leaned against the gym doorway, his sleeveless tank stuck to his chest from his own workout. One hand dropped to his prosthetic, giving his knee a rub. He caught Cade's glance and stood upright.

"What do you say to taking out your aggressions on something that can hit back?" Roman dropped his water bottle and towel on the bench and stepped onto the mat.

Cade frowned at the prove-yourself gleam in his friend's eye. "I was about to call it quits."

"Scared that I'll kick the shit out of you?"

"Something like that."

Roman's grin vanished, and his eyes went hard. "You afraid of getting your ass kicked by a man with one and a half legs?"

And there it was—the albatross Roman dragged around when he wasn't shit-faced drunk or on a mission kicking ass. It didn't take long after Roman's return from overseas to sense the change in his friend.

Dark moods. Self-imposed exile. Avoidance of people. As far as Cade knew, Roman hadn't touched a woman in years, and for the second oldest Steele brother, that was quite the feat. Since sprouting their first facial hairs, none of them ever hurt for female companionship.

Cade carefully contemplated his words as he unwrapped his hands. "I put in my workout. I'm good."

"Come on, Wright." Roman stalked closer. "Let's go at it like old times. First one on the ground unable to lift his head loses."

"We were a lot younger and a hell of a lot stupider back then. Concussion Syndrome's serious fucking business, man."

"That's a copout if I ever heard one, but you know what? Never mind." Roman grabbed his towel and bottle and took a swig. The smell that drifted Cade's way was definitely not water.

Unwilling to help his friend in his downward spiral, he conceded. "All right, Ro. Let's go. For old time's sake."

"Too late. I've got plans with people who aren't intimidated by a little scrap of fucking metal and plastic." Roman pushed past Knox on his way out of the gym.

"Was it something I said?" Knox asked dryly.

"It was something I wasn't keen on doing."

Knox's face grew grim. "I'd say talking to him is like talking to a brick wall, but there'd be more two-way conversation with a wall. The closer it gets to the anniversary—"

"The worse he gets. It's in what...two weeks?"

Knox nodded. "He'll go through his process and be back to his usual ornery self."

"If he doesn't pick a fight with the wrong person and get his ass beat."

"There's always that chance, but we can't help someone who doesn't want the help. Zoey's been working on him, though."

Cade snorted on a chuckle. "Then God help him.

My sister may look like a sweet poodle, but she's got the tenacity of Cujo. What's up? You didn't come here to make small talk about Zoey."

Knox leaned against the wall. "You ready for tomorrow night?"

Cade swapped his sweaty shirt for a dry one. "Got our backgrounds memorized. My place has been feminized thanks to Jaz. Oh, and remind me to thank her for that couples' game. I saw it this morning when I was pouring coffee into my travel mug and damn near burned off my balls."

"Actually, the game was my idea. Zoey and I have one that—"

"Stop right there, man." Cade held up his hand. "I read the back of the box, and I do not want to imagine my baby sister doing any of those things. You got me?"

Knox chuckled. *Bastard.*

"As for tonight, I'm good. Grace may be the people reader, but if there was one thing I learned as a detective it was how to loosen lips without beating the shit out of people. Everything will go off without a hiccup."

"And if you were working solo, that may be the case. But you're working alongside your ex."

"Not seeing how it's any different," Cade lied.

He'd spent the better part of the morning running through a wide range of potential ways for this to blow up in their faces, one of which was whatever they'd have to do to prove their loyalty to the Order.

Cade was an unknown despite Liam's magic making him look like the perfect candidate, and Grace had already Defected once. There was no way in hell they weren't going to be tested, and while Cade would do almost anything to get a job done, he drew the line at compromising Grace's safety.

"Do you really think I'm that stupid?"

"You want me to say that I'm worried? Fine. I don't like all the blanks, but I'm not afraid for myself." Cade threw his shit in his bag and zipped it up. "But I'm telling you right now, if shit hits the fan and I have to choose Grace's safety or getting the job done, I'll choose Grace."

"You won't get a problem here, but *she's* sure as hell going to give you a fight."

"There isn't a single one of you Steeles, other than your mother, that isn't a pain in my ass." Cade threw his foul-smelling towel at Knox's head, and he ducked, chuckling.

"I'm just keeping it real. This assignment wasn't going to be a cakewalk even if it had been Jaz going on the inside, but *now*?" Knox paused a beat. "I know there's shit about New Dawn and Rossbach that Grace keeps to herself. And maybe you know, or maybe you don't. But keep your eyes open. There's no telling where her head's going to be at. You better be serious about choosing her over the op. If you have to, throw her over your shoulder and haul ass."

Cade snorted. "Yeah, she'd love that."

"I don't care what she loves as long as she makes it out in one piece."

"You give her the same pep talk?"

"Damn straight I did." He rubbed his side. "And I have the forming bruise on my ribs to show for it."

Cade snorted on a laugh. "Woman's got wicked aim."

"Hell yeah, she does. She's a Steele." Knox clapped him on the back. "I'm headed out to meet with a potential recruit. You need anything before I go?"

"Nope. All good."

"Then good luck tomorrow. Watch your asses and do yourself a favor...listen to Grace. I know I give her a hard time, but she's trained in the psychobabble stuff, and she knows how these assholes think."

"You mean my skill for pyrotechnics isn't going to do us any good?"

"Not unless you guys *really* fuck the hell up."

Knox left, and Cade packed his gear before locking down the ops center. Up in Iron Bars, he waved a goodbye to Ryder, who was attempting to train yet another bartender, and headed out to his truck. He'd tossed his bag in his passenger side seat when a familiar vehicle pulled in front.

"Just fucking great." Cade slammed his truck door and waited as the older man stepped onto the curb.

Retired Army General Hogan Wilcox showed up like a cursed penny, at exact moments when Cade didn't have the patience to deal with him. Tired, on edge, and with adrenaline coursing through his veins from his workout, now wasn't the time to have a heart-to-heart with dear old dad.

"Knox isn't here."

"It isn't Knox I'm here to see. Heard about your operation happening tomorrow."

"And here I thought your dealings with Steele Ops were strictly monetary."

"They are. Brandt told me. Guess he needed reassurance that he did the right thing sending you boys in."

"And you're here to what? Check in? Pardon me while I shovel away the shit that's piling up around your feet."

Wilcox sighed, frustrated, but Cade didn't care. Just like he didn't give a rat's furry ass that the man had once been both revered and feared in Army history lessons, a reputation he'd gladly taken with him as the Army Chief of Staff.

Every time Cade looked at him, all he saw was the man who left his mother with two young children, one of whom was sick. Wilcox could dish up excuses until he turned blue in the face and empty his entire damn wallet. It wouldn't make things right.

Cade brushed past his father and reached for his door. "Well, it's been nice chatting. We'll have to not do this again anytime soon."

"Are you ever going to—?"

He spun around and froze. "What? Forgive you?"

"Your sister—"

"Doesn't have an unforgiving bone in her body. But unlike Zoey, I remember the day you left, or at least that part where you told me that you'd be back. Or did my eight-year-old imagination make that little bit up?"

Wilcox grimaced.

Cade had him. He knew he did.

"There was a lot that you don't get."

"I don't need to get you, Hogan, because I get *it*. You fathered two kids with a woman your family didn't approve of, and instead of fighting for the family you claimed to care about, you left."

"I did what I thought was best."

"And after Mom died you thought leaving Zoey in the child care system—with her condition—was the best thing?" Cade shook his head, disgusted. "Fuck-and-you."

Wilcox's face reddened. "Now wait a second, son."

Hands balled at his sides, Cade jumped the sidewalk and got within an inch of his father's face. "I am *not* your son. You gave up that title years ago."

"If I hadn't left, things could've been a hell of a lot worse for you and your sister."

"So you're sticking to that whole my-family-didn't-approve story, huh?"

"It's not a story. I was a pissant in the Army. Without my family's money, I had nothing to give any of you. I had no choice but to fall in line."

"Like a good little soldier, right?" Cade scoffed. "Count your blessings that you might be able to salvage something with Zoey, but I don't have the slightest urge to repair anything with you."

Wilcox followed him to his truck. "For God's sake, Cade, it's not like I left you and Zoey in the lurch. Gretchen took good care of the two of you. I made sure of it. And Zoey got the best—"

"Mention your little benefactor shit and I will lay you out right here. Paying her medical bills doesn't make up for being MIA." He climbed in his truck, not trusting himself with his sperm donor another second.

Once he'd pulled onto the road, he snuck a glance in his rearview mirror to see Hogan Wilcox staring after him.

Cade refused to feel sorry for the man who'd left them without a thought. It didn't matter that they'd lucked out with Gretchen adopting them. It didn't matter that Wilcox, from behind the curtain, paid for Zoey's mountains of hospital bills... or that he believed he'd done right by them.

He left.

No discussion. No warning.

As anger coursed through Cade's veins, his mind rewound time and swapped people and situations. It was suddenly like reliving what he'd done to Grace all those years ago: made a decision that affected everyone around him.

The realization only made Cade drive faster.

* * *

People hustled from store to store, some bogged down with so many bags Grace wasn't sure how they didn't collapse to the ground or roll down the escalator. Evidently the entire DC Metro Area had gotten bit by the holiday bug.

"What I wouldn't give to see Roman out here shopping with the masses," Grace joked as she and Zoey navigated the busy center aisle of Tysons.

"Yeah but you never will, because according to him that's what I'm for. And the internet. And gift card centers at the grocery store." Zoey grinned. "Now Liam on the other hand? I've seen the way he stops and stares at that bear-building commercial whenever it comes on. It wouldn't surprise me in the least if he shows up to make his own stuffed unicorn."

Grace laughed, easily imagining her cousin doing it. Unlike Roman, Liam wasn't deterred by large crowds, and Tysons drew people from everywhere, so many that the barely controlled chaos unnerved even her a bit.

A cold tingle creeped down her spine and sent her head in a slow swivel. It first happened when they'd stepped off the escalator, and it had come and gone for two hours since.

Zoey gently pulled her to a stop. "You need to spill it already. What's up?"

"I don't know what you mean," Grace lied, feigning innocence. She didn't want to put a damper on their girls' afternoon for nothing.

"Are you forgetting that I'm related to Cade, and virtually related to you and all your cousins? I can tell when you guys are scoping a place out without moving your heads. It's creepy as heck. *And* I've let you talk me into buying two outfits, and you haven't yet cracked a single smile."

"I just have a feeling. I'm not so sure that tail split off when we got to the parking lot."

When she and Zoey had driven into the parking garage, Grace had let out a sigh of relief that their tail had gone straight. Cade had taken center stage in her headspace ever since last night. There wasn't much room left for New Dawn stalkers.

"Okay." Zoey headed toward the food court.

"*Okay*? That's all you have to say?" She followed, setting her bags on the nearby table.

"Pretty much. If you have a feeling there's probably a reason for it, so sit your rear end down and do your creepy observer thing while I go get us pretzels."

"You want pretzels?"

"No, I want you be stationary in a sea of moving bodies so you can pick out another stationary body who seems a bit too preoccupied by two hot friends doing a little holiday shopping." Zoey's grin made Grace laugh.

"The guys really have taught you a thing or two, haven't they?"

"Yep. Now, cheese or no cheese?"

"Cheese, of course."

As Zoey left for the pretzel stand, Grace slowly eyed the crowd. There were a lot of interesting characters, but no one screamed ogler to her.

She was still casually people-watching when Zoey returned, innocently turning her body to look at the passing people. "Anything yet?"

Grace almost shook her head when she spotted him.

About fifteen yards away standing at a perfume kiosk, a broad-shouldered man in a brown leather jacket and black jeans quickly averted his gaze. The sales clerk approached him, and they talked briefly, the shopper shaking his head, and yet he remained in front of the perfumes.

"Perfume stand," Grace murmured to Zoey. "What do you think?"

Zoey casually fiddled with her purse on the back of her chair, slyly glancing up. "I think I've seen him before... when we were in the bookstore and then again standing outside the bathrooms."

Coincidences were possible, but in a mall the size of Tysons, it wasn't likely.

"Do you want to call the guys?" Zoey sipped on her lemonade.

Grace shook her head. "They'll draw needless attention. He's just surveilling, making sure Cade and I are who we say we are. We can keep shopping...maybe hit up Lacey's Lingerie."

"This is good, right? The sooner you get in, the sooner you can get the job done."

"Definitely."

Zoey's blue eyes narrowed behind her glasses. "Then why don't you look relieved? Are you nervous about going back? That's understandable, you know that, right? Those people stole years of your life, and don't get me started on that mother of yours."

Grace chuckled as her friend's disgust. She'd almost pay money to see her best friend go up against Rebecca Steele. Mother Dearest wouldn't stand a chance. "It's not even that. Not really."

At least that hadn't been what kept her up all night after Cade walked out of the bedroom.

"If it's not the job, then that means..." Zoey's eyes lit up. "It's my brother."

"No, it isn't."

Grace's eye twitched, and Zoey, being herself, immediately caught it. "You tall, gorgeous liar, you. It *is*. I see it all over your face, and don't give me that crap about training having erased all your 'looks.' Knox says that too, and yet I can tell when he's horny."

"He's always horny. You guys are like rabbits."

Zoey smirked, pink flooding her cheeks. "I'm not going to deny that, but we both know I'm right. Was it the Scandalous Desires game? Did you guys play it?"

"The scandalous what?" Grace asked, confused.

"Never mind. But you can't sit there and tell me that your broodiness this morning isn't about Cade. Did you guys 'fall back on bad habits'?" Zoey asked, smirking as she used Grace's own words.

"I knew I shouldn't have told you what happened six months ago."

"Technically, you didn't. I guessed. So is that it?"

"Nope. Definitely not."

"So he wanted to, and you dashed his hopes?" Zoey studied her carefully before choking on her drink. "Oh, my God. *He* was the one who cock-blocked *you*, wasn't he?"

A few people from nearby tables glanced their way. Grace grimaced, apologizing for her way too exuberant best friend.

"He did *not* cock-block me," Grace hissed.

"He turned you down, and you're *sulking*."

"I'm not..." Grace sighed. "Okay, yeah, maybe I am. I still don't see what the big deal was. It's just sex."

Zoey shook her head, laughing. "Sex is never *just sex* between exes. There's history too. Looks. Touches. Moments of time that will always be engrained in your mind. No matter how much time passes or distance there is, history will always be there. *Especially* during sex."

"They teach you that when you become a CSI?" Grace joked, ripping apart her pretzel. "He claims he wants...*more*."

"Such as...?"

Grace shrugged.

"Does he want to put a ring on it?"

Grace snorted. "No."

"Is he asking you to be the incubator for his children?"

"You're being ridiculous."

"Then what is he asking for in exchange for sexy naked times?"

Grace shoved a large piece of pretzel in her mouth. "A second chance. Or something like that."

Zoey waited a beat, then two. "That's it? And you can't give that to him?"

She *could,* in theory. Heck, she'd thought about it a million times since that day he left her apartment, but she always came around to the same problem. "I'm afraid of what will happen if I do."

Zoey flashed her a wan smile. "You guys were so happy for so long, Grace. Would it really be so bad to have that again?"

"It's not the good times that make me nervous, Zo. It's what would happen if it all goes sideways...again."

She'd barely survived losing Cade the first time.

She didn't know if she could handle it again.

CHAPTER
EIGHT

Thirty-six hours ago, Grace had been happily chugging along in life, working her stack of cases and avoiding the creepy agent three cubicles down from her own. She'd had her routine, her own space. Now, thanks to her cousins and their earlier game of Prepare the Undercovers, all she had was a blossoming headache and the lump of dread coiling her stomach.

With Liam as their ringleader, they'd grilled her and Cade for two hours—questions about their backgrounds, their current lives, and any possible curiosities that could pop up in social situations like the one they were about to step into.

Grace stood outside the nondescript brick building in Southeast and waited for Cade to come around the truck. He slipped an arm around her waist and leaned in to take a peek at the address written on the piece of paper.

"They definitely like keeping things low-key, don't they? Guess that's how they fly under the radar." He scanned the block, but there wasn't much to see.

It looked like any other DC street. Private residences intermixed with small neighborhood businesses, and yet Grace half expected the earth to open up and swallow her whole. A person-size sinkhole, or better yet, DC's very own Hellmouth.

Cade's fingers squeezed her hip. "What the hell put that look on your face?"

"Wondering if Rossbach's really the Master in disguise," she muttered.

"What?"

Grace pulled herself out of her self-imposed fantasy. "Huh?"

"The Master?" He waited expectantly for her to explain herself.

"Oh. *Buffy* reference. Sorry. Zoey and I binged the first season my first night here." She hiked her purse on her shoulder. "Let's do this."

"One second there." Cade eased her back. "Far be it for me to tell you how to do your job, but if *that's* your impersonation of a woman in love, we're going to have a problem, sweetheart. If you've changed your mind—"

"I haven't changed my mind."

"Your worry face says differently."

"I'm worried, just not about me." She gave him a pointed look.

He laughed. "Me? Hon, I didn't take on a leadership role with the 75th Ranger Regiment because I can't handle myself."

"That's what makes me nervous."

"Afraid you lost me."

"You're used to taking the lead, but this isn't an extraction in hostile-occupied territory—at least not yet. We're not rappelling off the face of a building or jumping out of a plane. What we need to do in there"—she pointed toward New Beginnings—"is a matter of the *mind*. This is *my* territory."

"Is this your way of telling me that I'm not tactful?"

"When was the last time you played anything subtle, or took the back seat and let someone else drive?"

He nodded. "Point taken. I'll follow your lead. But you got to do me a favor."

"What?"

He captured her chin between his fingers and tilted her face up toward him. Her breath caught as she automatically dropped her gaze to his mouth in time to see his lips twitch. Heat spread throughout her body, warming body parts that had previously been cold.

In all their preparation for tonight's assignment, one thing they hadn't mentioned was what happened the other night at his place. The memory of what she'd offered and what he'd turned down came flooding back—along with his little addendum.

"That little flush in your cheeks will do." Cade brushed his lips across the corner of her mouth before winding his fingers through hers.

"Was that really necessary?" She tried to sound annoyed but couldn't seem to find the heat.

"Yeah, it kind of was." Cade chuckled.

"Follow my lead, and don't go too far off script. I know how these people think."

It was how Grace avoided being sent to the Reconditioning Center more times than she'd been sent there. She hadn't magically disobeyed rules when she hit thirteen. She'd had a lifetime to study the best tactics to get herself out of tight jams, and she had that talent to this day.

Hopefully.

Grace led the way through the front door.

People decked out in sporty casual filled the room, their conversations at odds with the soft music filtered in from corner speakers. Small white lights wrapped around potted trees and plants gave the old bar a very comfortable and homey feel.

At first glance everything looked normal—including the people.

Cade eyed a couple who passed them, their heads bowed as they whispered.

"Doesn't this look cozy?" His mouth brushed against her cheek as he murmured in her ear. "There's an awful lot of people here for an informal recruitment drive. How are two people supposed to ferret through the horde and dole out golden tickets?"

"I don't think they are."

Cade's blue eyes lasered in on her. "You don't think Bethany and Thomas are the only recruiters here?"

"I think we'd be stupid to assume that they haven't planted current Order members in the crowd of hopefuls. People are more likely to talk without filters to people they think are on the same level. Even as hosts, Bethany and Thomas are one up."

"I never would've thought of that."

She smirked. "I know."

Chuckling, he looped an arm around her waist and nodded across the room where they'd caught their hosts' attentions. "Looks like we're on."

Bethany grabbed her husband's hand, and the duo hastily made their way over.

"You came!" Bethany leaned in, hugging Grace. "I was telling Thomas that I hadn't seen you two. I'd hoped you hadn't changed your minds."

Grace returned the embrace before stepping back to Cade's side. "We wouldn't miss this. It's not often that you meet another couple who thinks the same way that you do."

Bethany swept a hand over the busy room. "You'll definitely meet more like-minded people here. We couldn't have asked for a better turnout."

Cade put on an impressed face. "Where did you guys meet all these people?"

Thomas chuckled. "Bethany doesn't have a problem introducing herself to strangers . . . as you found out for yourself. We can't even go for a walk without her stopping to chat someone up. It's how we met our current dry cleaner and our future nanny—if we ever choose to have children down the line."

Bethany smacked him playfully. "I happen to think that people aren't kind enough to one another. It's been scientifically proven that a single smile can not only improve a person's mood, but their overall health. I consider it among my civic duties."

"I agree with that wholeheartedly." Grace nodded. "I once had an English teacher who was a perpetual grump, and I think he called out sick more times than he came to work."

"See! Proof!" Bethany linked arms with Grace and guided them deeper into the room, Thomas and Cade following close behind. "This really is the place for you to be, Grace. Everyone here has faced something in their past, a trial, or obstacle, and they've committed themselves to finding their new happy place."

Bile rose in Grace's throat, reading between the lines. Obstacles. Trials.

If she and Cade had already been accepted into the Order, the other woman would've called that *happy place* a New Dawn. It was Rossbach speak for the start-over. The fresh start. A new freakin' chapter.

"That sounds wonderful." Grace forced herself not to choke on the words. "You have no idea how incredible it is to hear that there are others who want the same things."

Bethany's smile couldn't have gotten any wider. "It is, isn't it? And our community grows every day. You just need to know where to look for us."

"Stephanie. James." Bethany stepped up to a tall, lithe blonde and a broad-shouldered man who oozed what Grace called the GI Joe gene from every pore. "I want to introduce you to Grace Steele and Cade Wright."

Stephanie gifted them a friendly smile and held out a well-manicured hand. "It's nice to meet you. I don't think we've seen you around here before, have we?"

Grace shook her head. "We almost literally stumbled into Bethany and Thomas twenty-four hours ago, and here we are."

"She does have a way of doing that, but she has an amazing track record, so if the two of you are here, you must be special."

Cade dropped a kiss on her temple. "I don't know about myself, but Grace is definitely one of a kind."

"Aw, that is so sweet." Bethany waved to someone across the room. "Now that I know everyone is in good hands, Thomas and I better keep mingling. A host's job is never done."

They all said quick see-you-laters, and Grace turned back to the other couple. "What about the two of you? How long have you known Bethany and Thomas?"

"For me it's close to eight months." Stephanie glanced at her male counterpart. "But James has been around longer. What's it been? A year?"

"And a half. I like to pop in whenever I'm town."

Cade shifted at Grace's side. "Does that mean you guys aren't from around here?"

"I'm local," Stephanie declared. "Actually, I work in the district attorney's office and James is—"

"From everywhere. Former Navy, so I got around."

Cade chuckled. "I called it before you even opened your mouth. Former Army."

"Let me guess. 75th Regiment?"

"That obvious, huh?"

James lifted a beer to his lips. "We worked with you guys a time or two. You fellas know your shit."

"Which means you weren't just Navy, you were on the SEAL teams."

"Guilty. Have any problems finding your niche when you got out? You always hear horror stories about brothers not being able to get their land legs back. Sad as hell."

Cade paused, earning him a look from Grace, but he recovered quickly. "That's the only reason I stayed in as long as I did. Re-upped at the last minute for another four-year tour because I damn near had a panic attack at the idea of being stuck on my ass."

Grace studied Cade carefully.

That hadn't been part of their practice, but he'd said it so casually that she couldn't help but wonder if it was true. Had he been afraid of that? It was possible. She knew each of her cousins had had an adjustment period after returning home.

"I hear you, man." James nodded. "I took a few security side jobs here and there...enough to feel useful. You?"

"Went through the police academy and worked my way up from beat cop to detective. I headed the Beltway Killer case."

Stephanie swallowed her sip of wine. "I thought you looked familiar. Those were some intense six months. I was one Clarion box away from becoming a brunette. Your sister was almost victim fourteen, wasn't she?"

Cade frowned, and he answered gruffly. "Yeah. Thanks to a lot of red tape and regulations made by people who sit behind a desk all damn day. The way everything went down's why I'm no longer with the DCPD. I'm a hell of a lot happier running a distillery with a few buddies of mine than I ever was carrying around those damn handcuffs."

"And what about you, Grace? What do you do?" Stephanie asked.

Grace feigned discomfort by shifting awkwardly on her heels. "I'm currently between jobs."

She gave Cade a faux nervous look, and he hugged her close. "Babe, I told you before and I'll tell you again, it's nothing to be ashamed of."

"I know. It's just..." She sighed and looked back to the curious couple. "I used to be with the FBI, but I quickly found out that their spouting about equal employment opportunities for all meant for everyone who'd been born with a dick between their legs. Pardon my language. I'm still a little sore about it."

Stephanie chuckled. "I went to Harvard Law School. I'm a blond woman with a genetic predisposition for big boobs. There wasn't a course that I took that I didn't hear at least a half dozen *Legally Blonde* references. On the daily. Trust me, I get it."

Grace returned her laugh. "Bethany wasn't lying when she said everyone here was from all walks of life, was she?"

"All very different but with very similar hopes and dreams. It's almost like an insta-family...except we *choose* to relate ourselves to each other." Stephanie studied her carefully. "Do you have any family, Grace? Other than your gorgeous fiancé here?"

Warning bells rang in Grace's head, confirming what she thought. *Stephanie and James are already part of the Order*. Cade's hand casually moved up and down her back, telling her that he realized the same thing.

"I do. I have an aunt I adore, and a few obnoxious cousins."

"That's it?"

"And a mother, but I haven't seen her in a long time." Grace swallowed audibly, playing up her nerves as Stephanie and James watched her like two hawks searching for prey. "I guess you could say that we had a falling out."

"I'm sorry to hear that."

"Me too. I was thirteen and hormonal. We had a fight—I don't even remember what about," Grace lied. "The next thing I know, I'm alongside the interstate, alone, with twenty bucks to my name."

"That must have been so frightening. Alone at thirteen?"

"That's putting it mildly."

James's face remained impassive, obviously not as sympathetic as Stephanie. His dark eyes lasered into her. "Why didn't you go back? After your head cleared? You don't think she would've shrugged it off as kids being kids?"

"I wanted to go back within the first few hours, but I didn't know how. Literally." Grace mimicked nervousness by increasing her blinking. "We lived in a . . . well, I guess the more mainstream term for it would've been commune. I'd been there since I was five, and there was never any reason to leave, so . . ."

"So you didn't know *how* to get back," Stephanie said.

"Exactly. The only thing that's come close to making me feel as safe as I did at New Dawn is Cade." Grace slid her eyes to him. "He got everything I was feeling because he did too. It was freeing."

"That's the saddest and yet the sweetest thing I've ever heard."

Grace laughed. "I didn't mean to go on and on about myself. I guess I've been feeling a little homesick lately."

"That's perfectly understandable." Stephanie looped her arm through Grace's and smiled. "Come on and let's introduce you two around to more of the group. I have a feeling that before the night is done, you're not going to feel the least bit homesick."

Stephanie was right.

As the night wore on, Grace's feigned homesickness turned to nausea. Each step, each couple she and Cade introduced themselves to felt like another inch of quicksand. By the end of the night, the only thing sticking above the flood line was her head.

And barely.

CHAPTER NINE

Grace jumped off the treadmill and barely refrained from breaking her nose, her legs having more in common with Jell-O than bone and muscle. Zoey couldn't even be blamed for her trip to the G Street community center. She'd gone all on her own, erroneously thinking she could sweat the last twenty-four hours out of her system.

If anything, her mind was even clearer—freakin' exercise hormones.

Zoey had been right. Sex would never be just sex with Cade, and thinking she could compartmentalize it hurt them both. It didn't mean she didn't want it to happen, but that she knew she'd regret it the second it did.

Maybe.

And then there was the off-the-cuff explanation Cade had given James the other night.

Grace didn't know if there was any truth to his fear of returning to civilian life, but if there was, it made her a Grade A jerk for cutting him off the way she had.

All servicemen and women went through an adjustment period after leaving the military. Some took to civilian life easily while others struggled to find their spot. She'd been so focused on her excitement for their future that she hadn't thought about Cade seeing it from the latter vantage point.

She wanted to ask him about it but didn't feel right bringing it up out of the blue.

As she shut off the power on her torture device, Grace immediately noticed Pepé Le Pew do the same from his treadmill in the corner. Her perfume kiosk admirer wasn't exactly stealthy, although he probably thought he was.

She'd ignored him as he'd trailed her around town— except for yesterday afternoon, when her curiosity had gotten the better of her. Thanks to a mischievous trip into Sonia's Sexy Sex Shop, she now knew Pepé had a thing for balls on a string.

Flinging her towel around her sweaty neck, Grace proceeded to guzzle a liter of water. Her cell rang in her gym bag, and she searched beneath her clothes, growling when it stopped and started again a few seconds later. Eventually finding it, she glanced at the unknown caller ID.

Finally.

"Hello?" she answered, keeping her voice cool.

"Grace? Hey, it's Bethany. From New Beginnings?" Bethany's voice came from the other end. "I hope I'm not bothering you."

"Not at all. Actually, your timing's perfect because you caught me before I went home and died."

"Are you okay? Do you need me to call anyone?"

Grace laughed. "Okay as I'll ever be after running five miles. Did I mention that I don't do prolonged bouts of exercise? I'm really going to regret this tomorrow."

"I don't suppose you want to postpone your death and meet me for coffee or something?"

Two days since the New Dawn social. *Not bad.* "Change it to a hot chocolate and you've got a deal. Where do you want to meet?"

"The Daily Grind? Do you know it?"

"Sure do." Especially considering it was only two blocks away. Coincidence? Probably not. "I can be there in twenty. Give me enough time to change into something that won't knock you out of your chair if you end up downwind."

"See you in a few."

Grace showered and changed in record time, throwing her hair into a messy bun. Twenty-five minutes later, she stepped into the neighborhood coffee shop, spotting Bethany in the far back corner. The brunette stood and waved.

"Sorry I'm late. It turns out I'm not the only one who tried Death By Treadmill today, so I had to wait for a shower."

"It's not a problem. I've always envied people who go out in the real world and exercise. I'm all about the home videos and the fewer the witnesses, the better."

Grace chuckled, momentarily forgetting this woman, although not directly responsible for Grace's life in New Dawn, lived for every word spoken out of the great Father Teague's mouth. Being a Seeker meant she'd paid her dues to the Order. It meant she'd proved herself a valuable member of the community. It meant that sweet, smiley Bethany Williams was nearly as dangerous as Rossbach himself.

They gave their orders to a waitress and waited for her to head back to the counter.

"I'm glad you called." Grace played up the uncertainty by fiddling with her napkin. "Cade told me not to hurry looking for a new job, but I'm going stir-crazy. The fact I resorted to exercise today to get out of the house proves it."

Bethany laughed. "I'm glad I could provide a distraction. And don't worry about the job thing. I'm sure something will come your way that's perfect for you."

"I wish I could be as optimistic as you. Right now I'd settle for something that would pay for my hot chocolate problem."

"Can chocolate ever be considered a problem?"

"Point taken."

The waitress arrived with their drinks, and Grace took a greedy sip.

Bethany leaned in to the table, looking very much like a woman with something to say. "So I have a confession to make."

"Isn't it a little early in our friendship for a tell-all?"

"It's not that kind of confession." Bethany chuckled. "Not that I didn't enjoy hanging out with you and Cade the other night, but I had an ulterior motive in today's meet-up."

Grace feigned curiosity. "Ooh. Intrigue. What's this motive?"

"You and Cade made quite the impression at the mixer the other night."

"There were a few people who left impressions on us too. James was a little *intense*. But Stephanie was an absolute joy…although I'm afraid I may have scared her off."

"Steph doesn't scare easily, and James was literally trained to be intimidating. But then again, you should be used to that with Cade. You said he was an Army Ranger, right? That's like the definition of intimidation."

"Yeah, but I'm pretty much immune to Cade's pound-against-the-chest tactics. Guess it comes with knowing him before he needed his first razor."

"Stephanie's actually one of the people who mentioned you."

Grace grimaced. "To ask you never to invite me to another function again?"

"Don't be silly." Bethany squeezed her arm and shook her head. "Actually, I hope you don't mind, but she told me a little bit about your history. I'm sorry to stick my nose where it doesn't belong."

"No. No. It's not like it's a secret or anything I'm ashamed of. It's just I don't usually go telling people about it right after exchanging names. It's not something that's widely understood, if you know what I mean."

"You mean about the commune?" Bethany asked.

She was digging for more information.

By throwing out an open-ended question, Bethany invited Grace to tell her more about her past life. It was the exact tactic they used in clinical psychiatric settings. She wasn't sure if it was something Bethany had been trained to do or if she'd stumbled on it by accident, but it didn't matter. Grace was about to give her the extra gossip she wanted.

"I described it as a commune because it's so hard to put into words that someone from the outside can understand. It's more than a plot of land, or even the people living on it. New Dawn was a way of life. A shared belief system." Grace cupped her mug and smiled wanly over the rim as she took a sip. "I'm still not explaining it well, so maybe I should shut up while I'm ahead."

"Please don't. Stephanie mentioned that you've been struggling being apart from them? From your mom?"

"Yeah, but Cade's helped fill some of that emptiness, and I adore my father's family. There's always going to be a hole, though. They don't quite *get* me like the people who lived in Sanctuary, and I didn't realize how important it was to surround yourself with like-minded people until I was suddenly on my own. Seventeen years and I've felt like an outsider every single day."

Bethany glanced around the coffee shop before dropping her voice to a low murmur. "What if I told you that you didn't have to be on your own anymore?"

"That's sweet, Bethany, and I'm sure you and Thomas have a great thing going at your place, but it wouldn't be the same."

"I don't think you understand what I'm saying. What if I told you that I was *with* the Order? Both Thomas and myself. And that we're active Seekers sent out by—"

"Father Teague." Grace thunked her mug to the table. It took a few beats and a discreet pinch on her thigh, but soon moisture welled and flowed over, wetting her cheeks. With faux flusters, she wiped them away. "Don't play with me. You have no idea how long I've hoped— just don't mess with me. *Please*."

"I'm not. May the New Dawn—"

"Shine upon you." Grace covered a gasp of shock with her hand. "I can't believe it. How...?"

"When I saw you in that park, you looked *so* familiar, and then when you told me your name, I *knew*. *I* was a child of the New Dawn too, Grace. As a matter of fact, my mother's one of Father Teague's newest Council members."

"Oh, wow." Grace feigned envy. Being a council member meant Bethany's mother would be in Teague Rossbach's inner circle. "From what I remember, Father Teague doesn't promote members to the council very often. You must be so proud."

"I am. Very proud. And it's because of my mother's status that we're occasionally able to speak. I mentioned you to her, and to say that she was excited would be an understatement." Bethany slid her hand over hers and squeezed. "You're no longer lost, Grace, at least not if you don't want to be."

Grace tried not to vomit on the so very clueless Seeker. "You have no idea how long I've wanted to hear those words. I can't even begin to describe how I feel right now."

Actually, she could—nauseated, ill, like ants crawled under her skin and made a home.

"And Cade? I wasn't sure how he'd feel about you contacting the council...or the Order itself."

"Oh, he'll be ecstatic. He knows all about New Dawn. And before you say it, I know divulging details about the Order is frowned on, but I knew what Father Teague instilled in me during my time with the Order would help Cade too. When he was discharged from the Army, he was nearly as lost as me."

Bethany studied her a moment before smiling. "That's what I was hoping to hear."

"Could you really get us into contact with the Order? When can we go? Tomorrow?"

Bethany chuckled before her face turned serious. "Soon. I promise. But for obvious reasons, we have to be careful. We can't risk accidently leading any non-believers into Sanctuary."

"No. I understand. Of course not."

Bethany looked contemplative for a few seconds. "While Thomas and I organize another pilgrimage, there is one small thing that the Order was hoping you could make happen. Not for them, of course, but for one of our flock."

Here it was.

The test of loyalty.

Grace had known it would happen. Nothing came free, and she'd been living on the Outside too long to be trusted right off the bat. Summoning every acting skill she ever acquired from summer drama camp, Grace nodded emphatically. "Yes. *Anything*."

"You didn't even hear what it is."

"Bethany, I've waited years to return home, and now that it can happen, I'm not letting anything stop me. You want me to fly to the moon, I will. You want me to break into the Pentagon? Consider it done. *Whatever* you need."

Bethany waited a beat before nodding. "We need you to break into the DCPD . . . and steal evidence."

Shit. It wasn't the Pentagon, but it was damn well close enough.

* * *

Cade's head pounded, seconds away from exploding onto everyone standing around the Steele Ops command center, and he wasn't the only one waiting for it to happen. All eyes were on him and had been since Grace practically sauntered into Iron Bars and casually asked for an audience with everyone.

She'd been too calm and rational for it to be anything good. And this definitely wasn't good, or bad.

It was a *clusterfuck* that only he seemed to be able to recognize. "There's no way I can be the only person to see all the horrible ways that this could go wrong."

"If we stick to the plan, nothing will go wrong." Grace stood in Steele Ops's command center, her arms folded across her chest, and brought her FBI game face. She wasn't backing down anytime soon. "We have to focus on our ultimate goal."

"If your goal's to get our asses arrested and hauled to jail, then what you're suggesting will definitely do the trick. Shit, Grace, I was a cop. Do you know what they do to cops in the general population? Tell me that you didn't agree to it."

"Of course I agreed to it. We wanted our golden ticket onto the Order compound, and this is it."

"A felony."

Zoey cleared her throat, trying to be the peacekeeper. "Let's take a breather and look at the big picture."

Cade tossed his hands in the air. "Take a breather, Zo? Really? This isn't something that can be solved with fucking yoga!"

"You're right," Grace snapped. "It can be solved by using our heads...and not the little one between your legs. If you would've listened instead of tuning me out the second I said 'steal,' you would've heard the rest of the plan."

Knox, mysteriously quiet up to this moment, stood and paced the room. "Your plan to work with the local PD?"

Grace nodded. "Director Vance already contacted the police commissioner to set it up. Bethany gave me the case number and location of the evidence. It's going to be a matter of bait-and-switch. Local PD will take the real surveillance used in the case and replace it with a duplicate. What we steal won't be the real thing."

"But whoever this case is against will still get off scot free," Cade clarified.

"Temporarily, yes, but Vance verified that all we're talking about here is a bar brawl. Someone got a little too free with his punches and destroyed a shit ton of property. The bar owner pressed charges for damages."

Knox rubbed his whiskered jaw. "Seems like a big deal for something that's usually settled out of court with the writing of a check. Who are they trying to protect?"

"Some New Dawn bigwig. And they expect to be looped in on the actual operation by video and audio feed, so we can't take the dupe and just hand it over to them. We have to go through the motions of stealing it so that they can see the show."

"Of course we do, because it wouldn't be a complete three-ring circus until that was the case," Cade muttered.

He was being an ass. He knew it. Judging by the room full of scowls aimed at him, everyone else did too. But he also knew Grace like he knew the back of his hand.

There was something she wasn't saying.

He studied her carefully, noting the subtle upward tilt of her chin. *Yep, definitely something.*

"What aren't you telling us?" Cade asked. "What are you so carefully trying to avoid spilling, princess?"

Her gaze snapped to him. "I've told you everything."

"I don't buy it." He narrowed his eyes on her, digesting her words all over again. "Even if Bethany didn't give you the name of this guy we're about to free, Vance would've when she looked into the case file. Is it someone you know?"

Grace's jaw clenched with quiet fury. If glares could drill through bodies, he'd be a human sieve. She knew exactly whom they were about to help, and she kept it quiet because he'd recognize the name too.

Cade didn't know a whole lot of cult members, so that whittled down his list considerably. "Who is it?"

"Who it is doesn't change the fact that this is what we need to do to get within sniffing distance of Sarah Brandt. If you don't like it, I'll more than happily tell Bethany that you're not so cool with the New Dawn lifestyle after all, and go at it alone."

Like fucking hell. No way was he letting her step back into this freak show without him as backup.

"Who are we about to help, Grace?" he asked again.

"Todd Winston."

The blank faces from her cousins told Cade they didn't know him from Adam. But Cade did.

His and Grace's "Story Time with Rhett" would be forever engrained into his memory vault, and so would the name of the man who had no problems killing his own flesh and blood—and bringing a young girl along for the ride.

CHAPTER
TEN

Grace took challenges head-on. She didn't balk, or hide, or skirt around issues, instead choosing to tackle them with single-minded focus and determination. Except when it came to this New Dawn case.

Survive suddenly became her new motto, and that had meant jumping into Cade's shower the second they stepped through the door to his townhouse. Pushing her forehead against the cold tiles, Grace prayed for the hot water to wash her memories down the drain, but it didn't work. Todd's face still held on like a leech.

Seventeen years ago, he'd been so enraptured by Rossbach's teachings. He'd been eager and entitled and so, so angry—a very deadly combination. There wasn't a chance in hell he wasn't a million times worse now.

Thinking of the countless other minds Rossbach and Todd had collectively poisoned, Grace shut off the water and toweled herself dry. She anchored the fluffy white towel across her body before coming to an abrupt stop outside the bathroom.

She blinked, unable to fully comprehend the scene in front of her, and blinked again.

Cade attempted to build a Jenga-like tower on the coffee table. It teetered precariously, and he cursed before making sure it stayed upright. It would've looked like the start of any regular game night...except for the fuzzy red handcuffs circling his wrists.

"Would you like me to leave you alone?"

"Shit." Cade's knee slammed into the table, knocking down half his tower.

Suppressing a laugh, she gripped her towel and padded barefoot to the empty box at his feet. On the front, a half-naked couple embraced passionately among swirls of glittery gold lettering. "Scandalous Desires...The Ultimate Intimacy Game for Couples."

"This isn't what it looks like."

"It looks like you're playing with that mystery game Zoey seemed to know something about."

"Okay, so maybe it is what it looks like, but I wasn't *playing* it." He attempted to clean up the fallen blocks, his movements hindered by the cuffs.

"I'm a profiler, not a prosecutor, but...really? The evidence is a little damning." Smirking, she picked up one of the fallen Jenga blocks and read the black inscription. "'Share the position which gets you to orgasm faster. Draw pictures for further explanation.'"

"I'm going to kill Jaz for leaving this here." Cade squirmed in his seat, tugging at the bracelets. "My skin itches from these damn things."

Grace picked up another block. "'Put on the fuzzy cuffs and wear them for the rest of the game.'" She couldn't suppress her laughter. "Looks like you already have that step covered."

"Seriously, Grace, is there a key in the box or something? I think I'm allergic to whatever the hell these things are covered in." Cade twisted his wrists, and she noted the red skin beneath the cuffs.

She shook out the box. "Nope. Empty."

Cade swore again, his curse earning him a chuckle from Grace as he grabbed the box and looked inside himself. "How the hell can there not be a key?"

"You could always write to the manufacturer and complain." Grace bit her lip and padded away toward the bedroom.

"Wait. You're not going to help me get out of these damn things?" he called after her.

"Your curiosity got you into them, surely you can get yourself out."

"If I could, I would've done it by now. And I wouldn't be asking you for help."

"They're plastic, Cade. Beast out of them."

"But then—"

"Then what?" She turned around before disappearing into the bedroom and leaned against the door, smiling coyly. "You can't play with them again?"

He narrowed his eyes, getting off the couch. "You're enjoying this?"

"Immensely, yes. It kind of reminds me of Johnny Franklin's birthday party when you tried cheating your way into a Seven Minutes in Heaven session with Heather Tooley and got Wilma Hutchinson instead."

Cade's mouth opened and closed. "How did you know I tried stuffing the hat?"

Grace smirked. "My talents at reading people were on point even back then. The question really is how could I have *not* noticed."

He stalked closer, each step that he took flipping Grace's stomach. "That goes to show what you know."

"Please. I saw you with all those extra pieces of paper."

"Yeah, you probably did." Cade stopped inches away. Heat poured off him in waves, but it was nothing compared to what was happening in his eyes.

Locked on her, they glittered with a faint trace of mischief and a whole lot of desire—blue-eyed molten lava. Grace had never been so aware of her lack of clothes until that very moment.

His gaze dropped to her mouth and back. "But it wasn't Heather Tooley's name I was stuffing in that damn hat."

"Then whose was it?"

"Yours."

Grace's breath caught in her lungs. Even while she mentally asked herself if it was the truth, she knew it was. Of the many things Cade Wright was, one thing he wasn't was a liar. Her body warmed from the small wave of hope his lusty gaze created, and she didn't know what to do with it.

"Don't look at me like that." Grace's soft demand didn't hold any kind of conviction, even to her own ears. Cade hadn't touched her and yet she tingled from her toes up, her towel chafing her hardening nipples.

"Look at you like what, Gracie? Like you've been *it* for me since the second you walked into my life? Why? So you can keep denying the truth? We're good together. Always have been and always will be."

He wasn't wrong, and, God help her, she didn't want to deny it either. Right then, her next breath wasn't as important as kissing him. She leaned closer, sliding her hand into his hair.

Cade stopped her. "I told you before, I want—"

"*Yes.*"

"Yes what?" He scanned her face as if trying to read her mind. "Because I meant it when I said that I don't want to be a next-morning regret."

"I don't want that either." Grace swallowed the lump that formed in her throat as she struggled with her words. "But I can't just jump into a relationship with you. I can't act like the last nine years never happened."

"I don't want you to. Past mistakes are how we learn not to make them again in the future." Cade slipped his joined hands over her head and trailed them down the center of her back. "We just need to be *us* and see where things go. If it leads to something more, great. If we find out that our issues are too much to deal with, then we part ways with no hard feelings. But I'm not going to lie, Gracie, I'm rooting for the first option."

Grace dropped her forehead on his chest and focused on what he was saying and everything she'd be putting on the line if she agreed. If they failed, there was no number of cases she'd be able to distract herself with to put the pieces of her life back together.

But if it worked?

Zoey had been right when she'd said that her time with Cade had been one of her happiest, and Grace wanted to be happy. *So. Damn. Bad.* Her job with the Bureau had filled one gap in her life, but there would always be a hole only Cade could fill.

"Okay." The word fell off her lips in a whisper as their gazes slowly met.

His eyes shone with a heavy need that was no doubt in her own. "Okay?"

"We'll try, but I'm going to ask you one really huge favor."

"Anything."

"Kiss me. Right the hell now."

Grace wasn't sure who moved first. Their bodies clashed together, tongues dueling in a frenzied search for more. They tumbled backward, her ass hitting the wall.

Using the extra support, Grace rubbed her body against his, fueled by the rough growl that slid from his throat. "You have no idea how much I've wanted this."

"Probably as bad as I did."

"I don't think that's possible. Legs around me. Now." Cade cupped her ass and pulled her closer.

She wrapped them around his waist, her towel pulling apart, revealing a scandalizing amount of skin.

Cade's gaze dropped between her legs. "Fuck me, you're gorgeous."

"You're not so bad yourself." Grace ran her mouth over his jaw, stopping to nibble his ear. "Now imagine all the places you could touch if you didn't have those pesky handcuffs on your wrists."

"Hold on," Cade growled.

"For what?"

"Beast mode."

Behind her back, the cuffs snapped. Cade's hands settled on her hips and instantly eased her body in a slow grind as he walked them to his bed.

Noting the broken links and the cuffs still on his wrists, she giggled. "I guess that's one way to solve the problem."

"That's me. A problem solver. Watch me solve another one." He tossed her onto the center of his bed, making her squeal, and tugged his shirt off.

The soft glow from the bedside lamp played over his broad chest. The man was gorgeous, and even if their arrangement turned out to have an expiration date, he was temporarily all hers—and she was going to enjoy every damn second of it.

Grace bit her bottom lip and scooted back, slowly working the knot on her towel. She timed her movements with his, pulling it apart as he shucked his pants and boxers down his legs. His erection bobbed in front of him, thick and hard, a drop of pre-come peeking out from the tip.

"See something you like, sweetheart?" He grinned.

"Do you really need to ask?" She urged him closer with a crook of a finger, but before he could cover her body, she took the length of him in her mouth.

He sucked in a sharp breath. "Holy shit."

His hand bunched her hair, pulling it away from her face as he watched her lips move around him. The lust filling his eyes fueled her even more as she tightened her grip and quickened the stroke of her tongue. Cade trembled in her hand before pulling away with a low groan.

"What's wrong? You didn't like?" she teased.

"Definitely wasn't the problem. I've spent months dreaming about coming inside that sweet body of yours, and I'll be damned if I'm going to shoot off prematurely." He leaned her back onto the bed as he fumbled in his bedside drawer, coming back up with a foil packet. He'd barely rolled the condom onto his cock when she rolled him over, changing their positions.

Cade didn't complain as she straddled his hips, teasing them both as she rubbed his length through her slit three, four times before finally...slowly...sliding him effortlessly home.

They groaned in unison.

Grace braced her hands on his chest and, despite her need rushing through her, forced herself into a slow, even pace. Pleasure coiled low in her abdomen, tightening her body. "You feel fucking incredible."

"Don't stop. Take it, baby. Take what you need from me." Cade's hands clamped down on her hips as he thrust from below, sensing her brewing orgasm. The only sound heard in the room was the wet glide of their bodies and their staccato breathing.

Sliding one hand up her torso and around her breast, Cade pinched her nipple with just the right amount of pressure to send her over the edge.

Grace's pleasure exploded. "Cade!"

"*Grace*. Fuck. Now." Her muscles squeezed him into a mutual release.

Their movements went from timed to uncoordinated as they road wave after wave of pleasure. Eventually, hard thrusts turned gentle and Grace collapsed on top.

She sighed, breathless. "Now imagine what would've happened if we'd played that little game."

Cade stroked a finger up her bare side. "We don't need a Scandalous Desires game to get our motors revving. We take off pretty well all on our own."

He was right. Grace just needed to be careful that she didn't fall off at the first sharp turn.

CHAPTER ELEVEN

Grace stepped into the Fifth Precinct, Cade close on her heels. The last time she'd stepped through these doors, it had been to take down a serial killer, and as horrible as it might seem, she half wished that were the case. Even though they'd planned this test of loyalty with the proper authorities, stealing evidence left a bad taste in her mouth.

She'd double-checked with Director Vance no less than six times that morning to make sure the original evidence had been duplicated and safely tucked away. There wasn't a reason to worry—except if she and Cade got caught.

Vance knew about the operation as did as the DC police commissioner, but that was it.

The more people pulled into the loop, the bigger the chance that someone slipped, and they couldn't chance it. Bethany and Thomas both listened and watched from the camera Grace wore on her lapel, and they needed to make everything look as authentic as possible because, unfortunately, they weren't stupid.

Cade's hand rested on the small of her back as he guided her through his old station.

He stopped and chatted with friends, one of whom

was Zoey's boss, Lieutenant Mason from CSI. As expected, it took them a good twenty minutes to make their way to the back of the building...and to the evidence locker.

"You guys are doing great, Grace," Bethany said into their ear comms. "In and out. Quick and easy. No one will even know that you've been in there."

"Are you're sure there's not going to be a problem cutting off the power? Because it just so happens that I left my invisible cloak in my closet."

Bethany chuckled. "We have it covered, don't worry. When you're in position, all our person has to do is hit the button and you're free and clear. Think of the big picture. You're helping a fellow Order member get one step closer to their New Dawn. There's no act more noble."

Except making sure that guy gets back to DC to see his day in court.

As if reading her mind, Cade cupped the back of her neck. His magical fingers rubbed away the forming knot just as they approached the evidence desk. "We got this, babe."

"Joe!" Cade addressed the older officer behind the chain-link screen and leaned against the counter. "How the hell are you doing, man?"

"Look what the cat drug in. How are you doing out there in the private sector? Civilian life, man. Scary thought."

Cade chuckled. "Are you kidding? I love it. I roll my ass out of bed whenever the hell I want to and then I get to experiment with alcohol. This is like retirement thirty years early. You've gotta be close to taking the plunge, aren't you?"

"Next year, but then what would I do? The sooner I retire, the sooner my ass will get dropped in the ground. Gotta keep busy to keep young, my friend."

"Ready whenever you are, Grace," Bethany announced in the ear comm.

"Ready," Grace murmured.

"On three."

Cade shifted, blocking Joe's view of the door. "How are the grandkids? Are your son and daughter-in-law going to give you that granddaughter you've been talking about?"

"One. Two."

The overhead lights blinked twice, before dousing the basement corridor in pitch black. In front of Grace, the door's security light went out. She tugged it open, careful not to make noise. "I'm in."

"All the way to the back. Second to last aisle on the left. Row S. Case file 52405." Grace snuck a glance back at Cade, who was "helping" Joe find his emergency Maglite. He dropped something, making the older officer shoot off a round of expletives.

"Your guy has the guard covered, Grace," Bethany encouraged. "You're doing great. Imagine how good it's going to feel to help someone in our community."

Grace held back a smart retort, because what it felt like was committing a felony, staged theft or not. She found row S, tucked her little pen flashlight between her lips, and scanned the box labels until she found 52405.

"Got it." She jimmied the tape open and grabbed

the copied thumb drive. "All this for this little piece of plastic?"

"That's all we need," Bethany affirmed. "Cade's still trying to distract his friend, but you may want to pick up the speed. He's getting a little antsy—the friend, not Cade. Your sweetie is cool as a cucumber."

Grace stuffed the drive between her cleavage and quietly returned the box. Three feet away from the door, Joe stepped into her line of vision, his broad back toward her.

She froze, afraid of drawing the officer's attention. Cade's gaze slid over Joe's shoulder, locking on her— and then he was gone. Something large hit the floor.

Cade.

"Shit, man, you okay?" Joe cried out and moved to help, no longer in Grace's path. "You trip over that box on the ground? I meant to stuff that away. Shit. I hope you didn't break anything."

"Go. Go. Go," Bethany ordered, chuckling.

She was glad one person was enjoying this.

Using Cade's distraction, she slipped silently out the door and nearly fell against the wall with a sigh. The police commissioner might know about their operation, but no one else in the precinct did. If they'd been caught it would be *real* handcuffs and an unsanitary holding cell.

"Good job, guys," Bethany congratulated. "Lights going on in three, two, one...voilà."

The overhead fluorescents blinked menacingly before coming to life. The rumble of the heating unit vibrated the floor, blasting stale air from the vents.

Cade stood behind the counter with Joe, helping the older man restack a tower of fallen files. "Looks like they figured out what the problem was. Something probably happened to the circuit breaker."

"Or it could've been the rats chewing on the wires again. We had the exterminator out here last month, but the little bastards still manage to sneak back in. Gotta love old DC buildings." Joe paused, looking nervous. "Oh. You probably shouldn't be inside the cage in case someone comes down to check on things."

"Can't be hanging out with the riffraff, right?" The two men shared a laugh, and after shaking Joe's hand, Cade met her at the hall corner. "Got it, babe?"

Staying in character, she gestured between her boobs. "Got it. Good job on the acrobatics there, slick. For a minute, I thought we were toast."

He slid her a coy smirk. "I think I may have bruised my ass on the way down. Maybe you can kiss it later and take away the sting."

Bethany laughed via the mic. "Job well done, you two. May the New Dawn shine upon you."

"And upon you as well." The words were bitter ash in Grace's mouth, and her hand, limp at her side, reflexively reached out for Cade's. He slid his fingers through hers and kissed the backs of her knuckles.

That small contact, however innocent he'd meant it to be, helped her breathe a little easier.

*　*　*

After Cade and Grace's *Grand Theft Evidence* at the station, Cade had been more than happy to hand over that little piece of plastic to Bethany and Thomas. Their evidence tampering hadn't come without a price. He'd felt it in the tremble of Grace's fingers. Saw it in the way she refused to meet his eye for too long.

Getting her alone, away from prying eyes, had been his goal after proving their worth to the Order. He needed to make sure she was okay, and she wasn't about to tell him the truth when they were surrounded by a crowd of people...especially when those people were their friends and family.

Which was probably why they were still at Iron Bars two hours after they'd checked in with Roman and the others.

Laughter spilled from one room to another, and as time passed, even more people made their way inside in an attempt to get away from the quickly dropping temps. The lounge was packed shoulder to shoulder, the tasting rooms in the back nearly the same.

It was as far from the alone time Cade had anticipated as it could get—and Grace, sitting with Zoey and Jaz across the room, hadn't looked his way in close to an hour.

Ryder's newest bartender reached across the bar to give a customer his drink, and the glass slipped from her fingers, dousing the front of her pants in vanilla bean vodka. It was the sixth disaster to happen within the last thirty minutes.

Roman sat down in the vacant seat on his left. "Ryder claims that she'll catch on quick."

"*Before* we run out of stock?"

Roman chuckled just as Ryder appeared behind the bar to help Emma clean up her latest mess. Bastard didn't realize he got starry-eyed gazing at the redhead.

"Everything at the precinct went off without a hitch? No problems?"

"Not a one—which makes me a little embarrassed for the state of DCPD's security features, and a lot more concerned about what other talents these New Dawn people have been hiding."

"Guess you and Grace will find that out soon enough."

Cade grunted and sipped his beer. If Bethany's appreciation over a job well done was any indication, they'd be getting that invite any day. Sarah Brandt would be back with her family. Job over. Peace reigns. And Grace no longer had a reason to stick around.

But hell if he didn't want to give her one, which was putting the cart light-years before the horse. He was surprised she agreed to see where things went with them. He didn't want to fuck it up by demanding more. Making edicts would lead to automatic failure and Grace telling him to go to hell.

For now he'd hold the course and hope for more mornings of waking up to her warm and very naked body. He'd enjoyed watching her gorgeous body glide into the shower instead of out of his apartment, which is what would have happened—and did happen—six months ago.

Thinking of Grace heading back to New York, Cade clutched his beer mug until his knuckles cracked.

A familiar laugh drew his attention across the room where Jaz, Zoey, and Grace had commandeered a corner table, a party sampler of flavored vodkas in front of them, and a flirty Cajun smiling down on them.

Tank whispered something in Grace's ear that made her laugh again, and he pulled away, shooting a smug smile Cade's way.

Bastard. If the guy weren't his friend he'd hate him. At the sound of another one of Grace's laughs, Cade changed his mind.

He hated Tank anyway.

An evil glint twinkled in Roman's eye. "You want to go over there?"

Fuck, yes.

"Nope." Cade watched Emma put way too much vodka in a Bloody Mary.

Roman stared over his shoulder, a shit-eating smirk on his face. "You got to see this."

"Nah. I'm good."

"Tank sure knows how to put on a show. I think it's the Louisiana bayou accent. Women lap it up like a damn Tootsie Roll Pop. Come on, man. You gotta at least take a look."

"I *really* fucking don't." Because God help Tank if he had his hands on Grace. And then if Cade strutted over there banging on his chest like a caveman, God help *him,* because Grace would kick his ass.

"Damn." Roman shook his head, his gaze still aimed across the room. "Guess the bastard's about to get lucky tonight after all."

"Fuckin' A." Cade was on his feet and already

halfway across the room before he realized the brunette sitting on Tank's lap wasn't Grace.

He shot Roman a hard glare and got a half shrug in return.

Grace chose that moment to turn her pretty golden gaze his way. Deer caught in headlights didn't describe how he felt. He told his feet to move, but they didn't obey. Around him, people swayed to the music filtering through the speakers, but he couldn't take his eyes off her.

Cade crooked his finger and got a subtle *who, me?* lift of her eyebrow. He wiggled his finger again and watched as Grace said something to Zoey and Jaz. Both women glanced his way, Zoey with an ear-to-ear smile and a thumb up.

Cade looked his fill as Grace closed in on him...if that was even possible. Her jeans were molded to her body, her heeled boots showcasing her mile-long legs. He reflexively licked his bottom lip and saw her gaze drop to the sight.

A smile played on her own lips as she walked up to him. "Please tell me that you didn't summon me over here."

"I didn't summon. I coaxed."

"And the difference is what?"

"No magic involved—unless you consider my animal magnetism a power."

Grace rolled her eyes. "If that's all you wanted to say..."

Cade caught her arm and gently pulled her back to him as a slow song came over the speaker. He brushed his mouth over the shell of her ear and nearly groaned when she sighed. "Dance with me."

"You? Dance? Who are you and what have you done with Cade Wright?"

"I told you that I'm not the same person I was nine years ago, and I meant it. This is me now. Cade 2.0." *This was him silently pleading with her not to pull away.*

This thing between them was so new, and not to mention fragile, that he half expected it to blow away. Hell, maybe he'd imagined it, which was why he waited with bated breath for her next move.

Her lips tugging into a small smirk, she slid her hands up his chest and linked them behind his neck. "What the hell am I going to do with you?"

"Right now? Dance with me. In another hour? Strip me naked and have your way with me." Cade eased them into a slow sway, and on every beat, the soft curves of her body melted against his even more.

He wanted to whisk her away right then, but instead, he savored the fact she stood with him—in public—and devoured him with her eyes. They weren't playing it up for New Dawn.

This was entirely for them.

Grace's fingers played with the hair along his nape. "Does this sudden need to dance have anything to do with a certain sexy Cajun?"

"*Sexy* Cajun?"

"Well, yeah. A woman would have to be dead not to notice—and I'm definitely not dead."

"No, you're definitely not." Cade breathed through a

rush of annoyance, stopping when she laughed so hard tears sprung to her eyes.

"You find something funny, sweetheart?" His voice rumbled his chest.

"Yeah, you." Grace snort-chuckled. "Seriously, Cade. I'm messing with you."

"So you don't think Tank's hot?"

"Oh, he's *totally* hot. But I've been too wrapped up in thoughts of taking this other guy home to really notice. Actually, I was crossing my fingers that he'd take me back to *his* place and ravage me."

"Ravage?"

"Mm. Total devouring." Grace nibbled her bottom lip, making Cade groan.

His cock twitched at the mental image she painted. "Just so you know, that guy you want to go home with is totally up for what you're suggesting—*after* getting one thing straight. This see-where-it-goes second-chance? It's just us. You and me. Cade and Grace."

"Temporary monogamy? How forward thinking of you."

Temporary. The word left a bad taste in Cade's mouth, but he'd gargle later. All that mattered at the moment was him and Grace being on the same page.

He leaned down and held his mouth mere centimeters away from hers, and she came the rest of the way. As their lips fused together, heat zipped through him. The kiss was hot, hungry, and over way too quick.

Her voice dropped low, heavy with lust. "I think I can handle that."

"Yeah?"

"Yeah. And I think…"

"What?"

"I think my phone's vibrating." Breaking the moment, Grace tugged her cell from her back pocket and flashed him a look at the caller ID. "It's Bethany."

Their gazes locked. They both knew what this meant.

New Dawn's light was already shining upon them, and yet all Cade could see was a dark cloud hovering right over their heads and the storm that was about to wreak havoc on their lives.

CHAPTER TWELVE

Drumming her fingers against her thigh, Grace fought not to look toward the driver's seat because Cade's worried glances only added to the nerves twisting her stomach.

This was *really* about to happen.

After seventeen years of being free of Father Teague's daily Blessings and her mother's nonstop disapproving lectures, she was headed back to New Dawn...and back to the people who stole eight years of her childhood.

Escaping the Rec had been easy compared to her time in Sanctuary. In the Order, you weren't one person. You were the *Community*, and every action was judged by how much it benefited the entire compound—or Rossbach. Not having known anything else, Grace had unwillingly accepted it as a way of life...but then she'd met her father's family.

Living with the Steeles, autonomy had been her biggest adjustment, and there had been times she'd gone a little overboard experimenting with it.

Okay, *a lot* overboard.

Skipped classes. Frat parties while, woefully, still in high school. The only reason she hadn't crash-landed while stretching her wings was Cade. He'd been her friend before anything else, and he hadn't hesitated to remind her on a daily basis that the Steeles were her second chance—and that she was blowing it.

Something had clicked.

Seeing the disappointment in Aunt Cindy's eyes, she'd buckled down with her studies and refocused her goals: to figure out why people made the choices that they did. *At what point did a simple couples' therapist turn into a sociopathic cult leader?*

Grace was a few hours away from finally answering that question.

Once again, Cade glanced her way, the sixth time in the last three minutes. They crossed a rickety one-lane bridge, and she sent up a silent prayer.

"With how often you keep staring at me it's a wonder how we haven't careened into a tree," Grace pointed out.

He didn't smile. "You've been quiet."

"You don't like it when I argue. You complain when I'm quiet. I'm beginning to think nothing would make you happy," Grace said.

Cade's frown deepened.

"Wow. Tough room. I thought at least you would enjoy that, Ro," Grace addressed her cousin who was about twelve car-lengths behind them in a nondescript black sedan with Tank in the driver's seat.

Her cousin's voice cursed from the comm link tucked into all their ears. "Too busy fearing for my life right now. This is the mountains of West Virginia, Dawson, not the fucking Indianapolis Speedway."

"Don't lose them. Don't get too close," Tank mimicked a whiney voice. "How about you pipe down and let me do what I do best?"

"Irritate me?"

Grace chuckled, their antics temporarily taking her mind off what they were about to do. After she and Cade met up with Bethany's New Dawn contact, her cousin and the sexy Cajun operator would keep a close distance, honing their inner hunters and making up camp outside the compound perimeter. They'd be their link to the outside world—and any surveillance toys they needed to get the job done.

Grace's gaze flickered to the rearview mirror, where the second car looked like a small dot. "I appreciate the eagerness, Tank, but our little plan is only going to work if you don't get spotted."

"This isn't my first rodeo, *cheré*. You and your fiancé there worry about being model New Dawn citizens and leave the rest to me and Roman."

"Just remember to ditch your comms the second you get to the meeting point," Roman reminded her. "There's no way they're not going to do a sweep to make sure you're not hot, and if they find the comms, this op is dead in the water right from the start."

Tank hummed his agreement. "And our camp will be four clicks away from the most eastern New Dawn perimeter. If that's still within their range, then we'll be at six. Or eight. Or ten. You get the idea."

They'd been through the plan a million times that morning alone. Grace could recite it in her sleep. "And if we can't meet up without compromising ourselves, don't do it."

"Exactly," Roman agreed. "If that means you guys have to go old-school and improvise Sarah Brandt's extraction, that's what you have Cade for."

Grace bit her lip to keep from laughing.

"Did you call me old?" Cade took the bait.

"No, your age is calling you old. I'm calling you resourceful. It's a compliment." Roman's low chuckle said otherwise.

"Yeah, well. Just remember that I'm only a year more resourceful than you, asshole."

Grace laughed, and it felt damn good. Almost as much as working alongside her family, and everyone associated with Steele Ops *was* her family. Even Tank and Jaz. Even Cade.

He slid her a look, and this time it was without the worry from before. His lips twisted into a grin as he linked his fingers through hers and brought them to his mouth. "We go in. We get Sarah. And we get the hell out. We got this, Gracie."

Every time Cade said "we," she got a surge of confidence.

"Damn right we do." As they crested a hill, an old, windowless building advertising live bait came into view. "We're at the gas station. Mics gone."

"Stay safe," Roman ordered.

Grace took both her and Cade's comms and stomped them with her boot. As she dropped the fragments into his lukewarm coffee, he pulled his truck into the gas station's stone lot. "Surprise, surprise."

He nodded toward the silver van and the familiar couple leaning against it.

Stephanie and James waited for them, the young assistant DA giving them a small wave and a sheepish smile. Grace honed her inner actress and waved back, muttering under her breath, "Wonder what kind of shit she does for Rossbach in the DA's office."

"Maybe we'll get lucky and find out."

Grace exited the truck, grabbing Cade's cold coffee cup, and dumped the contents—including two busted comm pieces—onto the gravel lot. She grimaced for Stephanie's benefit. "Nothing worse than lukewarm coffee."

"Except hot coffee." Stephanie grinned.

Grace gave Cade a playful smack on the chest. "See. I'm not the only one who thinks coffee could fuel a Hummer. He thinks I'm not normal because I'm partial to keeping my stomach lining where it's meant to be."

"Inhuman, babe." Cade dropped a kiss on her temple. "There's a difference."

"Not much of one." She turned toward the New Dawners. "*So . . .* may the New Dawn shine upon you."

"And upon you as well," Stephanie and James repeated.

The blonde wrapped Grace in a sheepish hug. "I'm sorry for all the secrecy. It's my least favorite part of bringing new—well, *old* and new—members to Sanctuary. But with the way the world is today it's even more important that the community remains free of Outside influence."

Cade shook James's hand. "It's not a problem. We're just excited to finally be on our way. With all the stories Grace has told me about the Order, I feel as though I'm coming home too."

"And you are." Stephanie smiled. "You two have an entire extended family eagerly waiting to help you find your path. But before we finish our pilgrimage we have a few inconveniences to get out of the way."

The other woman pulled a scanning device out from the van's cargo hold. Not unlike one of Liam's toys, it detected bugs and GPS trackers. "Cade, you're going to stay here with James while Grace and I hit the ladies' room. Then we'll grab your bags and get moving."

"We'll follow you in?" Cade asked.

"You'll have to come with us, but we have a very reliable friend who'll keep your truck safe while you're in Sanctuary."

"You mean I'll be seeing it again?"

Stephanie flashed him a puzzled look. "Of course. Unless you want to get rid of it. If that's the case, I'm sure Father Teague would help you with alternate arrangements when you're ready to trek back to the Outside."

Grace blinked, trying to clear her sudden confusion. "Do you mean that Order members come and go to Sanctuary as they please?"

Because it sure as hell wasn't that way seventeen years ago.

"After the Connection to the Order is complete and Father Teague feels as though you're ready to go in search of your New Dawn, of course." Stephanie chuckled. "I mean, you should know that, Grace. Your quest was the first one Father Teague blessed. Because of you, we have countless followers on the Outside working for the good of our community...and their New Dawns."

Cade's stare lifted the hairs on the back of Grace's

arm, but she wasn't sure which revelation was the worst one: the blatant lie Rossbach used to explain her abrupt departure or that there were Order members mixed in the general public—people who'd do anything for Rossbach's approval.

People who, like Todd Winston, felt owed.

People who didn't care what they had to do in the name of finding their New-fucking-Dawns.

A modest strip search and thirty minutes later, Grace still couldn't get Stephanie's words out of her head. But they all disappeared the second James held up twin black hoods. "For the ride."

"What? You guys ran out of peanuts?" Grace joked, her throat drying.

Stephanie patted her arm. "It's just precaution. Everyone gets one. It's how—"

"We keep Sanctuary safe."

"Exactly."

Cade squeezed Grace's hand and grinned. "Everyone gets one except whoever's driving, I hope. These roads aren't exactly a straight-line deal."

Stephanie chuckled and helped secure the hoods into place before guiding them into the back of the van. "Sit back and relax. Take a nap if you want. We'll be at Sanctuary in a little under three hours."

"I can't wait." Grace's stomach rolled.

She took five slow, deep breaths, and when that didn't resolve her nausea, she continued on for another ten. Cade settled into the seat next to hers, their shoulders rubbing. She slid her fingers through his and held on as if he were a life preserver.

And maybe he was.

The whirling thoughts in her head made her dizzy. But the one that settled on the forefront of her mind?

Her mother.

They'd never had a great relationship. She'd been a daddy's girl, through and through, her world caving in on her when he died. But instead of relying on each other to get through the tough times, Rebecca Steele uprooted their lives again and again. Until they reached Sanctuary.

A young, naïve Grace had been hopeful that her mother's newfound friendships meant they were finally done moving. Never in a million years would she have thought it could be so much worse.

Cade shifted closer, tucking her hooded head beneath his chin. "We got this, babe."

"Yeah, we do." Because they worked well together. She wouldn't be half as confident if it had been someone else sitting next to her, even one of her cousins. Despite all their history, in this one thing, Grace knew Cade would never let her down.

She wished that she could trust him with her heart as much as she did her life.

About three hours and a lot of backtracking later, James pulled the van off a severely potholed road and onto ground that couldn't be described as anything less than off-roading.

They bounced in the rear cargo hold, Grace sliding off the bench seat no less than four times before Cade shifted her onto his lap.

"You guys okay back there?" Stephanie asked from the front.

Grace grunted. "Okay, but in serious need of a bathroom."

"Then I have good news for you. We're here."

The van came to an abrupt stop. Doors opened and closed, and a soft murmur of voices droned on before the van's back door creaked open. James's firm hands helped her out of the back and onto shaky legs.

Her hood lifted. Grace winced, blinking against the harsh light from the setting sun, and as her vision adjusted, acidic bile rose in her throat. Her past collided with her present, and once she got over the aftershock, she cursed under her breath.

Mixed in with the crowd, and more notably around the compound's perimeter, were men and women decked out in tan-and-white camo...

And armed with automatic weapons.

At some point within the last seventeen years, Teague Rossbach had created his very own private militia.

CHAPTER THIRTEEN

Through his years with the 75th Regiment, and then with DCPD, Cade had found himself in some seriously fucked-up situations. He'd dead-dropped into alligator-infested swamplands. Led a car chase through a field of active land mines. And he'd never forget the Narcotic Nanas—a drug ring of not-so-sweet octogenarians who'd been smuggling heroin and angel dust through a downtown DC senior center.

But an army of private citizens dressing up like Rambos topped the scales.

Around them, people stopped and stared, more concerned about the new arrivals than the armed guards walking around the grounds.

"You forgot to mention that finding a New Dawn requires AK-47s," Cade murmured for Grace's ears only.

"Guess more has changed in seventeen years than I thought." Grace glanced around the commons. "But this can't alter our plans. Keep your eyes open for Sarah, and in the meantime, pray that those guys"—she nodded toward the guards—"are the biggest hurdle we come across."

Stephanie bounded over to them, smiling ear to ear. "It looks like we got here just in time for Evening

Nourishment, and I should probably warn you, I heard it's going to be a feast to celebrate the return of one of the Order's very own."

Grace turned a grimace into a smile and shoved down her sarcasm. "That's not necessary."

"Oh, hush. It's completely necessary, or Father Teague wouldn't have given the instruction." Stephanie hooked an arm through Grace's and led them toward the building where a group of people already headed. "I'm sorry we didn't get here in time to get you settled into your cabin, but we'll do that first thing after Nourishment. It's been a long day, and you two must be completely zapped."

"We get a cabin?" Cade asked.

"Of course. If we have the space for it, Father Teague likes to make sure couples are housed together. It can have a very positive influence on outcomes."

"And everyone else?"

"Our younger flock and those still single stay in something equivalent to a dormitory, but that too has positive sides. The more people surrounding you, the larger your support system."

Next to him, Grace muttered softly, "And the more chances for someone to turn you in for insubordination."

Cade couldn't believe the sheer number of people filing into the Nourishment Center. In the glorified mess hall, long tables were arranged in rows up and down the length of the room. And for the number of people— a hundred and growing—the crowd seated themselves with surprising ease.

More than one group glanced their way as they passed. Grace focused straight in front of her, or on Stephanie as they talked. The stark difference in her behavior compared to the light-headed chuckles in the car put him on alert.

They found open seats, and nearly immediately, in the back of the room, large double doors opened, and the murmur of voices instantly stopped. A couple in their sixties, dressed in slate gray robes, slowly strolled down the center aisle to an elongated table up front. Behind them came two middle-aged women and an older man.

"They're members of the council," Grace whispered for his ears only.

At the next arrival, Grace stiffened.

Her face paled as her gaze fixed on a man close to their own age. Wearing the same slate gray robes as the others before him, he scanned the room and stopped on Grace. The instant the man's mouth curled into a predatory grin, Cade knew who the bastard was.

Todd Winston.

It took everything Cade had to keep from crossing the room and throat-punching the fucker. Winston still smirked as he walked past them to sit with the other members of Rossbach's council, and then chairs scraped against the wood floor as people stood.

Unlike the gray robes of the others, the new couple entering the room wore bright gold, an intricate weave of silver ribbons wrapping around their waists in fancy belts. Salt-and-pepper hair helped peg them solidly in their early to mid-fifties, and the man smiled, licking up the adoration as if it were his damn dessert.

Teague Rossbach looked every bit the narcissist that Grace had painted him as. But in a complete contrast to the cult leader's smile, the woman on his arm frowned. Posture stiff, she looked over the room as if unimpressed . . . or bored.

Until her gaze slid over them.

Her eyes widened in surprise before her entire expression hardened in a calm, cool mask. Familiarity ran through Cade as the woman took the empty seat next to Rossbach.

Once dark as night hair.

Pale golden-brown eyes.

Strong cheekbones.

Fucking A.

Cade snapped his gaze toward Grace. The second he saw her face, he knew he'd guessed right.

Rebecca Steele sat at Rossbach's side—and looked like she was a lot more to the cult leader than a simple dinner companion.

Grace's mother never took her eyes off her daughter, and never once showed the smallest bit of relief—or happiness—that her daughter was back.

* * *

Grace paced the length of the small one-room cabin and waited for Cade. Following Evening Nourishment, James had approached, asking for a minute of his time. That was more than two hours ago, and while she knew

Cade could take care of himself, Grace waited for the other shoe to drop—on their heads.

Since Stephanie brought her to her and Cade's private "Haven," she'd been trying to wrap her mind around—and make sense of—everything around her.

New Dawn felt the same, and yet it seemed so different from the Order she remembered. It wasn't just the addition of a freakin' militia or the obvious growth in numbers.

It was the complete, total awe that flooded Teague Rossbach's flock as they listened to him give his evening blessing. They'd devoured every word, eyes glazed over in a look she saw way too often while working with the FBI.

Those looks, coupled with a charismatic sociopath like Rossbach, were a recipe for freakin' disaster. Grace and Cade couldn't find Sarah Brandt soon enough.

Someone knocked. Grace mentally hoped it was Cade looking for the right cabin, but before she tugged the door open, she knew it wasn't. It wasn't Cade. It wasn't a welcoming committee.

It was her mother.

Pulled tight into a low bun, Rebecca Steele's once illustrious dark hair had been overrun by silver streaks. Her mouth, bracketed with nearly twenty years' worth of wrinkles, tilted down into a severe frown.

But her eyes hadn't changed at all. They were filled with the same disgust that had been there for as long as Grace remembered.

She didn't budge from the open door, immediately forcing her mind to quiet. "Mother."

"It's really you." Rebecca Steele stood in front of her

daughter with no sign of moving. Not a hug. Not a smile. Not a *How have you been doing*? Or *My, look how you've grown.* Just an apathetic blank stare mixed with a hint of distrust.

For years, Grace had thought about the day she'd get a second chance to confront the woman who'd abandoned her all those years ago. Because that was what she'd done—even before choosing to stay in New Dawn when Grace begged her to leave.

Rebecca Steele abandoned her daughter the day officers came to their doorstep and told them of her husband's death. And she left her again when she fell in with the therapist from Georgia. And every day while living on the Order compound, Grace's mother slipped away more and more.

Until there was the only the woman standing in front of her now.

A stranger.

Sarah Brandt, Grace reminded herself. She and Cade were here to do a job, and that meant fitting in. It meant gaining trust. It meant painfully swallowing a lifetime's worth of backed up anger.

Grace held the door open a little and gestured to the room behind her. "Do you want to come inside?"

"I won't be staying long. I simply needed to be sure."

"Be sure of what?"

"That my selfish, insubordinate daughter really did return to New Dawn—to the very place she once claimed was slowly 'suffocating the life out of her.'" She paused a beat, waiting. "Did I remember that correctly?"

She had. But there'd been nothing slow about it.

"You did," Grace said, weighing her words carefully. "But that night was...difficult."

Her mother scoffed. "Paths to the New Dawn are never easy, Grace. That's why it was your duty to aid your fellow Order member to the best of your ability. And you failed. Abysmally."

Grace remembered, all too clearly. And put in the same position, she'd do it all over again—except she would have left with Rhett the first time he asked. Her mother called her act a failure. Grace called an act of humanity.

It took everything she had to not lash out, but there was too much riding on her ability to stay focused.

"I know," Grace forced herself to admit. "It's why I'm here. It's been seventeen years, Mom."

Her mother's golden eyes studied her. "I'm very much aware of the amount of time that's passed. You have no idea how much stress and humiliation your Defection caused."

"Is that why everyone seems to believe that I'd been sent away to find my New Dawn?"

"It's not like we could tell them the *truth*, and don't for one second think I'll let you either. Father Teague may believe that being on the Outside for so long without the support of your flock is punishment enough for your transgressions, but I don't."

"For a decision that she made when she was barely a teenager?" Cade's deep voice interjected.

Grace's mother stepped back, and Cade slowly walked up the cabin steps.

He glanced over her mother coolly, not hiding the fact that he didn't like her words. Grace almost felt bad for the other woman, because Cade unleashed every ounce of intimidation he'd learned from his time in the Rangers.

His gaze flickered to Grace and softened as he slid an arm around her waist. "I can't recall a single person who practices the same judgment that they did at thirteen. Lord knows I don't."

"People out *there*," Rebecca Steele added coldly. "But here in the Order, we hold our flock to higher standards, regardless of age, experience, or time spent at Sanctuary. If either of you are serious about reaching your New Dawn, it's something you'd do well to accept sooner rather than later."

She turned and traipsed down the stairs, obviously finished with the little reunion.

Grace closed the door and heaved out a sigh. "That sucked a lot less than I anticipated."

Cade cocked up a blond eyebrow. "Really?"

"Not really, no." It had gone about as well as she'd expected. The only shocking thing had been her ability to rein in her temper and not make the situation any worse. Nearly twenty years and Rebecca Steele was as self-righteous and delusional as she'd ever been.

"Tell me something good. What did James want to talk to you about?" she asked, needing to shift the subject off her mother.

"A job."

Grace blinked. "Say that again?"

"Seems like James is head of the armed henchmen patrolling the grounds, and he wanted to know if—

assuming Rossbach's approval—I'd be interested in using my knowledge in service of the Order."

Grace bit her lip, thinking of all the ways that could be a pain in the ass but also do them some good. "That could work in our favor."

"Seriously? You think I want to work for these assholes?"

"Yeah. I mean, you should. We don't know how long we're going to be stuck here, and like you pointed out, we're not exactly in Disneyland. Having you on the inside could help us get around better." She nodded toward the door. "As you can probably tell, I'm not exactly my mother's favorite person. Not so sure that getting on her good side's possible. Not sure she *has* a good side to get on, so every little bit helps."

If Rebecca Steele didn't have a good side seventeen years ago, there sure as hell wasn't one now. The longer a person was subjected to New Dawn's extremism, the more they lost pieces of themselves—and she knew that from firsthand experience.

Cade looked less than thrilled about her idea.

"You keep frowning like that and you're going to get wrinkles." Grace slowly closed the distance between them, easing her arms over his shoulders. "What's wrong?"

"I know what you're saying makes sense, but if I'm working with them, I won't be able to back you up if you need it. The whole point of this double op was to have each other's asses."

"We need to accept these small gifts when we get them because they're going to be few and far between."

Not to mention that this was likely to be the only one that they got.

CHAPTER FOURTEEN

Cade and Grace followed Stephanie through the New Dawn compound where camo-clad figures mingled with the regular people. Grace counted at least twelve sitting in the tree stands around the perimeter and figured there were probably more holed up in what Stephanie called the PC.

Protector Command.

She'd come close to letting a snide comment slip about the chosen title but hadn't because of Cade's hand tightening around hers. It was like he'd read her mind, which she hoped was a one-time thing, or else they were both starting the day sleep-deprived.

The night before, she hadn't been able to shut her brain off. She'd tossed and turned as her thoughts shifted from past memories to future scenarios and back again. When Stephanie knocked on their door this morning, Grace was more than happy to get up and get busy.

Until she mentioned some kind of test.

"What did you say this thing is again?" Grace hated surprises, especially when thought up by these people.

"The Enlightenment? It's just a way to help Father Teague decide where your skills are best put to use—

both while you're with us in Sanctuary, and when you're ready to take his teachings back to the Outside."

"So it's basically a job compatibility test?"

Stephanie chuckled. "Yeah, that's about it. For me, my Outside job with the DA's office is pretty self-explanatory. Order members can sometimes get into sticky situations while pursuing their New Dawn. But because of my job, I also happen to be a people person... which is why I'm an ideal escort."

Stephanie gave her an encouraging smile. "It's really nothing to worry about. For the two of you it's just a formality. I mean, the things we could do with an FBI agent and former Ranger are practically limitless."

That's what made Grace nervous, and judging by Cade's frown, him too.

"Everyone seems so happy here," he pointed out. "Is finding your New Dawn that easy for everyone?"

Stephanie's smile faltered. "No, unfortunately not. For some, there are a lot of Obstacles to overcome. The Outside can be a cruel, harsh place if you're not prepared. That's why Father Teague ensures every member has the tools they require before sending them to find their path."

"What about the people who find it a little more difficult?" Cade asked. "Is there tutoring or something that happens?"

"If a member of the flock requires a little more TLC, they're usually sent to the Reconditioning Center so they can get the extra help they need. And speaking of..." Stephanie nodded toward a two-story cabin structure set apart from the rest of the buildings, its back end abutting the forest. A petite brunette stepped onto the Rec porch, and even from this distance, the woman was unmistakable.

Sarah Brandt.

"Sarah!" Stephanie waved, encouraging her to join them. "I want to introduce you to the newbies. Grace. Cade. This is Sarah."

"Hi." Sarah nodded, joining them. "I heard a new van came in last night. I'd hoped to slide into the Evening Nourishment, but I was needed here."

"The Rec is Sarah's domain. She's great at handling our slightly lost members...knows the right push-to-nurture ratio to get them back on their path. The day she stepped into Sanctuary was a day the Order was given a huge blessing."

A blush crept up Sarah Brandt's cheeks. "Actually, it was just a Tuesday."

Grace laughed with the others. "How long have you been with the Order?"

"I've been in Sanctuary almost six and a half months now, but thanks to my boyfriend, Simon, I had access to Father Teague's wisdom before that. His words really resonated with me. They were how I knew this was where I was meant to be."

"Wow. Six months. Does that mean that you've already gone to the Outside to find your New Dawn?"

The vice president's daughter shook her head, still smiling. "I'll go on my journey as soon as I'm given Father Teague's blessing to do so. But for now, I'll remain here and serve our community."

"Your family on the Outside must miss you," Grace

asked with faux innocence and waited for the young woman's reaction.

Sarah Brandt's smile withered away, and the friendly sparkle in her eye turned dark. "No. I have no one on the Outside. My family is here."

The abrupt change in her tone made Grace blink before she caught herself.

Either ignoring the sudden shift in mood or not seeing it, Stephanie dropped an arm over Sarah's shoulder. "That's right. Here in Sanctuary, Sarah's been inundated with love and support, and she humbles us every day by giving it back by running the Reconditioning Center. I don't know what Father Teague would do without her."

Stephanie checked her watch. "Yikes. I need to get Grace and Cade over to the main house for their Enlightenment."

The eerie smile was back on Sarah's face as if it had never left. "Then go. Don't let me keep you. May the New Dawn shine upon you."

"And upon you as well," Grace, Cade, and Stephanie repeated in unison.

Stephanie hustled them through the main lodge, bypassing the dining room and what looked to be classrooms, most of which were already occupied. The deeper they went into the building, the quieter it got.

Stephanie stopped in front of a nondescript door. "This one's you, Grace. They ask that you remove anything metallic and have a seat in the chair closest to the door."

"Does this Enlightenment involve electrocution?"

Grace took out her earrings and tucked them into her pocket.

"Hardly." Stephanie laughed. "But it is sensitive equipment. Your evaluator will answer any and all questions that you have. Lord knew I had so many during my test that I could've filled up a three-subject notebook."

Grace linked her fingers through Cade's. "Do you mind if I have a word with Cade before we get started? Just for a minute."

Stephanie winked. "Not a problem."

Spotting an older man down the hall, she left them alone.

Cade was already shaking his head when Grace turned toward him. "I know what you're thinking, and no."

"How the hell do you know what I'm thinking?"

"You want to get yourself sentenced to the Rec."

Grace opened her mouth, then closed it with a sigh. "Okay, yeah, that's what I was thinking. But it's the perfect chance for me to get inside Sarah's head. You heard her out there, Cade. We need to know how genuine her desire to stay here is."

"Why? We can't leave this place without her, even if she's made it her permanent zip code. Brandt will roll heads if we had a chance to extricate her and didn't do it. I don't know about you, but I like my head where it is. Both of them."

Grace rolled her eyes. "I know we're not leaving without her, but if there's a chance we could talk sense to her and have her walk out on her own two feet, then that's the tactic we should try first. Brains over brawn."

"You really think you can break through six months of brainwashing in what? Twenty? Forty-eight hours?"

"I won't know until I try. We owe Sarah Brandt a solid chance before we break out the gag and handcuffs."

Cade speared his fingers through his hair. "I don't like the idea of you purposefully getting yourself in trouble just to get sent to the Rec. There's got to be another way."

"Trouble? Who said anything about getting myself in trouble? I'm supposedly eager to become the next model member of the flock, right?"

"Right," Cade dragged out the word, looking unsure. "What are you going to do? Ask for them to put you there?"

Grace grinned and patted his cheek. "See! You're gorgeous and smart!"

Cade cursed. "I think I liked the trouble route better."

"Zoey was right. You've turned into a worrywart in your old age. Keep it up and you won't have stomach lining by the time you hit thirty-five."

"Thanks to you and my sister, mine disappeared years ago." Cade palmed the back of her head and guided her mouth within inches of his before stopping. "*Please* be careful."

"I'm always careful."

Grace stood on her toes and closed the remaining distance. As her lips moved with his, a small hum slid out from her throat. Three days had passed since they'd wiped their slate clean and agreed to see where things went, and the intimate touches already came progressively easier.

It should freak her the hell out, and yet a warm glow of contentment put a smile on her face.

Cade protested her pulling away with a low groan. "Now you're just playing dirty—and trying to distract me from the fact that I won't have eyes on you for God knows how long."

"Uh huh. And it worked."

His concern jumbled her emotions, which wasn't a good thing considering she needed to go into a room and fool an evaluator into thinking she was determined to be a model member of the Order. "Keep yourself busy. I'll be back before you notice I was actually gone."

"Not likely," Cade muttered.

Grace waved to Stephanie, signaling that they were finished, and entered the room.

She hadn't known what to expect, but it wasn't the ominous metal contraption sitting on top of the lone desk. Wires jutted out from both sides, giving it a Dr. Frankenstein feel. But the older woman sitting behind it looked more like a grandmother than a mad scientist. Her stark white hair, pulled away from her face and wrapped into a low bun, was styled much like Grace's mother's. But this woman's gray robes identified her as a member of Rossbach's council.

Grace nodded, offering the elder a warm smile. "May the New Dawn shine upon you."

"And upon you as well, Grace. I'm Councilwoman Edith, and I'll be your evaluator this morning." She gestured to the seat across from her...and directly in front of the odd-looking machine. "Come. Sit. I assure you I don't bite."

"Are you sure *it* doesn't?" Grace gestured to the torture-tastic machine and sat. "So this is going to tell you where my place in the Order is going to be? Before, Father Teague put people where he felt they best fit."

"And he still does, but he relies on the evaluation to give him a starting point. We want your time here at Sanctuary to be a peaceful one so that you can better focus on the steps needed to take to reach New Dawn." She rounded the desk, a bundle of electrodes in her hands. "Our success rates have tripled since we've started implementing the evaluator."

"That's incredible." And more than a little scary. "And when you say success you mean..."

"The evaluator helps us identify possible Obstacles, and therefore allows Father Teague to develop an individual plan of attack for every Order member."

It was the "attack" part that didn't sit well with Grace.

The evaluator looked to be nothing more than an oddball lie detector, and thanks to the FBI, she'd been trained to beat them, graduating from Quantico with one of the highest success rates. Councilwoman Edith wanted to use it to sniff out her weaknesses, so she'd just make sure she didn't give her any.

At least not any that she didn't *want* her to have.

Edith brushed Grace's hair off her forehead and placed the electrodes on her face and arms. Even her legs.

"Wouldn't this go a lot easier if I just told you what my issues are?" Grace asked.

Edith smiled. "Even the most spiritually attuned persons can be blind to their Obstacles, and considering you already have a Defection under your belt, I wouldn't call you one of them."

Grace fought to keep her surprise off her face. "Why don't you think that I'd been sent away to find my New Dawn? That seems to be what everyone else was told."

"Because I had the privilege of sitting alongside your mother as she mourned your loss, and I hope you don't mind me being frank, dear, but she wouldn't be able to handle it again."

Grace snorted internally. Mourned for her own reputation was more like it, or the possibility of it interfering with her connection to Father Teague. But miss her? *Never.*

"I don't want that to happen either, Councilwoman. When I accidently stumbled on Bethany and Thomas, I told myself that I wouldn't squander this second chance. I'll do whatever needs to be done to make my mother proud, and to honor every single member of the Order in every action that I perform."

The older woman studied her, looking for authenticity, and Grace gave it to her in the subtle shine of tears. "I don't want to fail again, Edith. I'll do anything to prove that I belong here."

"Anything?"

"Yes . . . I'll even voluntarily serve time in the Reconditioning Center."

The Councilwoman slowly returned to her seat, and flipped on the evaluator. "I actually think that would be a splendid plan. At the conclusion of this evaluation, you'll report to the Rec for a minimum of a weekend of reconditioning. Once that sentence has concluded, we'll see if any additional time is warranted."

Checkmate.

Grace swallowed her smile and kept her face stoic. "I'd like that, Councilwoman Edith. Thank you."

"There's no need to thank me, child. Helping you to your New Dawn is thanks enough."

Grace didn't dwell on just how perfectly everything had fallen into line so far. She couldn't have planned it any better herself—which usually meant something waited on the outskirts to muck it all up.

CHAPTER FIFTEEN

Once upon a time, Cade had had an unforgettable run-in with a Russian intelligence officer known in wide circles as the Dentist, and not because of his overt love of oral hygiene. He'd come seconds away from his balls falling off in the frozen tundra. And he'd had tropical parasites pulled out from under his skin while stationed in a jungle.

None of it compared to being questioned for two hours by an eighty-year-old New Dawn member. The older man had touched base on everything—childhood friendships, the time he'd snuck out of the house to smoke his first cigarette. Then he'd broached the subject of the cause behind his and Grace's split nine years ago, and Cade had told the truth.

Him.

He had no delusions that he'd fucked up. He knew it. Grace knew it. He'd tossed away their six-year relationship because he hadn't been man enough to tell her that civilian life scared the shit out of him.

Within the regiment, you mattered. Your skills were put to good use, and your reputation as a badass came with the badge on your lapel. But the second you changed into civilian clothes, you became just another guy good with his fists.

There weren't too many occupations where that was checked off in the pro column.

A few of his buddies learned the hard way that private security firms weren't one size fits all. There were more bad operations out there than there were good ones, and after working with the best men and women the Army had to offer, Cade hadn't been about to compromise—not his morals or the lives of others.

So he'd eventually migrated to the idea of the police academy, thinking switching out one uniform for another would make for a smooth transition.

He'd been wrong.

Everything about working for the DCPD was different, the biggest factor being that it was mostly solitary. Only a select few got paired with a partner, and a hell of a lot rode on you following every rule and regulation right down to the dotted I. Winging shit as a detective was frowned upon by the higher-ups.

Winging shit as a Steele Ops operative was expected—and sometimes meant the difference between life and death.

Grace, though she'd only been with the team temporarily, embraced that concept with her stint to get inside the Rec, and her plan must have worked, because he hadn't seen her since their evaluations that morning.

But fuck it all if he didn't hate not knowing for sure.

"You realize the Evening Nourishment is the last meal of the day and not your last meal ever, right?" Decked out in the white-and-tan camo of the New Dawn Protectors, James approached from around the corner of the main hall. "I heard about Grace—which I'm assuming is the reason for the woe-is-me look."

Cade shook the other man's hand. "News travels fast around here."

"It practically flies at warp speed when someone takes their New Dawn seriously enough to volunteer to go to the Rec."

"She's damned determined to do things right this time around. The only problem is that I suddenly find myself with a lot of free time."

"That's why I tracked you down. Father Teague looked over this morning's evaluation and he's in agreement that we could use someone like you in Protector Command."

"Yeah?" Cade feigned a hopeful expression and grinned. "Does that mean I get my very own abominable snowman camo?"

James laughed. "Just wait until we change seasons, man. If you and Grace are around in the spring you get dog-shit brown."

"Perfect."

A few people nodded at them as they passed, and James gestured toward the PC quarters. "Walk and talk?"

They headed across the commons, most people giving them a wide berth. James either didn't care or didn't notice, but considering he worked on the teams, it was probably the former. He still hadn't figured out how a guy used to making life-and-death decisions on behalf of others got suckered into a life where no choice was really his own.

Everything was done for the Order. For Rossbach. For the New Dawn.

"I'm not gonna lie," James began. "Being with the PC isn't as glamorous as it sounds. It's a lot of sitting and standing, especially if you're working the surveillance room. Night shifts get rotated around among the team to keep it fair."

"And what about surveilling potential recruits on the Outside? Do those get rotated too?"

James paused a beat. "You pegged Quinn and Paul?"

"If one of them has a thing for perfume and the other drives like he's training for NASCAR, then yeah. We did."

"Priceless." James let out a barking laugh. "They were bragging for days that they bested an FBI agent and an Army Ranger. I should've known they were talking out their asses. I think Paul's working the desk right now. What do you say? Want to help me pop an ego?"

Cade smirked. "Got nowhere else to be."

Grace had told Cade to keep busy, and that's what he planned on doing. Her job was to get inside Sarah Brandt's head, and his was to get them all the hell out of here. His new title made slipping off the compound a hell of a lot easier.

"Can I ask you a question? It's something I've been wondering about since we first stepped off that van." Cade stayed casual, tucking his hands into his jeans.

"Shoot."

He nodded toward the guards in the perimeter tree stands. "What's with all the heavy artillery? Don't get me wrong, I'm a huge fan of having all the latest toys. I just didn't expect to see them here. Hell, how did you get them? Some of those AKs look like military grade shit."

"That's because they are."

Cade failed to wipe off his surprise.

James explained, "The Order has an in with someone in the State Department who works with their delivery system. When he's got a lot of product flying all over, he shuffles around paperwork and munitions until he's able to slip shipments out on the side."

"An in? You mean a member of the Order?"

James grinned. "We're everywhere, man. You probably already met a few before coming here and didn't even know it."

Cade made a mental note to have Liam alert their contact at State and nip that in the damn ass. Military munitions weren't made available to the public for a reason.

"Smuggling federal weapons is a big risk for such a little payoff. Sanctuary's remote location is a pretty decent security feature. Do you guys actually need all that firepower?" Cade asked.

"Father Teague wants to make sure Sanctuary's a safe haven, and that means preparing ourselves for all possibilities."

Grace had hit the nail on the head when she said that Rossbach's people would follow blindly, loyal to the Order to their own detriment. James believed what he said. This man who once risked everything, including his life, for his country, now risked it all in the name of *one* man. And he wasn't the least bit concerned by it.

Hell, he looked proud.

Cade kept him talking. "So video surveillance, perimeter security, and tailing prospective recruits. Does the PC do anything else? Any kind of hierarchy or chance for advancement?"

James slid him a smirk. "Already gunning for a promotion?"

"I have Ranger in my blood—always gunning for something."

"Then you'll be happy to know that there's always the chance of being selected into the Elite Guard."

"Elite, huh? That sounds promising." And a little bit eerie. "How do I sign myself up for that?"

"You don't." James led the way up the steps of the white barrack-like PC building. "Father Teague hand selects the members of the Elites because it's not for the faint of heart. They spend a lot more time on the Outside than they do here."

"Doing what?"

"Whatever the hell Father Teague needs them to do. If I hadn't served with some scary-ass people while on the SEAL teams, I'd say that the EG's were the scariest fuckers I'd ever met. Before you go climbing up the ladder, make sure you think it through. And talk it over with your girl. There's a reason why those guys don't have lasting relationships."

Cade really wanted to know what kind of missions Rossbach sent those men on, but it was clear that James wasn't about to say. Or he didn't know.

"Welcome to our nerve center." James tugged the door open and ushered him inside.

Despite the outside looking like an aged military

barrack, the inside of Protector Command headquarters was fairly updated with a small, open foyer. At the lone desk, a camo-clad guard looked up.

"Sir." Seeing James, he immediately stood. "There was an argument over at the new construction site. I sent Collins to break it up. He just radioed in that it was all taken care of."

"Good. Paul Novak, this is Cade Wright. I think you guys have already bumped into each other a time or two." James smirked, giving Cade a small nod.

Novak flashed Cade smug smile. "Yeah, you were a little too stuck in your head—and on your woman's lips—to notice me the first time around. I won't hold it against you."

. Cade cocked up an eyebrow. "Well, I do happen to like my woman's lips, but my head's just fine. So which one were you? The one who can't tail for shit or the one who has a thing for perfume?"

Novak's mouth opened and closed, looking like a fish yanked out of its water bowl.

James chuckled. "Guess you guys weren't as stealthy as you thought. Maybe we should send you two back to training."

"No way in hell were we spotted. Both you and your girl were oblivious." The kid, no more than nineteen or twenty, shot a glare at Cade.

Cade's irritation rose, and he glanced at the PC leader. "You said something about popping egos...may I?"

James looked almost eager. "Please. It would be a privilege to watch."

Cade turned back to the kid and, hardening his

glare, summoned every commanding officer he'd had in the Rangers. "First, that *girl* you mentioned is a fully trained former federal agent. She could drop you to the floor and have you wiping your ass with your nose in a split second. Second, the next time you or your buddy go out on surveillance duty, don't be the creepy stalker type unless you want to get pegged right away."

"I—"

"I wasn't done," Cade cut Novak off. "Third, when you're tailing someone by car, keep at least five car lengths between you and them...and it's probably a good idea not to use your blinkers and announce which direction you're about to turn. Also, parking directly across the street from an apartment building? Amateur move. Yeah, you can see the entrance, but the person you're watching can also see you. Would you like me to keep giving you pointers? I'm full of them."

Novak's jaw looked like it had been fused with screws.

"How old are you?" Cade demanded.

"Nineteen. Why the hell does that matter?"

"Because before you were wearing big boy underwear, I got my Ranger tab. I'd already jumped out of planes at thirty thousand feet, into hostile-infested areas, with little more than a damn pea-shooter to keep my head from imploding off my shoulders. I'd been a prisoner of war, escaped, and returned with a band of friends for a little payback on the men who thought it funny to hook me up to rusty battery cables. I held people's lives in my hands, the decisions I made literally a matter of life and death. What were you deciding fifteen years ago? To wear the Superman briefs or the Batman?"

This time, the kid wisely kept his mouth shut.

James cleared his throat, failing to hide his smirk. "Get Wright a badge made while I show him around the building. Make sure he has a level three clearance."

"Level three? He just got here and you're making him a three?"

His grin vanishing, James stalked up to the kid and stopped an inch shy of his face. "Make him a level three badge. If you have a problem with it, leave your PC camo on the desk and walk your naked ass right to the Rec. Got it?"

"Yes, sir."

James slipped past the desk and nodded for Cade to follow. "Good help is hard to find."

Cade chuckled. "I've been known to intimidate a few people, but you practically had the kid pissing his pants."

"It wasn't so much me as Novak knowing that he's on a three-strike system. He already has two. One more stint in the Rec and Father Teague will seriously contemplate booting his ass off Sanctuary. *I* know it and *he* knows it."

"Does that happen often? People leaving the Order completely?"

"Nah. By the time people get to Sanctuary, they've already shown the traits needed to be productive members. Novak's only here because of his parents. They've already achieved their New Dawns and moved on . . . he's not even close."

James scanned them through a set of double doors. They stepped into the modern, tech-savvy inner sanctum of PC headquarters. It reminded Cade of an updated version of the detectives' wing at DCPD.

Faux walls gave the appearance of separated rooms and a few office-like cubicles. A weapons cage tucked against the far-right wall, filled to the brim with AKs and ammo, could have supplied an entire forward operating base overseas and had leftovers to share.

James led the way through the room and at least a half dozen camo'd men—and two women—nodded in respect as they passed.

"Our main purpose here in Sanctuary is to keep the peace. Everyone here has the same ultimate goal of reaching their New Dawn, but that doesn't mean that their personalities don't...*conflict* sometimes," James said.

"And not to mention that it's a known fact that people get a little out of sorts knowing they're pretty far removed from civilization."

"Exactly."

"Basically what you're saying is that I'm a third level rent-a-cop."

James chuckled. "Pretty much, except we don't pay you for your services. We patrol the grounds, ensure there aren't any issues on the Outside that can affect Sanctuary. It doesn't happen often, but we do get an occasional straggler come through—sometimes a hunter or a nosy reporter. It's our job to turn them around and send them back on their way."

"Sounds thrilling."

The former SEAL clapped him on the back. "There's a reason why some of the guys climb over each other for a chance at the Elites. While what we do is important, it doesn't hold a candle to the excitement of the Outside."

James stopped in front of a room labeled "Surveillance." A lone guard sat in front of a dozen monitors. Each screen showcased a different part of the compound. There was one with a three-sixty view of the dining hall and two others from the main building. A few more showcased areas he didn't recognize, and two remained blank. One thing Cade noticed immediately was the notable blind spots from the cameras out on the grounds.

He could work with that.

"Where are those video feeds?" Cade nudged his chin to the screens he couldn't pinpoint.

"The two dead lines are the evaluation rooms. We don't have those running when no one's being tested," James answered. "And those others are our feeds into the Rec."

Big brother really was everywhere.

"Makes sense. So...a level three. Does it come with a fancy rank or something? Any perks?"

"Yeah, it means you can tell Novak to scrub the toilets with his own toothbrush if he pisses you off." James laughed. "I'll work on a new schedule tonight and fit you into the rotation, but I have to admit something, man. Your talents are wasted inspecting perimeter lines. I know you don't want to be apart from Grace for long periods, but you'd be doing me a solid if you helped train some of these newbies...or at least taught them how to tail people without throwing up blinking neon signs over their heads."

"Count me in. I do have a question about the Elites, though. If you run the day-to-day here in Sanctuary, who oversees them when they're out in the field?"

James's face twisted into a deep scowl. "Todd Winston. Don't ask me why Father Teague picked him, because I still haven't figured it out. The man doesn't know the difference between an IED and an AED."

The name burned like acid in Cade's stomach.

No wonder New Dawn had been eager to get Winston's legal affairs in order. Rossbach wanted to ensure that his go-to boy was at his disposal for whatever twisted mind games he had on his agenda next.

CHAPTER SIXTEEN

Not knowing what to expect, Grace pushed aside the uneasy twist of her stomach and hesitantly stepped into the Reconditioning Center. The last time she'd been there it had been nothing more than a one-room shanty with a single cot tucked into the far corner and a lingering smell of animal pee.

Now it was a two-story cabin structure with tattered sofas and chairs adorning a modest size living room. A fireplace took up a large portion of the back wall, and a narrow hall led from the front of the building to the small kitchen in the rear. One thing it was notably lacking was electricity.

The Rec isn't a vacation, Grace's mother told her the night she'd left New Dawn. It was a place of inner reflection. A place to figure out where you'd gone wrong and how you could do right. A place to solidify your resolve to find your New freakin' Dawn.

For Grace, it had been a place where she'd committed herself to putting everything these people stood for behind her.

Stephanie slid Grace an encouraging smile. "It's probably odd to be back here."

"Do you mean back in Sanctuary, or in the Rec?

Because I assure you, this is not the Reconditioning Center of my youth."

The New Dawn escort chuckled. "I wasn't around when you were, but the Rec has undergone a lot of transformation even in the time I've been here. A lot of it has to do with Sarah. She wanted to make sure it was a place conflicted members of the flock felt at ease and were far removed from the distractions happening elsewhere on the grounds. Fewer distractions means more chance to really self-reflect. And, of course, successful integration."

"And how do you know that someone's ready to be integrated back into the flock?"

"It's a joint decision made by the member themselves, Sarah, and Mother Rebecca."

The Rec had been her mother's brainchild more than seventeen years ago, so it made sense she still had her hands in it, but... "Father Teague doesn't weigh in on Rec assignment?"

"He's the one who gives the initial Rec sentence, but after that, he usually leaves the rest of the decisions up to Mother Rebecca."

Grace hid her surprise with an understanding nod. Rossbach not having his hands in *every* aspect of New Dawn life was a new little twist.

Three sets of voices drifted their way from the back of the house. They followed them, and the moment Grace and Stephanie stepped into the kitchen, everyone went quiet. Sarah Brandt glanced up, pausing her conversation with the young woman and older teen at her side. "Stephanie. And Grace."

Grace offered a purposely sheepish wave. "Bet this is some kind of record for you, right? Someone coming to the Rec after a few short days?"

Sarah chuckled. "From what I heard, you offered to come here. That's quite different than being sentenced as a reprimand." She turned to the two at her side. "This is Maria and David."

"Nice to meet you."

Stephanie glanced around. "You have two others with you, right?"

Sarah nodded. "Oscar and Levi are hauling water up from the river, but they should be here soon."

David shifted on his feet and stared at Grace. "You're really you, huh?"

Everyone chuckled, including Grace. "Last time I checked a mirror."

Sarah explained, "David was a fan of yours."

"A fan? I've been here less than twenty-four hours."

David's cheeks pinked. "Of when you were here before. I was only two, but my caretaker told me that I was your shadow when you helped in the nursery."

Two. So that would make him..."So you're about nineteen?"

He nodded, looking a little bashful.

That meant this poor kid had been here for the last seventeen years—or longer—with no familial connection, because Children of the New Dawn weren't reared by their parents. They were raised by the *flock*.

Grace herself, as one of the older children, often worked with the toddlers, and the longer she studied David, the more his unruly dark hair and big green eyes

morphed into a sweet young face she remembered reading to nearly every single night.

Grace cleared her throat, pushing away a swell of
emotions. "You had a favorite blanket. It was light blue
with a—"

"Sunshine patch on it. Yeah. That was me." He
smiled shyly.

New Dawn bred three types of followers: the anger-
ridden, the naïve sheep, and probably the most disturb-
ing of them all, the perfect blend of the two. The former
definitely fit Todd to a T. The eager to please Stephanie,
the sheep. A wary gut feeling told Grace that Sarah was
the latter.

But David?

Grace didn't think he belonged in any of the cat-
egories, and she wondered what would happen when
Rossbach realized he wouldn't get an obedient, mind-
less soldier out of the teen.

Stephanie clapped her hands, gaining everyone's attention. "Well, you're in good hands, Grace. I'm going
to leave you with Sarah, and she'll fill you in on all the
particulars. Either myself or someone else from the
flock will be checking in in a day or two."

She waved and skipped out of the room before Grace
turned to her three temporary roommates.

Maria, already losing interest, rifled through pots
and pans beneath one of the counters, and Sarah
handed David a rag and spray bottle. "Go wipe down
the table."

"But Evening Nourishment's not going to be for another hour."

"And when you clean the table, it'll be ready for you to set it." She slid Grace a small wink. "And don't forget to add another setting."

"Yes, ma'am." He trudged back to the attached dining room, grumbling under his breath.

"Can I help?" Grace offered. "Although I should warn you that I burn water."

"You any good with a peeler?" Sarah held out a veggie peeler and nodded to a small stack of potatoes.

"I can try."

"I'm going to go set the table," Maria mumbled and hustled after David, place settings in her hands.

"Was it something I said, or am I just that scary?"

"Maria's nervous around new people that come into the Rec. She has trust issues, which is why she's still with us in Sanctuary five years after her recruitment. To her, you're a wild card. She doesn't want to be linked to you by association and end up getting her Rec sentence extended." Sarah's mouth pulled up into a smirk. "There's a reason why David was so awestruck when you walked through the door. He's a teenager. He's rebellious. It's only natural he heard the stories about a particular young girl with the ability to find any kind of trouble in a three-mile radius."

Grace laughed, a real one this time. "It had to be at least five miles."

"Good to know," Sarah chuckled. "I'll make sure to stay on my toes around you."

"So you're like what? The Rec warden?"

"More like the resident assistant." She glanced up to the ceiling, where Grace immediately noticed the camera mounted in the corner. "*Those* are the wardens. The video feeds go directly to the PC. They're motion censored, so when anyone walks into the room, they turn on and record. They don't have sound capabilities—something David is very thankful for, since he tends to drop more than the occasional F-bomb. And FYI, there's one in everyone's bedrooms too."

"That's…" *Damn creepy.* "Thorough."

"You can say what you really think."

"I don't think I can. I don't want my voluntary Rec appearance to turn into a mandatory one."

Sarah laughed.

Not only did the vice president's daughter act like a woman who was happy staying with the Order, but Grace didn't see any sign of the woman who'd written rage posts calling for an all-hands-on-deck political mutiny. It was like they weren't the same person, and Grace had to wonder why.

She took her cue from Sarah and picked up her first potato. "Can I ask you what brought you to New Dawn? My mother physically brought me here to Sanctuary, but you said you're fairly new to the Order. If you don't want to talk about—"

"No, no. It's fine." Sarah's lighthearted smile stiffened. "To be honest, it was my boyfriend who introduced me to the Order."

"Is he here now? What does he do?"

"Simon's one of Father Teague's Elite Guards."

Grace racked her brain for any memory of the term and came up blank. "They're different from the PC?"

"Oh, *very* different." Sarah's face beamed, proud.

"Father Teague hand-selects the member of the Elites. They handle sensitive assignments for the Order. It's an honor, but it means that he's off Sanctuary quite a bit. He's due back sometime within the next few days, though."

"So he brought you here?"

Sarah nodded. "Before I met Simon, I wasn't happy with the life I was in. I just didn't know what to do about it until I ran into him at a coffee shop. He recognized the similarities in our hearts from the moment our eyes connected. And now, I'm here, and everything feels... *right*."

No doubt he recognized *her* too... and everything someone of her stature could bring to Rossbach's cause.

Oscar and Levi chose that moment to return with the water, and while they were more personable than Maria, they said hello and promptly disappeared to their quarters to wash up for Evening Nourishment.

With the meal nearly ready to be placed on the table, Sarah tossed her towel on the counter. "Let me show you to your room so you can wash up. Unlike the rest of the community, after Nourishment, we have a full evening of reflection. First together as a house, and then everyone will be sent to their private quarters."

"For more personal Reflections." At least that much hadn't changed—except for the cameras that made certain you didn't slack on your individual studies.

Sarah led her to a room that made a jail cell look decorative. A simple twin bed with stark white sheets was pushed against the wall, and tucked beneath the lone window, an empty desk was adorned with a plain metal basin and a pitcher of water.

"It's minimalist, but it's been designed that way to make it easier to focus on what's important." Sarah nudged a chin to a small corner dresser. "There's towels in there. I'll leave you to freshen up and see you downstairs in a bit."

Left alone to prepare for the evening meal, Grace side-eyed the wall-mounted camera and pretended she didn't care about its presence as she wiped down her arms and scrubbed her face.

Evening Nourishment at the main house was always a boisterous affair—at least after Rossbach's final Blessing of the night. So when Grace returned to the dining room a little less grimy than before, she hadn't expected the somber silence of Sarah and the four other Rec residents.

Everyone stood behind their chairs, heads bowed.

Grace stopped behind the empty chair next to Maria, and the other woman casually slid hers farther away. Grace resisted the urge to mess with her by sliding hers even closer and heard a small cough. Sarah Brandt's mouth twitched as if reading her mind.

A click sounded in the room, and then Rossbach's voice echoed from the speaker at the end of the table. "May the New Dawn shine upon you."

"And upon you as well," both the people around Grace's table and those in the main dining hall chanted in unison.

"*Duty* is something that we all possess," Rossbach addressed everyone. "Duty to your community. To your leaders, who strive every day to steer you in the right direction, to guide you on your path to your New Dawn.

But I and Mother Rebecca cannot do it alone. We must help each other. If it is within your power to aid a fellow member of the flock, you must do so without exception, for every New Dawn is precious. It's to be protected—at all costs."

As Grace listened, her stomach twisted into knots. It was the same old message that she'd heard seventeen years ago, but this time, she heard it with a federally trained ear.

It wasn't about the emotional freedom that came with forgiveness.

His sermon was about *unquestioned* loyalty. It fueled entitlements, encouraged them to be judge, jury, and executioner. It was about cold, unapologetic retribution without regard to the aftermath left behind.

Grace's gaze flicked over the people around the table. Most had their eyes closed, soaking up the words spewing from Rossbach's mouth. But Sarah Brandt stared at her clasped hands, a small smile on her face.

She not only believed every word that he said, but she was a woman with a solid, concrete plan. By the time Rossbach stopped talking, Grace was no longer hungry.

She pushed her food around on her plate and contemplated her next move. "So does—"

"We don't talk," Maria hissed.

Sarah gave Grace an apologetic smile. "She doesn't know that unless we tell her, Maria."

The other woman clamped her mouth shut.

"Evening Nourishment is our time to take Father Teague's words and apply them to ourselves. We solidify our resolve to finalize our Reconditioning and search within to identify our Obstacles and how to thwart them."

"I didn't know..." Grace turned to Maria, who looked near ready to pass out from all the out-of-the-norm meal talk. The poor woman truly believed her entire livelihood was on the line. "I'm sorry, Maria. I'll try to follow the rules more closely."

The other woman grunted and ate her dinner in silence.

The rest of the meal passed at a snail's pace, made even longer by the equally silent cleanup. After the last dish was put away, David led the way to the living room, where everyone chose a seat, most notably as far apart from others as the small room allowed. Grace took the plump chair on the left, positioning herself so she could observe the others without being obvious.

Sarah extinguished the lights, and opened the hutch that sat catty-corner to the fireplace to reveal a wide-screen TV, a far contrast from the rest of the Spartan Rec furnishings.

Rossbach blinked to life on the screen in high definition. "May the New Dawn shine upon you."

"And upon you as well," everyone in the room returned.

Startled, Grace glanced around, noting everyone's attention affixed to the front of the room.

"Your actions matter. *Decisions* matter," Rossbach began. "Being in the midst of Reconditioning means that you have made a choice that could've taken you so far from your New Dawn path that there is no going back."

Across the room, Maria's soft sniffle broke through the dead silence.

"We here at Sanctuary do not give up on our flock. You, my lovely people, are exactly where you need to be, and it is my firm belief that with careful nurturing, you'll once again rejoin your Order family. But you must commit yourself. You must be brave. You must be determined.

"Think of your Obstacle...picture it in your mind. Is it a person on the Outside who is blocking you from your path, or are memories of a particular place preventing you from moving forward? It could be one. Or both. Or more. But you *can* overcome it. You can overcome *them*. For the sake of your New Dawn and everything that you're entitled to, you must. Not. Fail."

Rossbach's recorded message droned on and on, and with each repetitive sentiment sounded less like a pep talk and more like a thorough brainwashing. Without a clock, she wasn't sure how long the video lasted, but by the time it ended, she wanted to claw off her ears.

Maria jumped up and hustled to her room, and the others silently followed.

Grace hung back, waiting as Sarah put the screen away.

"He's inspirational, isn't he?" A dreamy-eyed smile floated on the other woman's face.

He was something. And if this were any other assignment, Grace would be chomping at the bit to write a professional article on his personality traits.

"That happens every night?" Grace asked.

"And twice more during the day. It reminds us that

if our resolve is strong enough, and we're willing to put forth the effort, our New Dawn is only a few Obstacles away."

Grace knew she needed to ask her question even if she was already ninety-nine percent certain of the answer. "What's your Obstacle, Sarah?"

The young woman smiled, but this one, unlike the one earlier in the kitchen, left Grace cold.

"Obstacles are a private affair to be known only between the individual and Father Teague. But you'll know when I've finally reached my New Dawn." She reached out, squeezing Grace's clammy hand. "Soon, *everyone* will know."

CHAPTER SEVENTEEN

Ever since being granted his level three badge three days ago, Cade had made sure each of his PC shifts happened in the surveillance room. Not only did he get to verify the videos' blatant blind spots, but he got to keep taps on the Rec.

Specifically, Grace.

If he didn't know her as well as he did, he wouldn't have been able to distinguish her from the other five residents. They moved like robots, hopping from task to task, and mostly never saying a word to one another. And he *really* wanted to know what the living room was about. The camera angle focused on the front door and not the screen everyone's eyes were fixated on.

But after that evening's movie night, something changed.

The others went to their rooms, and Sarah and Grace stayed back. The two talked easily, but the tension in Grace's posture mixed with the exhausted dip of her shoulders was impossible to miss, and it didn't go away even when she hugged the vice president's daughter and walked out the Rec's front door.

That was two hours ago.

Now, Cade paced his and Grace's cabin, marking

each pass with a string of curses that would make his mother glower at him.

He'd barely heard the first squeak of the step when he flung open the front door and pulled Grace into his arms. "About damn time."

Curling his fingers into her hair, he held her against his chest and kissed the top of her head. Then her temple. Her cheek. And then he kissed her mouth.

Grace's hands slid up to his shoulders, and her lips opened, accepting the firm slide of his tongue. His body would have broken out into song if it could, every cell damn near vibrating. He hadn't realized the scope of his need for her until that very moment.

The tightness in his chest eased, and each breath came easier than the one before it. Grace Steele was his oxygen, and he didn't think he'd be able to survive without either of them for very long.

"Miss me much?" Against his mouth, Grace chuckled. "Maybe I should get myself sentenced to the Rec more often if that's the homecoming I'm going to get."

"Like fucking hell, sweetheart." He pulled back enough to close the door behind them, but he never took his hands off her. "Are you okay?"

"Never better."

Cupping her chin, he tilted her face up and scavenged for the truth.

She smiled, knowing exactly what he was doing, but the light didn't quite reach her eyes. "I'm tired. Physically. Mentally. And emotionally. But I'm okay."

"Christ. That place looked..."

"Weird as hell? Because that's how it felt." Her brain

slowly processed his words, and then his wardrobe. "Wait. How do you know how it looked? And why do you look like GI Joe?"

"Because you're looking at James's new right-hand man."

Her mouth dropped open. "I leave you alone for three days and you become New Dawn's perfect little pet?"

"I was always perfect, babe." He grinned, earning him an eye roll. "Besides, this means that once we pack Sarah up, I can get us out of this Twilight Zone undetected. It's like the stars are aligning."

Grace snorted and pulled away. "Until one gets snuffed out... which I'm pretty sure has already happened. Sarah Brandt isn't leaving voluntarily or quietly."

He winced. "It's that bad?"

"It's worse."

"How the hell could it be worse?"

"Because Rhett was right. Rossbach took the concept of happily ever after and put his own sick twist on it. Not only does Sarah Brandt feel that she's entitled to her New Dawn, but that it's perfectly acceptable for her to do anything to get it."

He didn't have to be trained in people's thought processes to know that was a very bad thing. "What's she going to do?"

"Whatever it is, it isn't good, and knowing how she felt about her father before she left, I can't shake the feeling that it has something to do with him."

For the first time, Cade noticed the dark circles under her eyes. The exhaustion he'd read from the video feed looked three times worse in person. He tucked a strand of hair behind her ear and let his fingers brush against her cheek. When she looked up at him, he fought not to take her pain away with a swift kiss.

"Go take a hot shower. Or a bath. Tomorrow after the night guard's swap, we'll trek out to Roman and Tank and give them an update."

"And Sarah?"

"She's not going anywhere right now. And if she's as deep into Rossbach as you think, then it's even more important that we get her the hell out of here. Go close your eyes. Just don't drown in the tub."

A small smile twitched her lips. "Maybe you should act as my lifeguard and join me?"

His cock went half hard at the invitation, but he wasn't so sure that was what she needed right now. "Rest up and maybe I'll do a little life-saving afterward."

"You don't want to have sex with me because I've been washing out of a basin for three days." She strutted away, putting a little extra sway in her ass.

"Goes to show what you know, babe, because you could be covered in mud and straight off an Iron Woman competition and I'd still want to have sex with you," Cade called after her.

Her soft chuckle floated back into the room and had him sucking down a groan. Truth was, he wanted nothing more than to follow her in there. If their time together had a shelf life, he wanted to savor every damn second, special assignment or not.

He wanted to earn back both Grace Steele's trust *and* her heart, and he wasn't going to do that with screaming orgasms, as fun as they may be. At that very moment, winning her over meant giving her time alone with her thoughts.

It meant letting her formulate their next step.

It meant stepping back to let her do her job.

After that happened, then *maybe* there could be orgasms.

* * *

The only thing better than soaking in a hot bath was sex, and only if that sex happened with Cade. But as much as she wished he'd taken her up on her offer to join her, she reluctantly admitted that she'd needed the time alone.

Even with her Rec history, she never could have envisioned the extent of Rossbach's brainwashing until she'd sat in that room with the others. Any lingering hope that Rhett's views on the Order's activities were biased disappeared.

If anything, things were way worse than even he'd thought, and it meant that the second she and Cade returned to DC, Grace needed a sit-down with Director Vance. There was no way the Order of the New Dawn couldn't be considered a public liability. Someone needed to step in and put a stop to it. Pronto.

At some point in her tub soak, Grace's eyes drifted closed. The stress of the last few days melted into the hot water, leaving behind nothing but a calm, soothing oasis until something shattered it. She woke up with a start and heard it again.

Cade knocked on the bathroom door. "You know I

was joking about drowning in there, right? Grace? You awake?"

"I'm awake." She shifted, her muscles clenching in protest. "But I seem to be a little...stuck."

Cade stepped inside, a smirk on his face until he took in her still nude form lying in the water. He cleared his throat, shifting his eyes away. "You need some help getting out?"

Initially, that was exactly what she'd planned. But seeing him standing in front of her, looking almost shy despite their history, sparked her devious side.

She looked up at him through her lashes and threw him her best seductive smile. "Or you could come in here with me."

Cade chuckled nervously. "Yeah, that's probably not a good idea. Then you're really not getting out of there anytime soon."

"I'd be okay with that."

"Grace," he said in warning.

Seeing he needed a little extra incentive, she slowly got to her knees. His gaze dropped to her wet breasts. "Fucking hell."

She hooked her fingers through the belt loops on his camo pants and tugged him closer. At perfect eye level, the telltale sign of his erection pushed against his zipper. "This looks really uncomfortable, and I think we should do something about it."

"You're not making this easy, Gracie."

"Good." She slowly worked the buttons of his pants, giving him time to pull away, but she knew he wouldn't. He watched her intently as she freed his already rock-hard cock and yanked his pants to his knees. He kicked them away and then ripped his shirt over his head.

"You look rather pleased with yourself, Special Agent Steele."

"Not yet." She leaned forward and ran her tongue over the drop of pre-come glistening on his cock. His hand lowered to the top of her head, and he hissed. "Now I am."

She licked him from base to tip before sliding him deeper into her mouth. Cade's fingers tightened in her hair, but he never pushed or guided. He let her control the pace, giving her an occasional groan for good measure. She palmed his ass and urged him deeper into her mouth.

Cade closed his eyes, struggling to hold back.

"Stop. Stop." He pulled away with a curse. His free hand stroked her cheek, brushing a lock of hair over her shoulder. "I want inside you when I come, but—fuck. I don't have any condoms."

"The FBI gives us regular screens. I'm clean. And I'm on the birth control shot." Her throat dried as she realized what she was suggesting.

Cade looked equally stunned. "Are you sure?"

"Do I have any reason to worry about you?"

"Fuck no. I never go without a condom."

She scooted back, making room for him. "Then come on in. The water's a little cool, but I think we can change that."

Cade stepped into the tub, and the second he sat, he pulled her onto his lap.

Grace straddled him. The change in position rubbed her nipples against his chest, making them tingle. "You feel so damn good."

"So do you." Cade threaded his fingers in her hair and brought her mouth to his for a hot, hard kiss.

The base of his cock, trapped between their bodies, brushed against her clit as she rotated her hips. Her body trembled and she did it again...slower...harder. "Oh, my God."

"Are you trying to make me come before I get inside you?" Cade ran his mouth down her neck. His palms cupped her breasts, holding them still as his mouth sought out its new target—her achingly hard nipples.

"I could say the same to you." Grace sat up on her knees, fisted his cock, and sank down on him in one hard drop of her hips.

Cade's hands clamped down on her hips as she eased her body into a slow, firm grind. "Fuck."

She couldn't form words and didn't know what to say even if she could. When they'd agreed to enjoy each other and see where things went, Grace had half expected the arrangement to fail miserably. There was so much *hurt* between them that it couldn't possibly work.

Hurt over his rejection of her. Hurt over keeping her distance from DC—and her family. It hurt when she returned home, feeling like an outsider with the people she cared about most. It hurt when she fought with Cade.

It hurt when they made love—because she knew how much time had been wasted.

It hurt because she'd never stopped loving him, and she didn't think she ever would.

Grace was so exhausted from all of the hurt. She wanted hope. She wanted trust. She wanted redemption. Most of all, she wanted *them*.

The idea of a future with Cade made Grace's body vibrate, but it scared her to death at the same time. They'd agreed to see where things went, but they'd been on the same path once before, and it had nearly left her in pieces.

"Look at me," Cade commanded softly. His blue eyes locked on her, darkening as he slid one hand up her arm and across her cheek. "I'm all yours, Gracie. Take it. Take me."

She almost asked him to clarify, but his body shifted beneath hers, the friction pulling a low groan from her throat.

Grace tossed her head back and enjoyed the sensation of his mouth feasting on her breasts. His thrusts lifted higher, plunging deeper into her body, and with every drop of her hips, the pleasure surged closer to the breaking point.

Cade's fingers flexed on her hip, and they both erupted in a loud cry of each other's names. He dragged her mouth down for a kiss she felt right down to her soul, and Grace knew right then...

If there really was such a thing as a New Dawn, Cade Wright stood right in the middle of hers.

CHAPTER
EIGHTEEN

Cade stood at the easternmost corner of the New Dawn compound, counting the number of things he'd rather be doing than waiting for a man to sneak away from his post to take a dump.

There were a million of them, and they all involved—in some way, shape, or naked form—the woman crouched at his side. He practically heard Grace's impatience as her twitching knee bounced against his.

"I thought you said he always leaves around now?" She checked her watch for the third time in as many minutes.

"Guess he forgot to set his timer. I don't know what to tell you. He's done it for the previous three nights. Maybe he stopped taking his Metamucil or something."

She snickered before remembering they were supposed to be lying low. Insanely smart and a gifted people reader, but the woman didn't have a tactical bone in her gorgeous body—except for her fondness for her handgun.

"You're eager to get to Roman so he can put Magdalena in your hands again."

"Not just Magdalena. I'm hoping he'll have some

hot chocolate too, because I'm freezing my nips off out here."

Cade's gaze automatically dropped to where her breasts were hidden beneath four layers of outerwear.

Grace chuckled. "Eyes are up here, Cade."

"I wasn't searching for your eyes."

Even hidden in shadows, he caught her rolling her pretty brown orbs. He didn't care. He grinned. Something had changed last night, maybe while they'd been in the tub, or later in the night when he'd woken up to find a warm, soft Grace wrapped around him like his own personal body pillow.

He wasn't sure when the hell it happened, but he was opportunistic enough to take advantage of it while it lasted—and he prayed it lasted a hell of a long time. Forever would be good with him. But for now, he'd take it one day at a time.

He'd gotten up early this morning and plotted their way out to the guys' campsite, but the plan relied heavily on Riley taking his regularly scheduled shit break. An hour into their wait, and his toes were starting to lose their feeling too. Too much longer and they'd have to scrap their plan and try again another night.

"Ten more minutes and we'll go around the south side and see if we can breach the perimeter line from there," he suggested.

"I don't think we'll have to." Grace nudged her chin up toward the tree stand where the PC guard shifted, antsy on his perch.

James's henchman climbed down from his position and disappeared behind a wide, snow-tipped pine tree.

"Stay on my heels." Carrying nothing but themselves, Cade led the way through the thicket of trees. The four clicks out to Roman and Tank's campsite would be easy. It was the way back, bogged down with a few extra toys, that would be the real trick.

They trudged through the woods silently, not taking any chances that New Dawn had changed things up on them at the last minute. They made it about three clicks when the sound of a goose stopped them cold.

They stood in position and heard the call again.

Grace scoffed. "Seriously? Do those idiots realize that we're in the West Virginian woods in the middle of freakin' December?"

Cade snorted. "Don't think they care."

Six feet away, Tank stepped out from a ground-mounted hunter's blind, a camouflaged hidey hole that snipers used to bunker down for the long haul. "About damn time you guys showed up. We thought you ditched the fam and joined New Dawn for real."

"Don't even joke." Grace speared him with a glare, but it softened when the Louisiana native tossed an arm over her shoulder. She grimaced, shrinking away. "And you've obviously ditched soap and water. When was the last time you showered?"

"When did you guys head out here?"

"Ew. Stay over there—*please*."

Laughing, Tank led the way through heavy underbrush. "We made camp a good five clicks farther than any of your new friends dare to venture. These guys may be armed to the teeth, but they're not the adventurous sort."

"Pretty sure that's saved for his elite squad," Cade said humorlessly.

Tank cocked up an eyebrow. "He's got an elite squad?"

"From what I hear. So you might want to retire your goose calls in case they're not as stupid as their home-bound friends."

"Noted. So..." He slid them a coy smirk. "...did you guys have to participate in any ceremonial orgies or anything?"

Grace growled and stormed past.

Tank chuckled. "Was it something I said?"

"You better be careful, man. She's cold, chocolate-deprived, and already said the first thing she's doing when she gets to your camp is grab Magdalena."

Tank's face paled. "Shit. I better go apologize."

"I would if I were you." Cade chuckled as his team-mate jogged to catch up to her.

They walked another hundred yards and over a small rise until the campsite came into view. A collection of tents made a U shape with a fire pit in the center and a canopied table. Against a far tree, rope and twine were nailed into the bark, wild game hanging from the branches.

"You guys really went above and beyond to sell the hunters angle, huh?" Cade asked.

"Needed something plausible in case your friends stumbled on us." Roman stood by their makeshift table, handing Grace a steaming mug. "It's a good thing you guys showed up when you did. We were a day out from storming the place."

"No, he wasn't," Tank tattled, sitting next to Grace.

"Maybe not. But Knox's check-ins were really starting to chafe. He doesn't like you guys being in there without communication." He nodded toward a small pack on the ground. "And speaking of comms...call me Santa. There's a sat phone in there, a pair of .22s, and that access card Rhett Winston gave you guys."

Grace snatched the bag and peeked inside. "Tell me that my girl is one of the .22s."

Roman's lips twitched. "Your Mag is safe and tucked inside, along with a nine-millimeter. There's also a few nondescript bugs you can plant over the compound. Liam will help us keep tabs on everything from back at HQ. Have you made contact with Sarah Brandt yet?"

Cade deferred to Grace, who clutched her hot mug like a lifeline. "Remember that thing I warned you guys about?"

"You warn us about a lot of shit, cuz. You're going to have to be more specific."

"She's not going to see this as a rescue. As a matter of fact, she's going to fight us like hell. She practically worships Rossbach and my mother."

Roman's face hardened. "What the fuck does your mother have to do with this?"

"Guess who's married to him? Or his concubine? Or fuck-buddy? Or whatever the hell they call each other? She's the *Mother* Rebecca to his *Father* Teague."

"You can't be fucking serious."

Cade pushed Tank over on the bench seat and took the spot next to Grace. "Oh, she's serious, and that woman's every bit as vile as we imagined. Every time she speaks, I become more and more amazed that someone like her could raise someone as incredible as Grace."

"That's because she *didn't* raise me. Thank God," Grace muttered.

Roman and Tank went quiet.

Cade turned to his friends, noting Tank's eyebrows lifted high into his hairline. Roman simply stared him down, his dark eyes drilling a hole through him. Neither of them were slouches in the perception department, and if Cade sensed the difference between him and Grace, they could too.

But Roman wouldn't question it—at least not in front of Grace. "So Brandt's daughter isn't going to be happy about the family reunion. Does that mean you think we should leave her alone and give the vice president our condolences?"

"Fuck no," Grace exclaimed, her eyes widening. "We need to get her out from under their thumb, pronto. I'd bet my badge *and* Magdalena that she sees her father as the Obstacle between her and her New Dawn, and she'll do anything to get it. And I do mean *anything*."

"You think she'd do something to the vice president of the United States? To her own dad?"

Grace shrugged. "Sometimes hate and love aren't mutually exclusive, and nothing's more convoluted than familial relationships. In Sarah's eyes, Pierce Brandt is what's standing between her and the life she deserves."

"Then why the fuck are we going to deliver her to his damn doorstep?" Roman asked. "I mean, what the hell do we say? *Here you go, Mr. B. Oh, and by the way, your daughter may or may not want to knock you off. Good luck with that.*"

"No!" Grace smacked her mug down and stood. "We're going to take her back to civilization, and then we're going to get her the freakin' help she needs to figure her shit out!"

No one said a thing until Grace stormed away, cursing a blue streak.

Roman stood to follow, but Cade stopped him. "I'll go."

"You really think that's a good idea?"

"Yeah, I do."

Roman shrugged but didn't argue. "Great. Because I really like my balls where they are."

Cade followed the cursing to one of the two larger tents. He paused outside. "You got Magdalena's safety on or off?"

"Go away, Cade."

"Oh well. I like to live dangerously." He stepped through the flap moments before Grace turned her back, but he didn't miss the dampness on her cheeks. *Shit.* One thing that always gutted him was the sight of her tears. "Grace."

She wiped at her face, cursing. "Do you *never* listen?"

"No. Ask my mother. It's something I've had a problem with ever since I reached double digits."

Cade waited two feet away, wanting *her* to turn to *him*. Hell, he needed it. He could push her for answers, and she might even give in and tell him what was going on in her head, but it wouldn't mean as much as if she trusted him enough to come to *him*.

Head bowed down, her shoulders heaved with the effort to control her breathing. "We have to get her out of there. And the way she thinks...it's not entirely her fault."

"I know."

She turned, this time not bothering to hide the moisture rolling over her cheeks. "I don't think you do. Given the right situation, or if I'd stayed in Sanctuary longer, I could've been her."

Hearing the break in her voice, Cade closed the distance between them in three long strides. Cupping her cheeks, he angled her face toward him so she couldn't look away. "You never could've been her. Not in a million years."

"There's a reason why Todd asked me to the cabin that night. Because he saw something inside of me that made him believe that I'd help him. Hell, that I'd be *happy* to help him to do God only knows what to Rhett."

He thumbed away her tears. "No, he forced you into that situation because he's an asshole. And unlike him, you knew it wasn't right. Rhett Winston's alive today because of you. He said so himself."

She flashed him a pathetic smile. "You're just saying that so I don't beat myself up over it."

"No, I said it because it's true. We'll get Sarah Brandt away from your mother and Rossbach, and then we'll get her the help she needs. I promise. We're in this together." Cade dropped his forehead to hers and prayed she believed his next words. "Gracie, you can trust me."

She closed her eyes and whispered, "I do."

Cade's entire world trembled beneath his feet.

After he'd broken her trust nine years ago, he never thought he'd be able to get it back. Even despite their fragile agreement, he hadn't fully let himself believe a second chance with her was possible, no matter how much he wanted it.

But he saw it—in her words and in the soft golden depth of her eyes as she hesitantly met his gaze.

She trusted him.

Now it was up to him to make sure she never regretted it.

CHAPTER NINETEEN

The previous night on her and Cade's trek back onto the compound and into their cabin, Grace had felt lighter—and that was saying something, since they now had to orchestrate a kidnapping. She'd believed that she could trust him, and that dynamic change in their relationship would definitely take time to get used to.

Relationship.

The word made her twitchy, and not because she couldn't see herself with him.

Because she *could*, and they hadn't once mentioned what would happen between them beyond the *right now*. It was a conversation they needed to have soon—just not when she was less than an hour away from having to kiss her mother's ass.

"You worried about having to make nice with Mother Dearest?" Cade's voice tugged Grace out of her daze.

"You a mind reader now?"

"No, I'm a Grace reader, and the worry is plastered all over your face. We already know what we're dealing with when it comes to Sarah. You don't have to make nice with Rebecca to get your foot in the door."

"No, but if our plan to get Sarah off the compound

is going to work, I need to gain her trust, and to gain her trust, I need a reason to stick to her side that doesn't involve sitting in front of those damn brainwashing videos."

"That's not happening again," Cade growled. His white-and-tan Protector Command camo fit him like a well-worn glove, and she couldn't help but ogle the way his abs flexed as he tugged on his boots and pushed to his feet.

"I know, but people don't exactly hover around the Rec unless they have a reason to. My mother can give me one." *Unfortunately*.

She wasn't eager for another mother-daughter talk, but it was a necessary evil. For all that Rossbach controlled around Sanctuary, Rebecca Steele wasn't without her own pull.

Grace didn't expect it to be a simple matter of asking for a favor either. Drunk on what little power Rossbach had given her, her mother would make her work for what she wanted. She just wasn't about to tell Cade that, because he already didn't like the idea.

"So you have a PC shift after the Morning Meal?" Grace asked, hoping he didn't call her out on the abrupt change of subject.

"Yep. Perimeter detail. I'm hoping to nudge that southern cam over a bit. That way we'll have a bigger blind spot to work with on our way out."

"Just don't be too obvious."

"Well, damn, and here I was going to ask James to hold the ladder."

"Funny." Grace tossed his coat into his face, making him laugh.

They bundled up and headed outside, where Sanctuary residents were already awake and active, a few filing into the main building across the compound grounds. James stood outside, talking to another uniformed guard.

"Looks like I have a little brown-nosing to do myself." Cade pulled her into a quick, hard kiss. "Don't go kicking anyone's ass, no matter how much he or she may deserve it."

"You're really sucking all the joy out of my day. You know that, right?"

Cade smirked and crossed the commons, giving her an exquisite view of the way his fatigues cupped his backside. She let herself admire the sight before she focused on Operation Kiss Maternal Behind.

She didn't have to go too far. Less than twenty yards away, her mother and Sarah stood talking, looking amiable and downright friendly. Grace trudged through the snow and prepped herself for contact. Five feet away, she plastered a fake smile on her face. At three feet, she threw up her invisible protective shields.

"Mother. Sarah. May the New Dawn shine upon you."

"And upon you as well," Grace's mother and Brandt's daughter chimed in unison, but only the vice president's daughter seemed to mean it.

Sarah smiled. "I hope you had a restful evening... and a warm one. It was frigid last night."

"It was pretty cold, but Cade and I managed."

Rebecca Steele's glare landed on her with all the weight of an anvil. "Getting a late start to your day, are you not? It's awfully close to the beginning of the Morning Meal."

"There's still a few minutes. You're standing here, and Morning Meal doesn't happen without Mother Rebecca in attendance, right?"

Shit. She hadn't meant that to sound as bitchy as it came out—or maybe she did.

Her mother's eyes narrowed. "Father Teague shouldn't have rushed your Reconditioning. I think you would've benefited from a few more weeks—at the very least."

"Technically, it wasn't reconditioning. I *asked* for that time in the center." Grace kept her voice neutral.

"So I heard. But that doesn't mean you should've been granted permission to leave."

Sarah gave Grace a warm smile. "Actually, I think Grace is well on the way to finding her own path. Even Maria warmed up to her by the third day, and we know that's near impossible."

This time, Grace's grin was genuine. "I knew I'd wear her down eventually."

"It has nothing to do with wearing her down. She finally saw what I saw in you the moment we first met."

"My charming personality?"

"The Order. You may have stumbled off your path, Grace, but the Order has always been inside you. It always will be."

Not if she could help it. She'd perform an exorcism if she had to to wash her hands of it.

Grace duplicated the dreamy look on the other woman's face. "Now I just need to find my place within the community. Cade's thrilled to be part of the Protector Command, and like him, I'm a doer. This waiting around for the results of my Enlightening is driving me bonkers."

"I have an idea, and of course, it would be with your permission, Mother Rebecca, but what if Grace were to help me with little things around the center? Not only could she be an extra set of hands, but it'll give the residents hope to see that regardless of how far off the path you've physically traveled, you can always find it again."

Rebecca's gaze shifted between the two young women. Her mother wanted to say no probably more than she wanted her next breath, but she also worried how it would look to others.

Always concerned with appearances, Grace thought, waiting to hear her answer. Refusing Grace a position in which she could help other members of the flock would raise more than a few eyebrows.

Grace summoned every last bit of faux innocence she could muster. "That would be incredible if I'd be allowed to do that."

Her mother lifted her chin staunchly and turned to Sarah as if Grace weren't even there. "Against my better judgment, I'll agree to it, but if there's the slightest issue, I trust that you'll report it to me immediately? And I do mean the smallest. There's no reason to wait until something festers out of control."

By *it* she meant Grace. "Standing right here, Mother," she joked, waving her hand. "And there won't be any issues to report."

Her mother snarled, "You are your father's daughter,

Grace Ann. Trouble follows you around like starving ants at a picnic."

Grace bit back a retort in her father's defense.

Truth be told, she barely remembered him. He'd died overseas when she'd been so young that her memories were distorted with vague recollections and stories she'd heard from her aunt Cindy and her cousins. But to hear her aunt tell it, she'd been a daddy's girl from head to toe, dragging his old uniform cover around like a security blanket.

More than one time—or a dozen—she'd wondered what her childhood would have been like if he'd come home from that tour. A family man through and through, there'd be no way he'd let his wife and daughter live on a commune, and she couldn't help but think he'd have a field day putting Rossbach in his place.

She would have had a parent who actually gave a rat's ass about her.

Rebecca Steele looked at Grace expectantly, waiting for the heated reaction that thirteen-year-old Grace wouldn't have hesitated to give in defense of a man she'd barely known.

Instead of giving her mother ammunition and a reason to send her straight back to the Rec, she conjured another reply. "I'm not the same person that I was before, Mother."

She was better prepared. She was armed with years of study. And she now knew how her mother's mind worked.

"From this moment onward, you will address me as *Mother Rebecca*," her mother commanded. "Any further breaches of etiquette and you *will* be sent back to the Reconditioning Center without the luxury of knowing it's a temporary sentence. Do I make myself clear?"

"Crystal."

With a huff, her mother stormed off toward the dining hall, her golden robes dragging through the slush.

Grace blew out a heavy sigh, catching sight of Sarah's sympathetic look. "I'm sorry you had to see that. My . . . Mother Rebecca . . . seems to have an abundance of memories but is in short supply of forgiveness."

"I don't see it that way. I know that she and Father Teague can't play favorites, but you're her daughter, Grace. She wants what's best for you."

Rebecca Steele didn't give two hoots about her daughter, not twenty-six years ago, not seventeen, and not now. But Sarah was so deep in her hero worship that she'd explain anything away that challenged her idea of Mother Rebecca.

Grace took Sarah's mention of motherhood and flipped it around. "Your parents must feel the same way too, right? Want what's best for you? Have you talked to them since you've been here? They must miss you."

Sarah's smile vanished like a flick of a switch. "No. They don't."

"But they have to—"

"No, They. Don't." There was no sign of Sarah's earlier friendly demeanor. "I know you mean well, but my parents are *nothing* like Mother Rebecca and Father Teague. They're loyal only to their own greed, and don't care who they hurt in their desperate attempt to get *more* . . . more power, more money . . . more influence over people less fortunate than them. People like my parents are the reason I'm in Sanctuary today."

At least Sarah and I have that in common, Grace thought dryly.

"I'm sorry you feel that way," she said sincerely.

"Don't be. It's because of my past that I can now prepare for my future. And the same goes for you. You are who you are right at this very moment because of everything and everyone that came before. Accept it. Own it. And let it guide you to your path."

That was scarily good advice if only she didn't mean it in a twisted, fucked-up, felony kind of way.

* * *

During a perimeter check with Novak that evening, Cade had been able to nudge the southern camera to the exact position he wanted. All he and Grace needed now was to give Ro and Tank a heads-up, locate Sarah Brandt, and get the hell out of Oz.

The sooner, the better.

Cade rubbed his temples, his pounding headache making his eyes throb. The bright light of the surveillance screens and his annoying "trainer" didn't make the pain any less. "I think I'll go take another stroll around the grounds and make sure everything's still good."

Novak looked at him as if he had double heads. "Why the hell would you do that? We can see the compound from right here. Plus we already have guys outside."

Because if he didn't move—and soon—he was going

to lose his shit. And probably on the kid in front of him. He wasn't built for sitting on his hands.

Voices in the lobby drew Cade's attention just as his colleague shot to his feet, the most he'd moved in at least four hours. "Get the hell up."

As Cade slowly stood, Todd Winston walked into the room with none other than Teague Rossbach himself.

"Gentlemen. No need to be so formal." Rossbach gestured for them to relax.

"May the New Dawn shine upon you, Father Teague," Novak droned.

"And upon you as well." His eyes shifted toward Cade before glancing back at the surveillance equipment. "I trust everything is running smoothly."

"Smoother than cool silk, Father Teague. You have no worries about the safety of Sanctuary while I'm on duty."

Cade nearly rolled his eyes. At this rate, he'd have to pull the kid from the cult leader's ass and administer CPR.

Rossbach turned back toward Cade. "I'd hoped to see you adjusting to your new role here. I know we run things quite differently than they do on the Outside. The change can be difficult for people at first."

"Actually, sir, it feels as though I've always been here. Not much adjustment needed. It's good to wake up in the morning and feel useful again."

"And we're more than happy to help with that." He nodded toward Winston. "Our Elite Guards could use someone with your talents. I'm sure it won't be long before you're having a discussion with the councilman here."

Cade faked awe. "Wow, sir. That would be incredible. James wasn't able to tell me a lot about the EG, but I learned enough to know that it would be an honor."

Todd Winston scowled, not in the least sugarcoating his disgust at the idea. "Don't let Father Teague's compliment blow up your head. There've been plenty of good men who've tried to keep up with the harsh demands of the EGs, but very few have passed."

Cade really wanted to punch this asshole. Instead, he let the jerk's comment slide. A little. "I passed my RASP training with flying colors. I'm sure I'll do fine with your men, Councilman Winston. I'm sorry. I pegged James as a Navy guy from the second we first met, but I can't seem to ID your service branch. Who did you serve with?"

Winston ground his teeth. "I bring something entirely different to the table."

Rossbach ignored the silent pissing contest in front of him and walked toward the surveillance exit. "Thank you both for doing such a fantastic job, but if you'll excuse me, there's a matter that I need to attend to. Todd. With me."

Winston followed his boss, but not before throwing a death glare back at Cade. He couldn't help it; he waved, chuckling internally.

Guess Grace wasn't the only one who caused problems.

Cade casually peered around the corner in the direction Winston and Rossbach had gone. They were already out of sight, and with nothing in the back of the building except for the break room, he wasn't exactly sure what kind of business Rossbach intended to have.

But he sure as hell wanted to find out.

"I have to hit the latrine," Cade announced.

"The what?" Novak was back to stuffing his face with something that smelled suspiciously like pork rinds.

"I need to go take a piss. That okay?"

"Yeah. Sure. Whatever." He kicked his boots up on the table. "Don't take long."

He planned on taking however long he wanted. Shift change was in ten minutes, and if he played his cards right he wouldn't have to stare at video screens any more tonight.

Cade followed Rossbach's voice, stopping just before he stepped into the almost-empty break room. Peering around the corner, he watched Winston slide a metal shelving unit to the side, revealing a security-sealed door.

"Funny how that wasn't on the grand tour," Cade murmured.

Winston pulled a key card out of his pocket, not unlike the one his father had given Grace, and brushed it over the scanner. It flashed green before unlocking with a soft hiss. Cade barely caught a glimpse of stairs before Winston and Rossbach stepped through it and the shelving unit slid back into place.

They didn't come back.

Ten minutes passed, then twenty. After thirty minutes of lurking in the break room, the new shift of arriving guards threw him questioning looks. He clocked out and headed back to the cabin, already forming a plan to get on the other side of that door.

Halfway up the cabin steps, Grace screamed.

Fists raised and prepped to go to war, he burst through the door. Except there were no Elite Guards. No Teague Rossbach or Todd Winston.

There was just Grace, lying in bed, the sheets twisted around her body as she battled a faceless enemy.

"Grace." He sat on the edge of the bed and gently touched her arm.

"No! Don't!" Grace jerked away, her head whipping from side to side. "Please don't!"

"Grace, baby, it's just a nightmare." He brought her hand to his lips, and keeping his voice low, cooed her name until her violent movements slowly stopped.

Her eyes, foggy with sleep, flickered open. "Cade? You're back?"

"Yeah, and none too soon. You were kicking the shit out of the bedsheets when I got here."

She glanced down at her sweat-dampened skin and grimaced. "That hasn't happened in a long time—at least not that I know of."

"It's to be expected, though, right? Being here must bring back a lot of memories."

"Yeah. That's probably it." She pulled away, and Cade felt the loss immediately.

He wouldn't let his disappointment show and risk pushing her away even more. Instead, he followed her to the bathroom and leaned against the doorjamb as she splashed cold water on her face.

"I may have found a use for that key card Rhett gave us. I saw Winston and Rossbach use a similar one to slip through an unmarked door back at the PC, and I doubt it was to watch ESPN Zone."

"Okay, let's go." She headed toward her boots.

"I love your work ethic, babe, but it's not happening tonight."

"There's no time like the present."

"Actually, there is, which would be when I'm on duty and can make sure that we're not spotted."

"There's no way there's anything good behind that door, Cade. Not with Rossbach *and* Todd involved. This may have started with getting Sarah Brandt back to her family, but we can't ignore what's happening here. This place is a powder keg waiting for the stroke of a match."

He raised his hands in mock surrender. "I'm not arguing the point, but if whatever's behind that door is as big as I think it's going to be, we're not going to want to sit on it. We're going to want to move."

Grace didn't look convinced.

"Hey." He slowly eased his arms around her waist and ducked his gaze to meet hers. "We both want the same things here—Sarah safe with her family and Rossbach unable to hurt another person. But I'm the tactics guy, remember? It's my job to take our goal and figure out the best way to reach it. Waiting twenty-four hours before we tackle the door—and Sarah—is it."

"Okay."

"Okay?"

"If you think waiting until tomorrow night is really the best course of action, then we'll wait."

She met his gaze, but she didn't *see* him. Her mind was somewhere else, and if he had to venture a guess he'd say it had something to do with whatever had been chasing her in her sleep.

When they'd been together the first time around, he'd been an expert at keeping away the demons, but after nine years apart, he was out of practice. If he tried to bring her back to him—and failed—he wasn't sure what he'd do.

But he had to try.

"I know we promised that we'd take things between us one day at a time...that we'd see where things went and if they took us in the same direction. But I'm not gonna lie, Grace. I *want* to move forward, and I hope to God that you're right there next to me. But that can only happen if you talk to me." Cade swallowed the hard lump that was slowly forming in his throat. "Talk to me, Grace."

"I...can't."

He'd barely heard her, but the words still sucker punched him in the gut. He stepped back, his arms dropping. "Okay then. I understand."

"No, I don't think you do."

"It's too much too soon. I get it. You warned me, right? You told me that you couldn't make any promises."

"Cade—"

He held up his hand. "Grace, it's okay. I'm a big boy. I can handle a little disappointment."

Fuck. Knowing she still didn't trust him and realizing that she might never wasn't disappointing. It was an ice pick through his damn chest. He turned, unable to meet her eyes and risk her seeing how much it wasn't okay.

"Stop walking away from me!" Grace cried, her voice cracking.

Cade whirled around.

Tears poured down her cheeks, dripping off her chin. "Why are you always walking away from me? Why does everyone always leave?"

The agony on her face tore him apart, and he couldn't keep his distance.

CHAPTER TWENTY

Cade gave Grace ample time to run away, but her feet remained rooted to the spot. He pulled her into a hug, and her tears soaked through his shirt immediately. She couldn't bring herself to stop, her emotions running high ever since she'd woken up from her dream.

Her *nightmare*—watching Cade walk away.

His cheek brushed the top of her head. "I'm right here, Grace. I'm right here next to you, and there's no place on earth that I'd rather be."

He meant what he said, and although she believed him, he couldn't understand her fear. Hell, sometimes she didn't understand it herself. She'd interviewed serial killers and didn't flinch. She could go twelve rounds with Teague Rossbach *and* her mother and still have energy to spare.

But reliving the pain of watching him walk away brought her to her knees.

"You have no idea how hard it is to be the one *waiting*. *Always* waiting." Grace took a deep breath and hesitantly met his worried gaze. "I waited for my mother to just *once* choose me over a cult. Too afraid of all the unknowns, I waited until something horrible nearly happened before I cut ties with the Order. I waited to embrace a family who loved me because I wasn't sure if I could be the person that they expected me to be. And after I *finally* let someone inside, I waited at home while you put your life on the line for your country."

Grace's head told her to shut up while she was ahead, but she couldn't. She'd spent a lifetime keeping her mouth closed, of letting things—the important things—fester inside of her.

If she wanted to break the cycle, she needed to shatter it to a million pieces so she could never put it back together and fall back on old habits.

She needed to break it to move forward.

"I waited for you so we could start our lives together...and when you showed up the weekend of my graduation, and I saw that look on your face, I knew. Somehow I *knew* that you were going to tell me that I needed to wait even longer." The tears in her eyes made Cade's face fuzzy. "I couldn't wait anymore, Cade. I just...couldn't."

"Why didn't you tell me that's how you felt?" His voice dropped a few octaves, heavy with the same emotion that made it difficult for her to speak too.

"Because I'm me. My first instinct is to react first and deal with the fallout afterward—Gracie the Lion, remember? Except when I finally talked myself through all of my own nonsense, it was too late. The plane was already up in the air."

Cade searched her face for answers. "What are you saying?"

"I'm saying that I got tired of just *waiting*. That day

you left my apartment, I summoned my inner Andretti and got pulled over no less than four times, but when I got to the base, your Boeing was already wheels up. You were gone."

His hand slid up her bare arm and over her shoulder before cupping her cheek. His thumb brushed over her bottom lip, drawing her eyes closed. "You followed me."

"I did."

"Why?"

The words stuck in her throat, unwilling to come out. Saying them made her more vulnerable than she'd ever been with New Dawn.

"Why, Gracie?"

"Because I knew that for you, I'd wait forever." Grace's heart stumbled over itself as she waited for his reaction.

At thirty years old, she'd never once been this honest. With *anyone*. It was freeing and terrifying all at the same time, and yet her chest felt a little lighter. No matter the outcome, she'd laid it on the line...taken the next step entirely out of her hands and placed it in Cade's.

He opened his mouth a split second before a trilling alarm pierced their eardrums, the tense moment broken.

Grace winced. "What the hell is that? A tornado siren in the mountains?"

Cade peeked out the heavy curtains and cursed. He was already half shrugged into his coat when Grace slid into hers, following him onto the porch.

People slowly poured out of their residences, all flocking to where five tall shadows accepted the barrage of hugs being thrown their way. A pajama-wearing Sarah flew out of the Rec and into the arms of one of the new arrivals.

"Looks like Rossbach's Elite Squad just returned home," Cade murmured what she had just realized.

"Grace!" Sarah Brandt waved in their direction, a tall broad-shouldered man at her side. She grabbed his hand and dragged him toward her. "*This* is Simon. Simon, this is Cade and Grace. Mother Rebecca's daughter."

Reynolds's dark eyes gave Grace a critical assessment that left her a little on edge.

Sarah, oblivious to the tension, squeezed his hand like he was her lifeline. "Mother Rebecca signed Grace to help out at the Rec, so that means I may have a little extra time on my hands. We could start our hikes back up again, and I could—"

"No."

The vice president's daughter blinked. "But—"

"I said no." Reynolds shot his girlfriend a glare. "I'm not back for long. Winston brought us in for a quick breather, and then we're headed back Outside. We've talked about this before, Sarah. Duty comes before *anything* else. Even us."

Tears welled in the young woman's eyes, but she blinked them away. "I know. I...I'm sorry."

Simon Reynolds was awfully lucky Magdalena wasn't sitting on Grace's hip.

Tucking her hands casually behind her back, Grace

restrained herself from going for a nose shot that would make her cousins proud. But, damn, it was hard. "I have to round the team up for a briefing." Without another word, Simon left, leaving behind awkward silence.

Sarah broke it, shifting uneasily on her feet. "It's been a long few weeks for him. Being part of the EG is a pretty high-stress job."

"I'm sure," Grace agreed with a nod. *But it didn't give him the right to be an ass.*

"I have a few things to finish up before I can call today's to-do list completed." Sarah's smile came back albeit a little hesitantly as she headed back to the Rec with a wave. "You guys enjoy the rest of your night."

When she was out of earshot, Cade grunted. "That was real hearts-and-flowers shit. I can totally see how she fell for him."

"Asshole or not, him popping up in Sanctuary just made our job that much harder."

Rossbach and her mother stepped through the cheering horde of people, but where Rossbach's attention drifted toward the return of his trained henchmen, Rebecca Steele's locked on her daughter.

A chill immediately ripped through Grace's body. But it had nothing to do with the quickly plummeting temperature and everything with the calculating expression on her mother's face.

It was a good thing Grace and Cade were in their final New Dawn hours...because that was the look of a woman about to blow shit up, and Grace didn't want to be within fifty miles of the blast zone.

CHAPTER TWENTY-ONE

The celebration the night before had lasted about an hour. Glorified superheroes to the flock, Rossbach's Elite Guards had strutted around the grounds shaking hands and puffing their chests out like peacocks. And then there had been Rossbach's grand speech with Mother Rebecca standing dutifully by his side.

Duty and honor. Yadda, yadda, yadda. A proud New Dawn.

What the fuck ever.

The longer the man had droned on and on, the more Cade realized this not only changed their plan, but it moved up their timeline. They needed to make sure everyone was on the same path, and that had meant another trip out to Roman and Tank's campsite.

It also meant no time alone to discuss what Rossbach's Elite's had so rudely interrupted. For now, he'd hold on to the fact that even though Grace hadn't spouted off about love sonnets and happily-ever-afters, they were definitely leaning in that direction. At least more than they had been one short week ago.

Roman—the observant bastard—watched Cade like a hawk the moment he and Grace stepped into their tent, and he hadn't let up in the last hour.

"If you have a problem with my plan, speak up." Cade finally dared his friend to disagree.

None of their options gave him the warm fuzzies, which meant they had to pick a tactic that sucked less than the others.

Roman wasn't convinced they were picking the right one. "I'm just worried your idea's a little too ambitious. We can focus on Sarah Brandt's extraction and then send in a second team to do a sweep of Rossbach's basement haven."

Grace was already shaking her head. "That's not going to work and for a multitude of reasons. For one, Sarah's *going* to be missed. She runs the Rec, for God's sake. And second, Rossbach and my mother aren't stupid. When it's realized that Cade and I are MIA too, the dots are going to be connected pretty quickly, and the moment that happens, whatever information's lying around in that basement is gone. We have one chance at this, and I'm not about to waste it."

Cade nodded. "Plus, I have a feeling that we won't want to sit on whatever intelligence is down there. Rossbach messed with these people's heads more than we originally thought. There's no telling what kind of twisted shit he has happening down there."

"Exactly. Don't make me pull rank on you, Roman. Remember which one of us has the shiny gold badge." Grace locked her cousin in a hard stare. "I want whatever Rossbach thinks he needs to hide behind a hidden door, because whatever it is isn't good."

Neither one of them blinked for nearly thirty seconds.

"Fine." Roman sighed. "But if you can't reach that basement without detection, you have to bail, treasure trove of evidence or not. You can't extract shit if one of those EG bastards catches the two of you."

Grace dropped a noisy kiss on Roman's cheek. "See. Things go so smoothly when you guys just agree with me. You should do it more often."

Roman snorted and stood, nodding to Tank, who was already packing up their campsite. "We'll finish tidying things up here and meet up with you at the rendezvous point. With any luck we'll all be sleeping in our own damn beds by morning."

Across the tent, Tank chuckled. "Thank God, because you have one hell of a deviated septum, my friend. I don't think a grizzly growls louder than you snore."

They all laughed except for Roman. "Glad you all find this funny, but let's not lose focus, okay? You guys need not only to get into that basement, but to get Brandt away from the boyfriend."

"Sometimes you worry too much, Ro." Grace stood and tugged on her coat. "That's why Cade and I make the perfect team. He can Ranger us into that basement, and I'll mind-lure Sarah away from Asshole Simon. If only all assignments were so easy."

Cade and Grace said their goodbyes and left Roman and Tank to prepare for every possible kind of extraction.

"Easy, huh?" Cade slid her a coy look, smirking.

She shrugged. "You think I was going to admit that we're putting way too much trust into Rhett's key card getting us through that door? Hell no."

They trekked back to Sanctuary in silence, Cade's new position with the PC making it easy to slip through the perimeter and into their cabin undetected. He'd barely shrugged out of his black camo and into PC tan when someone knocked on the door.

Grace caught his eye. "They wouldn't be knocking if they'd seen us sneak back onto the compound. Right?"

"You tell me, Special Agent Steele." He nodded for her to step out of the line of sight and opened the door to a vaguely familiar Order member. The older man thrust a slip of paper into his hands and walked away without a word. "This place keeps getting weirder and weirder."

"What is it?" Grace hovered over his shoulder, and when he opened the note, she grabbed it out of his hand and read it herself. "Are you fucking kidding me?"

"I don't know. I wasn't allowed to read it," Cade joked dryly.

"Here. For your literary enjoyment." She shoved the note back at him and stomped her way to the bathroom.

He glanced down at the handwritten note. "Mother and Father Mind-Bender are inviting us to a nightcap? What the fresh hell is this?"

"Damned if I know. What could the witch possibly have to say to me that she hasn't already?"

Twenty-five minutes later, they stood outside Rossbach's personal quarters, a cabin that from the outside looked a lot like their own except on a larger scale.

Cade gave Grace's fingers a firm squeeze. "We're here to have a little nip, and then we're gone. How long can that last? An hour?"

"If you seriously think that we're here for drinks and chitchat I don't know how you ever got your Ranger tab. Isn't the 75th Regiment supposed to be the *elite* of the elite?" Grace looked at the door as if a tiger lay in wait behind it. "She has a motive. I just don't know what the hell it is yet."

"Then I guess we're about to find out." He kissed her temple.

She'd barely rapped on the door when it opened underneath her fist.

Rebecca Steele stood in front of them, looking like an older version of her daughter except for the scowl on her face. She stepped aside and gestured for them to come inside. "And here I thought you'd found a better use of your time this evening."

Grace opened her mouth, but Cade settled a hand on her shoulder. "Not at all, Mother Rebecca. Last night's excitement ran into today. We were about to turn in for the night when we got your invitation."

"Cade! Grace!" Rossbach stepped out from a back room, smarmy smile on his face. Either the man had a closet full of gold robes or he just wore the same one over and over.

Both options skeeved Cade out.

"Please. Sit with us." Rossbach gestured to a small table where a small plate of desserts and four empty wineglasses sat. "I'm sorry we haven't been able to do this sooner, but as you could probably tell, there's a record number of our flock nearly ready to search out their New Dawns. It's exciting times, but a great responsibility."

"We're eager to make that transition ourselves, aren't we, sweetheart?" Cade pulled out Grace's chair, and they all sat.

Grace nodded. "Definitely. I've wanted this for a long time."

"It takes more than a desire for it," Rossbach added, taking time to fill up everyone's glasses. "It takes a strong will, determination, and a willingness to do whatever needs to be done."

"All of which we have."

Rebecca Steele brought her wine to her lips and locked her sights on her daughter from over the rim. "Determined individuals don't wipe their hands of things when the slightest obstacle steps into their path. Tell me, Cade, did Grace tell you about the circumstances around her Defection?"

Grace stiffened in her seat. "He knows—"

Rossbach cut her off. "I believe Mother Rebecca's question was made to Cade."

Grace snapped her mouth shut, but her hands fisted in her lap. Beneath the table, Cade unobtrusively slid his hand over her knee. "I know why she was sent to the Reconditioning Center, yes."

"The worst thing a member of the flock can do is deny another a chance at their New Dawn," Rebecca stated coldly. "But I can't say that my daughter's downfall came as a shock. By that point, she'd already pushed the boundaries of our rules for years, and with every disobedient behavior, her own New Dawn became further and further from reach."

"I was a *child*," Grace announced.

"Age is not an excuse, Grace. Those who study so-cietal patterns can see distinguishing characters as far back as infancy. You, my dear daughter, are destined to push away the things that matter most in your life. Isn't that what happened between you and Cade nine years ago?"

Cade froze, and next to him so did Grace.

They'd expected New Dawn to look into their past, but the glint in Rebecca's cold expression told him that wasn't where she'd gotten the information.

She confirmed it when she looked him dead in the eye. "How did you describe it during your Enlighten-ment, Cade? That she goes through the motions of life while always waiting for the other shoe to drop? I'm gathering that to mean that she never fully commits herself to any one thing or person."

"And whose fault do you suppose that is?" Grace snapped.

Her mother laughed. "*Mine?* Are you really trying to pin your shortcomings on me? I'm not the one who Defected. I'm not the one who let my obstacle veer you from your path."

"And what exactly is my Obstacle, Mother?"

"*Yourself.*"

Rossbach cleared his throat, breaking the sudden si-lence. "It's not too late to conquer your self-destructive ways, Grace. But it *will* take sacrifice." His gaze flick-ered over toward Cade and back. "In order to begin your life anew, you must shed the old."

A cold feeling settled in Cade's stomach. "What ex-actly are you proposing she shed?"

"Everything from the Outside...starting with the imposters who've called themselves her family for the last seventeen years." Rossbach drilled his dark gaze into Grace. "Only *we*, the *Order*, can put you on your path. To believe otherwise would be foolish."

Grace's chair screeched as she pushed it back and stood. "Those *imposters* gave me everything I wanted in life and more. And they did so without degrading me or attaching conditions. They didn't want me around because of what they could get me to do for them. They brought me into their family because they loved me."

Grace's mom scoffed. "Everyone's actions are fueled by a system of wants and desires. It's human nature."

"You're right. But what makes the difference is whether or not they're driven by love...or greed. I'm pretty sure you're very much familiar with the second motive. So you can take your offer to help me find my New Dawn and you can tuck it...because I already found mine. And they're my family. My *real* family."

Grace stalked out, slamming the door behind her.

Rebecca Steele didn't look the least bit shocked, or flustered, as she turned toward Cade. "If you care for my daughter as much as you claim, you'll make sure she changes her mind."

He slowly got to his feet and glared at the woman across the table. "I wouldn't get her to change her mind even if I could."

"That's a true shame."

Fuck it. He and Grace were leaving in a matter of hours. "If you never had any intentions of being a real mother, then you should've left her with the woman who was more than willing and able to do the job."

"Am I to guess that you mean my late husband's sister? I can only imagine what Grace's fate would've been if I had dropped her on the Steeles' doorstep all those years ago. Cindy could barely handle the four ruffians she birthed herself, much less an insolent, disobedient child such as Grace Ann."

Cade's knuckles cracked as he fisted his hands. "There isn't a day that passes that I'm not thankful for her stubbornness. That gorgeously hard head of hers is the only reason she became the incredible person she is today, despite having you as a role model."

"That is quite enough!" Rossbach stood, red-faced and livid. "You will show Mother Rebecca the respect that she deserves!"

"I am." Cade ignored the string of angry shouts as he slammed the door behind him.

It was way past time they got the hell out of this shit-hole.

And it was *way* past time that he made sure Grace knew just how serious he was about their future together.

* * *

Grace wasn't sure whose ass she wanted to kick more: hers for falling for her mother's divide-and-conquer tactic or her mother's for being deviant enough to think of it. Rebecca Steele's talent for smelling blood in the water had gotten better through the years, and at the mention of Grace and Cade's past, she'd sniffed the first drop.

At the mention of Grace's family, she'd smelled a damn feast.

Her mother could attack all she wanted. Grace had years and a hell of a lot of training to let most of the worst roll off her back. But come at her family?

That had struck a nerve.

It was either get up and leave or whip out the badge and handcuffs and ruin any chance of putting a whole lot of bad people behind bars. For now, she needed to count on Cade to make the peace and move on to the next phase of their plan—to find a *legal* reason for her to whip out her badge and handcuffs. Or at the very least, to gather enough information for a judge to give her one.

Grace grabbed the tactical bag from beneath the bed and tossed it onto the mattress. She'd barely checked Magdalena's ammo clip when the knock came.

"Grace?" Sarah's voice sounded muffled through the door. "Hey. I saw you walk across the courtyard, and I just wanted to make sure you were okay. You looked upset."

Crap. It wasn't as if she could play asleep. She'd literally walked through the door a minute ago.

Tossing the bag back beneath the bed, Grace schooled her expression and opened the door. "Sarah. Hey. No, I'm fine."

"You didn't look fine." Sarah looked genuinely concerned. "I just wanted to let you know that I'm here.

You don't have to be a Rec resident in order for us to talk."

This *so* wasn't the plan—at least not for another hour, until after they checked out Rossbach's mystery door, but Grace couldn't pass up this opportunity. "You're right. It's been a pretty rough day, but I don't want to keep you from Simon. I know you haven't seen each other in a while."

"Actually, I was taking a little breather from Simon when I saw you."

"A breather? Why? Is everything okay?" Because if the jerk did anything to hurt her there'd be an opening in Rossbach's Elite Guard.

"Everything's fine. He's just been a little different since last night."

"Different how?"

Sarah shrugged. "Not really himself. He mentioned not being able to finish an assignment, and I think it's bothering him. We'll figure it out, and if we can't we'll go to remediation with Father Teague. But I didn't come here to talk about me and Simon. Something's bothering you."

More than she knows. Grace prayed she wasn't about to make a terrible mistake.

She opened the door a little wider. "Want to come in from the cold?"

"Definitely." Sarah smiled and kicked the snow off her boots before stepping inside the one-room cabin. "So what's got you in a funk? Men troubles? Female troubles? Or—"

"Maternal troubles."

Sarah nodded in understanding. "So I'm guessing tonight didn't go as either of you had hoped."

"You know about tonight?"

"I knew your mother planned to invite you over for a heart-to-heart talk. I'm sorry that it didn't go as either of you had hoped."

Grace snorted internally. "My mother doesn't *do* heart-to-hearts. We've never been close, but after my father died and she relocated us to Sanctuary—and Father Teague—she's disappeared completely."

"I'm sure it was difficult to have your life uprooted as a child, but she did it all for you. To give your life a purpose. To give you a supportive, devoted family."

"I had that—*after* I Defected from the Order."

Sarah's mouth dropped open, her surprise too acute to be fake. "*Defected*? I don't understand. Father Teague sent you on your journey to find your New Dawn…to confront your Obstacles."

"No, Sarah. I left after being sentenced to the Rec for not helping Todd torture his own father. I ran for my life…and for my humanity."

Grace struggled to keep a rush of emotions at bay. It was the first time she'd said those words aloud, but they needed to know how far gone Sarah Brandt really was. They needed to know if she was a danger to others…or just to herself.

Emotions whipped through Sarah too fast for Grace to identify them all. "If Father Teague doled out punishment, then it must have been justified."

"Punishment for not harming another person? Do you know how that sounds?"

"It sounds like he cared for Todd's future, and you, as his friend, should have too." Sarah's chin lifted as she threw a hard glare at Grace. "You cannot blame others for your shortcomings."

"I did what I did *because* I cared. I wasn't about to sit by and watch Todd become a monster, and there was no way I'd let Rhett Winston become a victim. They were *family*, Sarah. Can you stand there and tell me that you'd be able to do that to your parents? To your father?"

"Our family is made up of those we choose to bring into our lives...not a household that we were born into." Sarah's mouth twisted into an angry snarl. "Father Teague and Mother Rebecca are my true parents—the people listed on my Outside birth certificate can go to hell for I care...and they soon will."

Sarah's tone chilled Grace to the bone.

She meant every word.

"You're right about family being the people you choose to surround yourself with," Grace agreed. "They're the ones who want nothing but the best for you. Who support you in everything that you do."

"Exactly." Sarah nodded emphatically.

"But real family asks for nothing in return but your love. They sure as hell don't ask you to harm others or put yourself at risk for their own personal gain. You can still step off whatever path Rossbach has put you on, Sarah," she suggested gently. "You don't have to become his puppet."

"*Puppet?*" Sarah stalked closer, her green eyes—which were a lot like her father's—hardened. "You don't get it, do you? If I help Father Teague reach his New Dawn, I'll finally be more than someone's trophy. I'll be his *pride*."

Grace's stomach twisted into a knot. "What did he ask you to do, Sarah? And how high is that cost?"

A slow, cold smile slid onto her face. "It doesn't matter. The only thing that does is that in helping him find his New Dawn, I'll also be getting mine. And there's no one on this planet that's going to stop me."

Wrong.

Grace was.

Slipping her hand to the small of her back, she slowly eased Magdalena out from the band of her pants. "I'm really sorry to hear you say that—you have no idea how much."

Sarah Brandt's gaze dropped to the gun. "What do you think you're doing?"

"Like you, I'm doing what I have to."

And then she'd hope that Cade could undo the kink she'd just put in their plan.

CHAPTER TWENTY-TWO

Cade couldn't get back to his and Grace's cabin fast enough, and not just because he wanted to make sure Grace was okay after the scene with Rebecca and Rossbach.

They needed to get their asses moving. Pronto.

He took the steps to the cabin two at a time and entered the cabin. "Don't hate me, but I may have—fuck-and-me." Cade blinked, and when the sight in front of him didn't disappear, he didn't know whether to laugh or curse again.

Grace paced the room while a gagged Sarah Brandt sat on the floor, handcuffed to one of the bed's legs. The younger woman squirmed and shouted, the noise muffled.

"And here I was about to apologize for mucking up our plans." Cade smirked.

"You're laughing? *Seriously?*" Grace looked livid and more than a little freaked out.

"What would you like me to do? We can't exactly put this shit back in the box from which it came. I'm sure you have as much a reason for veering away from the plan as I did."

Grace stopped pacing. "What do you mean? What did *you* do?"

"Voiced my displeasure with Mother Dearest and probably bought myself a year in the Rec if we don't hustle our asses. We need to get into the basement sooner rather than later."

Grace looked from a narrow-eyed Sarah and back to him. "And what are we going to do about her? We can't take her with us."

"I could always check out the mystery door myself."

"No."

"But—"

"*No*." She drilled a finger into his chest. "What happened to that whole we-stick-together thing?"

He palmed her hips and guided her closer. "I still mean it. But if things don't go our way I'd rather be the only one to get caught. That way you can still get Sarah out of here."

"Very noble of you, but that won't work. Because if they catch you, who do you think they're going to go look for next? And I may be able to bench press my own weight, but Sarah's not exactly a helpless toothpick. I'd never be able to drag her to the rendezvous point on my own."

"Then we leave her here and swing back on our way out." Grace didn't look sure about the suggestion and, hell, neither was he. He pinched her chin between his fingers and nudged her gaze to his. "I'm tactics guy, remember? It's all good. It'll probably take Rossbach at least an hour to calm your mother down enough to start thinking about punishments. By the time she does, we'll be long gone."

A string of muffled squeals drew their attention to Sarah.

Grace cursed. "Fine. But we can't let her sit here out in the open like this."

"Pretty sure the sink has some pretty hefty piping underneath it."

Five minutes later, they'd secured Sarah to the bathroom's plumbing and Cade had shrugged into his PC camo. "Give me a full fifteen minutes to get the night guard out of the PC headquarters and disable the cameras. From that point, we'll have maybe ten more until James gets an alert. We can't dawdle."

"No dawdling. Got it. I'll be at the back door waiting for my invite inside. And our bug-out bags?"

"I put them into position earlier this morning when making rounds." The supplies were hidden around their possible extraction routes. All they had to do was grab and go, and if anyone eventually found the spares, it wouldn't matter. They'd be gone.

"Then I guess we're all set."

Before stepping into the field where shit had the potential to get real damn quick, Cade always shared a good-luck fist-bump with his team. It was a superstition that he'd started way back in Basic. But he didn't want to bump knuckles with Grace.

He paused at the door and spun her into a kiss. He'd meant it to be quick, but the second his mouth covered hers, his body and brain had another idea. Her hands slipped around his neck, and her pink tongue flicked out, brushing against his.

He groaned. "You're killing me."

"You're the one who initiated it, so that's on you." She reached behind him and opened the door, letting in a rush of cold air. "Go. Your fifteen minutes starts now."

Cade hustled over to the PC post, and as he'd expected, the place was deserted except for one lone twenty-something kid sitting in front of the security feeds.

"Hey. Adam, right?" Cade asked. He kicked the snow off his boots and hung up his coat.

"Fuck." The PC guard startled, his feet dropping to the ground with a heavy thud. "You scared the hell out of me, man. I didn't even hear you come in."

Or see him walk through the front door.

Cade chuckled. "Sorry about that. Guess it's a side effect of Ranger training. But, hey, thanks for picking up my slack. That was a real solid thing for you to do. I owe you one."

"Uh...what?"

"My post." Cade nodded to the screen. "I'm still in that needing-to-impress phase, and I couldn't have done it if I'd missed my shift."

"I think you're confused. This is my scheduled night."

"Nope. Trust me, I'd much rather be hanging out with my lady. Maybe you never got the updated schedule?"

"Updated? I didn't know they changed it. Maybe I'll give James a—" The kid reached over for the phone.

"If you don't want a whole night off, I'll head back, but I don't think it's worth waking James. He wasn't in the best mood earlier today."

"Shit. Yeah, no. You're right. I don't know how I

could've missed a night off, but I'm all for it." The kid stood eagerly. "Thanks. I owe you one."

"Don't thank me. Just doing my job."

The kid hightailed it from the building. Cade waited a solid minute after the door closed and sat at the computer hub. Thanks to watching Liam perform his keyboard magic more times than he could count, it wasn't difficult to take the videos offline. One screen flickered off, then another. Before long, all the cameras showed black-and-white fuzz.

"Showtime." Cade hustled to open the back door, located on the far end of the break room.

"About damn time." Grace stood, teeth chattering as she stepped inside. "Another minute and my eyelashes would've adhered to my eyebrows."

"Didn't think I'd have to practically bribe the kid to take the night off. The blocker's up. You got Rhett's access card?"

She tugged it out of her back pocket. "Yep. Let's hope this is our golden ticket. Where's this door?"

"Over here." He led her over to the shelving unit and slid it aside easily.

"How very Sherlock Holmes. I'd be impressed if I wasn't a little worried what Rossbach's keeping down here." As Grace swiped the badge over the scanner, they both held their breath until the red light flickered and turned to a solid green. The door unlocked with a heavy *whoosh*.

"Like magic." Cade handed her the second flashlight from his belt loop. "Do you want to lead the way or should I?"

Grace gave the dark void a less than thrilled look and stepped aside. "Please. Feel free. If the monster beneath the stairs grabs you first, I'll have time to get away."

Cade snorted and flicked on his light. "Watch your step."

The stairs creaked ominously as they descended. Cobwebs clung to the support beams over their heads, one catching in Grace's hair.

She batted it away, wrinkling her nose. "One thing Rossbach and Winston definitely weren't doing down here was spring cleaning. I don't think this place has seen a dustpan in about ten years. Maybe longer."

Reaching the bottom floor, Cade scanned his flashlight around the large room. It was as big down here as it was upstairs, except without the post-fab walls dissecting the place into smaller sections.

Grace nodded to their left. "Let's divvy up. Start on the far ends and work our way to the inside."

"Sounds good to me." Cade went right. Boxes stacked two or three high were tucked into corners, some tightly sealed but others overflowing with coats and clothes. "What the hell are Rossbach and Winston doing down here in this mold trap? Organizing a clothing drive?"

"I think I found your answer," Grace said from across the room. "You need to get over here. *Now*."

The urgency in her voice had him hustling over to where she stood in front of a large table. Topographic maps and building blueprints littered the surface. He picked one up. "None of this makes sense. This map's from some rural area in Texas, and this blueprint is for a residential condo complex. If he's angling to make some kind of big terroristic statement, targeting soft spots like these ones aren't going to do the trick."

"He's not going for big. He's going for personal." Grace brushed past him, her attention focused on something on their left. "Cade."

"Yeah? We running out of time?" He rummaged through the small stack of additional blueprints, trying to find some kind of link from one to the other.

"We aren't, but someone is, and it looks like a few people have already reached their expiration dates."

"What do you me—?" His gaze caught on the board she was studying.

It almost looked like the murder board they made during the Cupid Killer case. They'd used an entire wall in the department meeting room and pinned up collected data and information, even pictures and relationships of all the BCK victims. It was a visual way to see everything in one spot instead of having it tucked away in multiple files.

This was different.

Six eight-by-ten photographs were pinned up in a row. All appeared centered around a different lone figure. And all but the last two images were marked with blaring red X's.

"Is this what I think it is?" Cade asked.

"If you're thinking it's a hit list? Yeah. Pretty sure we found out what Rossbach's Elite Guards do for him when they're on the Outside." She dug a camera from her coat pocket and went down the line, snapping pictures. "These guys are all wearing different military uniforms, and you're more of an expert than me, but they look dated. I don't think these are too recent."

Cade studied the three pictures already crossed off. "Good eye. The first one's Navy. The second one is definitely Army. And the third is a Marine. And if I had to make a guess, I'd say they're all about twenty years old. Rossbach wasn't even in the military, so how would he have crossed paths with any of these men? And what the hell could they have done to him that would've signed their death warrants?"

"If you want me to list all the reasons, I'll be here all day. They could've looked at him wrong, or failed to give him the respect he believes he deserves. But my guess is it's more personal." Grace aimed her flashlight on the fourth pic, and Rhett's profile came into view.

"Bet Rossbach threw that one up after Rhett escaped."

"Because if he wanted to, Rhett could easily destroy everything he's worked for." Grace paused at the fifth picture and made a noncommittal grunt. "This picture's not as clear as the others. It's further away."

Cade shifted down to the fifth image.

She was right. Taken from a distance, and at an angle that didn't give more than a half-ass side view, there was no identifying the person's face. The only thing that could be seen at all was the back edge of a military-grade Jeep... and a hell of a lot of sand.

Instead of a red X, the second-to-last image was marked up with a large—and literal—question mark. "He doesn't know this one's identity."

"But he knows the last one." Grabbing Cade's hand, Grace drew him closer to the last pinned target.

His mind slowly registered the familiar face staring back at him.

Like the others, it was dated, probably at least twenty-five or more odd years old, but he'd recognize those blue eyes anywhere. Hell, he saw them every time he looked at himself in the mirror.

It was Hogan Wilcox.

His father.

CHAPTER TWENTY-THREE

Grace had known Rossbach's room of mystery wouldn't be an immersive shrine to early nineties boy bands, but she hadn't expected to find a half-completed hit list either. Or that she'd know two people on it.

As they'd made their way back to the cabin to pick up Sarah, Grace had watched Cade carefully.

His relationship with Hogan Wilcox—if it could be called that—was tumultuous at best and nonexistent at worst. But it wasn't for lack of trying on the former Chief of Staff's part. Grace expected that the reason the retired Army General became Steele Ops's financial backer was to rebuild the connection he'd lost when he left Cade, Zoey, and their mother.

Zoey had slowly accepted the former general's reappearance over the last couple months. Cade not so much.

At the mention of Wilcox, he shut down, making Roman look talkative by comparison. And Grace didn't have room to complain about the tight lips. She wasn't much better when it came down to talking about the woman who gave birth to her, but it didn't negate the fact that she *wanted* Cade to talk about it.

To her.

Eventually.

Right now they had a vice president's daughter to kidnap.

With a silent timeclock ticking away, they found Sarah right where they left her. Seeing them, she sat straighter, her eyes narrowing in on them in hatred.

"If you don't like the handcuffs, then you shouldn't have plotted the world's downfall," Grace chided, not in the mood for the drama. She crouched down to her level. "We're going to go for a little walk. You're *not* going to run. You're *not* going to cause a scene. And you *are* going to stay on your own two feet. I don't want to drag you through the snow, but I will if I have to. You got it?"

Despite the death-ray glare she gave her, Sarah nodded.

Grace secured a second pair of handcuffs around her wrists before unlocking the first set and helping her get to her feet.

Cade came around the corner, one of their bug-out bags in hand. "All set to get back to reality."

They stepped out from the bathroom when someone knocked on the door.

"Grace?" A familiar deep voice called from the other side. Simon Reynolds knocked again, making the entire front door rattle. "I'm looking for Sarah. You seen her around?"

With quick reflexes, Grace secured Sarah's gag into place. "Do *not* make a noise or this *will* end badly for someone. Do you hear me?" She caught Cade's eyes and mouthed, "What do we do?"

"Back window."

Each taking one of Sarah's arms, they veered toward the far wall, where a small single-pane window barely let in a ray of moonlight.

"That's gonna be a tight fit. Are you sure you're going to be able to get through?" Grace asked.

"We'll make do. You first, and then I'll send our special package down to you. And I know I don't have to express to you how quiet you need to be..."

"And yet you felt the need to mention it." Grace tucked Magdalena back in her holster and nudged the window up, grimacing when it let out a hearty screech.

Simon Reynolds's shadow could be seen pacing through the slat beneath the front door, and it paused before he knocked again. "Grace!"

"Go," Cade urged. "Light and quick."

Grace sucked in a groan as she hoisted herself through the window. The wood frame bit into her fingers, making her realize that she'd taken off her gloves to handle the handcuffs. It was too late to go back for them now.

Ignoring the splinters gouging into her palm, she swung her leg over the edge and counted to three before plummeting the five feet to the ground. Her knees buckled from impact, but she stayed upright, looking up just as Cade struggled to get an uncooperative Sarah through the same window.

Grimacing, Cade held on to the young woman's arms and slowly eased her down. She squirmed and kicked at the back wall, jarring his shoulders.

"Just drop her," Grace whispered. "I'll catch her."

Sarah twisted. Her gag dislodged, and she immediately whipped her head—and her mouth—toward Cade's arm. And bit.

"Fuckin' A." Cade cursed. "She bit me!"

"Simon!" Sarah screeched.

"Let go!" Grace ordered. "Now!"

Cade dropped Sarah into her arms. Grace immediately stifled her screams with her hands as Cade quickly flung himself through the window and retied the gag firmly into place. "There's no way he didn't hear that."

On cue, voices drifted their way from around the corner of the cabin.

Cade tossed Grace their sat phone and hoisted their squirming cargo over his shoulder. "You better ring the guys and tell them that we're coming in hot—and with a few friends. And do it while your lovely ass runs as fast as it can."

* * *

If he hadn't been concerned about the sound of barking dogs closing in on them, Cade would have marveled at Grace's speed. She charged through the underbrush, paving their way off this damn mountain, their hope for a quiet extraction long gone.

His hand throbbed from where the vice president's daughter nearly bit through his tactical glove, but he wasn't about to make another rookie mistake. Hell, they couldn't afford it, because he was a thousand percent certain Simon Reynolds and his Elite Guard buddies were the ones on their tail.

No way did he want to stick around and see how well trained they were or weren't.

Grace glanced at the handheld GPS and nodded toward a familiar snow-covered rise. "This way."

Digging her hands into the dirt, she pulled her way up the embankment until a large shadow hovered over them, extending a hand.

"About damn time you showed up to the party. Food's getting cold." Tank yanked Grace up the last two feet before taking a squirming Sarah Brandt out of Cade's hands.

"Careful. She bites."

Tank chuckled. "Good to know. Guess she wasn't up for coming along quietly, huh?"

"Damn near lost my fingers," Cade complained. "Funny how all that New Dawn complacency flew right out the window."

"Rexie smells something," someone shouted in the distance. "This way!"

"Fuck."

"Change in plans." Tank passed Sarah back to Cade, snatching the hat on her head. "Head south. Roman's waiting with a few supplies. I'll lay a false trail for the pooches to pick up, and then I'll meet up with you guys later."

"You sure separating right now's a smart idea?"

The faraway voice shouted, this time a little closer.

Cade cursed. "Okay, yeah, that's probably a good idea."

Tank flashed a wink and took off, heading in the opposite direction to the one they needed to go. This time, Cade took the lead.

His boots slipped on the slick ground, making the mile trek down toward the valley more than a little interesting. When they reached the rolling river that bisected the two mountains, he let out a soft sigh of relief.

Grace braced her hands on her knees and panted, each heaving breath creating a steam cloud around her head. "We lost them, but I don't know how long that's going to last."

"Hopefully long enough to get off this damn mountain. We have about another mile before we meet up with Ro."

"Fuck, I'm never going to feel warm again. I think my organs are turning to ice."

Cade chuckled as they walked downstream. "It'll be my personal mission to warm you back up again the second we're alone. And speaking of our lack of privacy right now, someone got awfully docile. Can you check her?"

She peeked under Sarah's head of hair. "She passed out...probably from the rush of blood flow to her head."

"Can't say that I'm sorry about that...but what I can say with one hundred percent certainty is that I'm going to have to buy one of those doughnut cushions, because my ass is one big black-and-blue."

"There goes that idea I had for later."

Cade smirked, about to tease back when something snapped in the distance. They both froze, and they heard it again. Cade lifted his finger to his mouth and nodded Grace left, away from the riverbank.

Simon Reynolds's voice echoed through the trees,

"It's cute how you think we're going to let you get off this mountain."

Grace tugged Cade behind a fallen log. Ten yards away, the Elite Guard slowly stalked through the forest. Cade scanned the area and didn't see anyone else. Reynolds was alone.

"I know you were in the PC basement. I know what you saw. Hell, I was the one who planned out each one of those kills right down to clean-up." Simon chuckled. "Man, what a rush. There's nothing like the feeling of righteousness when you know you're about to correct a wrong, or the look of pure desperation when the other person realizes they're about to pay for their misdeeds."

Reynolds stepped through the thicket, not trying to be quiet. "And speaking of misdeeds. You two snuck downstairs before I could update our little board. There's one more red X to go with the others."

Reynolds stopped fifteen yards away and scanned the area around him. "When was the last time you saw your buddy Rhett, Grace? I bet it was a while ago, right?"

Grace sucked in a breath, and Cade reached out, squeezing her fingers.

"Now *that* was a retribution that had been a long time in the making."

A gunshot erupted. Cade pushed Grace down, but the bullet flew wide over their heads, colliding with the tree to Simon's right. He whipped around, and brought his own gun up, shooting wild. Someone drilled another barrage of bullets into the ground right in front of his feet.

He stepped back.

Another round of bullets pushed him backward even more as dirt and snow sprayed up, hitting him in the face. His back foot, landing on a slick moss-coated river rock, slipped out from under him. Reynolds's arms flailed as he fought for balance, but it didn't work. He teetered backward and tumbled ass-first into the rushing river.

Two seconds after the splash came the goose call.

Grace dropped her head onto Cade's leg and laughed. "Oh, my God. Those two and their damn goose calls."

"You may want to put a little hustle in your bustle, kids, because our little firefight's only going to bring the asshat's friends that much faster," Roman's voice called out.

Grace trudged up to her cousin and planted a noisy kiss on his cheek. "Don't tell the others, but you're officially my favorite."

"You mean I wasn't before?" Roman teased dryly before breaking out into a grin.

Tank joined them, surprisingly out of breath for the former Special Forces operator, and reached to take Sarah's load off Cade's shoulder. "I hate to break up this reunion, but I don't know how long those pups are going to be fooled."

"I can't go back to DC." Grace's protest turned all their heads.

"Grace—" Roman interjected.

"Yes, you can," Tank said in unison.

Grace spun around to Cade, those gorgeous—and

determined—brown eyes drilling into his. "*I can't*. I need to make sure Rhett's okay."

"Reynolds could've been playing you to try and get you to react. Rhett's picture wasn't crossed off."

"That doesn't mean they didn't get to him. They've been back less than a day. Maybe they didn't have the time to mark it up." Grace dropped their bug-out bag by her feet and started rummaging through it, pulling out an extra flashlight and a bottle of water. "I can go myself. Take Sarah and head back with Roman and Tank. That way you can check on your dad."

"Like fucking hell am I leaving you alone on this mountain—or alone *period* with those New Dawn assholes out there," Cade growled.

Her brown eyes snapped up to his.

"Don't throw those pretty brown-eyed daggers at me," he protested.

"I'd be throwing real ones at you if I had any in my possession."

She probably would. He was grateful Roman's favorite throwing knives were probably tucked away and out of her reach.

"Do you seriously think it's a good idea to go traipsing up a booby-trapped mountain in the middle of the night?" Cade pleaded to her common sense.

"No, which is why I'll find somewhere to lay low until daylight. But just *hoping* that Rhett's okay isn't an option, and you don't know me as well as you think you do if you think it is."

Oh, he knew her, probably better than himself.

"Then I'm going with you. Roman and Tank can manage taking Sarah back."

Roman cleared his throat. "Someone want to clue us the hell in? What the fuck did we miss, and what's this about Rhett and General Wilcox?"

Grace tossed him her camera. "Get that to Liam, but make sure Director Vance is looped in. Rossbach's using his Elite Guards as a hit squad, and by the look of it, they've already knocked their list of six down to three. Rhett and Cade's dad are two of the remaining."

Tank whistled. "Who's the third?"

"Don't know," Cade interjected. "But it also looks like Rossbach doesn't know yet either, so we have a bit of time on that front."

"He doesn't know the identity of someone he's trying to have knocked off? Interesting."

"Which is why you need to give that camera to Liam. Four of the men in those pics are wearing military uniforms, so I'm hoping it won't take him long to get hits."

"And the fifth?"

"Civilian clothes, but I'm about ninety percent sure that it was taken on a base somewhere. There's a small corner glimpse of what looks like a military grade Humvee."

Roman didn't look thrilled at the idea of splitting up, but he didn't argue. "We'll look into it, and I'll get the General on the horn the second we step off this mountain. Not sure how he's going to react to the info that someone's gunning for him, though."

Cade did. He might not know his father very well, but he knew enough to know that they'd have nearly the same reaction. "He'll sit out on his front steps with a banner over his fucking head saying *Here I am, fucker. Come and get me.*"

"You're probably right." Roman chuckled. He tossed Cade a set of keys. "We have a backup car about three miles south, just off an old logger trail. It's nothing fancy, but it'll get you where you need to go. There's a bag in the trunk with some clothes and cash. Make sure you check in the second you can without compromising yourselves. I don't want Zoey hounding my ass worrying about you two."

Cade smirked, knowing it wasn't only Zoey who would worry. "We love you too, man. We'll be careful."

"One more thing." Grace slid a glance to a still unconscious Sarah. "She's not the same person that Brandt remembers. She's a danger to herself, and especially to him. She needs professional help. Vance has access to all my Bureau contacts. There's a doctor in Arizona who specializes in cult victims. We need to contact her."

Roman grimaced but nodded. "The VP's not gonna love that."

"I don't care what he does or doesn't love. It's what she needs."

"Got it. Vance. Contact. Professional help."

Cade shrugged their pack over his shoulder and automatically reached for Grace's hand. The gesture didn't go unnoticed by either of their friends, but he didn't care. "I think we've all spent way too much time on this damn mountain. It's about time we get off."

CHAPTER
TWENTY-FOUR

Grace glanced over her shoulder for the third time in as many minutes, half expecting Simon to pop out from behind a tree any second. Something like a little river water wouldn't deter a man like him from dusting off and getting back on his feet.

And coming after them.

If she were warm with a sufficient amount of chocolate in her system, she'd be up for the challenge, but she'd lost feeling in her hands fifteen minutes ago, and her stomach growled out its displeasure at not having been fed.

Grace hurdled over a fallen log and glanced into the woods behind them—again. This time, Cade caught it.

"Our ride out of here should be around the corner."

"Good." She waited a beat before pointing out what had been bothering her for the last hour. "Simon shot at us."

Cade slid her a questioning look. "Is there more to that statement?"

"Roman fired that warning shot and Simon immediately started shooting blind into the trees. If the three of us hadn't been crouched down, any one of us could've been hit. He knew we had Sarah, and he risked hitting her."

Grace wished she'd broken his nose when she'd had the chance. *Bastard*.

Cade's hand settled on the small of her back. "Soon, thanks to you, Sarah will be with people who actually care about her well-being. Getting her out of there was the first step. Everything that happens next is up to her and her family."

Knowing he was right didn't make her worry any less.

The road Sarah was about to travel wasn't a smooth one, and she wouldn't wish it on her worst enemy, much less someone who could've been a good friend if they'd been in different situations.

They stepped out of the thicket of trees and onto the dirt-lined logging trail.

Cade nudged his chin to the left. "There's our chariot."

"Chariot" was an understatement. Mud brown with more than a few holes rusted through the exterior, their getaway car looked Grace's age. Or hell, a few years older.

"Roman can't be serious. He said this thing would get us where we needed to go. I didn't realize he meant we'd have to propel it forward ourselves as if we lived in Bedrock."

Smirking, Cade dangled the set of keys in front of her. "Do you want to do the honors or should I?"

She gave the car a wary once-over. "It's all yours. The less I have to touch the interior the better."

Cade chuckled. He popped open the trunk and tossed her the black bug-out bag stashed beneath the spare tire. "While I drive, you see what they gave us to work with. It should be pretty standard. Clothes, cash, guns, and ammo. Everything you need for a fun party."

The second they belted up, Cade took off.

He was right. They had all the necessities, including a map of the DC Metro area, some bottled water, and a few packs of beef jerky. At the sight of the dried teeth-breakers, Cade's eyes lit up.

"Hand those things over before I gnaw my arm off." He bit into a big clump and groaned. "Better than a New York strip."

"I'll have to take your word on that." She opened up a bag of nuts and searched the GPS coordinates for someplace out of the way for them to lie low. Options were seriously lacking in this area. "There's a motel about ten miles out from here, but there's another one about five miles away from where we'd need to park and hike up to Rhett's cabin. My vote is for the one closer to Rhett. It'll make getting up at first light that much easier."

"And on the off chance Reynolds wasn't blowing smoke earlier, it'll probably be the first place that Rossbach's EGs check."

She hated that he was right, but she sent him an annoyed glare anyway. He slid a hand over her knee and squeezed assuredly. "We'll take the extra distance into consideration when we come up with the morning plan. We'll get you up that mountain, Grace. I promise."

She believed him as much as she believed Rhett could handle himself, but it didn't make her worry any less. He was family, one of the first constants in her life, and she didn't know what she'd do if he wasn't there anymore.

The slow rub of Cade's hand and every stressful minute of the last few days weighted Grace's eyelids until she couldn't fight the exhaustion anymore. She fell asleep and woke up to the sound of their chariot's brakes screeching as Cade pulled to a stop.

"We there?" She yawned into her elbow and glanced at the interstate motel that could have starred in every B-rated horror flick. "Oh, wow. You sure you don't want to keep going?"

"I don't think the other one would be much better." Cade chuckled. "It's this or the back seat, and my vote's for the place that doesn't give us frostbite if we have to take a piss."

"This place will probably give us gangrene instead. Or a fungal infection."

Cade headed into the front office and came back out in less than five minutes. He grabbed the bug-out bag from her and tossed her the keys to room 3C. "Would you like me to carry you over the threshold, my lady?"

"No, but you're definitely slaying any dragons—er, cockroaches—that we may come across. As a matter of fact, we're sleeping in shifts. With the lights on."

Cade chuckled. "Where's that Steele sense of adventure?"

"In a five-star hotel."

The interior could have been worse, but not by much. Bright blue carpets contrasted with the pink floral bedspread on the single queen mattress, and the patterned wallpaper looked straight out of the seventies. But overall, it was cleaner than she expected, the smell of bleach hanging in the air.

Cade tossed their bag on the bed. "Shower first, or would you like to partake in our beef jerky feast? I'd run across the street to get something, but it's just a cow field. I saw a vending machine in the office, though."

"I think I'll shower and sleep. I'm too tired to chew, especially jerky."

"While you're cleaning up, I'm going to check in with Roman and Steele Ops, and then maybe hit up that vending machine. We may need a little more sustenance in the morning—and a cavalry." He walked to the door but paused. "And Grace?"

"Yeah?"

"Take Magdalena into the bathroom with you . . . just in case."

"Already planned on it." After Cade left her alone, Grace dug through their bag, pulling out a nondescript T-shirt and a pair of men's boxers. She set Maggie on the toilet lid and got undressed while the water warmed up, and then she scoured every inch of her body, averting her eyes from the questionable black smudges rimming the tiles.

Possibly-toxic mold be damned, her skin felt shiny and squeaky clean by the time she shut off the water and slipped into the spare clothes. She opened the bathroom door and crashed into Cade's hard body.

His hands gripped her hips, preventing her from falling on her ass. "Did you leave any hot water for me?"

She glanced back at the still steamy bathroom. "Maybe?"

Lust darkened his eyes and fueled her own, but with everything that had happened in the last twenty-four hours, acting on it wasn't a good idea—at least not until they finished that heart-to-heart talk where she basically admitted that he'd been—and always would be—the love of her life.

His gaze paused on her lips before dropping to where her wet hair dampened her soft gray T-shirt. "It's late. It's been one hell of a long day, and tomorrow's going to be a lot of the same. Probably more."

"And your point?"

"That as much as I want to finish yesterday's conversation and act on that look in your eye, we're going to have to take a rain check. We need to be well rested in order to deal with whatever comes at us next."

The telltale firming of Cade's cock brushed against her stomach spoke volumes for what it thought about that idea. "I'll probably be asleep the second my head hits the pillow."

She wasn't.

Listening to the shower from beneath the pink floral comforter, she tossed and turned, trying both sides before ending up flat on her stomach. No position helped. She eyed the floor, seriously contemplating giving it a try until she spotted the mystery stain two feet away. "Yeah, I'm not that brave."

She returned to her left side when Cade stepped out from the bathroom, a cloud of steam billowing out behind him. Water droplets clung to his bare chest, and his towel, halfheartedly wrapped around his waist, looked ready to drop at the faintest breeze.

He grabbed a pair of boxers from their bag and slid them on beneath the towel. Two seconds later, the mattress dipped as he climbed into the bed behind her. Heat radiated off him, warming her skin as he tucked an arm beneath her head.

His mouth, a hair's breadth away from her ear, brushed her skin. She shivered. "You were supposed to be asleep before I finished."

"I guess turning off my brain's more difficult than I thought." She rolled over to face him, putting their faces a mere inch apart. "Did you check in with the guys?"

"I did. They were back at Steele Ops and in the process of contacting the vice president when I called, and I'm pretty sure Director Vance is on her way over."

"And then they're taking Sarah to Dr. Preston? The cult specialist in Arizona?"

He hesitated. "Knox and Vance have it covered."

"You're dodging my question." She narrowed her eyes. "Why are you question-dodging?"

"Don't use your mind-reading power on me, Special Agent Steele. You may not like what you end up stumbling into."

"I don't need to like it. I just need to know." She pushed him onto his back and propped her chin on his chest. "Start talking, Wright."

He tucked a stray lock of hair off her face, his fingers brushing against her cheek. "Evidently Brandt wasn't thrilled about Arizona."

"Too bad. She *has* to go. It's important for her to—"

"Babe, I know. You're preaching to the choir here.

Neither Vance nor your cousins are pushovers. Let them do what they do. You're either here or there—you can't be both."

His words echoed in her head. He hadn't meant them as an accusation, but guilt still rushed over her. She sat up and tucked her knees to her chest. "You should be with Roman and the guys in DC. You should be with your father."

"I'm exactly where I need—and want—to be."

She opened her mouth to argue, but Cade palmed her cheek, silencing her with his thumb. "Knox already sent people to track Wilcox down, and everyone there is more than capable of questioning the old man about his connection to Rossbach."

"You know that's not why I think you should be there."

Cade's hand fell away as he sat up, turning to face the wall—and giving Grace his back. Every inch separating them felt like a mile, and she longed to close that distance. But just as he'd given her space during the last week, she needed to do the same.

It was painful and it sucked, but she waited for him to give the verbal invitation.

"I know what you're thinking, but you're wrong." Cade's back rippled with tension as he leaned his arms on his knees. "He is *not* my father."

"He may not be the one that you remembered when you were little, or the one you imagined every day since, but he *is* your dad."

"No, he's the man who abandoned his family," Cade snapped. "And for no good reason other than that he was a coward. He left my mother alone with two small children, one of whom was chronically ill, and he didn't look back—not even when our mom died. Anonymously throwing money into Zoey's healthcare doesn't negate the fact that he wasn't there."

"You're right. It doesn't." Grace understood the anger. Her entire life she'd lived knowing that her mother couldn't give two hoots about her, but from what interaction she'd had with the former general, Grace knew that wasn't the case with him.

Deep down, Cade knew it too.

"*Five* surgeries." Cade's voice was thick with emotion. "Zoey suffered through five open heart surgeries— six if you count the valve replacement this year. She's been subjected to countless more procedures and setbacks. He could've stepped forward at any point in time, and he didn't—even after his stuck-up snob of a family was long gone."

Grace's palm itched to touch him, but she stayed back, giving him time to work through his emotions. "You're right."

"I know I'm right. And you think I should what? Forgive him? Forget all the hell we went through until Gretchen came into our lives?"

"You shouldn't forget. You should learn from it." They *both* should.

Sometimes there was a delicate line between throwing your opinions in someone's face and gently steering them into looking at something from a different perspective. Nerves rolled through Grace's stomach as she contemplated on how to do the latter.

This was *the talk* before the *talk*. The one that would, hopefully, make any discussion about a future together that much easier.

Steadying her breathing, Grace slowly crawled across the bed and onto Cade's lap, her legs straddling his. His hands dropped to her hips, but he refused to meet her eyes.

She tilted his face up to hers, and the pain floating in his blue eyes cut her to the quick. It felt it as if it were her own—and it was. As much as she'd tried ignoring it, and denying it, she loved Cade Wright.

She was *in* love with him and had been ever since that day she first knocked on the Steeles' front door and he answered it with a snarky attitude. She'd loved him years later, even when he'd broken her heart.

And she loved him now.

She'd love him *always*.

And if there was any chance of a future together, they couldn't hide behind the past and pretend that it hadn't happened. Not now. Not ever.

"What your father did was wrong," Grace admitted. "He made a bad decision, made it out of fear, and he wasn't the only one to suffer the consequences. His actions affected you, and Zoey, and Gretchen, and everyone who loves you. But it's not so different from what happened between us nine years ago."

Cade stiffened, but Grace preempted his defensiveness, stroking her thumbs over his cheeks. "Why did you re-up with the Army? After we already had our entire lives laid out in front of us... you showed up to my graduation having already sold your life away for another four years."

"That's completely different."

"The situation's different, but I'm not so sure the motive is." Grace fought against welling tears, unsure if she was ready to hear the truth, but knowing she needed to. They'd already spent way too much time and energy avoiding what was right in front of them. *"Why?"*

Cade wiped away her tears, but as soon as he did, more fell.

His Adam's apple bobbed. "I didn't know who I'd be without the Army. I didn't know if I could be someone who deserved you in his life. I didn't know if I could be the type of man who you'd proudly calls yours. I made the decision I did because I loved you too damn much to risk fucking up your life."

"Both your decision and Hogan's were made from the same place—fear, and love." Grace bit her lip and prayed he'd understand. "Don't they *both* deserve forgiveness and a second chance?"

Grace's chest ached as she waited for his response. More than anything, she wanted him to say yes. Anger for her mother had once ruled her life and her every decision, and she didn't want that for him—regardless if he felt the same about their future together or not.

"You're right," Cade murmured.

Grace's heart beat so hard she wasn't sure if she'd heard him correctly. "I am?"

"You sound surprised." His mouth twitched into a small, slow smile. "The truth is, I'd started seeing a few blazingly obvious similarities between me and the old man a while ago, but I ignored it. And him. I should've known that you'd catch on, though."

"Yeah, you should've." Grace brushed her mouth over his, initially meaning the kiss to be sweet and quick. But on contact, Cade's hand slid into her hair. She angled her head and deepened the embrace, gently nibbling on his bottom lip and making him groan.

Nothing tasted sweeter than his lips. Nothing made her body come alive more than his touch. Nothing made her feel more complete than *him*.

"You still need that rest we talked about," Cade murmured against her mouth.

Temporarily abandoning her hair, he slid his hands beneath her oversized T-shirt, his knuckles running up her torso. Every additional inch of skin he exposed elicited a new wave of goose bumps.

"Uh huh." Grace pulled the offending shirt off and tossed it aside, leaving herself sitting astride his lap, naked from the waist up. "But I also need you."

They'd made love more times than she could count, but this time it was as if she were experiencing it for the first time.

He cradled her breasts in his palms, slowly bringing his mouth to each hardened tip. Grace tossed her head back on a moan, fingers clutching his shoulders for support. She rolled her hips, her panty-covered mound brushing against his hardening cock. It twitched at the contact and caused her to rub her body harder.

Cade supported her ass and with a growl, spun them around and pushed her back onto the mattress. "Fuck, baby. I need you now. I need you *always*."

A quick shedding of the rest of their clothes, and Cade had her—*all of her*. While feasting on her lips, he slid effortlessly into the hot depths of her body. One slow, deep thrust turned into a second. They moved in sync, Grace unable to tell where one ended and the other began as they met thrust for thrust.

They kissed. They touched. They shouted their way through a massive—shared—release. And as they cried each other's names, Grace knew this was more than a second chance.

This was more than overcoming their past.

This was their homecoming.

CHAPTER
TWENTY-FIVE

Grace flexed her stiff back and immediately felt the hard erection nestled against her backside. Behind her, Cade murmured something unintelligible, pulling her closer, and she eagerly went, melting against him. She smiled to herself as memories from the night seeped back into her consciousness.

"I think she's having a sex dream, because that grin screams naked naughtiness," a deep, familiar voice proclaimed from way too damn close.

Grace's eyes snapped open.

Registering a looming shadow hovering over her head, she whipped out a defensive fist, her knuckles catching on the nearest object.

"Fucking A! Oh, shit." That same familiar voice wheezed as if having difficulty breathing. "I can taste my testicles. That's probably a bad thing, right?"

"I told you that you should've kept your distance. Maybe next time you'll listen to me," a feminine voice chided.

Grace's brain slowly defuzzed, taking in the sight of Liam, hunched over, deep-breathing as if he were teaching a Lamaze class. "What the hell are you doing?"

"Watching any chance of little Liam juniors go down the drain. *Fuck*."

Jaz leaned against the wall and rolled her eyes. "I wanted to call you on the sat phone when we parked—like a normal person. Brainiac here wanted to try his hand at old-school lock-picking."

"And it was disappointingly easy. All I needed was a credit card." Still grimacing, Liam reached for the nearest chair. "I need to sit down."

"What the hell's going on?" Cade asked, sitting up.

Thank God they'd gotten dressed at some point during the night, because as much as Grace loved her cousins, she didn't love them *that* much.

"You called for the cavalry, and the cavalry came," Liam explained with a tight smile.

Cade looked from Liam to Grace and back to Liam. He chuckled. "She nailed you in the 'nads, didn't she?"

"Fuck, yeah." Liam adjusted himself, wincing.

"Be thankful I made her tuck her gun in the drawer instead of under her pillow."

"Don't even joke, man."

"Who's joking?"

To demonstrate Cade's point, Grace slipped Magdalena from the drawer and watched Liam's face pale.

Chuckling, Jaz tossed Grace another pack, and she caught it midair. "Clothes that will actually fit you, unlike the gorilla-wear I'm sure Roman tucked in that bug-out bag."

"You're a life-saver, Jaz Curva."

"And a sweetheart. Why does everybody always forget how sweet I am?" the former Marine sniper teased dryly.

"Maybe because you're sweet like those Extreme

Sour Heads." Liam dodged her punch, laughing harder as he headed for the door. "The bus pulls away in ten, kids, so I suggest you put a little hustle in it."

Grace didn't need ten minutes. Eager to get out to Rhett's cabin, she was dressed and sliding into the passenger seat of a thankfully rust-free sedan in five.

Jaz navigated the West Virginia roads like she did life—full of flair and without apology. Grace white-knuckled the corners and closed her eyes when the Marine flew by stragglers she claimed drove slowly enough for a turtle to pass.

"Bet you're sorry you didn't let me drive, aren't you?" In the rear seat, Liam leaned back as if he hadn't a care in the world.

Grace recited more than a few prayers on their travel into Maryland, but they got to Rhett's mountain in record time. As Cade gave Liam and Jaz the run-down on what to expect, Grace hopped out from the car, her eyes dropping to the snow-packed mud fifteen yards away.

Her stomach plummeted and twisted into giant-sized knot. "Someone was here."

Cade followed her line of sight and pointed to a second set of tire marks. "Two sets of someones."

He and Liam crouched by the tracks, faces grim.

"These are fresh." Liam dipped his finger into what looked like a dark spot of oil. "And I'm talking within the last two days. Anything older would've been covered up by the snow this area got three days ago."

"We have to get up there." Grace spun, ready to charge up the mountain.

Cade snagged her elbow. "Whoa. Pause. Wait a sec."

"Rhett may not have a second. I swear to God, Cade, if you tell me to stay with the car I'm going to—" Her threat died when he held out Magdalena.

He waited for her to take it, eyebrows raised expectantly. "I didn't think you'd want to go anywhere without your trusty friend, and you left her in the bag."

Grace took the Mag and tucking it at the small of her back, smiled apologetically. "Sorry. Guess I got hit with a little tunnel vision."

"Happens to the best of us." He smirked.

Liam grimaced. "Seeing you guys cozy in bed together was traumatic enough. Can you stop being so nice to each other? It's freakin' me out a little bit."

Grace and Cade both shot him dubious looks.

"What? It's true. Ask anyone. Ask Jaz." He turned to the sniper, who was pulling out a vicious looking rifle from the trunk of the car.

At the mention of her name, Jaz glanced up. "Personally, I like it. I may not act it, but I'm a big fan of happily-ever-afters. I don't think there's a rom-com movie that I haven't seen."

"I'm so glad that fifty percent of you approve," Grace interjected, "but can we get the hell up that mountain now? It's bad enough we had to wait to morning."

Her words seemed to snap everyone into gear. They rebundled into heavier winter outerwear and loaded up on whatever weapons they'd be able to hike with easily. Knowing the mountain and Rhett's security like the back of her hand, Grace took the lead.

Unlike the tire tracks, half the boot prints had already been filled by blowing snow, but the trail was definitely there. They hadn't been the only ones to come up this way. The real question was how much of a head start did the others have?

Less than a mile from the cabin, their surroundings transformed from luscious fauna to charred earth. Trees not blown to bits stood like petrified statues, and the punji pit on Grace's left had been disturbed from the explosion.

Liam whistled. "Damn. I thought my neighbor hated visitors—and she threatened to electrify her welcome mat the next time I knocked on her door."

"Rhett definitely likes his personal space." Despite Grace knowing what surprises her friend had for unexpected guests, she was still left a little speechless—and worried. Especially when she located the trail again outside the blast radius. "Whoever came up here really wanted to get to Rhett's cabin, and they weren't letting a little fireworks stop them."

Cade's hand landed on her shoulder.

Once upon a time she would have immediately shrugged it off, but she covered it with her own hand and squeezed, thankful for the silent support. "He knows how to take care of himself."

"He sure as hell does. He may have been way out here alone, but he was no sitting duck," Cade reminded her.

Grace mentally reminded herself of that fact as they hiked the rest of the way, but what little comfort the words gave her died the second the cabin came into

view. The left half of the porch and the front of the
house had suffered the same fate as the trees.

A faint stench of smoke and ash still hung in the
air, but no secondary fires or glowing embers meant
they'd missed the action by at least twelve hours. Probably more.

"Careful," Cade warned as they approached the
stairs. "There could be additional devices that could
still go off."

"He only put one on the steps, and as you can tell,
it was triggered already. The rest of the cabin's clear."
Not waiting for him, Grace held her breath and slowly
tightrope-walked what was left of the steps' framework.
The wood creaked ominously, flakes of timber breaking
off beneath her weight. Once at the top, she took a
breath and turned back to Cade. "Your turn."

"Yeah, I'm not feeling that lucky today." He gripped
the edge of the undisturbed side of the porch and
tugged his oversized body up and over. "Jaz, Liam. You
guys go around back. See if you catch sight of anything."

"On it." Jaz nodded and turned the corner.

Grace was torn with wanting to see Rhett and afraid
at what she'd find if she did. It was hard to tell if the
busted furniture and destroyed computers were because
of the explosion or because of a fight—until she found
the large pool of dried blood in the kitchen.

Blood—*but no body*.

Liam's whistle pierced the air. "You guys may want
to come out and see this!"

Grace and Cade stepped out of the undisturbed rear

of the cabin and looked to where Liam pointed into the snow. "There's an old blood trail leading from the cabin to right here and then it stops, which means that whoever was bleeding either miraculously healed themselves, or—"

"He was carried out," Grace finished.

Her cousin gave her an apologetic look. "You sure your EG friends didn't bring a souvenir back to Sanctuary? You said they were having a celebration when they got back..."

Grace's gut instinct told her that wasn't the case. "No, Sarah admitted that their assignment didn't go as planned—on two separate occasions. At the time, she had no reason to lie."

For FBI field investigators, lack of a body was good news, and while she was more than thankful they didn't find Rhett among the rubble, she couldn't help but wonder where the hell he was...and what he was preparing to do.

* * *

Grace had been hired to do a job—work with her cousins to return Sarah Brandt to her father—and technically, she'd completed her assignment. Mission accomplished. Father and daughter reunited. As soon as Director Vance signed off on her report, nothing stopped her from jumping on the first available flight back to New York.

Nothing except Cade Wright—and her about-to-explode head.

In the bottom dregs of Steele Ops's operation center, a modern-day, testosterone-fueled showdown was in full swing. Knox and Roman squared off with the VP's security detail, and then Brandt himself glared accusingly at Director Vance. Growled warnings and ultimatums were hurled back and forth from both sides, but not a single person heeded them.

Grace's body ached from physical exertion of hiking up and down two damn mountains. Add in her worry over Rhett and all the shouting around her, and she was *done*.

Grace slipped her fingers into the corner of her mouth and whistled—*loud*. Everyone came to an instant stop and looked her way. *Finally*. "Oh, good, I have everyone's attention."

Roman yanked on his ear, wincing. "Shit, that was loud."

"Then maybe you shouldn't have taught me how to do it."

She glanced around the room, not sparing anyone her death-ray glare, including a red-faced Vice President Brandt. Jake Corelli opened his mouth to say something—again—and she took a move from Aunt Cindy's playbook and simply lifted one dark eyebrow.

The Secret Service agent's mouth snapped closed. *Cute and smart.*

"It seems to me that there's a whole lot of talking—and shouting—happening from both sides of the ring here, and the only one who has any right to talk right now is *me*."

"Now wait a minute—" Pierce Brandt interjected.

"Sht." Grace pinched her fingers by her mouth, another Aunt Cindy favorite.

If Director Vance hadn't been within Grace's peripheral vision, she would have missed her boss's slight twitch of the lips. Thank God. Because she'd just mimed for the vice president of the United States to zip his damn lips.

She'd spent the last hour detailing their findings about Rossbach's hit list. She'd bullet-pointed the many ways New Dawn and its members posed a threat to the public. Then she'd gone into explicit detail on how Rossbach and her mother rewired people's brains to not only accept their views on revenge and lethal retribution, but to condone their actions, no matter how violent they may be.

It still wasn't sinking into Pierce Brandt's head.

Grace barely contained her usual go-to method of knocking sense into her cousins—a kick to the solar plexus—and remained a respectable three feet distance from the vice president. "Sir, I'm not sure how to rephrase this so you understand the severity of the situation—and your daughter's mind-set."

"I understand perfectly well, Special Agent Steele. I called in a favor to have you handle my daughter's extraction, and you performed your job. Thank you."

"You called me in because I know how cults like the OND work. Throwing Sarah back into your world as if she'd never been part of them is dangerous."

Brandt got to his feet as if prepping to leave. "In danger with the world's finest security guarding her? That's absolutely ridiculous. She'll be the safest she could possibly be. New Dawn will never get to her again."

"They already have, sir." Grace glanced at the director and took her boss's slight nod as a green light to take off the kid gloves. "I didn't say she was *in* danger. I meant she *is* dangerous. To herself. *Especially* to you. Sarah's physical body may look the same to you, sir, but I assure you, her mind isn't."

Brandt's mouth tightened, his expression darkening. "That's absurd."

"No. It's not. What's absurd is you thinking that she's suddenly going to jump back into her old life after months of being brainwashed by those people!"

A pin could have dropped in the room and sounded like an explosion.

All eyes froze on her. Cade shifted at her back, and even though he didn't touch her or say a word, his strength fueled her own. Something had changed back in that motel, and suddenly she didn't want to withhold anything—not her thoughts or her feelings, and definitely not her words.

"I know, sir, because it was expected of me." Grace sent an apologetic look to her cousins. They all watched her with various degrees of guilt. "It's not your fault. None of you." Her gaze drifted toward Cade, looping him into the group. "This is something I should've come clean about seventeen years ago, but for Sarah Brandt's future, I'm doing it now."

Cade wrapped his fingers around hers and squeezed. "Better late than never, babe."

Pierce Brandt sighed impatiently. "While this is all

very touching, and I do appreciate the sentiment behind it, I don't see what this has to do with Sarah."

"I wasn't miraculously saved the night I Defected from New Dawn. Or when I walked into the Steeles' house. As great as my family is, their love didn't suddenly cure me. The first psychiatrist didn't *get* me. Neither did the second. No one understands unless you've lived in the life, and I'm telling you, Mr. Brandt, what Sarah needs more than anything right now, including you, is Dr. Preston. Her expertise with cult victims is the only chance you have of getting your daughter back."

"My daughter wouldn't hurt a fly." Brandt lifted his chin defiantly, but his voice no longer sounded so sure.

"*Your* daughter wouldn't. Rossbach's loyal follower would. There isn't anything she wouldn't do in the name of New Dawn."

Grace prayed he listened, but she saw deep in his eyes, he couldn't. Or wouldn't. It was the reason she'd stayed in the Order as long as she had. No one wanted to think bad of someone they cared about. And despite not wanting to admit it, she had cared about her mother and the people of Sanctuary in some way. They'd given her the only life she'd known up until returning to DC.

The vice president turned to Director Vance. "Are you charging my daughter with anything, Director?"

Vance's shoulders lifted with her silent sigh. "No, sir. Not at this time."

"Then I'm taking Sarah, and I'm leaving."

"Sir, I strongly encourage you to listen to Special Agent Steele. If she believes that your daughter would benefit from time in a facility designated for this specific issue, then I think you should consider it."

Brandt spun around, red-faced and livid. "She's not some lab rat! She's *my daughter*—who my wife and I have spent a lifetime raising and supporting! I will not have anyone talking about her as if she's damaged goods."

Grace cleared her throat. "The most supportive thing you could do right now for Sarah is take her to Arizona."

"Your job is officially done, Special Agent Steele. Thank you, but goodbye." The vice president stalked out, his security detail with him.

"Corelli."

Jake Corelli lagged behind. He sighed as if knowing what she was about to say. "I'll try to get through to him, Grace, but he's pretty set in his ways. You know I can't make any promises."

"In the meantime, you *need* to keep an eye on her. Right now Sarah has zero emotional attachment to the vice president. There's no telling what she'd do to get back to the people she considers her real family."

"Yeah, I'm getting that. I'll up her detail. She won't be able to take a piss without us knowing."

Grace waited until Corelli left before turning to Vance. "Please tell me that we're not letting this go, ma'am."

"I don't want to. You know I don't, but without concrete—or at least highly motivational—evidence that what you saw is indeed a hit list, I'm not so sure I can authorize—"

Liam strutted into the room looking like the Cheshire cat.

"It's highly motivational evidence that you want, Director? How would this suffice?" He tossed a file onto the table in front of them, and everyone automatically drifted closer. "Let me give you the highlight reel. Our three marked men all served in different branches of the military—and all three have been found dead within the last four months."

Grace picked up one of the backgrounds on the victims. "Sometimes I hate being right."

"And that's not all. According to their records, they've never served together. Never been stationed even remotely near the same bases. Hell, the same countries. The only thing they do have in common is that their service records mysteriously end about twenty years ago."

That piqued Director Vance's interest. "What do you mean 'end'? They were discharged?"

"I mean the paper trail stops cold. No duty stations. No promotions. No demotions. And no official discharge from the service. That means these guys had either worked as a magician's disappearing sidekicks, or—"

"They worked black ops," Roman spoke up. "And depending on where they worked and who they worked alongside, you can't—and won't—find a paper trail because there isn't one. They don't keep them for a reason."

Vance pulled her attention away from the files. "Okay. I agree, this definitely sounds ominous, but that doesn't mean that these men were—"

Liam cut off the director. "Actually, if you hold that thought for one more minute." He dropped in front of his computer, and all the information spread out on the table now appeared on the oversize wall monitor. "Target one: Christian Gains. Former Navy SEAL. Died in an apartment building fire three months ago."

"Unfortunate, but not exactly nefarious."

Grace immediately saw what Liam did. "The blueprints we found in that basement were for that building complex. I recognize the builder's logo."

"Bingo," Liam verified. "And the fire was recently ruled an arson. The investigative report also confirms that both fire exits on Gains's floor appeared to have been sealed shut. There was no way he was getting out of there unless he went free-diving from his bedroom window."

Cade cursed. "Gains couldn't have been the only person on that entire floor."

"He wasn't. The same fire claimed the life of an elderly couple and a twenty-two-year-old bartender."

A wave of nausea rolled through Grace. "Rossbach doesn't care who gets hurts in the process of him finding his New Dawn, and his Elite Guards don't either. They only care about their final target. What about the other two men?"

"Matt Striker. Hit and run. And the most recent, Doug Unger, was shot in a supposed robbery gone wrong. All different. All fishy. And all way too damn convenient if you ask me."

Director Vance studied Liam's findings with a critical eye and finally nodded. "What does Hogan Wilcox have to do with these men? And who is the mystery man in the sixth picture?"

"That we're still trying to figure out." Liam slid an apologetic look toward Cade. "We got half a forest ranger division tracking Wilcox down, but it turns out ice fishing doesn't really happen in well-populated areas. At least not the General's favorite spots. Once we locate him, we're hoping he'll shed some light on this."

"And if we're right about this, the General's life is at risk too." The director sighed and pinned Grace with a hard stare. "I want you to take a team back up that mountain. Bring Rossbach in for questioning, and hopefully by the time that happens, we'll have more answers."

"You want me to take lead of a team?" Grace tried—and failed—to hide her surprise. "I've never done that before, ma'am. I—"

"Just managed to pull off a great undercover assignment, kidnap the daughter of a political figure, and get us intelligence that could help out wipe out a national threat. Something tells me that you'll be just fine running your own team."

"That wasn't all on me, ma'am. All of that happened because of my cousins . . . and Cade."

"The fact that you don't want to take credit for it, Special Agent Steele, tells me that my original assessment is spot-on—and that we need to have a talk about your future at the Bureau."

If it weren't for the director's pleased smile, Grace would have thought she'd bought herself another stint on her boss's shit list. She accepted the compliment as the high praise it was meant to be. "If I'm taking a team up, can I request to have Steele Ops as a backup?"

"You sure as hell can. I'll have an operations team assembled within the hour." Director Vance drilled Grace with her no-nonsense, determined stare. "I don't have to tell you how much I want Rossbach brought in, do I?"

"No, ma'am, you don't."

No one wanted a pair of handcuffs on Rossbach more than Grace—and she'd bring a few extras in case her mother felt left out.

CHAPTER
TWENTY-SIX

Grace soaked in the loud family chaos surrounding her and tried living in the moment instead of replaying the events of that morning's operation. Sanctuary had been deserted when she'd gotten there with the FBI–Steele Ops teams, and judging by the abandoned food left sitting out and the fire roaring in the ovens, it had been a quick evacuation.

They'd known they were coming.

Strike that.

Her mother had known *she* was coming—and she'd even left behind a personally addressed note in the cabin that she and Rossbach had shared.

YOU are my Obstacle, Grace Ann. You shattered my New Dawn first with your birth, and then again with your Return. I cannot allow that to happen again.

Beautifully maternal and such a crock of poo. Still, the sliver of paper practically burned a hole in her jeans pocket, but not because she believed the words.

That quaint little love note penned by her mother put her life into perspective and made Grace realize— more than she ever had before—that family really was who you wanted them to be. And she couldn't have picked a better group of people.

Zoey and Cade battled it out over a game of foosball, their shouts and back-and-forth smack talk fueling the cheers and jeers of their audience. Liam walked the room and collected what looked to be monetary bets, and Tank and Jaz looked way too eager to spill each other's blood during the next round.

After the disappointing raid on Sanctuary, it seemed only natural for them all to end up back at Aunt Cindy's place. It was comfortable. It was familiar. It was home. Cade and Zoey's mom had hustled over, steaming trays of meatballs in hand, and the food and drink hadn't stopped since.

This was the family she'd always been meant to have. Loud. Supportive. And above all else...accepting.

"Your plate looks suspiciously empty there, sweetheart." Aunt Cindy set a serving dish full of cannoli onto the table. "Grab some of these babies, and I'll block the hungry horde with my Mom glare."

Grace laughed, pulling her aunt into a hug. "Let the hungry horde have their dessert, Aunt C. I'll bust out of these pants if I eat one more bite."

"As if. You've lost way too much weight since the last time I saw you."

"You mean the other week?"

Aunt Cindy frowned, hitting her with that Mom glare she'd mentioned. "You know damn well that's not what I was referring to. I get that you're not Betty Crocker, but they do have takeout in New York City from what I hear."

"They have takeout everything in New York—and delivery—at all hours of the day and night. It's amazing."

"Then you have absolutely no excuse not to do a better job at taking care of yourself."

"You're right, I don't." Her agreement took the bluster out of her aunt's sails.

Cindy scanned the room and shook her head at her sons' antics.

Grace hadn't known what to expect of her father's family when Rhett dropped her off on their doorstep seventeen years ago. They'd been loud and brash, privacy as foreign a concept as was the common decency of leaving the room to drop a gas bomb.

And she thanked God for every second of it.

Slipping in behind Aunt Cindy, she wrapped her arms around the woman who might not have given birth to her in the biological sense, but who birthed her all the same—the *real* her. "I love you. I know I don't tell you that enough, but I'm incredibly lucky to have you in my life, Aunt Cindy."

"Oh, honey." She turned and trapped Grace's face between her palms before kissing her forehead. "I love you too. And you don't need to say it, sweetheart. I know."

"Yes, I do. And I'm sorry it's been so long since I've been home."

"You're home now." Cindy wiped away the tears she hadn't even realized she'd shed. "And you know me, I don't like to pry in my children's lives, but..."

Grace laughed: One, because she loved hearing her aunt lump her in with her cousins. And two, because it was what the older woman always said seconds before she pried. "And what kind of non-prying questions are floating around in your head right now?"

Cindy's gaze slid to the foosball game where Cade graciously admitted defeat to his sister. "A woman can't help but notice that things have seemed a little *warmer* between you two since you walked through the door."

"Maybe that's because you keep the thermostat set on eighty-four," Grace teased.

"Oh, hush now."

Grace's gaze strayed to where Cade armed Tank with a few strategic pointers on the fine art of Steele basement foosball. "You're right. Things are definitely warmer. I just don't think I should be talking about it with you before I've had a chance to talk about it with him. But you can get that look out of your eye right now."

"What look? I don't have a look."

Grace smirked at her aunt's faux innocence. "You most definitely do, and it says that you're already planning to buy out an entire department store of all their baby clothes. Trust me when I say that babies are *not* happening any time in the near future unless they come from Knox and Zoey. I've killed three houseplants in the last six months. I can't be trusted with another living person. At least not for a good long while."

"Maybe it's me, but it's probably not good form for an FBI agent to admit to committing murder." Cade's voice swiveled both Grace's and Cindy's heads.

He reached past them and grabbed a cannoli, kissing Cindy on the side of the head. "Please tell me you have more of these."

"There's some upstairs already on a plate with your name on it."

"And did you hide it in our new spot? Because I'm pretty sure Liam sniffed out the old one."

Grace's lips twitched as she soaked in the play between the two of them. "You conned my impressionable aunt into cannoli smuggling?"

"I did nothing of the sort. It was her idea. I just went along with it."

Aunt Cindy flashed Grace a wink and left them alone—at least as alone as they could be.

"You looked awfully serious over here a minute ago." Cade popped another cannoli into his mouth and watched her carefully.

"You were busy getting your ass kicked by your baby sister. How did you even notice?"

"You were watching me?" Cade's mouth kicked up into a naughty grin as he stalked closer.

"How could I not? You were bent over the table. The view was too good not to ogle." Grace held her spot until the toes of his boots bumped against hers.

As his hands settled on her hips, her body automatically swayed toward his. Surrounded by their families wasn't exactly the time to have the long overdue heart-to-heart, but she couldn't help needing to feel him.

Her gaze dropped to his mouth. Just thinking about kissing him made her lips tingle.

"Careful, sweetheart. You keep looking at me like that, and everyone in this room's going to get a show," Cade growled, his chest rumbling.

"I'm not so sure I'd be against that," Grace admitted cautiously.

"*Really?*"

She chuckled nervously and ignored her increasingly sweaty palms. "I wasn't talking about giving them a floor show. I meant I wouldn't be against them knowing...about *us*."

Grace's heart pounded in her ears. She wouldn't be able to hear Cade's response even if he'd spoken. The way he looked at her, his blue eyes lasered in on hers, stirred something deep inside her.

Hope.

Need.

And an overwhelming desire to start her life over—*with him*.

"You want there to be an *us*?" Cade brushed his knuckles over her cheek, the soft touch pulling a sigh from her throat. "An *us* in the future?"

"More than anything." She opened her mouth to admit for the first time in nine years that she loved him—that she was *in* love with him and she'd never stopped. Not even for a second. But the *Who's the Boss* theme song rang from her back pocket.

Across the room, Liam and Knox laughed. "Think your ass is ringing, Grace."

She knew it was, and she'd never been so tempted to ignore Director Vance's phone call. "I have to..."

"Get it. I'm not going anywhere."

She really hoped he meant that.

"Director," Grace answered the phone. "We haven't found Wilcox yet, but we're close to—"

"You're done out there in DC," Vance replied succinctly. "I'm officially opening an investigation to look into Teague Rossbach, Rebecca Steele, and all of the

OND, and I want you on it. Your flight back to New York's scheduled for two p.m. tomorrow."

"*Tomorrow*? Can't I work from here?"

"If I wanted you to work from there I would've made that a viable option, Special Agent Steele. No, the people I want on the team are based there and that's where you'll be. I'll meet you in the New York satellite office by late afternoon. *Tomorrow*. Or you can forget about that promotional opportunity I was going to speak with you about."

"A promotion?"

The director hung up, not giving Grace a chance to react much less counteroffer or ask questions. By the time she slipped her phone back into her pants, whatever breaking revelations she and Cade had been about to divulge disappeared.

"I…" She forced herself to meet his gaze. "I have to go back to New York."

"Tomorrow. I heard." His face was devoid of any emotion…except the slight flicker of anticipation—and something else. "And it sounds like a congratulations are in order too."

A promotion.

A few months ago that news would have come with music and joy-dancing in her underwear. Instead, a hefty elephant sat on her chest…and he brought along his entire herd.

* * *

What goes around comes around.

That's all Cade could think about as he waited for

Grace to say something—anything. It almost felt like time had rewound nine years and swapped their bodies for good measure. Nine years ago, he'd been the one to choose career over them, and now she had the opportunity to do the same thing.

And he could see in her eyes that that was exactly what she was about to do.

Cade stepped back, and when Grace reached for his hand, he pulled away. It was a dick move, but he couldn't touch her and then watch her walk away.

Her hopeful expression fell. "My job's in New York, Cade. I *have* to go."

"You're right. It is. And not to mention that you've got a shiny new promotion lighting your way back."

"That's it?" She paused a beat. "That's all you're going to say about it?"

Her dark eyes filled with something akin to pain, but all Cade could feel was the ice pick stabbing through his chest. *Fuck, it hurt to breathe.* "What do you want me to say? That I don't want you to leave DC?"

"That would be kind of great, yeah." Grace's raised voice earned them more than a few glances from their families. The room got noticeably quiet, but it was too late for discretion. "Or maybe that we can figure something out... put our frequent flier miles back to good use."

"We did the long-distance thing before, and look how it turned out. I want *more* for us, but I'll be damned if I'm going to order you not to go back to New York. The only thing that'll do is bring us a whole lot of misery, and I'm sorry, but I won't be responsible for hurting us yet again."

He'd once taken Grace's decision away from her and tossed all of their plans out the window because he'd been a coward. No matter how badly he wanted her to stay in DC, he refused to make her sacrifice her future again.

He refused to do that to the woman he loved—and he did love her. With every ounce of his soul and every inch of his being. Wherever she lived and whatever job she had wouldn't change the fact that she was *it* for him. She was *it* seventeen years ago, and she'd be *it* for seventeen years in the future.

Hell, she'd be *it* forever.

Moisture welled in Grace's big brown eyes, and he almost caved. He almost dropped to his knees and wrapped his arms around her waist, begging her to stay. But he'd sworn to himself that he'd never again be that selfish asshole who hurt her.

Silent tension filled every corner of the Steeles' basement, and from somewhere across the room, a clock ticked. Fitting since it felt like Cade waited for one of Rhett Winston's bombs to go off.

Roman cleared his throat, the first one to speak. "Maybe you guys should take a walk or something…"

"That sounds like a good idea," Zoey agreed, her voice a lot more hopeful than Cade felt. "Fresh air cures everything, right?"

"It won't cure this, Zo." Cade couldn't tear his eyes off Grace. "And besides, Grace probably has a lot of packing to do."

A tear streaked down Grace's cheek, and he stuffed his hands in his pocket to avoid brushing it away. A second tear fell, and then a third. Every fallen drop ripped Cade's insides apart more than the next, because Grace Steele didn't cry.

She didn't show weakness.

And right now, she was baring her hurt for both their families—and him—to see.

"You're right. I need to get back to Zoey's place and get my stuff together." She gave him her back and hugged her aunt first. "I love you. I'll swing by in the morning before I head off to the airport, okay?"

Cindy squeezed her tight and shot a motherly glare at Cade from over Grace's shoulder. "Stay for a little longer. We just started putting out all the dessert and I'm sure—"

"I'm super tired, Aunt C. I've hiked up and down so many mountains in the last few days that my body's about to stage a shutdown." Grace slowly made her way around the room to each of her cousins and Zoey.

It was the right thing to do, Cade told himself on a mental loop.

But as Grace disappeared upstairs with a final wave, the eight glares blasted his way—one of which was from his own mother—told him that he was the only one who thought so.

And he wasn't so sure he believed it completely himself.

CHAPTER TWENTY-SEVEN

Within an hour and a half of leaving Aunt Cindy's, Grace had slipped into Cade's townhouse to snatch the things she'd left behind and not only got to Zoey's blessedly empty apartment, but corralled everything into a single suitcase.

Super Packer, thy name is Grace Steele.

If she could put her life in order as well as she did her underwear and cable-knit sweaters she'd be all set.

Grace took pride in her ability to read people, and her knack for anticipating a person's actions before they even decided on any made her the most successful profiler at the Bureau.

Yet somehow she hadn't been able to predict Cade. The most important—and potentially life-changing—read of her life, and she botched it. Not a little. Not a moderate amount. She screwed it up in a mega, they-never-should've-remade-*Dirty-Dancing* kind of way.

"Now what, Grace?" She stared at the closed suitcase on Zoey's bed as a rush of emotions hurtled through her like a freight train.

Her knees buckled, and she sat before they gave way. The pain she'd experienced nine years ago had nothing on the throbbing ache in her chest now. It hurt to breathe, and it worsened each time she mentally replayed the scene in her aunt's basement.

She'd wanted him to ask her to stay in DC more than she'd wanted anything in her life, even to be rid of New Dawn. And he'd wanted to. She'd seen it in his eyes, but he stopped himself because he didn't want to take her choices away from her.

The stupid, self-sacrificing jerk.

It was as if they were doomed to be repelling magnets, always moving in the opposite direction. Damn it, she was done with pushing away from the things she wanted most. And she wanted her job, her family, DC, *and* Cade.

And she wouldn't accept anything less.

Grace wiped away a fresh set of tears, summoned every ounce of her Steele stubbornness, and got to her feet. Cade didn't want to take her decisions away from her?

Then he wasn't about to start with this one.

She grabbed her cell and flipped through her contacts for the one person who could give her everything she'd ever wanted. Five minutes and a formally drafted email later, and Grace was sliding into her shoes with renewed determination.

Her cell rang. Zoey's name flashed on the caller ID, but Grace let it go to voice mail, choosing to stay focused on Operation Cade. The phone rang again just as the security system beeped, signaling it had been disarmed.

She chuckled at her best friend's eagerness. "Sorry for not picking up, but I don't need a pep talk, Zo. I'm not taking no for an answer. Your brother's never going to know what hit him."

Grace stepped out of the bedroom and caught a fist to the face. Pain exploded through her jaw, and her body stumbled sideways.

"Told you that I'd see you again." Simon Reynolds fisted his hand in her hair and slammed her face first into the wall.

Colorful stars burst across Grace's vision as she fought to remain upright. She drew her elbow back in a sharp jab and followed it up with a backfist. The sound of crunching bone reached her ears moments before Simon cursed, stumbling back.

"Good to see you too, Simon." She grabbed the back of his shirt and this time rammed *him* headfirst into the wall. The plaster dented, leaving behind an asshole-sized divot. She reached toward her side holster before realizing it was empty.

"Looking for this?" Six feet away, Todd Winston inspected Magdalena with interest, but it was the Colt pointed in her direction that held the majority of her attention. "Gotta hand it to you, Grace. You have lousy taste in men, but great taste in guns."

She blinked away the trail of blood that ran into her eye. "Why don't you give it back to me and I'll show you how to use it."

Todd laughed. "I always did like your sense of humor. Remind me again why we stopped being friends? Oh, that's right. Because you're a lying, back-stabbing *Defector*."

"Better to be a Defector than whatever the hell it is

that you are. What, Todd? Did you bring Simon along for the ride so that he could do your dirty work?"

"Simon came along for the ride so he could have a piece of you himself."

Reynolds's beefy arm banded across her throat from behind. Grace gasped, digging her nails into his flesh as he dragged her toward the kitchen and threw her into one of the chairs. "Go ahead and move, bitch. Give me a reason to end this right here and now."

"Go to fucking hell."

Simon grinned. "Already been there, baby. It's pretty nice if you ask me."

Todd growled impatiently. "Tie her the fuck up already."

Grace took turns glaring at them each but paid enough attention on Simon's rope tying to know that it wouldn't be easy to escape. The binds bit into her skin until her fingers tingled, but she wouldn't wince and give him any satisfaction.

Todd chuckled. "Quiet for the first time for as long as I've known you. I'm not gonna lie. It's eerie."

"You want me to talk?" It wouldn't take much to get him to spill everything he knew about Rossbach and the Order...and the men pictured on the basement wall. "Let's start with how you're either incredibly brave or ridiculously stupid to show your faces in DC. People are looking for you." She slid a warning glance to Simon. "*All* of you. If you haven't been spotted yet, it's just a matter of time."

"We're good at disappearing...as you and your fellow FBI agents are aware." Todd waited a beat before smirking. "Yeah, that's right, *Special Agent Steele*. We saw you and your buddies ransack our Sanctuary...as if you weren't in enough trouble with the Order after stealing one of our most beloved flock members."

Grace feigned cool indifference. "Trouble? I got a promotion out of it."

Simon growled seconds before his hand whipped across her face. The lip that had been split a few minutes ago opened wider, blood dripping off her chin.

She shot him a glare. "I'd really like to see you try that when my hands aren't tied."

"It would be my fucking pleasure," Simon hissed.

"Enough," Todd bellowed. "She's just trying to piss you off enough that you make a stupid mistake. Don't fucking play into it."

Grace snorted. "Yeah, that ship has already sailed away. You two made a stupid mistake by assaulting a federal agent."

"The Outside and their laws have no hold over us."

"But their maximum security prisons certainly do—or at least they will when I make sure that your asses are thrown inside of one—right along with your precious Father Teague."

"Keep talking. Every word out of your mouth shows just how clueless you really are." A slow smile slithered onto Todd's face.

This time, Grace's disgust wasn't fabricated. A chill slid down her spine, freezing her completely, when Rebecca Steele stepped into the foyer.

Her mother didn't flinch or miss a beat as she eyed her daughter tied up like a Thanksgiving Day turkey.

Todd stepped back, and Simon dipped his head down in a show of respect—all things anyone in the Order would do when their leader stepped into the room.

It took Grace about five seconds to put the scene together and come to a realization that would have knocked her off her chair if she weren't tied to it.

"*You?*" Grace couldn't hide her shock. "This entire time it's been you?"

Her mother laughed. "That's right. *Me*. Is it so difficult a concept for you to grasp?"

In theory? *No*.

If forced to list every single one of her mother's personality traits and cross-check them with possible occupations, a devious cult leader would definitely be on top, right along with people who suckered you into buying time-shares that you can't afford.

But Grace wasn't sure how she hadn't seen it until *now*.

It had all been in front of her face—the violent shift of the Order, Rebecca's concoction of the Rec and the way she made certain she had control over it by appointing someone that *she* could control. The list went on and on—and Rossbach probably didn't even know that he'd been played.

All this time Grace had been working on the assumption that *he* was the sociopath when in reality it was her mother. Rossbach, and Sarah and Todd and all the others, were nothing more than well-controlled sheep, and probably from the second her mother stepped foot in Sanctuary.

"That's impressive," Grace lied, ignoring the roll of

her stomach. "And I bet Teague probably believes that everything you've put into motion was all his idea."

"Of course. It wouldn't serve my purpose well if he realized just how inconsequential he really is in the grand scheme of things. This way, he stays in the dark, blissfully happy as long as I make sure that he makes the progression to his New Dawn."

"Wow. Those are the words to a love song if I ever heard one."

"Love doesn't get things done, Grace. Under Teague's guidance, the Order was nothing more than pathetic hippies happy living out their sad lives away from civilization. *I* gave them something to strive for. *I* gave them a path in which to direct all that pent-up energy."

"You mean you gave them the green light to turn their self-righteous anger into violence. That's not exactly back-pat-worthy stuff, mother. It's unethical, immoral, and illegal."

Her mother's mouth dropped as if smelling something foul. "I ask myself every day how half your genes came from me, and I still don't know the answer."

Grace parried Rebecca's glare with one of her own. "And I thank God every day that my Steele genes are the more dominant of the two—especially now that I know who and what you really are."

"Very smart, daughter, but your cute little mind tricks aren't going to work. I'm sticking to my plan, and nothing you say, or do, will stop me. Simon?"

He stepped forward, an eager look on his face. "Ma'am?"

"Take post in the outside hallway and make sure we're not interrupted."

"But...you said—"

She whirled around on him. "I *said* guard the door."

Reynolds grudgingly left the apartment, but Todd remained, standing off to the side like an obedient zombie waiting for his master to give him instructions. Her mother ignored him as she turned her attention back to Grace.

"Now where were we? Ah yes. Your existence," her mother began. "Not only does it keep me from my New Dawn, but our entire community is in upheaval because of your actions. That cannot go without punishment. If we let it slide, it undermines the hopes and dreams of everyone that we've sworn to protect."

"Gonna take me back to the Rec?" Grace taunted. "In case Todd didn't tell you, it's swarming with FBI agents."

"We both know you're far beyond the Reconditioning Center. You always have been. Even when we first arrived at Sanctuary." She curled her lips in disgust. "Ugh. You'd been so *needy*...so obsessed with your own wants. It was *disgusting*."

"I was *five*! What I needed was my *mother*, but you made sure she wasn't available—even before you took us to the Order!"

"The Order was the best thing I could've done for you. It was your lack of acceptance that kept you on the fringes of finding your New Dawn."

On the coffee table, Grace's cell chimed with a text. Her mother picked it up and read it. "Liam would like you to know that General Wilcox has been located, and it appears as though they're close to finding a link between the killed servicemen."

Shit.

She should've put the screen lock on her phone like Liam had been telling her to do for months.

One second her mother was across the room, and in a blink of an eye, she stood in front of Grace, burrowing the cold metal of Todd's gun into her forehead. "Is that what you're doing now, Grace? You're actively preventing Father Teague from reaching his New Dawn? *When will you stop*?"

Grace stared her dead in the eye. "I'll stop the second you're not able to hurt another living, breathing soul and not a moment before."

Rebecca screamed. "With every New Dawn come sacrifices!"

"They're people, not sacrificial lambs!"

"They need to be punished!" The cold, unflustered woman Grace had known for her entire life transformed into a red-faced powder keg that was about to explode. Snarling, Rebecca angled the gun at Grace's temple. "In your death, you honor me with my New Dawn, and it's about damn time that you honor the woman who gave you life."

"You may have given me life, but you did not give me *a* life." Grace slowed her breathing and summoned every ounce of love she had for her family—and that included Cade. It wrapped around her like a warm blanket, keeping her safe against the hate staring down at her.

Grace lifted her chin and stared Rebecca Steele in the eye, refusing to give her the fear that she wanted to see.

Rebecca seethed. "How dare you dis—"

Behind her, a window shattered.

All hell broke loose as the front door crashed open. A FBI tactical team barreled into the apartment. People shouted and barked orders, but Grace's fuzzy head couldn't register them all.

Her gaze landed on the wet red blotch blossoming on her mother's gun arm, and she slowly connected the sight of the blood and the breaking glass.

Sniper.

"Grace." Ryder's voice echoed as if he stood in a wind tunnel. "Grace!"

A large body pushed through the sea of federal agents. Her cousin crouched in front of her, gently tugging her chin up before addressing someone behind her. "Winston. Cut her out of these things."

"Damn it, kid. Did I not tell you to stay the hell out of trouble?" Rhett's hands gently snapped the ropes away.

"You're okay…" Grace's voice sounded foreign to her own ears.

"Yeah, I'm okay. I had to lie low for a bit before tracking down your family. I never expected to stumble into this shit storm outside. I think you've taken over my role as a trouble magnet."

Grace's knees buckled, tumbling her into someone's open arms.

"Fuck," Rhett cursed. "I'm not so sure that all this blood is Rebecca's."

"We need an EMT over here," Ryder shouted. "Now!"

Grace fought against her dimming vision, but her head swirled too fast to keep her eyes open. "Cade. I need to talk to Cade."

"You will, kiddo. You just got to keep it together for a little longer, okay?"

"My mother. A . . . sniper?"

Ryder's hand slowly pushed away her hair. "Jaz. And don't worry about Rebecca Steele. She's not going to be able to hurt you or anyone else ever again. I promise."

On cue, her mother's vulgar curses echoed through the apartment. Grace wrestled her eyes open long enough to see a handful of FBI agents strong-arming not just her mother into handcuffs, but Todd Winston too.

"Simon . . . ?"

"Already in the back of a squad car, cuz."

"Good." Grace nodded less than a second before darkness washed over her, and this time she couldn't pull herself back out.

CHAPTER
TWENTY-EIGHT

Two hours earlier, Hogan Wilcox had strutted himself down to Steele Ops headquarters with an easy "I heard you were looking for me" and plopped his ass in a chair as if he didn't have a worry in the world.

At least until now.

Wilcox might have been a difficult man to read, but Cade saw the concerned narrowing of his eyes. *Finally.*

"You're seriously going to sit there with your mouth clamped shut?" Cade asked, exasperated. "After everything I've just told you?"

He'd spent all night wailing on a heavy bag and cursing himself for letting Grace walk away. Now her words from the night at the motel came back to bite him in the ass too.

She'd been right. When it came to his father, he'd held on to that anger so long it had become an automatic physical response. If he ever wanted to move the fuck forward, he needed to break the cycle—and it needed to be him who did it.

Cade sat across from Hogan and nodded to the five pictures they'd taken from Sanctuary. "We got a mystery man, you, and three dead former military with questionable service records. You got to give me a little more than you were all *work buddies*."

"We were friends, and we worked together."

Cade ground his teeth. "I got that much. These three men have already been systematically hunted down and assassinated. Whatever beef Rossbach has against you all is obviously a big deal—at least to him. And you don't look the least bit worried."

"I can take care of myself, son."

He bit his tongue to keep from reminding Wilcox that he wasn't his son. *He was.* The man may not have raised him, but his stubbornness ran through his own veins, and as flawed as they both were, they had one other thing in common.

They weren't afraid to haul out the big guns.

"You're on Rossbach's radar." Cade nodded to the picture. "And unfortunately, not everyone working for him is a total idiot. How long do you think it's going to take for him to figure out that there's a connection between you and Zoey?"

His father flinched, the first time in hours he'd showed signs of faltering. *Bingo.*

"Didn't think of that, did you, Pops? Well, *I* did. If the bastard's smart enough to identify and locate you and three former black ops soldiers, then he's smart enough to realize that one of his targets has a brand new shiny family."

"Is Zoey okay?"

"Zoey's fine. But she won't be totally in the clear until we understand what's fueling Rossbach. Why does he think that getting rid of you is going to give him his happily-ever-after?"

"I've never met the man at any point in my life, and that's the damn truth."

"And yet we have three dead men with a potential for two more."

Leaning heavily on the table, his father sighed. "I can't tell you specifics. I can't tell you our mission goals or the details of our assignments." His gaze flickered to the mystery man image. "And unless there's some kind of national emergency, I can't tell you *his* name."

"So you were part of a team?"

"I was the team lead, yes."

"I'm not asking for your daily journal. I'm asking for a motive, so we can create a plan of attack."

His father took a deep breath and nodded. "We were out on another assignment when our unit got word that human traffickers were about to send a convoy through our area. Normally we would've let the local authorities handle the situation, but then there came word that one of the people being trafficked was an American woman who'd been in the area working for an NGO group."

"And?" Cade coaxed for more.

"And we were told by our COs back in the States to let the locals handle it as usual."

Cade already guessed where this was heading because, hell, he'd been in a situation a lot like it. Brass and politicians thousands of miles away made decisions about in-field tactics and people's lives all the damn time. "I'm going to take a wild guess and say that your team didn't listen to those orders."

Wilcox scrubbed a hand over his face, looking a lot older than his fifty-some years. "No, we didn't. Our base command had us follow the caravan. We couldn't leave them—*none* of them—to those monsters."

"You executed a takedown."

"We did recon. We planned. We ran drills. We had a local who was able to get a little friendly with the traffickers and get exactly the intel we needed for a night raid. We couldn't have had a more perfect setup, but one of those bastards ended up with a case of the shits. He pegged one of our guys on his way to take a dump, and all hell broke loose. We flipped immediately to our backup plan, but at that point, there wasn't a single prisoner that wasn't panicking, including Addison Parker. She ran straight into the gunfire."

Addison Parker. The name didn't ring any bells in the background they'd dug up on Rossbach. "Who was she to Rossbach?"

The conference door opened, and Grace strode in. "His fiancée."

Cade's attention snapped to her, and his stomach dropped.

A dark purple bruise covered her left jaw, and another was already forming higher up on her cheek. Her hair, a tangled, matted mess, was pulled back, clumped with what couldn't be anything else but blood.

"What the fuck happened?" He rushed over to her and, cupping her face, brushed his thumb over her swollen lips.

She winced.

"Shit." He pulled his hand away, realizing that after

the way they'd parted, she probably didn't want his dumb ass touching her. "I'm sorry."

"I'm not." Instead of throwing a punch, she latched onto his hand with both of hers and held him close. "And what happened? Let's just say that Mother Dearest had second thoughts about leaving without saying goodbye."

"We'll get back to actual details in a minute. Why aren't you in the hospital?"

"Because she's a damn Steele." Ryder walked into the room with his brothers, Tank, and Jaz close on his heels—and Rhett Winston. "I told the EMTs to dose her with Versed and throw her in that damn ambulance, but she pulled that soothing voice shit and had them agreeing with her in less than five minutes. Freakin' witch magic."

Grace was already rolling her eyes. "Please. It's a slight concussion—which I've had before, thanks to growing up with four stupid cousins."

Rhett muttered something under his breath that sounded a hell of a lot like, "And a bullethole."

Cade's vision went red. "You were fucking shot!"

Grace threw Winston a glare. "No, I was *grazed*, and I'm not so sure it wasn't from the exploding glass."

Her mother. Bullets. Exploding shit. Cade ran his hands down her arms and froze at the sight of the rope burns circling her wrists. He nearly went nuclear.

"Nope. Up here, big guy." Grace tugged his gaze back up. "You with me?"

"Yeah."

"Good—because I'm not going to lie. I have a splitting headache, and I really don't want to repeat myself."

"Okay." He braced himself to hear a whole lot of shit that was going to piss him off and steered Grace into the chair next to his father. "Sit and explain."

"My *mother* put the twist behind the twisted mind of New Dawn. The whole idea of retribution and payback? Hers. Every demented thought about duty and rights and serving the good of the Order? All her the entire damn time."

"You're fucking shittin' me." Cade apologized when she flashed him an annoyed look. "Sorry. Let's get on with whose necks I have to break for hurting you."

"You don't have to break anything, because Rebecca, Todd, and Simon Reynolds are already in FBI custody, thanks to an off-duty agent spotting Simon not too far from Zoey's place."

"Well, I beg to differ about that." Cade slid Ryder and Rhett a look. "And when the hell did you two come into play?"

Rhett, hands shoved deep in his pockets, looked like he'd gone a few rounds with a heavyweight boxer himself. "After the showdown at my place, I went looking for Grace and ended up running into Ryder here. He took me to the apartment, and when we got there, the FBI already had the place surrounded."

Cade took a moment to process everything, and then he went through it all again for good measure. "And Rossbach?"

"He's still on the loose—and dangerous," Grace pointed out. "He may not be the mastermind, but everyone in the Order still worships him as if he were. Vance is personally interrogating Todd and the others now, so she'll probably have his whereabouts sometime within the hour. She's freakishly good at prying information out of people."

Director Vance.

Cade couldn't help but think about the last time they'd mentioned Grace's boss. "I thought she ordered you back to New York."

"Yeah, well, those plans changed this morning." Grace's swollen mouth tilted into a small smile. "That explanation's going to have to come later. Right now, we need mystery man's identity."

Cade's father stood. "You know Rossbach's motive. Isn't that enough to help you catch him and put him away? Hell, use me as bait."

"No," Cade growled.

"Why the hell not? My actions made this mess. Besides, there's no way in hell those New Dawn bastards are getting to *him*." Wilcox nodded to the unknown target. "Of all the people on this earth, he's one of the best protected in the world."

"That sure of yourself, huh? Why? Does he live in Timbuktu or some equally remote location?"

"Hardly. He lives right here. In DC."

"And you think that makes him untouchable?"

"No, but the constant Secret Service presence does."

Cade registered his father's words at the exact time Grace did.

"Secret Service?" they asked in unison.

Wilcox nodded. "I've always found it ironic that our duty station commander, the one who made up his own security measures, suddenly had to submit to someone else's."

A bad feeling twisted Cade's insides. "Is this the same duty commander who gave you the orders to raid the trafficking ring that killed Teague Rossbach's fiancée?"

"One and the same. But from what I hear, Brandt's significantly increased his detail these last few days. The only people who can get within sniffing distance of him are his family."

Grace released a string of profanities. "*Sarah*. Rossbach and my mother were waiting for the right time to send her back home so she could do their dirty work for them—two New Dawns for the price of one quick and dirty assassination."

"The Elite Guard isn't going to take out Brandt. His own daughter is."

CHAPTER TWENTY-NINE

Grace dialed the number to the White House switchboard and listened to the same irritating message as the last four times she'd tried: *Your call cannot be connected. Good day.*

She growled, shoving her cell in her pocket. "I think that switchboard operator blocked my number!"

"Maybe you shouldn't have asked the last one if his brain was the size of a pencil eraser." Cade glanced at her from the driver's side, a small smirk in place as he weaved their SUV through the busy DC traffic. "They probably have you on some kind of watch list now."

Grace shot him a glare. "When someone tells you the vice president's in danger, you should transfer the damn call, or at the least, jot down a freakin' message. Not give some scripted response and offer to transfer you to the Visitor Information Center."

"Just sayin' there's a big difference between vinegar and honey, sweetheart."

"I wouldn't have to worry about the acidity of my sarcasm if you guys had a direct link to your *client*."

"He's the VP. He's not exactly difficult to find."

"Yeah? How's that going for us right now?"

It wasn't. Not even Vance, who was leading the

charge to find Rossbach, had been able to get through to the vice president. They had to do this the old-fashioned way and hope for the best.

Grace took a deep breath. Even with the two-ton weight hanging over their heads, she wouldn't want to be anywhere else besides in that car sitting next to Cade. Leaving him and her family behind just wasn't an option, and once Sarah was in custody and on the road to recovery, she vowed to have a sit-down with everyone who was important to her.

Cade was first.

She loved that he didn't want to be the driving force in her decisions, that he wanted her to do what was best for her, but the truth was that *he* was what was best. Everything that happened after she'd phoned Director Vance back at Zoey's place confirmed she'd made the right decision.

Grace could have her job, her family, *and* her man—and she wasn't settling for anything less.

She pointed toward a side street that ran along President's Park and butted up to the White House grounds. "Go through here and pull up to the guard shack."

Cade turned the SUV and grimaced, warily looking at the armed guards squared off along every inch of the building and beyond. "Why the hell couldn't we have had this break last night when there wasn't a state dinner? I feel like we're already in a sniper's crosshairs."

"We probably are. They guard this place to the nines when there are so many dignitaries in house."

Cade grumbled. "If we miraculously don't end up shot, do you seriously think Brandt's going to welcome what you have to say about his daughter? He could've listened to you the first time around and he didn't. You think that's going to change now?"

"Maybe. Maybe not. But it doesn't mean that I'm not going to try." Otherwise, the vice president would find out firsthand how right she'd been about New Dawn, and by then, it would be too late to turn back time.

"Stop slowing down! There's the guard shack!" Grace pointed to the left.

"I'm going eighty miles per hour. Do you want me to plow *through* the building?"

"Will it get us there any faster?"

"You're going to get us shot by Secret Service." Cade cursed, but did as she asked. He flew straight up to the guard shack and came to a loud, screeching halt. The two guards inside immediately aimed their guns in their direction, both barking orders.

Grace whipped up her hands, her FBI credentials facing them. "FBI Special Agent Steele!"

"Do not lower your hands!" the first guard barked while the second, gun still aimed into the SUV, spoke to someone on the radio.

"We need to get into the White House!" She moved to open her door and both men gripped their guns tighter.

"Don't move!"

Cade snapped, "Fuck, Grace, do what they say!"

"We don't have time for this." Grace plastered her creds on the front window. "Use your frontal cortex, gentlemen. *Read. The. Badge.*"

They stared at her credentials a good ten seconds before the second guard nodded to the first. They reluctantly got into position, one at each door. "Get out. Very slowly, and keep your hands where we can see them."

Grace frowned. "And how exactly are we supposed to get out without using our hands? Pull the latch with our tongues?"

"Fucking hell," Cade muttered.

The agents glanced at each other and came around Cade's side first, one manning the door and the other with his gun aimed into the front seat. Two more guards ran out from behind the gate and did the same with her.

Grace kept her creds opened and raised. "We need to get into the building. Vice President Brandt's security is compromised."

"I assure you, ma'am, the vice president's safer than he's ever been."

"And I assure you that he's not. Call whoever you need to call, but we need to get into that damn building. Now."

Another guard frowned, his gun never wavering. "That's the White House, ma'am, not just any *damn* building."

Grace took a deep breath and cleared her head and her agitation. *Honey instead of vinegar.* "Agent Jake Corelli. Brandt's head of security. Get him and tell him that I'm out here. Tell him what I told you."

One of the newer guards turned away as he softly spoke into his radio. A minute later, he came back. "Are you armed, ma'am?"

"Back holster. A .22 Magnum."

"And there's a Colt on my right side," Cade added.

The guard nodded to one of his buddies, who then came around and patted them each down, taking the weapons out of their holsters. She gave Magdalena a longing glance but kept her mouth shut.

Once the guards were satisfied they were clean, the one with the radio nodded. "Agent Corelli will be waiting for you inside the east entrance."

"And your friends aren't going to make it rain bullets?" Cade eyed the snipers standing on top of the building, assault weapons pointed toward their position. "Because I really don't feel like getting shot today."

"You're good to go, sir."

Grace took off, every inch of her body protesting the run. Cade kept an easy pace beside her until they reached the building.

A tuxedo-clad Corelli opened the back door. "What the hell happened to you?"

"Someone called me ma'am and took away my gun," Grace joked dryly.

"You're either ridiculously brave or courageously stupid, Special Agent Steele."

"I'd go with both options," Cade grumbled.

Grace chose to ignore both men. "We don't have time for egos. We need to make sure that Sarah Brandt's secure, and that the vice president's in a safe room." At the man's silence, Grace's internal alarm system blared. "You're not giving me the warm-and-fuzzies, Corelli."

"The vice president is in a room with the president of

the United States and dozens of foreign dignitaries and their security details. He's in as safe of a room as there's ever going to be."

"And Sarah? You didn't say that *she's* secure."

Corelli paused. "She's at the dinner."

Grace couldn't believe her ears. "I told you to watch her! Letting her get gussied up to play the part of the dutiful daughter is not keeping an eye on her."

"She *is* being watched. There's a detail around her at all times," Corelli said defensively. "Look, I tried doing what you asked, but the vice president's not exactly receptive when it's something he doesn't want to do. For what it's worth, he did send her to *someone* who cleared her."

Grace scoffed. "After what? One meeting? The girl's been brainwashed to justify all actions done in the name of the Order. That means she's deceptive enough to lie convincingly when she needs to. She probably has a better chance of faking her way through a polygraph than you do."

Realization flickered in the agent's eyes.

"Follow me." He hustled them through the halls of the White House, shouting into his radio. "I need updated positions on Papa Bear and Baby Bear. Right now."

Cade touched Grace's elbow as they followed hot on Corelli's heels. "We better be right about this, or else you can forget about that promotion, and I'm going to be sentenced to Leavenworth."

"First, you're not in the Army anymore, Rambo. They won't send you to Leavenworth. And Vance isn't going to fire me."

"So sure of yourself, are you?"

"As a matter of fact, I am. Promotion, remember?"

They stopped outside the State Dining Room while Corelli barked orders to his team, but Cade didn't take his eyes off her. "Look, I didn't say anything the other night because I'm an asshole, but…congratulations. I know you've worked hard for this, and there isn't anyone who deserves it more."

The pained look on his face told her what she needed to know.

"That means a lot to hear you say that," Grace said truthfully, barely suppressing her nerves. "It comes with a lot more responsibility, and relocating is always a pain in the ass, but that part won't last forever. And I have four built-in personal movers. Actually, six. You and Tank aren't escaping manual labor."

"No. You're right, it's…wait." Cade blinked. "Relocating?"

Grace took his hand, and their gazes collided. "*Relocating*. Permanently. To DC."

Corelli cleared his throat and tossed open the door. "Look alive, kids."

Grace reluctantly pulled her attention away from the man she loved and onto their surroundings. "Oh. Wow."

Dignitaries galore spread throughout the room, dressed to impress in glittery gowns and fancy suits. Her ripped shirt and yoga pants, not to mention the multicolored bruises, made her stand out like a sore thumb.

Those nearby cast them curious glances.

"Guess I'm a little underdressed," Grace murmured.

Corelli waved to someone on the other side of the room. "The vice president's on the private balcony with—" His eyes snapped toward the balcony in question and cursed. "Clear the room and get the president to her safe room. *Now*!"

Both suited and plain-clothed Secret Service leaped into action, causing more than a stir among the guests. People panicked from the flurry of activity, some running to the nearest exits and other freezing like statues. Across the room, the president was whisked away.

"Is that the balcony?" Grace noted six armed and serious-looking Secret Service agents stealthily approaching a set of French doors.

Corelli nodded. "Sarah's on the landing with her father . . . and she's armed."

"Tell them to stop their approach."

"Are you fucking serious? Did you not hear me say that she has a gun?"

"Grace." Cade touched her hand. "Maybe you should let them—"

"No. I know she's not herself, but I know she's not as far gone as my mother. So far she hasn't done anything wrong except want to be cared for. She's desperate. I can work with that."

Corelli frowned. "You're asking me to risk the vice president's life."

"I'm asking you to *trust* me."

Corelli looked to Cade, who shrugged. "Brandt trusted her enough with his daughter to bring her into this. I'd do what she says, but that's just me. Well, and the VP."

"Fuck," Corelli cursed, then nodded. "Everyone hold," he spoke into his mic. "I repeat, make no moves toward the target."

He turned toward Grace. "I really hope you know what you're doing."

"So do I."

CHAPTER THIRTY

Grace stood outside the balcony doors and took a deep breath. Behind her, Cade talked to one of her cousins on the phone and hung up. "Roman said that Vance took Rossbach into custody about five minutes ago. Evidently our buddy Todd sang like a canary when threatened with jail time."

"Good. I can use that to our advantage."

Corelli stepped over. "Here."

"A flak jacket?" She glanced down, accepting the heavy black vest.

"Before the vice president sealed the door, Agent Reed caught a glimpse of Sarah's gun. It's 3-D printed, but the bullets sure as hell aren't. It'll do as much damage as one bought straight from the assembly line."

"That's how she was able to sneak it in?" Cade spun Grace toward him and double-checked the buckles on the vest.

"Looks like. I can't tell you how pissed I am that we didn't take this more seriously. I thought we had her covered."

Grace felt a little sorry for the Secret Service agent. "Failure isn't an option for her. She would've found a way around whatever security you could've put in place."

"Still doesn't make me feel any better."

A thought struck Grace. "Wait. You said Brandt closed the door on his detail? Before or after she showed the gun?"

"After. Why?"

"Did she order him to do that?"

Corelli thought about it before shaking his head. "I don't think so. He just did it. Why?"

"Because even though she obviously intends to hurt him, he's protecting her." Pieces of a plan slowly formed in Grace's mind. The rest she'd have to make up as she went.

"Grace." Cade squeezed her fingers, pulling her attention to him.

"Don't tell me not to do this, Cade," she warned.

"I'm not. Just . . ." He cupped her cheek and dropped a hard kiss to her lips.

Grace slid her fingers around the nape of his neck and into his hair and poured everything she had into that kiss. Every intention. Every promise. Every last breath.

When her chest ached from lack of oxygen, Cade rested his forehead to hers, panting as heavily as she was. "Be careful. *Please*."

"I'm always careful. Besides, I have a lot to look forward to when I step back into this room. At least I hope that I do."

"You do." Cade flashed a nervous smile and reluctantly stepped back. "Now go perform your magic."

Grace took a cleansing breath and gently eased down the door handle. "Wish me luck."

"You don't need luck."

"Do not come out here!" Sarah's voice screeched.

"Sarah." Grace softened her voice. "It's me. Grace. Mother Rebecca's daughter. You remember me, right?"

Sarah scoffed. "I don't think I'll ever forget the person who carried me away from my home."

"Technically Cade did the carrying, but...yeah. I'm sorry about the way things played out," she said truthfully. "I wanted to talk to you about it...about what you're about to do."

"The time to talk was in Sanctuary. Now it's time to fulfill my duty."

"It's your duty that I want to talk about, Sarah." Grace turned back to Cade and got a supportive nod. "Please?"

"F-fine. But you b-better be alone...and unarmed."

"I am. I promise." She waited a beat and then opened the door wide enough to step through. Unlike Brandt, she didn't close it all the way, giving the agents inside a backup plan if this one exploded in her face.

"You can't stop me." Sarah Brandt stood in the center of balcony, aiming a white plastic, although no less lethal, 3D-printed gun at her father with a shaky hand. The vice president stood stock still, eyes wide with concern as he watched his daughter. "I have to do this. For me. For my New Dawn...and for Father Teague's."

"I know you feel like you don't have any other choice, Sarah, but you do," Grace began carefully. "Think about what you're doing right now. Think about how this could end."

"With me and Father Teague getting our New Dawns. *Everyone* deserves their New Dawn."

"Even at the expense of another's life?" Grace stepped forward one slow step at a time. Pierce Brandt shifted nervously on his feet, for once wisely remaining quiet.

"That's far enough." Sarah's hands trembled.

Grace stopped, lifting her hands. "Okay. Okay. Just...can you answer that question? Why is one person's life more important than another? Why must your father die so that Father Teague can be happy?"

"Because everyone—"

"Deserves a second chance. You're right. They do. But *this* isn't the way to go about it, Sarah. You can't take away someone's second chance to give someone else theirs. That's not how life works...or happiness."

Tears ran down Sarah's cheeks. "It has to! There has to be some kind of payback system! Otherwise someone—"

"Will always be hurting." Grace's heart ached for the other woman. Confused. Desperate for something she didn't think could be hers. "Lethal retribution isn't the answer."

Sarah's hands trembled more.

Grace calmed her voice despite the fact that every muscle in her body was prepped to move. "Can you lower the gun a little bit for me? Just a little. And take a deep breath. You don't have to look at me, but take a deep inhale and let it out slowly."

It took a moment, but the other woman listened, and her trembling abated.

"Good. Now, I want you to help me think through something, okay? We're just going to have a little think tank...you and me."

"O-okay," Sarah said reluctantly.

"You think, that by harming your father, you'd not only be that much closer to your New Dawn, but you'd be helping Father Teague, right?"

She nodded. "Mother Rebecca said it was a sign that my Dawn was linked to his—that once I overcome my Obstacle, everything else would be a smooth road to the life I deserve."

Grace mentally cursed her mother out all over again.

"That's a nice thought, but that's not reality, Sarah," Grace said gently. "Life is never a smooth road. It's full of swerves and surprises. Some good and some maybe not so good."

"But she said—"

"I know what she said, but you and me are the only ones here right now, remember? We're putting our heads together." Grace waited for Sarah's slow nod. "So what happens if you or Teague face another Obstacle? Does that mean that you both have the right to hurt someone else to make it go away?"

"No...it...I-I don't know."

"Then where does it end? Where does the cycle stop?" Grace took a small step closer, and when Sarah didn't recoil, she took another. "What happens to the loved ones, Grace? If you hurt your father, what happens to your mother? In the name of *her* New Dawn, is it acceptable for her to eliminate the persons who took her husband away?"

"I..."

"Causing pain is never the way to a life of love. The only path *to* a life of love is to live your life *with* love." Grace stepped within grabbing distance but made no move to snatch the weapon. She slowly placed her hand on Sarah's shoulder.

"Grace," Cade warned, watching from inside the building.

Tears poured down Sarah's face as she looked Grace in the eye. "I want that... I want a life with love."

"I know you do. We all do. But this isn't the way to get it." She slid her gaze to the vice president where he stood frozen into position, his face pale and forehead sweaty. "Really look at your father, Sarah. He wants you to be safe. He protected you by closing the door and separating you from the agents inside. He wants you to be happy. He loves you. Unconditionally."

"I do," Pierce Brandt choked out, his words roughened by emotion and a healthy dose of fear. "Your mother and I love you so much. I know I disappointed you somewhere down the line, and I promise... with all my heart... that I'll do whatever it takes to make it up to you."

Sarah stared at her father.

"I love you, Sarah."

Grace counted to five, then ten. Every second that ticked by, she prepared to lunge for the gun... but then the vice president's daughter melted. On a heavy sob, she dropped the gun to her side and sunk to her knees.

A dozen armed Secret Service agents stormed the balcony. Grace inserted herself between them and

Sarah, gently easing the gun from her hold moments before Vice President Brandt rushed forward.

"I'm so sorry, Daddy," Sarah sobbed into her father's chest. "I'm sorry. I don't know how...I just..."

"It's okay, sweetheart. I know. We're going to get you the help you need. I promise. We'll make it all better." He cradled her against him, tears dripping off his chin. His gaze caught Grace's from over Sarah's head and mouthed a silent thank-you.

Her body still buzzing from the run of adrenaline, Grace shimmied past the relieved security detail and back into the ballroom. It was easy to spot Cade. The only person in the room other than a few other guards, he leaned heavily on a cocktail table, his head bowed so she couldn't read his expression.

Grace approached him even more carefully than she had the vice president's daughter. "So...mission accomplished. Bad guys taken care of and a family reunited. Everything else will fall into place with time."

He looked up, his heated gaze nearly knocking her back a few steps. "You realize that could've backfired in a stupendous way, right?"

"It could've, but it didn't."

He pushed off the table and stepped closer. "You were so close to her that your flak jacket wouldn't have done a damn thing if she'd have fired."

"I know."

"And yet you did it anyway."

"I knew I could get through to her."

"And what made you so damn sure, huh?" Cade demanded.

"Because in any other time or place, she could've been me. She has people who care about her, who genuinely want what's best for her, and for whatever reason, she couldn't see it. She just needed reminding. We both did."

Cade's face lost its hardness as he studied her. "And what made you come to this grand realization?"

"Knox and Ryder and Liam and Roman. Zoey. Aunt Cindy and Gretchen. *You.*" Grace walked closer until her shoes bumped into his, and she looked up, refusing to pull her eyes away from his. "Ask me why I requested Vance turn my promotion into a transfer to the DC office."

Cade's throat worked overtime, and he swallowed loudly. "Why?"

"Because I love you. I'm *in* love with you and I have been since I was a surly thirteen-year-old who thought the world was against her. You didn't tell me to stay the other night because you didn't want to take my choice away from me, but *this* is my choice, Cade. *You* are my choice."

For a second, he didn't move, and Grace questioned her people reading yet again. Nerves rolled her stomach, making her feel like she was going to puke. But then he cupped her chin between his fingers and held her hostage with every emotion that showed on his face.

"What was it that you said to Sarah?" Cade asked, his blue eyes bright with unshed tears. "The only path *to* a life of love is to live your life *with* love."

Grace nodded, barely able to form words or even breathe. "I did say that, didn't I?"

"You're my path, Grace Steele. You're my life. You're my *forever*."

She smiled through the barrage of happy tears pouring down her cheeks.

Grace had spent years denying her heart what it really wanted, and having it right in front of her was more than a little surreal. Sliding her hands up Cade's chest, she ignored the swarm of people around them. "I really hope you know what you're getting yourself into. I have it on good authority that us Steeles are a decent-sized handful."

He chuckled. "Try two handfuls."

As his mouth descended onto hers, Grace knew she wouldn't change a thing about her past even if she had the opportunity. It all brought her to *this* moment. It brought her Cade. It brought her the life that she was always meant to live.

It brought her unconditional *love*.

EPILOGUE

Christmas music played in the background, mixing in with laughing conversations and good-natured insult swapping, one more outrageous than the next. Add in the sweet smell of cinnamon, and it was a typical Steele-Wright holiday.

Typical... except for the fact that once the festivities were over, Grace wasn't hopping on the next plane back to New York.

Female laughter drew Cade's attention across the room to where Zoey howled at something Jaz said, which was no doubt aimed at one of the guys. A feast was in the process of being laid out. Liam and Ryder were already circling the table, eyeing the goods, and Grace stood off to the side with Knox and Rhett. But Rhett seemed to be the only one listening to what the eldest Steele brother had to say.

Grace watched Cade, her lips twitching mischievously. He was dying to know about the midnight surprise she'd teased him about before they'd walked through the door.

"I like that look in your eye, son." Hogan Wilcox grinned, making his way over.

Not long ago, Cade would have walked the other

way, but with Grace's help and her talent for knocking his head on straight, he accepted his father's hand.

"Glad you could make it," Cade said sincerely. He caught Zoey's smile from across the room and winked at his sister.

"I was glad to get the invitation... and doubly glad to see what I expected for a while now." Hogan glanced toward Grace. "She's a good woman."

"She's the best." Cade cleared his throat and flexed his fingers around his beer. *One step at a time*, Grace had told him. And the first one was always the hardest. "I'm not offering weekend fishing trips or anything right now, but I'm not against grabbing an occasional dinner together. Or maybe a few beers and a hockey game."

The former Army Chief of Staff blinked, at a loss for words. "I...I'd really like that. A lot."

"Good." They talked a little more before movement across the room caught Cade's attention. He excused himself and met Grace halfway, easing his arms around her waist and pulling her snugly against his chest.

"Everything okay?" Her eyes flicked across the room where his dad joined Roman.

"It would be better if you told me about my midnight surprise."

She chuckled. "They call it a surprise for a reason. You'll get to open it later. Actually, I came here to ask you if you planned on eating any of the food that's piling up in the dining room."

"Hell yeah, I am."

"Then you may want to run into the kitchen and

help with something... or at the very least make it look like you are, which is what Liam's doing."

He glanced over her shoulder. "It looks like everything's under control. Why mess with perfection?"

"Because this year we've instituted a new rule: you don't help, you don't eat."

Cade narrowed his eyes. "Something tells me that you're the mastermind behind this new rule."

She shrugged, slowly easing out of his embrace. "Guess that means Tank gets your share of the food, because he's making his mama's cheesy potatoes."

"That bayou bastard's cooking something?"

"Mm. And it smells absolutely sinful."

"Like hell you say." Cade stayed on Grace's heels back to the kitchen. No way would he let that asshole soak up all the female adoration.

Zoey's mouth dropped as she clunked a stack of dishes onto the counter the second he walked into the kitchen. "Oh, my God, it worked!"

Grace smirked. "Of course it worked. I told you, *open book*."

He was missing something, and judging by the stunned faces all around him, it was something big. He shifted his attention from Grace to his sister. "Why do I feel like I've been conned?"

His mother plopped dishes into his hands. "Not conned, dear. Played like a fine-tuned orchestra instrument."

"What's the difference?"

Zoey chuckled. "The latter is more fun to watch."

Everyone laughed.

The room was cramped, loud, the temperature near sweltering between the number of the people and the overworked oven. It was barely controlled chaos, but Cade wouldn't have had it any other way.

"You find this is funny?" Cade eyed Grace.

"Ridiculously funny." She giggled, her brown eyes lighting up nearly as much as the lights from the tree in the other room.

He slowly edged her against the doorjamb. "And here you almost managed to get yourself on the Nice List."

"The Nice List is overrated." Her gaze flickered above them to where a sprig of mistletoe hovered over their heads. She nestled closer, slowly lifting her mouth to his, and murmured, "Later tonight, I'm going to show you just how much fun the naughty list can be."

Keep reading for a peek at the next book in
the Steele Ops series,

Fatal Deception

Coming Spring 2020

CHAPTER
ONE

The ten-item list of things Roman Steele wanted to do today didn't include visiting Tru Tech Industries. Hell, it didn't make the top one hundred. Yet his dumb ass stood in the same spot it had for the last twenty minutes.

Anyone who wanted to slip something into the government-sponsored research lab short of a herd of elephants would find it all too easy. Barely old enough to sprout facial hair, the guard manning the security checkpoint flirted with a smiling redhead, oblivious to the long line of annoyed people prepping to stage a revolt. The man in front of Roman muttered under his breath and pushed right past the checkpoint.

Undetected.

Roman slid his younger brother a glare. "You've got to be fucking kidding me."

Chuckling, Liam shrugged unapologetically. "I told you it was going to be a lot of work."

"This isn't a lot of work. This is miracle-type shit— and I'm certainly no fairy godmother."

"Tell me about it, although I wouldn't mind if you swapped the 'fuck off' sign hanging over your head for pink-glittered wings. Seriously, dude. You could've at least dressed for the occasion."

Roman glanced down at his jeans and T-shirt. This *was* him dressed up.

His everyday wear consisted of either workout clothes or Steele Ops black camo. Considering that the private security firm he ran with Liam and their two other brothers, Knox and Ryder, had an emphasis on *private*, strutting the DC streets in tactical gear wasn't the best idea.

They'd officially opened their doors last year, converting the historic Keaton Jailhouse in downtown Alexandria to house both their business ventures. Iron Bars Distillery and Beer Garden took up the first three floors and had quickly gained in popularity within the community. But beneath the feet of their vanilla vodka–loving customers, Steele Ops ran like a well-oiled machine.

Anti-terrorism. Covert extractions. They got shit done that the government couldn't do thanks to bureaucratic red tape or lack of manpower. And only an elite few knew of their existence, one of them Army General Hogan Wilcox, a former member of the Joint Chiefs of Staff—and his teammate Cade's father.

Wilcox was how they'd been roped into the risk analysis assignment at Tru Tech Industries.

Crossing his arms over his chest, Roman glared at the still-oblivious guard while talking to Liam. "I don't need to wear a suit and tie like you to know that it's a damn miracle this place hasn't had a security breach to date. Remind me again why you wanted me to tag along. You're the tech guy. If there's holes in their system you're going to be the one who finds them."

"Because two heads are better than one—even if that second one is yours." Liam smirked. "It's not like you had big plans today...or dare I say...a *date*."

Roman slid his brother a glare. "And how the hell do you know?"

"Because the day ends in a 'y,' big brother."

Liam wasn't wrong. Roman couldn't remember the last time he'd had a night out with a woman, or even a quick—naked—rumble in the sheets. Thanks to their Steele genes, Roman and his brothers had never struggled to find female companionship when they wanted it. The problem was that he *didn't* want it.

Not really. He didn't experience stress relief from sex any differently than he did from wailing on the heavy bag for an hour, or making a detour to The Cage. And anything more than a quick romp was off the table.

Been there, done that, had the below-the-knee amputation to prove it.

Relationships required trust, and the only people he counted on to mean what they said were his family and his team. *End of list*.

Liam cleared his throat as they took another step to the front of the security line. "I just have one request. Let me do the talking. We both know that when you open your mouth, chances are high that you'll piss someone off."

"I should probably be offended by that comment, but I'm not," Roman joked dryly.

Of his three brothers, he was definitely the more solitary of the bunch. Knox, as the oldest, often paved the way, and Liam, as the youngest by a few years, often fought to keep up. Ryder usually bounced in between the two, eager to benefit from both worlds.

Roman simply chose to make his own path. He'd gone from Army to Special Forces, to being hand-selected for an international special team assignment—black ops shit at the kind of CIA installations that don't exist.

Don't ask, you better not tell, and if you do, your ass is grass.

Roman hadn't needed that damn IED explosion and the loss of the bottom third of his left leg to make him untrusting. Living three years of his life on a black site where everyone had a hidden agenda did it just fine.

"I'll keep my people skills on the down-low," Roman agreed. "At least until someone says or does something that's too stupid to ignore."

Liam snorted, his gaze shifted to the older man approaching them who couldn't be anyone else but Roger Carmichael, Tru Tech's CEO, and the man who had called them about the possible threat against a building full of biological hazards.

* * *

Focused on the petri dish in front of her, Dr. Isabel Santiago steadied her hand and applied a drop of the FC-5 virus to the latest batch of vaccine hopefuls. The task was easier said than done, which had nothing to do with her bulky biohazard suit and rubbers gloves and everything to do with the "music" filtering into the lab through the speakers.

"I think those headaches you get have something to do with your playlist," Isabel joked, knowing her friend and doctoral student, Maddy Calhoun, would hear from the clean room.

As Isabel's safety spotter, Mads didn't need to be in the Legion's lab, and often caught up on homework or read. Tonight, however, she'd changed tactics.

"Oooh, funny. You should give up your genius creds and join the comedy club circuit. You *owe* me, Isa." Maddy leaned in to the two-way mic that allowed them to have a conversation through the lab's safety panes. "Do you have any idea what I could be doing on a Friday night? Or *who*?"

Beneath her headgear, Isa snortled. "That neighbor who lives on the floor above you? What's his name? Clint?"

Maddy wrinkled her nose. "Yeah, no. Been there and not doing that again. Don't get me wrong. He was drop-dead gorgeous, and the things he could do with his tongue? *Have mercy.* But afterward? There was nothing. I shit you not, Is, but we were looking up at the stars and I commented on the Milky Way, and he thought I wanted to drive to the nearest 7-Eleven for a candy bar."

Isa swallowed a chuckle. "It couldn't have been that bad."

"It so, so was. But stop trying to change the subject. I expect payment in full for tonight."

"I let you play your...music."

"Not cutting it. I had a big night planned for the two of us. I'm talking slinky dresses, drinks, and did I mention that the place was owned by brothers? *Brothers*, Isabel. Hot gods all derived from the same gene pool."

"Sorry to kill your plans of debauchery, but I really needed to assess this latest batch of vaccines. I shouldn't be much longer. Maybe we can forgo the slinky dresses and hot gods and just grab a quick drink on the way home."

Maddy pouted. "Not the same thing."

It wasn't.

As sad as it might be to someone with Maddy's social stature, viruses were Isabel's life. Ebola. Smallpox. She worked on all of them and a lot more in the name of the United States government. Most researchers waited their entire careers to be given the opportunity that Tru Tech Industries had given her: her own basement lab equipped with all the latest toys and gadgets. But all the tech and responsibility came at a price.

Her personal life.

Behind Maddy, the light above the Legion's private elevator flickered on, visually alerting them that they were about to get a visitor. Only a select few personnel had the clearance to visit the Legion, so when Tru Tech's CEO, Dr. Roger Carmichael, stepped out of the elevator, Isabel wasn't surprised.

Until two men followed him.

Neither of them belonged at Tru Tech, much less in the lab. Dressed in a tailor-made gray suit, the man on the left could have stepped off a billionaire romance cover. Light brown hair curled over his collar, and his bespectacled hazel eyes lit up as he surveyed the room.

Where guy number one looked the part of a board-room flunky, his sidekick was the complete opposite.

Well-worn jeans hung off a trim waist, and his dark hair hung loose, hitting his impressively broad shoulders. Everything about him, from the leather jacket and the days-old scruff covering his square jaw, screamed trouble.

And then his gaze flickered up to hers.

Isabel froze. Steel gray, and with the power to penetrate through multiple layers of protective polyglass, his eyes conjured something in her that she hadn't felt in a damn long time.

"Un-freakin-believable," Isabel muttered.

She shut down the sudden libido rush and exchanged it for annoyance. The Legion wasn't on the company's tour for a reason. One misstep or distraction could have catastrophic results, and that was something she reminded Carmichael about on the daily.

Grimacing, Maddy eyed Isa as she cleared her workspace and secured the FC-5 samples back into their pressurized containments. "I know that look. It usually comes right before—"

"I'm stepping into decontamination, Mads. I need to have a little chat with our CEO."

"*That*." Maddy remotely opened the lab door and sealed Isabel into the decontamination room, where she was immediately blasted from all sides with the foam germicidal cocktail meant to kill any possible lingering contaminants.

After a ten-minute decon, Isabel stepped into the clean room, where Maddy waited. "Honey is sweeter than vinegar, Isa."

Isabel took a moment to tug her braid of dark hair out from beneath her lab coat. "I'm not going to give him vinegar."

Her grad student blew out a relieved breath. "Good."

"I'm giving him a good dose of reality."

"Oh, boy."

Isabel kept Carmichael in her sights as she calmly walked across the lobby.

He looked away from his visitors and saw her approach. "It's as if I have the power to make people appear just by speaking their name. Gentlemen, this is Dr. Isabel Santiago, our lead virologist here at Tru Tech."

Mr. Boardroom smiled, flashing a set of impressive dimples. "What exactly does a virologist study, Dr. Santiago?"

"Viruses," Isabel said tersely.

The suited man laughed, but Mr. Leather Jacket frowned, looking less than impressed with her smart-ass comment. Mouth pressed into a tight line, he studied her. His gaze was a million times more potent without a barrier, sending a small shiver down Isa's spine. The sensation wasn't entirely unpleasant, but definitely unwanted.

Carmichael shifted uneasily on his feet. "I have to say that Dr. Santiago put my recruitment skills to the test, but with a whole lot of persistence, I eventually lured her away from bedside medicine."

"With the promise that the Legion was *my* lab, *my* rules." She slid a look to the two visitors and back to her theoretical boss. "I don't consider guided tours to any random Joe that swaggers off the street proper use of our security guidelines."

Mr. Leather cocked one gorgeously dark eyebrow. "I assure you, Dr. Santiago, I don't swagger."

His friend chuckled. "Actually, sometimes you do, although I'd classify it more like a strut."

Isabel's lips twitched, and she fought to contain her smirk.

Mr. Leather didn't seem to find it funny. "And how do you know that we're not new Tru Tech employees getting the lay of the land, Dr. Santiago?"

"Mr. . . . ?"

"Steele. Roman Steele."

Isa forced herself to meet his gaze. "I know, Mr. Steele, because unless I'm mistaken, that's a tailor-made Valentino your friend is wearing, and tailor-made anything, much less Valentino, doesn't happen on a researcher's salary. And you're . . . you."

She bit her tongue before admitting that men in her line of work oozed pen ink from their pockets, not testosterone from their pores. Twelve years in the United States Army taught her to recognize a soldier when she saw one, but Roman Steele hadn't been a basic private.

He looked like a man used to giving orders and having them obeyed . . . and Isa was more than happy to remind him that not only was he now in the private sector, but he stood in *her* world.

Carmichael broke the rising tension with a throat-clear. "It's getting late, gentlemen, and I'm sure Dr. Santiago would love to get home at some point tonight. If you'll follow me, we'll head back up and collect your things."

With a parting warning stare, Isa's boss led his friends back toward the elevators. Roman Steele glanced back seconds before they stepped into the Legion elevators, and Isa couldn't help it. She wiggled her fingers in a girly wave until the doors swallowed him whole.

It took five whole seconds for her to realize Maddy was way too quiet.

She turned to her friend, whose mouth was practically agape.

"What the fresh hell was that?" Maddy asked.

"What was what?" Isabel pretended not to understand.

"That!" She pointed to the elevator, which was now on its way back to the main lobby. "That man was a visual vacation—and I mean the Bahamas, Jamaica, and the Virgin Islands all rolled into one deliciously hot inclusive destination, and you treated him like a weekend trip in an RV park."

"I think that's a little overkill, don't you?"

"No. No, I don't."

The elevator beeped, signaling a returning visitor.

"Oh, good." Maddy sighed, turning her toward the door. "You can apologize and maybe he'll be up to do more than undress you with his eyes."

Isa opened her mouth to object because, first, she

had nothing to apologize for, and second, she didn't want Roman Steele undressing anything of hers—with his eyes or his hands.

The elevator dinged as it reached the basement floor, but it wasn't Carmichael and his visitors that stepped out. Frank, the soon-to-be-retired security guard specially assigned to the Legion, glanced her way.

"Perfect timing, Frank." Isa smiled, always loving the time of the night that the older man made his rounds. "Can you please tell Maddy that I don't need a vacation—in more ways than one?"

Frank's wide, panicked eyes shot her way a split second before someone pushed him from behind. The older man crashed into the table against the wall and hit the ground as four men stepped off the elevator.

Isabel's brain didn't completely register the intrusion...not until the one nearest her aimed his gun at the center of her chest, clear blue eyes locked on her through the slits of his black ski mask.

"Going somewhere, Dr. Santiago?"

ABOUT THE AUTHOR

April blames her incurable chocolate addiction on growing up in rural Pennsylvania, way too close to America's chocolate capital, Hershey. She now lives in Virginia with her college sweetheart husband, two young children, and a cat who thinks she's a human-dog hybrid. On those rare occasions she's not donning the cape of her children's personal chauffer, April's either planning, plotting, or writing about her next alpha hero and the woman he never knew he needed, but now can't live without.

To learn more, visit:
AprilHuntBooks.com
Twitter @AprilHuntBooks
Facebook.com/AprilHuntBooks

EXTREME HONOR

Piper J. Drake

HONOR, LOYALTY, LOVE

David Cruz is good at two things: war and training
dogs. The ex-soldier's toughest case is Atlas, a
Belgian Malinois whose handler died in combat.
Nobody at Hope's Crossing kennel can break
through the animal's grief. That is, until dog whis-
perer Evelyn Jones walks into the facility . . . and into
Atlas's heart. David hates to admit that the curvy
blonde's mesmerizing effect isn't limited to canines.
But when Lyn's work with Atlas puts her in danger,
David will do anything to protect her.

Lyn realizes that David's own battle scars make him
uniquely qualified for his job as a trainer. Tough as
nails yet gentle when it counts, he's gotten closer to
Atlas than anyone else—and he's willing to put his
hard-wired suspicion aside to let her do the same.
But someone desperate enough to kill doesn't want
Lyn working with Atlas. Now only teamwork, trust,
and courage can save two troubled hearts and the
dog who loves them both.

Keep reading for a bonus novel by Piper J. Drake!

To Matthew.
For believing in me. For your support,
patience, and caring, thank you.
大好き—*Daisuki*

ACKNOWLEDGMENTS

To Courtney Miller-Callihan: Thank you for your confidence in me and your never-ending patience.

To Lauren and Dana: Thank you for working with me to polish this story and make it even better.

CHAPTER ONE

David Cruz studied the woman standing in the front waiting area with equal parts irritation and interest. The room had an open design to accommodate dozens of owners and their dogs comfortably—enough space to prevent tussles the humans might not be able to break up without a trainer's help. Of course, the area was empty of other people and dogs at the moment and this little bit of trouble filled the room just fine on her own. Her neat dress suit had to have been tailored to a fit so exact, it might as well have been a military dress uniform. And she wore it as if she was ready for inspection, her posture perfect with her shoulders straight, her chin up, and her hands easy at her sides. If her thumbs lined up with the side seams on her skirt, he'd have wondered if a cadet had gotten lost from the nearby military academy.

The severe gray fabric didn't leach color from her face, though; instead the contrast set off her peaches and cream complexion. Made him think of a dish of ice cream on a hot day. And even standing still, she radiated energy. Charisma. Like she could burst into motion at a moment's notice and heaven help the man who got in her way. He had an urge to step right up and see if she could run him over.

Not likely, but it'd be fun to let her give it a try.

"Look, Miss…"

"Jones. Evelyn Jones." Her sharp tone cut across his attempt to address the current issue with any semblance of calm. "Any and all documentation you might need is right there in the folder I handed you. If you'll verify it instead of wasting both of our time trying to send me away, I'll be able to get to what I've been sent here to do instead of standing around engaging in a pissing contest."

Well, she'd come in ready for a fight.

Head held high and standing as tall as she could, her hackles would've been raised if she'd been a dog. The mental image was entertaining, to be honest, especially since her blond hair was pulled back in a no-nonsense ponytail combined with the stylish poofed-up effect. No idea why women did that but hell, she looked good.

And he did take a minute to appreciate her as she was: compact, curvy, and hot enough to catch the attention of every male on two legs walking the property. But her impact on the four-legged variety remained to be seen.

He could do without her glaring attempt at intimidation, though, and he wondered whether he shouldn't send her sweet ass right on back out the door. If she crossed her arms over her admittedly impressive chest or otherwise altered her body language to increase her aggressive stance, he would. If her attitude was enough to scratch his temper, the dog she was here to see would rip her to shreds.

"Your credentials aren't in question, Miss Jones." He raised his hand to forestall another interruption. He'd had plenty of experience with her kind of sprint-out-the-gate, establish–credibility-immediately personality. It didn't intimidate him one bit but he also wouldn't be rushed. "As I was about to say, you could wait here and be run over by the incoming class of two-year-olds or you can come on in to the office area and have a cup of coffee while I make a few calls."

She blinked and her cheeks flushed. "I...of course. A cup of coffee would be appreciated."

Somehow, he doubted that considering the sour tone of her voice. It took some effort not to grin at her discomfort. "Glad you decided to come along. The two-year-olds aren't a bad batch but their handlers are in some serious need of training. Go figure."

The corner of her very kissable mouth quirked. "Isn't it always the human side of the pair in need of the real training?"

Now, they had some common ground after all. At least when it came to civilians.

But if he wanted to be fair—and hell, who did?—Military dog handlers needed heavy training at the beginning, too. Especially if they wanted to reach the level of excellence required of a special forces working team.

He led her past the receiving desk and down a short hallway to a smaller area with chairs arranged for easy conversation. They had one of those little one-cup coffee makers and she seemed fine fixing up her own mug. He preferred his coffee brewed in a real pot and none of those handy automated gadgets managed a strong enough brew.

The whole host-and-good-manners thing dispensed, he headed for his office. "If you'll just wait here..."

"It would save time if you showed me Atlas. I could introduce myself to him while you're making your call."

He halted; his temper simmered back up to the surface. "With all due respect, Miss Jones, you're not meeting Atlas until I've straightened out exactly what is going on here."

"It's fairly straightforward. I've been brought in at the request of the Pentagon to work with the dog you refuse to introduce me to." At the edge of his peripheral vision, her movement caught his attention. A slight raise of the chin. "It would save you time if you would take my suggestion before I make a call of my own."

He studied her for the few seconds it took for his irritation to cool enough for polite conversation again. All bravado and possibly some real bite behind her threat. It depended on exactly who at the Pentagon had contracted her.

"You could save us even more time and leave now." He turned to face her, calling her bluff. Lesser men backed down immediately under his glare. Took her a full five seconds to drop her eyes. "As far as the United States Air Force is concerned, Atlas was placed under the care of Hope's Crossing Kennels with me as his official trainer. Currently, I'm willing to go through due diligence and consider a joint effort if your consulting credentials are confirmed. But if you truly did your homework on Atlas and this facility, you would know you either work with us or you are escorted off the property. This is not a general kennel where consultants are allowed to stroll in and work independently."

After all, Hope's Crossing Kennels wasn't just a training facility for domestic pets. And the trainers who lived here weren't civilians.

He strode into his office and resisted the urge to slam the door behind him. Bad enough she'd goaded him into a pissing contest. Instead, he managed a creditable quiet close without shooting her a dirty look as he did so. He stepped around his desk, fired up his computer. Logging in always took longer than he'd like. Then again, there wasn't a computer system fast enough to keep up with the advancing demands of security and surveillance needs and the equipment he had installed throughout the interior—and exterior—of the kennels gave him constant streaming feed whenever he needed eyes on a particular part of the property.

At the moment, Miss Jones remained seated and sipping her coffee. Good. Even better if her very attractive behind stayed put. It'd be a damn shame if she took her bluff further and did something stupid, like wander off.

Gaze trained on the video feed, he reached for his Bluetooth earpiece and made sure his smartphone was connected. "Call Beckhorn."

A few rings. "Beckhorn here."

Beckhorn always recognized Cruz's number so it wasn't a surprise when the man answered right away. Cruz was glad his longtime friend had been free enough to take a call at all.

"Please tell me you didn't send her." Not likely, since Beckhorn was at Lackland Air Force Base down in

Texas. But hell, influence didn't always have to do with geographic location.

A pause. "Unless I forgot I sent you a stripper for your birthday, I got no idea what you are talking about here. And I'm sure as hell I don't know when your birthday is off the top of my head."

Shouldn't. But he did. Visuals of Miss Jones doing a sensual striptease superimposed the real woman still sitting on the edge of a chair just outside his office. A lot of potential there, but he'd best file the fun thoughts for some later time tonight.

"A Miss Evelyn Jones arrived today with a very official statement of work to provide consultation for Atlas." And didn't that just chafe his butt. He was the best military dog trainer on the East Coast. He didn't need a...dog whisperer.

"Huh." Beckhorn had a few other choice utterances. Man hadn't lost his touch with the creative expletives. But then, men like him and Cruz tended to not lose the survival skills they'd accumulated over multiple deployments. "Send me scans of the documentation. I'll need to track it down but I'm gonna say up front I'm not surprised."

"There's a reason you flew me down there to meet Atlas." Cruz probably didn't need to remind Beckhorn but it could always be said for the benefit of the lady who'd left her seat and was now standing with her ear pressed against the door. Maybe he'd raise his voice a notch or two for her benefit. "The dog comes first. I won't waste time playing nice with any handpicked consultants if it compromises the dog's progress. If she's a help, she stays. If she's a pain in the ass, she's out."

Especially when some of the work he needed to do with Atlas went beyond the dog's recovery and more into what had happened to his handler. He didn't need some consultant tangling things up.

"Agreed. No worries from this angle." Beckhorn sighed. "Let me follow the audit trail and figure out what officer brought her in. Atlas is a high profile dog. Between the news spot and the articles published about him, the military is going to spare no expense to do right by him. But it also means others are going to want to make doubly sure Atlas has the best care out there. I'm surprised you don't have half a dozen consultants from various military offices and a few choice senators pounding at your door."

"This isn't about news coverage." Cruz tried to keep the growl out of his voice. "It's about giving Atlas what he needs to recover from where he's been."

And what he's lost.

Some people might not give a dog credit for emotions, but Cruz had seen dogs exhibit unfailing loyalty and selfless courage in the face of danger for the sake of their handlers. They experienced emotions. They loved. Deeply.

Atlas had seen awful things. Hell, so had they all. But Atlas had lost his handler—his partner—a man the dog had given his everything to. The dog deserved some sort of peace for the rest of his days if Cruz could help him. And Atlas's handler deserved to have the truth behind his death exposed, if anyone could find it.

"Based on your twenty-four-hour report, Atlas hasn't improved much." Beckhorn cleared his throat. "Not expecting you to work miracles, but one of those would help your case in working with the dog solo."

"I'm not going to rush the dog." Cruz stood up and began to pace, irritated. Oh, not with Beckhorn, but with higher ups always convinced throwing more resources at a problem would lead to faster results. "He'll come around in his own time. I'm letting him get to know me and the facilities here. Not as structured as a military base, not as chaotic as a normal home."

"What are you going to do with the consultant?" Beckhorn tended to choke on the last word, but then, he had a thing about private contractors. Miss Jones might be different, but then again, she might not.

"I'll give it some thought." And he wasn't committing to anything. High-ranking sponsors from DC or no, if Atlas didn't like her, Miss Jones was out the door.

And it was about time to address the way she was lurking on the other side of his.

*   *   *

The door opened so fast under Lyn's hands, she pitched forward before she could catch her balance. She came up against a hard, very well-muscled chest.

Smooth, poised, graceful even. All things she wished she'd managed but definitely was not.

He wrapped big hands around her upper arms and set her back on her own feet. Cheeks burning, she forced herself to look up into his face. His brows were drawn close over his steel-blue eyes in the most intimidating scowl she'd ever encountered. No sense in fumbling for excuses. "I figured giving in to my curiosity about whatever you were doing was better than succumbing to the urge to go meet Atlas."

A noncommittal grunt was his only reply.

Good. Because she was fresh out of ideas for how to recover the professional manner she'd strapped on this morning as armor. She fussed with her suit, straightening the fabric and brushing away imaginary dust, as if setting her clothes to rights would bring back her confidence.

"For what it's worth, the doors around here are surprisingly soundproof." It would be the closest she'd admit to having pressed right up against the door trying to hear something, anything to give her a clue as to whether this man would cooperate today or if she'd have to escalate back up to her sponsor, the man who'd signed her contract, her employer. Thinking of the man in those terms made her grit her teeth.

And she wanted to talk to him like she needed a hole in the head.

David Cruz quirked his very sexy mouth in a half-smile. "Good to know. Maybe I'll cancel the order on the white noise generators for the offices."

Lyn blinked. "Overkill for a kennel, isn't it?"

His dark eyes fixed her in a somber stare. "We've all learned here to be prepared for every conceivable situation. It's kept the people, and some of the older dogs, alive when others didn't make it. We like to keep up the practice."

Oh man. Mental note to do some more research on Hope's Crossing Kennels. All her employer had given her was a newspaper article on Atlas, the hero dog returned from overseas, and the address for the kennel he'd been transferred to. She'd walked in ready to deal with the usual blustering egos. Strong personalities were a given with trainers working with dominant dogs all the time. But taking in the man that was David Cruz, really looking at him...

Lean and wiry, Cruz didn't seem to have an ounce of extra flesh on him. Everything about him was sharp, from the way he responded to every sound around them to the way his musculature showed through his snug tee. Cut wasn't the word for it. She thought she'd seen some fitness guys on the Internet call it shredded? Oh yes. His bronze skin and dark hair, combined with his brooding expression, stole her mental filter, leaving her with no sensible words from the start.

She was messing up this entire project and what she really wanted was to do the only thing she was good at: helping dogs. She'd turned down two private training contracts to clear her schedule for this. Her services were in high demand. And damn it, she could help Atlas.

But she'd made a mistake trying to bulldoze her way through Cruz. She shouldn't have tried to get around him or walk over him. Her employer would've sneered at her and cited a serious tactical error. But she wasn't military and she didn't have to maneuver her way to steady footing again the way others might. She could give a little, compromise, adjust to the situation and change her approach. And she could open her mind and learn before trying to shower everyone with her expertise.

"Has the status with Atlas changed?" She kept her tone soft, trying not to make it sound antagonizing.

Cruz's brows drew together and if it was possible, his expression darkened further. "How do you mean?"

She treaded carefully. "Newspaper article said he was

pining away for his handler who died overseas."

A long pause. "He's eating."

Her heart skipped and then sank. It was a good sign if Atlas was eating. Bad news was they might not need her after all.

"To be fair," Cruz continued, "he's only eating on command. He won't eat if someone's not watching to make sure he does."

Lyn struggled to keep a politely positive expression. No gloating. No anything that might shut Cruz down again. "I appreciate your honesty."

"Yeah well, I try not to lie unless absolutely necessary."

But he hadn't had to share the whole truth either. Was he giving her a chance?

Whatever she said next might mean the difference between seeing Atlas and seeing her way out the front door. Her employer wouldn't be happy and she wouldn't be either.

Atlas's story had struck a chord with her. He'd gone to hell and back on the commands of someone he trusted, with unwavering faith he was doing the right thing. And that person was suddenly gone. Her father had always guided her to do the right thing. When he died, her world had been filled with a lot of people telling her what to do and every one of them had their own selfish motives in mind. It'd stopped being about the right thing and warped into presenting the right illusion.

Be real. Every dog recognizes a fake. And good men can see through it too.

"I'd really like to help." Honest. Simple. All the other

reasons paled in comparison to this.

Cruz pressed his lips together in a hard line. She thought for a moment he'd say no. Fighting the urge to let loose an avalanche of reasons why she could and reiterate every point on her résumé supporting her expertise, she forced herself to stay put and wait. Five years rehabilitating abused animals in New York City and four years working as a private trainer to some of the most difficult human personalities on the West Coast had taught her patience.

"You've worked with dogs suffering from PTSD before." He made the statement a question.

"Yes." Quite a few in fact, but with a man like Cruz, she was getting the sense that less was more, at least when it came to credentials. He could and would check out her résumé later. He'd see her years of work, her awards and appearances at training conferences, in the paperwork.

No more bragging at this point and no more blustering.

"Let's go."

She didn't have a chance to thank him, only hurried to keep up as he took long strides down another hallway and through a solid built door. They came out in the hallway to a set of kennels built directly against the main building.

Every one of the dogs came to alertness.

Cruz came to a stop at one. "We're not going to do the usual introduction and sniffing. I'm going to open up the kennel and bring Atlas out. I'm going to hand him off to you and I want you to do exactly as I did for him. Then you're going to give him back to me."

Lyn nodded. This was new to her. It didn't matter because she was up to handling anything this man might ask her to do. What mattered was Atlas.

Cruz gave a quiet command and opened up the kennel. A moment later he was leading a beautiful, muscled dog out into the corridor. The dog stood squarely on all fours and had the elegant lines characteristic of the Belgian Malinois breed. His proud head was chiseled and in good proportion to his body. There wasn't an ounce of extra flesh on him and in fact, he looked slightly gaunt.

Still, even among the working dogs she'd met, she wasn't sure she'd ever encountered a dog with this air of...fitness.

But there was something missing. Atlas was aware and responsive, but he didn't have the indefinable energy the other dogs around her were projecting. He wasn't engaged, vibrating with eagerness. Intelligence was unmistakable in his expression but there was no air of inquisitiveness. As if he didn't care.

Another murmured command and then the man bent down. Picking up Atlas, he wrapped his arms around the dog's chest and hindquarters in a secure hold. He then lifted what had to be around 70 to 75 pounds of solid dog and turned to her.

Lyn swallowed hard.

She held out her arms, watchful for Atlas's reaction. He remained calm in Cruz's arms and didn't even look at her. As the trainer stepped forward, she copied his hold on the dog, ignoring the accidental brush of Cruz's arms against her breasts. Once Atlas was securely in her hold, Cruz stepped away.

Atlas's fur was surprisingly silken and soft under her hands. She resisted the urge to bury her face in his shoulder. God, he was a magnificent animal. Gorgeous, and so very sad. Her heart ached . . . and so did her arms.

How long was he going to have her hold Atlas? She leaned back slightly to try to take more of the weight in her back and legs as her arms strained.

She would not drop this dog.

"Okay." Cruz stepped forward and took Atlas from her.

As the dog left her arms, Atlas turned his head and touched her cheek with a cool nose and sniffed. Once.

"Huh," Cruz grunted. He stepped back and set Atlas on his feet. Then he returned the dog to his kennel with quiet praise.

Lyn waited, trembling a little. She should probably add some weights to her daily fitness routine. If Cruz had noticed how hard it had been for her, he might not . . .

"We start tomorrow."

"Excuse me, what?" She'd heard him. Only, it wasn't what she'd expected.

"That's the first sign of personal response I've seen out of him." There was a wry note in his words. "I'll take help where I can get it. You're staying at a nearby hotel?"

"Yes." Excitement zinged through her.

"Good. Give me the address and leave the attitude you came here with back at the hotel room." Cruz scowled at her. "This, right here, the you I see right now with the dogs is the person I want to see at oh-five-hundred tomorrow morning."

She wasn't going to argue, not when she basically agreed with him. It was going to be such a relief not to have to walk around with attitude for armor. Any soldier her sponsor had ever introduced her to had been a world-class asshole. The attitude had protected her, given her a way to stand up and not be treated as a doormat...and it was exhausting. But it seemed as if David Cruz was a different kind of military man and for the first time, she looked forward to working side by side with one.

But she was not going to say "yes, sir."

"You got it."

A grin spread across his face, lighting up his whole expression and doing evil things to her libido. "Well, you might be one of the better things that's happened all day after all."

Wow.

CHAPTER TWO

"Seriously? You've been here for days and it's a woman who gets your attention?" Cruz stood in Atlas's kennel, leaning against the doorframe.

The dog in question lay in the far corner, probably enjoying the cool cement beneath his belly. Not that he didn't have the option of a cushy bed over in the other corner.

Right now, Atlas wouldn't even look at Cruz and the dog seriously appeared to have no shits to give on the current topic of conversation. He'd been that way since Cruz had returned from seeing the very pretty Miss Jones out to her car and hadn't moved in the several hours while Cruz was out working the other dogs under his care.

'Course, Atlas rarely moved, based on Cruz's experience both in having observed the dog back at Lackland Air Force Base and in the days here at Hope's Crossing. The dog might as well be a statue unless given a direct command. Then he'd obey, but it was like giving a robot orders.

When Cruz had seen Atlas respond to Jones, there'd been a spark. A ghost of the young dog Cruz had trained years ago.

And he would latch on to any incentive to get the dog to respond.

"Well, we'll see how you do with Miss Jones tomorrow morning." Not even a perked ear. Then again, Atlas didn't know the pretty stranger's name yet and it occurred to Cruz that he wasn't on a first-name basis either.

Been too long surrounded by just men and dogs.

Oh, he'd dated on and off since he'd arrived in Pennsylvania. A couple evenings here and there in Philly. He'd had a few hot women but nothing had lasted more than a few sweaty nights, and he had no plans to change the trend.

"I bet the club scene isn't your style either." Cruz preferred to spend some time every day hanging out in Atlas's kennel, talking. Gave the dog a chance to get to know him again, become used to his presence as a companion and not just as a temporary handler or his once-upon-a-time trainer.

But the indefinable moment when a dog chooses a new master? Hadn't happened yet. Not with Cruz or Rojas or Forte, the three best dog trainers on the East Coast. It'd been Calhoun that Atlas bonded to and now his handler was dead.

And contrary to bills of sale or certificates of ownership, it was always the dog's choice as to who his next master was going to be.

"We'll see what Miss Jones prefers to be called on a

first-name basis." He wouldn't admit out loud, even to Atlas, how curious he was about the things she liked to be called. Not as if Atlas was going to go around telling anyone stories.

His smartphone vibrated in his back pocket. Cruz reached for it and gave the picture password lock screen a tap and a swipe in the right places to get past the security. A little more effort than the usual pin or swipe to unlock apps that came standard with a smartphone, but maintaining higher security was a habit he didn't intend to let go.

An alert flashed across the screen.

"Hold the fort, Atlas. I'll be back."

In moments, Cruz strode into his office cursing. His computer was still running and it took less than a few seconds to authenticate and gain access past the screen saver protection.

A few seconds too many.

Whatever virtual intruder had tripped his network security was long gone. Best he could hope for was to follow any tracks left behind to trace whoever it was back to their source. 'Course, the person had only been nosing around the edges of the security system. They hadn't stumbled into it the way a random Internet intrusion would occur. No, whoever it was had known this system was here and had been testing to see just how sensitive the security measures were.

He glowered at his screen as he attempted to trace them back to their IP, only they'd gone through several servers. And by the time he did locate the originating IP, he cursed even more. Random computer terminal in a cyber café in Japan. Not likely.

Weird.

He didn't like weird. Nor did he believe in coincidences, so he locked down his computer again and pushed away from his desk, rising and heading for the door. Something like this didn't happen randomly, considering the other new things here at the kennels. There was Atlas's arrival and the circumstances around it, Miss Jones arriving to insist on working with Atlas, then this.

Atlas's handler had died for a reason, one Cruz was still looking for. Apparently there were other people looking for it, too.

"You headed out?" Forte passed him in the hallway. The owner of Hope's Crossing Kennels must've been breaking for lunch after a morning of teaching basic obedience classes.

"Yeah. We've had a security issue. No physical incursion, just a minor blip on the network. Secured now but I want to follow a hunch." Cruz didn't linger.

Forte called after him, "Let us know if you need us."

"Will do."

He and Forte had served together overseas. They'd gone out with less information in the past. Likely Forte would want answers later but it was good to be with people who wouldn't hold him up with questions when he was on the move.

Cruz crossed the front parking lot and headed for the private drive where his car was parked alongside the other trainers' vehicles. On his way, he glanced at the front drive and what could be seen of the trees lining the perimeter of the extensive property. His security wasn't just computer system based. He'd designed it all, from the access to any of the buildings to the kennels to the perimeter of the grounds they were built on. It'd been designed to maintain privacy in a civilian area but easily upgradeable if there was need, and they'd never had multiple nibbles until today.

There was only one new person, unexpected and unannounced, who'd shown up recently and she'd been there this very morning.

He entered the address to her hotel on his smartphone and set the GPS to direct him there.

Her attitude had been one thing, but her threat about calling her backers in the Pentagon? Maybe she was more than a simple civilian dog trainer. And maybe her interest in Atlas had grown from more than just the news coverage about his situation.

A man developed hyperawareness to survive overseas and there was a fuzzy line between hyperawareness and paranoia. Miss Jones arriving the way she had and hinting at high-ranking backing hadn't just gotten under his skin. Something was off.

Time to seek her out and ask a few pointed questions about her reasons for wanting to work with Atlas. And if any of her answers came across the slightest bit shady, she was out. Hell, he was tempted to keep her out of it based on his doubts here and now.

In his experience, any doubt whatsoever could mean the difference between success and failure, coming home alive and…not. Atlas's handler hadn't come home. And the circumstances around it were enough to make Cruz proceed with extreme caution.

He'd suffered a momentary weakness in telling her she could work with him on Atlas. Seeing her face soften when she'd gotten near the dogs—the way all her walls came down the minute Atlas was in her arms—had made Cruz think she really had come to help the dog.

But if the incursion on their network had been her, she must've gone straight back to her hotel and jumped online to start hacking into their system.

And she was good, too, if she could make it look like she'd done it from the other side of the world.

Well, he recognized her for what she was and he would be damned if he was going to wait until tomorrow morning to call her on it.

* * *

Lyn wiped sweat from her brow as she exited the elevator. She'd spent more time on the elliptical than normal, trying to outrun her thoughts on Atlas and her impressions of David Cruz. There was a lot to process from what she'd seen today. It didn't seem as if there'd be enough time to do the follow-up research she had planned before calling it a night. Through it all, she was sure she was missing something important about him. It was the kind of important that could eat away at a person and cause insomnia. The only cure she had for it was to burn off the anxiety eating her up and clear her head to track down the useful bits of information. Thus the visit to the hotel gym.

Bleh. So now her legs were about as useful as limp noodles and she wasn't sure she was even walking a straight line down the hallway back to her hotel room. But her mind was clearer and she already had some search strings in mind once she got in front of her laptop.

Everything about David Cruz shouted military. Not

uncommon for kennels providing trained working dogs to military and law enforcement. But most of the trainers she'd met hadn't had the edge Cruz had.

His level of tension as he walked into a room had been enough to make her nervous, an awareness of everything around him. She'd seen men like him on military bases, fresh back from deployment, but not a trainer working at a kennel out in the middle of suburbia.

But he wasn't a raging jackass either. And she'd come to associate the attitude with the kind of soldier. It was probably unfair, but it was exactly why she'd left home as soon as she'd gotten accepted to college and never gone back for more than a brief visit. The men her stepfather introduced her to had all set her teeth on edge with their overbearing demeanors and the way they patronized her.

David Cruz hadn't done any of that. If anything, she owed him an apology for the way she'd greeted him.

She barely glanced up as a man turned the corner at the far end of the hallway and walked toward her, then passed by without a word. Pausing at her door, it took two tries to slide her room key but finally she got the green light and turned the handle. As she walked inside, a loud thump made her look up from her phone.

Panic shot through her as a man dressed all in black straightened, her laptop bag in his hand. For a moment her mind froze.

What? Who?

She started to shout, but a hand covered her mouth as a hard body crowded her from behind, forcing her farther into the room and making her drop her phone.

She stumbled forward and another hand grabbed her left arm, twisting it behind her back.

Oh God. Her thoughts scrambled and scattered. This wasn't really happening.

The man already in the room walked toward her, his lips stretching into a leering grin. The rest of his face was hidden by a ski mask. He looked her over from head to toe and then his gaze settled somewhere south of her face.

"It's really too bad you came back." His voice sent chills down her spine and she struggled.

No. No, no, no, no!

Her captor only tightened his grip until pain shot through her shoulder. What should she do? What could she do?

The other man leaned close and the stench of cigars choked her. "I'm not gonna lie though, Miss Jones. I'm kinda glad you did."

She stared at him, shrank away as he ran a tongue over his top lip. It was all going in slow motion and she gagged in disgust.

"We weren't supposed to let her see us." The words rumbled in the chest behind her head.

"And she won't see our faces." The other man reached out and fondled her breast, pinching her nipple. Twisting. Pain and revulsion shot through her. She couldn't get away. "But we can show her a couple other things before we leave. Seems a shame to let the bed go to..."

Stop!

Lyn kicked out, hard, her foot catching the front of his shin.

"Ow! You bitch!"

Desperate, she bucked against her captor. The back of her head contacted with a hard jaw and she heard teeth snap together. A grunt of pain.

The pain in her shoulder seared through her and she didn't care. She needed to get away. Now.

A door crashed open and the weight of her captor slammed into her as they both fell to the floor.

"Hey!" the other man shouted.

An angry roar was all she could make of the newcomer. There were sounds of punches thrown as she struggled to see, trapped as she was. Then feet running past her.

The weight lifted off her as the man above her scrambled to his feet. She rolled to her back and drove her feet upward, catching him in the gut.

"Oof!"

"Fuck. Let's go." Both men ran out the door.

She sobbed.

A hand touched her shoulder and she flinched away. *No!*

"Hey, hey! It's okay. You're safe now. I won't hurt you." The statements were repeated over and over again. Slowly, the voice seeped through her panicked thoughts. She knew the voice.

David Cruz was crouching down in front of her.

She couldn't catch her breath and the sobbing wouldn't stop. She swallowed hard and tried to take a deep breath. Then another.

"That's it. Nice and easy. Take your time." Cruz crooned to her, his words soft and patient. "I'm not going to leave you. You're safe."

Good. Safe was good.

"I'm going to call the police now, Miss Jones."

"D-don't. Please."

Cruz's brows drew together. "Why shouldn't I call the police?"

She shook her head. "No. I mean, yes. Call the police. Just..."

He didn't seem to get angry at all. He only waited, watching her. His gaze trained on her face, not touching her. Not doing...things.

"D-don't call me 'Miss Jones,' please." The last word came out in a whisper. She'd have nightmares, for a long time. And the way the other man had said her name was going to haunt her forever.

"What should I call you?" So gentle. Was this how he won the trust of his dogs? She wouldn't blame them for trusting him.

"Lyn." She shifted, trying to move her left arm, and winced as the sharp pain came back.

"Easy there, Lyn. Call me David. Can I touch your shoulder?"

The sobbing hadn't stopped yet and tremors took over her body as reaction set in. Logically, she could register what was happening to her. Take a step away from herself and compartmentalize to catalog the damage, hear what David was saying to her. But she wasn't up for intelligible speech yet. She only nodded in response to David's question.

His touch was feather-light and still, it took effort not to shrink away from him.

"It's okay. You've been through hell just now. I won't ask more questions until the police get here." His check was gentle but thorough, and strangely her shakes steadied when he touched her but started up again as soon as he sat back on his heels. "Nothing broken or dislocated, but he had your arm wrenched behind you in a nasty hold. I'm betting the paramedics will still want you to have it in a sling for a few days."

She blinked up at him.

"I'm calling in 9-1-1. They'll dispatch both police and ambulance. You should be looked over."

For the first time, she took a long look at her hotel room behind him. Everything, all her belongings, had been tossed across the room. She hadn't brought much with her but she had packed for an extended stay. All of her clothes, her notes, were strewn everywhere.

Fear rose up in any icy wave and clawed at her throat.

"Why were they here?" They had to have been looking for something.

David shook his head. "I was about to ask you the same. This looks too thorough to be a random robbery."

The one man had said something…

"One of the men, the one holding me, said I wasn't supposed to see them." And she wouldn't think about what the other man had said. Not yet. She'd tell the police when they got there and David could listen then.

"That so? We're going to have to see what the police think." Somehow she suspected David was leaving things unsaid.

Biting her lip, she wondered whether they were going to come back for her.

"They won't get to you again, Lyn." David responded as if he'd heard her thoughts. "And you did great in here. I only heard a minute or two, but you let them know you weren't going to give in without a fight. You were very brave."

Then why did the word "stupid" come more immediately to mind?

An awkward silence settled between the two of them. It stretched out until she fished for something, anything, to say. "I might be late tomorrow morning."

A surprised bark of laughter yanked her gaze back to him. He smiled at her, warm and comforting. And she wanted to slip into the curve of his arms to ward off the chill.

She'd only met him this morning and already she was going to ask him for more than she should. But what else was she going to do?

"Will you stay with me?"

He reached out a hand slowly, giving her plenty of time to watch the approach, and then cupped her cheek. "I'll be right here, the entire time. If you need to go to the hospital, I'll go with you there, too. Okay?"

"Okay."

CHAPTER THREE

How is she?"

Cruz craned his neck to look out the window. "Physically? She's a trooper. Arm's in a sling for a few days but she insisted on starting with Atlas at oh-five-hundred this morning."

That despite his assurance to her that it was completely fine for her to have started later. She'd mentioned she might be late, damn it. She should have taken the time for herself.

"That so?" Beckhorn's voice held equal parts surprise and admiration. Cruz shared it. "How's Atlas doing?"

"He's acknowledging her existence." And didn't that chafe his ass just a little bit. "She's out walking the perimeter with him now."

Speaking of, the pair came into view finally, far out across the grounds. Atlas kept pace with Lyn's short stride, adjusting to her changes in speed and coming to heel when she paused to check out flowers or whatever.

Dog still maintained an air of disinterest, but he was out there with her and not laying on his belly in the kennel.

"So he's making progress." Beckhorn pressed for more.

"Baby steps, my friend." Cruz chuckled. "Don't go reporting him as recovered any time soon."

"This mean you don't want me to keep digging into who sent her?"

Cruz leaned back in his chair, considering. Her fear had been real the night before. Terror, really. "She was damned shaken up last night. Take a look at the debrief I sent you, off the record. Someone was looking for info she didn't know she had. Or maybe she didn't have it yet."

"She's a liability." His friend made a grim noise.

"I had her check out of the hotel and gave her a place to stay here where I can keep an eye on her." He didn't entirely trust her yet but he was sure she hadn't been faking anything the evening before. Her reactions had been genuine.

"You're going to keep her around?" Beckhorn whistled, low and long. "Is she that hot?"

"It's not about that and you know better." Of course, Lyn chose to bend over right about then, checking out a pretty wildflower or weed or something, and he got a faraway view of her shapely rear.

Okay, she was hot.

But he wouldn't keep a liability around just for that. He had Atlas in mind.

"Yeah, yeah," Beckhorn continued, oblivious of the view. "What's the plan now?"

"We both know there was something to the way Calhoun died." It was a big part of the reason Beckhorn had called Cruz so soon for Atlas. He'd needed someone he could trust to oversee the dog's recovery before something unfortunate occurred. "Accidental friendly fire, my ass."

"It's the 'accidental' part in question. We both know it wasn't friendly even if the round did come from one of ours." Beckhorn's tone went flat. "What we need to do is both prove it and find out why. Calhoun reached out to you just before he died and whatever drunk text he sent you pointed to Atlas."

"At the time, the message hadn't made any sense so I assumed it was a drunk text." Cruz swallowed hard on the guilt and self-recrimination there. Not sure what he could've done from across a damned ocean but he still felt he should've realized something was wrong and helped his friend stay alive.

"It still doesn't make any sense." A string of curses followed. "Look. No ripping ourselves up for what we would've, should've, could've. We do the right thing now."

"Yeah." Cruz nodded even if Beckhorn couldn't see.

Lyn resumed her stroll and Atlas took up position by her side. Dog might play like he wasn't interested in the woman but he was engaged and Cruz would take whatever help there was to be had.

Of course, he might have more in common with the dog than he'd prefer to admit.

Last night, she'd suffered a bad scare. Things could have been far worse if he hadn't shown up when he did. He'd been ready to rip her a new one when he'd come to her door, ajar only because her phone had landed in the entryway. It'd taken seconds to change gears from being angry with her to charging in to help her.

He'd have still gotten through, but it would've taken longer for him to realize what was going on and to break down the door. She'd been very lucky.

In those moments, he'd become someone else. The man he used to be. The stranger he'd locked down after he'd returned from deployment. When he'd heard her in danger, he'd gladly embraced the old rage and the cold calm to rush the door. Eliminate the threats.

"You still there, man?" Beckhorn brought him back.

A cold chill passed through Cruz as he realized he'd come to his feet. Maybe he hadn't completely put the other him to rest yet, but it'd take some time to ease back and he hadn't been all too relaxed as it was. It'd been why he'd come to spend time at Hope's Crossing. "Yeah. Here."

Now. Just a minute ago? Not so much. Seemed like Miss Evelyn Jones had a way of pushing all sorts of buttons with him without even trying to.

"You wanna share what you're thinking? I can almost hear the gears turning in your head."

Way across the field, Lyn had come to a halt. It was Atlas's posture that got Cruz moving. "I'm going to have to call you back."

* * *

Atlas noticed the stranger first. Lyn thought it might be one of the other trainers, but in seconds it was clear he wasn't. She'd met both through the course of the day and neither of them had the same build or stance. Dressed casual in dark jeans and button-up shirt, the stranger came through a thick grouping of trees out of nowhere. He caught sight of her and grinned. She recognized it. Oh God, she'd recognize that grin anywhere.

Fear rushed through her and she stumbled back a step, instinctively bringing her hands up to ward off the stranger without thinking.

A deep growl broke through her shock and Atlas surged forward, ripping the leash off her wrist before she could close her hand securely back around the leather.

"Atlas!" *Oh no, no.* She couldn't leave him, wouldn't. Last night, the intruders didn't seem to have any weapons on them, but this man might.

But he blanched white at the sight of the oncoming dog. He backpedaled a few steps and then turned and ran straight back through the copse of trees.

Atlas plunged through after him.

Lyn ran after them both.

"Are you crazy?" The bellow came from behind her but Lyn ignored David and kept going. His angry shout was gaining on her. "Stop! I got this."

Reckless, more afraid for Atlas than anything, Lyn sprinted through the trees and came out in another field. The stranger lay on his back, yelling in pain with Atlas over him. He'd only made it halfway to the fence.

"*Los! Los!*" David caught up and passed her by. "*Los!*"

Atlas didn't let up.

"I'm just lost! I came in here by accident!" The man was shouting.

David let loose a curse and turned to her. "Lyn, come here."

Her heart in her throat, she ran to his side. She should say something, tell Cruz who the man was.

The man's screaming became shriller and words scattered from her mind.

"Here, focus here." David's words cut across the awful sound. "You can do this. Go to Atlas, grab his collar, tell him '*Los*.'"

"What? I..."

He grabbed her good arm and gave her a light shake. "Quick. Before he gets through this guy's guard. Atlas can and will kill. You need to do this."

His gaze caught her, steel blue and hard. Not cold. Urgent.

She nodded.

He let her go then and she stumbled toward Atlas. She needed to get to him before he killed this man.

"Not on his left, go to his right."

Obeying David's instructions, she changed the direction of her approach.

Atlas was so fast, he was a blur. He had the man's forearm between his teeth and was shaking his head back and forth. As she hesitated, there was a sickening crack.

"*Los!*" The word fell out of her mouth as she lunged forward and grabbed for Atlas's collar. "*Los*, Atlas, *los*!"

Atlas released his hold and she dragged him back as the man crab-walked away from them on one good arm. David was on him in a split second.

"I'm going to sue! You're all crazy here! I'm going to sue!" The man babbled as David hauled him to his feet.

He was covered in blood and his arm hung at an awkward angle.

Lyn swallowed back bile and knelt down next to Atlas, keeping a firm hold on his collar. She couldn't stop shaking. "Good boy, Atlas. Good boy."

Atlas's attention was on the man and he whined with eagerness but stayed with her.

"Lyn." David sounded calm, completely ignoring the threats of the injured man. "Take Atlas back to the kennel and check him over."

"What about..."

"Police are en route. The silent alarm went off when he broke the perimeter. I'll wait here for them; you take Atlas back. Go around the trees so I have you two in my line of sight."

That, she could do. The farther away she could get from the man, the better. "Okay."

She fumbled for Atlas's leash with her bad arm, ignoring the ache in her shoulder. Didn't want to chance letting go of his collar until she had the leash in hand. When she stood, she had to tug twice for Atlas to come with her, but he did.

They made it a couple of yards before she noticed Atlas was walking funny. She turned to look him over, bending to run her hands over his chest and shoulder.

"Oh no." She'd thought the blood splashed across his chest belonged to the man. But as she ran her hands through his fur, her fingers found a gouge in his flesh.

Sirens approached in the distance and two men came running from the main building. David's partners.

"What happened?" Forte skidded to a stop next to her and Atlas gave a warning growl. Rojas continued on past, toward David and the intruder.

"Easy," she murmured to Atlas. Not good if he went for one of the trainers. Not good. They needed them. "He needs help. He dove through the trees over there and must've gotten torn up on his way through."

"Seriously?" Forte started to kneel but halted and straightened as he took in the dog's posture. "Okay, Lyn, he's not going to make this easy. I need to talk you through this."

"What do I need to do?" Too much time was passing and Atlas was hurt.

"Kneel down and get your arms around him. Don't lift him. Don't hurt yourself. Just hold him. Talk to him. Let him know it's okay for me to take him from you. If you don't, he's not going to let me touch him."

It wasn't what she'd been expecting. But she didn't waste time waiting for an explanation. She squatted in the grass next to Atlas, murmuring soothing nonsense phrases as she did. His growl quieted but he didn't take his gaze off Forte. Copying what David had done the day before, she wrapped her arms around Atlas's chest and hindquarters. Her shoulder ached but she ignored it. Instead, she kept talking to Atlas, coaxing him to calm and listen to her.

When his posture relaxed, Forte kneeled next to them both, nice and slow.

"It's okay. He's going to help." She kissed Atlas's head, whispered against his fur. "Good boy. Good boy."

It wasn't what the dog was used to hearing, but his ears turned back in her direction. He was listening.

Forte got his arms around Atlas, keeping up a steady soothing monologue of his own. The dog remained still with the handoff, heavy panting the only sign of his distress.

"Let's get him to the main building. We've got a triage room." Forte's words were grim. "Grab the phone out of my back pocket. Vet's on speed dial."

Embarrassed, Lyn fumbled at his backside as he strode across the field. "Which...?"

"Left cheek, my friend. We're friends now, right?"

A laugh slipped out before she had too much time to think. One more fumble and unintentional grope and she had the phone. It was easy to find the vet on speed dial. She was in the top five favorites on the front screen and labeled as "Vet."

Easiest thing to do in the last twenty-four hours.

* * *

Cruz strode through the doors of the triage room they kept on site. Atlas lay on the table and Doc Medicci was shaving away the fur around a nasty slice across his shoulder.

Forte stood by, helping with the now calm dog.

And there was Lyn.

He zeroed in on her. "Is any of that blood yours?"

"I'm sorry," she whispered, her gaze locked on Atlas. "He went right through the trees and must've tore himself up on a branch. It didn't even slow him down."

"It's not the first time we've seen something like this." He was concerned. Of course he was. But the intensity and prey drive these dogs had resulted in accidents like these in the past. In this case, Atlas had moved to protect Lyn.

Currently, Cruz was fairly overwhelmed with the need to take care of her himself.

"Relatively superficial this time." Medicci didn't even glance up from her work. "I'm not finding any other damage. I'm going to put on a dissolving suture. Keep it clean and restrict him to light exercise until it heals. If it gets red or irritated, call me."

In short order, Atlas was back on his feet.

"Go get cleaned up, Lyn. He's fine now and you're swaying on your feet." Forte's tone was gentle, not angry.

Cruz caught Forte's attention and his friend gave him a brief nod.

"Let's go." Cruz reached out for Lyn and herded her toward the door, careful not to touch her.

Did she realize she was shaking?

"The man. He was the same from yesterday." Lyn's voice trembled. She took a breath and the rest came out in a rush. Atlas padded over and leaned against her leg. "He had a ski mask on but I recognized his grin. The way he looked at me. It was the same guy, I swear."

Cruz clenched his teeth against the wave of anger as it washed through him. He sucked in cooler air as he struggled to rein in his temper. He hadn't recognized the man, possibly because the man's expressions through the ski mask the night before and the grimace of pain he wore today when Cruz had gotten a good look at him were vastly different. But he could understand why Lyn had recognized the grin. And he wanted to wipe the guy from the face of the earth for putting that kind of fear into her with just one expression.

"I'll update the police." Forte's cool helped anchor

him. "You go on and wash up or Sophie will have all our heads for not showing up to dinner."

His heartbeat pounded in his ears, but he focused on Lyn. "They'll handle it for now. Let me take care of you."

Not going to think about his words too much. It was what he meant, so he said it.

The cabin he'd put her in late last night wasn't far. Its proximity to the main building and kennels was the reason he'd given it to her in the first place.

When she fumbled at her pockets for the key, he reached up behind the lamp fixture high above the door and pulled out the spare. Once he had the door open, he kept an eye on Atlas. The dog didn't signal that he detected any humans.

In fact, Atlas had simply walked along with Lyn calm as you please, as if he hadn't broken training and gone after a man not so long ago.

They entered the cabin and he flipped on the light, then nudged her toward the kitchen.

Once he had her there, he turned on the brighter kitchen lighting and turned to her. "Let me get a look at your wrist."

She held both hands out to him, palms up.

"Don't strain your shoulder." He tucked her left arm back in its sling. As gently as he could, he touched the angry red abrasion around her right wrist.

"He didn't mean to do it."

"He had other things on his mind." Cruz agreed. She must've tried to hold Atlas when the dog had lunged after the intruder. Atlas had literally ripped the leash off her wrist. "Any sharp pain when I do this?"

He bent her hand at the wrist, carefully testing the range of motion.

She shook her head. "I don't think anything is broken. Only lost a couple of layers of skin is all."

"Well, let's make sure it heals up quickly." He put a hand on either side of her waist and hoisted her up—hiding a grin as she squeaked—and sat her on the kitchen counter. First of all, he liked her sound effects. Wondered what others she might have. Second, she didn't flinch at his touch. A good sign she was recovering from the previous night's scare even better than she might notice herself.

Atlas gave a short bark.

"*Af.*" Cruz watched as the dog's ears came forward, considering. Then he lay down on his belly, head up, watching.

Dog definitely had a thing for Miss Lyn Jones. And wow had Atlas woken up. The difference between yesterday and right now was night and day.

Cruz shook his head.

"I'm sorry." Lyn shifted on the counter.

"No. Not you." He turned and pulled a go bag from under the sink. A quick rummage inside and he pulled out one of his personal med kits.

"What is that? How do you know where things are?" Lyn craned her neck to see around him. "Is every cabin stocked like this?"

"No." Setting the kit on the counter beside her, he opened it up and pulled out a few supplies.

"Then how do you know where everything is?"

"This was my cabin."

She paused. "Oh, um."

He waved a hand toward the rest of the cabin. "It was more secure, so I put you here and I moved out to the guest cabin closer to the edge of the property."

"But you had to move all your stuff?" She sounded uncomfortable.

"Not really. I don't keep much aside from essentials." He realized he was starting to scowl, but it wasn't because she was making him angry. Why was it that the woman could be attacked twice in less than twenty-four hours, hurt both times, and worried about him having to move his stuff? "It really is okay. I prefer to be farther away from the main house anyway. Too many guests on the property once the basic obedience classes get started."

"Okay." She was chewing on her lower lip, still concerned.

Saying more would only make her think on it harder so he decided to drop the topic. Nice to know she did care about putting others out of their way. He'd have done it regardless, all things considered. But it made it better to not be taken for granted.

"We're going to clean your wrist and get the blood flowing a little. Then I'll get some antibiotic ointment on it."

She didn't comment. Her dubious frown made him smile though.

"Trust me, I know what I'm doing."

"You're not going to tell me it's not going to hurt, are you?" She narrowed her eyes.

He shrugged. "It's not gonna tickle exactly."

"Joyful." She held out her wrist to him.

It took less time to clean her wrist under cool running water in the sink than it had to patch up Atlas. Her skin was delicate, smooth and silken to touch. If her wrist was this soft, he couldn't help but wonder about other, more tender places.

Nope. *Keep on task*, he ordered himself. He patted the area dry and spread the antibiotic cream over the abrasion as gently as he could.

"For such big hands, you've got a really light touch." Her words were slurred a little. She must've been coming down off the adrenaline kick. Considering last night and today, she had to be exhausted.

"Yeah?" He wrapped sterile gauze around her slender wrist, mostly to remind her not to bump it into things.

"Your fingertips are calloused, a lil' rough."

That didn't sound like a compliment. "Sorry."

"No, I like it. It feels kinda good on my skin."

Her heart rate had picked up, fluttering at the pulse point under his touch.

"Yeah?" The urge to slide has hands over more delicate areas increased and he couldn't help running his thumb along the inside of her arm.

Awareness grew in her gaze and she bit her lip as she nodded.

He leaned toward her, focused on her plump lip caught under her teeth.

"What else do you like?"

She opened her mouth to answer but he didn't plan to let her get a word out. Maybe later. He bent his head to capture her lips.

And seventy-five pounds of fur jumped up on his side.

"The hell?"

Lyn gasped. "Atlas!"

"*Af.*" Mindful of the dog's injury, Cruz gave Atlas a gentle shove.

The dog dropped back to all fours, his tongue lolling. Looking from him to Lyn and back again, Atlas lay back down on his belly.

Jealous. Damn dog was jealous.

CHAPTER FOUR

"Rest. Relax. For how long?" Lyn sat on the couch in the main area of the cabin, tapping her fingers on the windowsill. It wasn't as if she'd broken anything.

David had left only a few minutes ago. And to his credit, he'd mentioned something about lunch as he'd left.

It was already past mid-morning so unless he planned to starve her, lunch couldn't be too far off.

Patience had never been one of her virtues, though.

"At least he left you with me." She turned away from the windowsill and studied Atlas.

The dog lay stretched out on the floor with his head on his paws, as close to her perch on the couch as possible. He'd opened his eyes and lifted his big ears in her direction at her movement.

"You are my job, after all." She continued to consider him.

His attitude really had changed overnight. The look in

his eyes was still somewhat reserved in her opinion, but he was more obvious about listening to her. Not as aloof or disinterested as yesterday, or first thing in the morning, for that manner.

Good signs, all of them.

David was a good dog trainer. She had no doubts after having seen him greet the other dogs at the kennel. Every one of the dogs in the care of Hope's Crossing Kennels jumped to their feet at his approach, eager for a word from him or the chance to work. His body language was always relaxed, confident. He moved with the kind of easy readiness—potential for explosive action in every muscle—that commanded respect. The dogs were sensitive to it, acknowledged him as a dominant in the territory. With him, there was no question as to who was in charge.

"But you need more than clear leadership," she murmured to Atlas. He blinked and blew a huff of air out of his nose.

She held out her hand in a loose fist, the back of her hand toward him. He considered for a long minute before lifting his head and extending his nose. One sniff. Then he returned to resting on his paws again, looking away from her. Not interested in more than acknowledging her.

"It's good to have this time to get to know you." She always talked to dogs when they were relaxing. If she'd been working with him instead of enjoying quiet time— and there was a difference—she'd give him clear and concise commands instead of conversational commentary. Even eager-to-please dogs still needed to understand what it was a human wanted them to do and they didn't precisely speak human. They learned to recognize short commands combined with body language. Any human could speak a command, in any language, and it'd still take a dog a minute to really understand what the human wanted unless the human copied a known trainer exactly in words, tone, and gestures. Then the dog probably made an educated guess.

"You're smart enough to know what we all want from you," she murmured. "But obedience and working aren't what you want to do right now, are they? You've lost your heart."

She didn't blame him. Being heartbroken was something she could understand.

"I've never had my heart broken by a boyfriend, mind you." She leaned her head back against the couch's arm rest. Confiding in dogs was one of the most secure ways of getting something off her chest. And opening herself up to them gained their trust in return, every time. "I think human hearts break, too, when the people we live for disappoint us. Like our parents. I have trust issues."

Of course, if David was to walk in, he'd probably think he was interrupting a therapy session. Only she was the one on the couch talking about her emotional baggage while Atlas was the shrink listening.

There was a method to what she was doing, though. Atlas was getting used to the cadence and tone of her voice. Her scent surrounded him in this room. And every movement she made was being cataloged in a library in his mind associated to her. The introduction process was a long one, and the more time the dog had to interact with her, the more comfortable he'd be because he'd know what she was likely to do.

Her phone rang, the tone bringing her bolt upright in her seat. Atlas was on his feet beside her, his entire body tense and his ears forward at alert. A low growl rumbled from his chest.

"Sorry, Atlas. Easy." She took a deep breath, calming herself so the dog would take her cue and go back to resting.

Damn it. As much as she hated the distinctive ringtone—or rather, the caller it was assigned to—she figured she better answer it before the caller decided to blow up her phone again.

"Hello, Captain Jones." Neutral. She was going for a nice, civil exchange.

A pause. "I have repeatedly instructed you to call me 'Father.'" The voice on the other end was surly.

Make no mistake, his feelings weren't hurt. In her twenty-eight years of experience, he'd gone around in a perpetual state of dissatisfaction with the world. Well, at least twenty-five. Theoretically, the first few years of her life hadn't been formative in terms of actual memories. Her mother had married him when she'd been just a toddler.

Instead of arguing the point, she decided to go for pleasantries. "I hope you've been well. Is there a reason you're calling?"

"Don't try to sidetrack me, miss. Each time you insist on your lack of respect for familial ties, it becomes more of a habit. One of these days you're going to do it in front of admiralty and the reflection on me will be absolutely inappropriate. I will not have it." His words came low and fast, as they always did whether they were speaking face to face or over the phone. Given the choice, she preferred the distance. Then she could pretend the admonishments didn't give her cold chills anymore. The impact of his intense, quiet speeches was worse for her than all the screaming in the world.

"You're one promotion away from Rear Admiral." She commended herself for a cool, even delivery there. "Surely your service record outweighs the impact of a few words from me."

Besides, he hadn't ever let her call him "Daddy" or "Dad," and not "Papa," ever. Not what had come naturally to her as a child. It'd always been "Father" for as long as she could remember. Proper. Formal. And pronounced properly as soon as humanly possible.

"It's amazing you ever graduated from college." His words dripped with disgust. *Oh, what a surprise.* "Even basic classes and interaction with professors should have demonstrated that perception is a distinct advantage in every situation. Never underestimate it."

What will people think? echoed through her childhood. "Of course. I do remember those lessons from you."

"Then apply what you learned." A command, not a request. With him it was never a request.

She waited. He'd called her and she'd asked why. He could either continue to rant or actually get to the reason for this contact in the first place.

"I was informed you experienced an attack." Was that a note of discomfort? Surely not.

"There was an incident at my hotel last night. I gave a detailed report to the police." She waited to see where this was going.

There was an intake of breath. "Did you see your attackers well enough to identify them?"

A leering grin flashed across her mind's eye. Her heart kicked hard in her chest and she swallowed the sudden taste of bile. Atlas was on his feet in front of her, pulling her focus with a somber stare.

She was safe. Atlas had made sure of it.

Regaining her composure, she stood and tried to walk off the residual nerves as she answered, "Not last night."

Maybe her stepfather was concerned? Hard to tell with him, but there was always room for surprise in the day.

"No? It would have been useful if you could give a sketch artist something to work with."

Ah. Of course. How easy it was to find a shortcoming. "The man I saw was wearing a ski mask. The other attacker came from behind and I never saw him."

This was her stepfather's chance to express concern. Two attackers. Didn't he wonder how she'd come through in one piece?

"As your point of escalation on your current contract, I was notified about the encounter and your physical status but not given the details of the sequence of events." He paused. "I assume you were able to trigger an alarm of some sort to call for aid."

Actually, no. And if Cruz hadn't arrived when he had, she wouldn't have been able to. Something she was going to fix, and soon. Maybe one of those tiny, super loud air horns to carry in her purse. "Not quite, but help was close by and the police were called as soon as possible."

She was reluctant to mention Cruz saving her. It wasn't that she wasn't thankful. She was. But the idea of admitting to her stepfather that she'd needed rescuing stuck in her throat. She should have been more aware of her surroundings, should've been able to guard herself better. The nature of her job had her traveling alone most of the time and right now the idea of staying in a hotel gave her more than a moment's hesitation. Suddenly cold, she shuddered.

"You've changed to a hotel with better security?" It was more of a statement than a question. Another assumption.

He made those a lot. And basically considered you an imbecile if you hadn't done what he considered the most logical, best, or expedient thing to do.

This time, she was fairly certain he would be surprised but not disappointed. "Not a hotel. I've moved into guest accommodations directly on Hope's Crossing Kennels property."

Silence. Then, "Is staying on the premises a common practice when you are consulting?"

Oh no, judgment could stop right there. "With private clients, of course not. However, this is a professional kennel facility and it makes absolute sense to be as near Atlas as possible while I work with him. It maximizes my access to him and the increased exposure could potentially speed his recovery."

There, refute that *line of reasoning.*

"Indeed." Another pause. "And security is sufficient on the premises?"

Was he actually concerned for her safety? She checked her incredulity. She was getting petty and letting it go was still a work in progress. Recent years working on her own had helped her maturity in dealing with him but this contract and the sudden uptick in conversations dragged up too many old habits. It was time to think more constructively. "Security here is better than most hotels. Gated entrance, video surveillance, and dogs with various levels of advanced training." She paused. It seemed thorough to her so she considered what else might be useful information to provide before he needed to prompt her again. "One of them has been caught."

"How?" His voice turned sharp.

Puzzled, she answered, "He showed up here at the kennels while I was working with Atlas this morning. Atlas apprehended him."

And she was incredibly proud of Atlas. She paused in her slow pacing around the room and turned to give the dog a soft smile. He was still in front of the couch, sitting now.

"Ah." Her stepfather cleared his throat. "I wasn't aware. It's not likely you were targeted at random at the hotel, then. Do the police know why this man seems to have targeted you specifically?"

"That's a good point." It galled her to acknowledge it because any time he had one it was an assumption he was right about all things, in perpetuity. "The police took him into custody. I haven't heard anything more."

Silence.

"I guess you were only notified about last night's incident so far?" She was walking out on thin ice and at any minute it was going to crack under her feet.

She didn't want to think about the attack last night or the man showing up this morning. But there was a reason he'd come after her and there was another man still out there. It might be more trouble for Hope's Crossing Kennels and she didn't want to repay their generosity in letting her stay with the danger. Uneasy, she started to pace again. Maybe she should discuss this with David.

"I'm sure I'll be notified shortly. I'll also take steps to ensure there isn't a delay in this kind of update in the future." So matter of fact.

If he only said it was because he cared, it'd make all the difference. Instead, he made it sound like he was just making sure he could call in expedient damage control in case she managed to embarrass him. She used to think he was planning a political career the way he worried so much about appearances. But the two of them had never been on the same page, so neither understood the other's aspirations.

She'd given up trying to share a long time ago.

"You were the one who wanted to be involved in this particular military case." He had to bring it up. "There are quite a few eyes on the dog. He's been prominent in the news and other media outlets."

Of course. "I'm making good progress for having only recently met Atlas."

"Good. I expect personal status reports." Crisp. Maybe even cheerful? For him.

There was quite the range of moods from him today. She couldn't remember the last time she'd been on the phone with him for this long.

"Via e-mail?" she asked hopefully. *Please*. E-mail would be so much less awkward than phone calls.

"Secure e-mail correspondence with me, always. Use the encryption program I sent you." He sounded distracted now. Already done with her and on to the next thing.

Actually, she was relieved. It'd been a weird conversation. "No problem."

Still, she was surprised he was interested enough in Atlas and her work to request actual status reports. Of course, this was the first time her line of work had overlapped with anything remotely related to his, and as the main holder of her contract she supposed it did reflect directly on him.

"I'll send you some background on this kennel and the man working with you on the dog."

She blinked. "I'd planned to research both the kennel and the people I'm working with already."

"The research should have been done in advance, but you wouldn't have the resources to access much more than names and public record." He made it sound so dismissive.

Well, she wasn't a private investigator and as a civilian, she was limited to what a good Internet search could find for her. He had another point. She was never going to be someone to spite herself by turning down valuable information just because of where it came from.

"Background information would be helpful." There. As close to a thank-you as she was going to manage through gritted teeth.

"Remember. Your performance reflects on me and that dog is a military asset. Conduct yourself professionally." His admonishment sparked her temper again. "The man you're working with is former military. Don't let him run over you on this case. Men like him are still military even after they've left active duty. Arrogant sons of bitches. Do not let him take credit for our family's work."

Hello, pot, calling kettle black.

And there was no way her stepfather could know about the...almost moment between her and David. Something she hadn't had a chance to think about, but she should. Until she did, though, her stepfather needed to recognize this project included real souls. Not just assets listed on a report. "That dog's name is Atlas. And I am always professional. I'm very good at what I do."

Damn. Too much. She shouldn't have taken the bait. Shouldn't have gotten defensive about her abilities.

"We'll see." He ended the call.

Of course. He always had the last word. And damn, but it'd left her reaching for a comeback again. Too slow. Flustered. He'd won that round.

She tapped her foot, restless. Atlas hadn't budged from his spot over by the couch, but he was sitting up and watching her. Another good sign. Even if he wanted to maintain a little detachment, he was tuned in to what she was doing and what her moods were. Engaged. Very positive considering yesterday he'd been completely disinterested in life in general and people specifically.

No harm in continuing a bit of therapeutic venting in Atlas's direction. Dogs were excellent listeners. "I lived and breathed to please my stepfather when I was a kid. He was never home. The few times he came back, I wanted to show him everything I'd done while he was gone. How good I'd been. And somehow I got it into my head that if I could just do well enough in school, win enough awards, excel at sports, then he'd come home to stay. Every time he left again, it broke my heart." Her eyes grew hot and she blinked against dryness. The tears had long since burned away when it came to this set of memories. "When he finally sat me down and informed me how very little I mattered in the bigger picture of his career and his life with my mother, my heart was in pieces on the floor. I was extra baggage. Someone else's genetic contribution to the continuation of the human race. And out of honor, he'd see to it I had the basics to grow up and contribute to society. That was it."

She huffed out a soft laugh. Atlas gave her one of those doggy raised eyebrow looks.

"By the time I realized I had nothing to do with his decisions, I thought I hated him. Really. It took a long time to realize no matter how mad I was at him, how much I said I didn't care, I was waiting for the one time he'd say I'd proved him wrong or made him proud." She chewed on her lip. It'd been a bitter taste, admitting it to herself. "He's not a bad man. His priorities are different from...basically the rest of the warm-blooded, caring portion of this world."

Atlas settled back down on his belly, his head raised as he continued to listen to her.

She stepped toward him and crouched down to sit back on her heels within arm's reach of him. "We're all assets to him. We each go in one of two buckets: useful or useless. And to be honest, even if I built my career on my own and in spite of his doubts, I still want to prove to him I'm not useless."

She sighed. And Atlas sighed too.

"I want to say it's not a primary driver." Studying the beautiful contrast of black in the tan of Atlas's face, calm settled over her. "And it's not. I came here for you and your story. Just reading what happened, I wanted to get to know you. And now that I've met you, I want to see you happy again."

Because broken hearts could heal. It wasn't a whimsical child's refuge, it was her very real belief and she wanted it for Atlas.

CHAPTER FIVE

Cruz hesitated at the door to his cabin, now guest quarters. Atlas hadn't sounded any kind of alarm at his approach, but then the dog knew his step. If there was a window open somewhere, the dog might have caught his scent, too. Also familiar. It would've been confirmation: someone who belonged was on his way and not a stranger.

He shouldn't be disappointed Atlas hadn't given a warning bark on the approach of a known human.

But Atlas was waking up from the pining he'd been doing. Engaging with the world and people again. Maybe it was unfair to expect leaving him with Lyn Jones for an hour or two would trigger a full transformation in the dog, but Cruz had kinda hoped it'd be that easy—for Atlas's sake, and so they could make more progress in tracking down the mystery of his old friend's cryptic message.

Atlas's handler, Calhoun, had sent a random text to

Cruz in the middle of the night a while back. It hadn't made any sense. Cruz had assumed it'd been a drunk text, honestly. Then Calhoun died. As far as Cruz was concerned, the message and the tragedy were connected in a bad way, no matter what the official report said. Cruz needed Atlas to puzzle out Calhoun's message and his old friend deserved having his last request fulfilled.

One step at a time. He'd see how things had progressed with Lyn and Atlas first, then figure out his next actions. Considering how he'd left Lyn, there was a spark he needed to follow up on there, too.

Juggling the packages he carried into his left hand, he freed up the other to give a quick knock. Lyn's soft acknowledgment came from inside, not directly on the other side of the door but definitely in the main room. He let himself in.

"Brought some choices for lunch." Stepping inside, he noticed the guest cabin was mostly dark. The only light was streaming in from the windows. Plenty to see by, but a relief from the midday sun beating down outside.

"Smells good." Lyn had been...sitting? She rose from the middle of the floor and Atlas came to stand on all four feet as she did it.

Funny.

"I've got a couple of choices from our favorite sub shop. Cheesesteak or meatball parm. Which would you like?"

Her eyes widened.

Shit. Maybe she didn't like either option.

"Are you a vegetarian?" He probably should've asked before they'd made the lunch run but he'd been in a hurry to tuck her away someplace safe and get back to the police who'd responded to the call this morning.

She blinked and placed her hand on her belly. "No. I was just hoping you hadn't heard my stomach growl when the word 'cheesesteak' came out of your mouth. I'm starving."

Good. Otherwise, he would've been making a second run out for food because he sure as hell wasn't going to let her go hungry as a result of his lapse in thought. Generally, he tried to be considerate and shit. With this woman, though, he was constantly off his game.

Atlas stood in the middle of the living area watching him, expression and body language decidedly neutral.

Well, the pair of them had him off balance. Cruz might have a chance to regain it if they could avoid an encounter requiring police follow-up for more than twenty-four hours. All things considered, anyone would be a little unhinged.

He headed for the small kitchen table in the breakfast area. "Let's not keep you waiting anymore."

Pulling the foil-wrapped subs out of the bag, he placed the cheesesteak in front of her and took the meatball parmesan for himself. Plenty of napkins went in a pile in the middle of the table. Added bonus, he flipped open a carton containing French fries drowning in melted cheese.

Lyn pulled out a chair and glanced back at Atlas mid-motion. The dog's ears swiveled forward. Cruz bit back his first impulse comment and waited to see what she did.

She gave a slight shake of her head. "Atlas, *auf*."

The dog hesitated and then lay down on his belly, head still up.

"*Blijf.*" She gave the dog a long look and then turned, seating herself.

Atlas watched her back and glanced at Cruz. Then the big dog set his head between his paws, turned away from the table as if he hadn't wanted any people food anyway.

Cruz approved. No way was he going to feed any dog in their care this kind of junk food. And yes, he saw the irony. But the dogs at Hope's Crossing Kennels were fed balanced meals based on their weight and level of activity. Cheesy, greasy, bombs of comfort food were not figured into their dietary plans.

She glanced up to meet Cruz's gaze. "I did some research into the command you taught me earlier. Most of my clients have their dogs trained to respond to English commands but Atlas and I have been figuring out how to work with the Dutch vocabulary he recognizes."

He'd planned to work with her and Atlas on that after lunch. On one hand, her initiative was on point and he approved. On the other, he was inexplicably irritated at the implied censure in her tone. As if he'd meant to keep her communication with Atlas limited or been testing her. She was probably fishing to see if he'd been doing just that but he wasn't going to take the bait and respond.

Whatever passive–aggressive crap she was anticipating, he didn't play those games. So he remained silent and kept his expression neutral, continuing to set out their lunch.

"I'm not going to lie; I'm really interested in trying this." Lyn quit staring at him and unwrapped the cheesesteak. "I've never had a real Philly cheesesteak anywhere near Philadelphia."

Cruz raised an eyebrow. "Your work doesn't bring you to Pennsylvania very often?"

She shook her head. "I'm mostly on the West Coast. Seattle, Portland, several cities in California."

She had the sandwich up and had turned her head to the side, trying to fit the entire end in her mouth. As long as they were being honest, Cruz really enjoyed watching her try. How much a lady could fit into her mouth was always an interesting question.

And he was definitely going to hell for that thought.

Then her eyes shuttered closed as she had her first bite and chewed. "Mmm."

His pants suddenly got a hell of a lot tighter. "Good?"

"Oh yeah." She chewed some more, savoring. "That is really good."

"Have some cheese fries." He pushed the carton over to her and got up to get them each a glass of water. She looked like she was about to inhale the cheesesteak and he wanted to be sure she had something to wash it all down before she choked.

He also needed time to get his stupid grin under control because watching her enjoy a simple sandwich was incredibly entertaining. In all sorts of ways.

"What kind of cheese is this?" Lyn asked. He glanced back to see her studying the end of a coated fry before popping it into her mouth.

Bad, bad pictures flashed through his head. *Jesus*.

"Cheez Whiz." Not his favorite, but then Rojas had been the one to actually go for the food. "It's one of the favorites on-site."

"One of?" she asked even as she took another bite.

Even eating messy, she was cute. Hot. Both.

He returned to the table with glasses of water and sat down again. "Everyone has their taste. I like my cheesesteaks better with real provolone."

"Hmm." Another bite and a very thoughtful look of concentration as she pondered. "It wouldn't go over the fries as easily."

He nodded. "True. I still like the fries better with Cheez Whiz."

She sighed, studying her now half a sandwich. "It's too bad this is so very *bad* for us."

"Doesn't hurt to enjoy once in a while." Life could be short. Painfully so. Living for the moment helped. This was fun, much improved from her indirect attitude earlier. "If you like it that much, we'll have to make sure to take you into Philly and have you order your own at one of the classic places for them."

She chewed some more, swallowed, and took a sip of water. "Aren't the best places Pat's and Geno's?"

He shrugged. "Probably the ones you hear about most often. There's Jim's on South Street too. A lot of places in Philly do a good cheesesteak. I like Tony Luke's on Oregon Ave."

The cheesesteak in her hands had more of her attention than his words did. No issue there. He liked a woman with her priorities straight.

There was a lot to like about Lyn Jones from what he'd seen over the last day, and he'd rather focus on the positive. The way she could enjoy a good sandwich every bit as much as a swanky meal in an expensive establishment was high up on his list of good things about her so far.

"You think Atlas would do well on a socialization

walk through the city?" She was back to the fries and looking at him with a clear, crystal green gaze. He decided not to tell her she had cheese on the corner of her mouth, or that he wanted to kiss it off.

"Maybe not today, but not out of the question later this week if he keeps improving." He glanced at the dog, who was steadfast in trying to ignore them. Normally he didn't eat in front of the dogs. No need to tease them with what they couldn't have. But it didn't hurt their training to have temptation around them sometimes. "I was thinking maybe I'd take you out to dinner and give him the night off."

She swallowed. Hard. "Dinner. Like a date?"

Ah. Maybe not. "That was the idea. Maybe I read things wrong but I thought we had a moment back there."

"Oh." Her fair cheeks flushed pink. "No. Yes. We did. I just..."

"It's okay if you'd prefer not." He schooled his expression to carefully neutral. She was important to helping Atlas and he didn't want her to feel uncomfortable working with him just because he'd asked her on a date. Dumb idea anyway.

She bit her lower lip but had the grace to look him directly in the eye. "You're a very nice man, David. And I can't thank you enough..."

He held up his hand. "No need to thank me."

He'd slam his own head into a wall before letting her accept a date with him as a thank-you for what any decent person should've done for her. Interested in her? Yes. But everything in him rebelled at the idea of pressuring her. He liked his women willing and he didn't exactly have a problem finding them. This just needed to quit being so damned uncomfortable.

"I'd like to keep things at the professional coworker level... and friends. Is that okay?"

How could he say no? He wasn't an absolute dick. And besides which, his priority was Atlas. The dog needed for them to work well together and David wasn't about to let his hormones screw anything up.

"We're good." He gave her what he hoped was a reassuring smile. "Totally professional and no hard feelings."

She let out the breath she'd been holding and gave him a small, unsure smile.

He pushed the fries closer to her and handed her a napkin. "Have another fry. You'll need the energy this afternoon working with our friend here."

* * *

"Agility?" Lyn studied the course. It wasn't the standard agility course she was used to seeing but rather a more rugged course. There were items specific to K9 training like the broad jump, catwalk, and brick wall jump. The Catch-A frame was completely new to her. The car door jump and window jump were actually painted in more realistic colors as opposed to the standard white. The equipment was familiar to her but not part of her usual clientele's goals.

David took the lead off Atlas. "He can do all of it. Easily. The question is whether he wants to."

She nodded. A dog learned exponentially faster with internal drive. Incentive could help too, but a trainer learned to align training with the natural drive of the dog for the best results. Which meant finding a situation in which the dog wanted to perform a particular action.

At the moment, Atlas was sitting next to David and not even looking at the agility course. Not interested.

"What're we using for incentive?" She'd used treats usually for clients, but the K9 and military trainers didn't always have the same practices.

David pulled a tennis ball from his pocket. Atlas watched the slow arch of the ball as it crossed the distance between them. Lyn was happy she caught it. It would've been insanely embarrassing if she'd dropped it considering how much time David had given her to catch it.

"He gets this after completing each exercise." David lifted his chin toward the ball in her hands. "Then we'll see if we can get him to do the whole course for the ball."

She raised her eyebrows. "That's assuming a very fast learning curve."

He shrugged. "This is all review for him. He used to run a course like this for the sheer joy of doing it. If we get him back into a mood to do it at all, I don't think it'll take long for him to demonstrate how easy this is for him."

She laughed. Atlas did seem to have his fair share of pride. "Okay."

"Walk to each obstacle and give the command. Let's take them one at a time and see how much he needs to obey."

"Obedience." She frowned. "We haven't confirmed he's consistently obedient yet."

Only a few commands this morning and during lunch. Every time, she'd seen the pause, the consideration, as Atlas had *decided* whether he wanted to obey.

"He's still got solid obedience." David spoke with utter confidence, almost irritating. "There's a delay but he doesn't ignore commands. He just doesn't care enough to execute immediately."

She frowned. The delay in behavior might not be a big deal in the civilian world. Some regular owners might not even think twice about the delay even if it became a habit. But... he could be testing her. "The delay isn't acceptable for military work."

David shook his head, no hint of whether he'd been leading her to saying so or not. Just responding. "Not at all. But then, at his age, he might not be redeployed at this point. It really depends on how well he comes through this."

So cold. Matter of fact. She kind of hated David a little bit for the way he casually talked about Atlas like that. As if it was all about practicality and not about an injured soul.

Her heart ached for Atlas. Part of her wanted to cut him slack, let him have the leeway in his training to ensure he'd be allowed to retire and enjoy life here. But Atlas was a working dog. He might not be happy no longer working. It had to be up to him. Find his balance again and working might be what he lived for.

"You do basic obedience with every dog here, right?" Seemed as if she'd seen the other trainers working with various dogs. Both Alex Rojas and Brandon Forte had been out with various dogs all morning.

"We make sure every working dog here trains for

thirty minutes in obedience every day. Then they spend time in their specialization." Still brisk and all business, David pointed toward the kennels. "Any puppies Rojas breeds are also taught basic obedience as a package deal with the buyers. We use the time in the basic obedience classes to confirm the new owners are a good fit for our dogs."

Good practice, assessing the owners to be sure they could handle the dogs they were purchasing. The trainers were less likely to lose track of a puppy somebody might decide to abandon. Too many people purchased a dog, invested in training, then dropped it in a shelter rather than admit to the breeder they'd decided they didn't want the dog anymore.

Perhaps she was reading too much into his tone. He was being practical but maybe he wasn't uncaring. She realized she was biased because of her dealings with her stepfather, looking for callousness in David. But David had been very generous with answering questions. Especially considering she'd turned him down earlier, he could've taken a completely different tack. She appreciated his willingness to really work with her.

"How many of your puppies go to private homes?" She'd thought they specialized in working dogs.

David studied Atlas. "Not every dog is suited for military or K9 work. We start assessing temperament right away and do our best to find good homes for the puppies not suited for working. They start training early and we watch them for the right combination of prey drive, aggression, intelligence . . . all of the traits necessary for them to be successful."

"And those same traits make them difficult home

pets." High aggression and intelligence made for destroyed homes when those same dogs became agitated in a high-density neighborhood or got bored while owners were away at work or even on short errands. It was amazing what level of destruction a single dog could do in the wrong environment.

David's grin drew an answering grin from her. It was ridiculous how much of a difference his expression made from his previous attitude and how happy she was for them to be on the same page when it came to training. She'd butted heads with other trainers in the past and the experience had been frustrating. She'd really thought he would be another one of those when she'd first met him. This—and seeing him with Atlas—was proving her wrong in the best of ways.

It'd been the right decision not to go out to dinner with him. This level of professionalism was something much better, even if he was also one of the most distractingly attractive men she'd ever worked with.

"Well, I might not have the same commands you'd use." She figured it would be best to clarify before she confused Atlas. "I did look up the basic Dutch commands but I need to do more studying."

David swept his arm out toward the course. "Let's give it a try and take those spots where we run into them. I can give you the correct command if Atlas is looking like he's up for the course."

Good point. First step: see if the dog was actually willing. This entire exercise could end quickly if he only walked up to the first obstacle and sat there.

"All right. Let's give this a try."

CHAPTER SIX

Please tell me you're not going to keep her here on a gorgeous Saturday while the rest of you all pretend it's just another day of the week."

Lyn looked up at the speaker, an extremely attractive Asian woman with way more energy than anyone ought to have at 0500 on a Saturday morning. Seriously, the woman literally exuded vitality.

"Sophie, we are holding no one hostage." From his position behind the breakfast counter in the communal kitchen, Brandon poured a new cup of coffee. He added cream and sugar then held it out to her.

He was going to give her caffeine? Seemed like a questionable choice.

Lyn wasn't a morning person by nature. Most of her clients preferred to meet at reasonable times in the morning, like nine or ten. However, Hope's Crossing Kennels had a much more active routine than the average home owner. The trainers were up and beginning morning chores by 0500, as they put it. The early morning was filled with feeding, then basic obedience for the working canines and the boarded guest dogs. Later in the morning, people would begin arriving for obedience and agility classes with Alex while Brandon and David took the working canines through specialized training. The afternoon went along the same lines, with various dogs getting individualized attention. Evening saw people arriving for more classes into the night.

The trainers of Hope's Crossing Kennels easily worked sixteen-hour days, with long breaks in the slow times of the afternoon to balance out their long hours.

Lyn's involvement was solely regarding Atlas but she sure as hell wasn't going to sleep in when David was up and getting started with the freaking dawn. What she hadn't anticipated was how ragged she'd feel once the weekend hit and they were all still getting started right on time.

One never appreciated sleeping in on the weekends until one couldn't. It'd been especially hard to climb out from under the comforters this morning. The guest bed was warm, cozy and comfortable. David's bed.

Lyn took another sip of her own coffee. No good could come of her brain being allowed to continue half-asleep at this moment.

"You all may continue with your routine," Sophie was saying, coffee mug in hand and a stolen piece of bacon in the other. "But your guest here might not know there are options for her. Like actually leaving kennel grounds and enjoying a day off."

"We take days off." Alex sat at the table across from

Lyn and gave her a grin. She lifted her mug in acknowledgment.

Sophie scowled in his general direction.

David slid a plate of eggs sunny side up and bacon in front of Lyn and her attention snapped to the wonderful smell of breakfast. She lifted her fork. "Thank you."

"No problem." David was already digging into his own plate of food.

He'd been incredibly considerate through the entire week. Breakfast was always like this at the kennel. They ate together, went through the day's schedule and any potential issues. Lyn was included as a contributing member. Maybe not one of the inner circle, but a part of a team. It was refreshing, interesting, as compared with the solo work she usually did in her training and consulting business.

"The least you could all do is introduce us properly." Sophie had a plate of breakfast by now and she seated herself.

Brandon sat next to her, absently passing a plate of iced breakfast rolls over to Lyn before offering it to Sophie, too. They smelled heavenly and Lyn immediately bit deep into golden, pillowy goodness. When blueberries burst across her tongue, complemented by the vanilla lemon icing, Lyn closed her eyes to focus every fiber of her being on enjoying the flavors.

Alex chuckled. "Pretty sure Lyn's going to be your friend forever if you keep bringing baked goods on your visits while she's here. And you know who Lyn is because as soon as you noticed we had a guest you followed Brandon around until he told you. Not sure any other introductions are needed."

Lyn finished chewing and swallowed, coming up for air before taking another bite of happiness. They all accepted the other woman with an easy air of long acquaintance. She was like a little sister, running around bugging her big brothers for attention. Brandon glanced at Sophie as she reached over him for salt and quickly stuffed his own breakfast roll in his mouth.

Well, mostly big brothers. There was something else going on there but it wasn't Lyn's thing to get into the middle of those situations.

"Lyn, it's a pleasure to officially meet you." Sophie extended her hand across the table. "I'm Sophie and I do the accounting for the kennels."

"She also keeps giving us all reason to keep up our cardio, otherwise her baking would make us fat." Despite his commentary, Alex helped himself to another sweet roll.

Lyn quickly wiped her hands on her napkin and reached out her right hand to accept the handshake. "You made these? They're incredible."

"It's a hobby." Sophie's slender hand caught hers in a firm grip.

Nice. Lyn hated limp handshakes.

Sophie gave her a friendly smile. The sort of open, genuine smile Lyn couldn't help but return. "I was going to do a little shopping in New Hope today. Why don't you join me?"

"Oh." Lyn glanced at David. "I don't want to miss any work with Atlas."

"Today's his rest day. No plans besides easy exercise time and relaxing with him." David didn't look up from his plate. "You can always spend time with him after you get back."

The week had been interesting, learning how to take Atlas through the various specialized training. They'd only covered agility and scent training this week, with one session on bite work. David had asked a friend from the local police force to come and wear the big protective suit when they'd done the bite work.

It'd been frightening and fascinating to see Atlas spring into action. She'd worked with K9s in the past but Atlas, as an Air Force military working dog, was on a different level. His aggression was higher if at all possible, and his speed was heart stopping. Plus, there'd been a distinct difference between biting to apprehend the way K9s did and biting to kill the way a military working dog needed to.

"Can we speak privately for a minute?" She put her fork and knife on her plate. "So we're on the same page about Atlas."

David didn't respond but pushed his chair back and rose.

In minutes, they were down the hall in his office. She still couldn't stop blushing when she looked at the door. Eavesdropping hadn't been the greatest moment of her life.

"Is this because of yesterday's bite work session?" She wasn't going to waste time circling the question.

David met her gaze directly. "What is this? And why do you think it is?"

"I was surprised by the directive to bite to kill." She'd been transparent about it because it seemed to be the way they worked best together. "I've appreciated the way we've been able to work together up to yesterday but it seemed like yesterday's session broke something."

Silence. Then David sighed and dragged a hand through his hair. The gesture only made her want to run her own fingers through.

"It was a reminder about how different civilian dog behavior is from what we need Atlas to be for military work." David didn't sound happy about admitting it. "And your anxiety can transfer to the dog. Atlas needs to be able to do those things without hesitation."

Atlas hadn't seemed to hesitate or consider at all the day before. In fact, Lyn had been elated because his response had been the best she'd seen all week. "There was no delay in Atlas obeying any command yesterday."

"No," David agreed. "Not a fraction of a second of hesitation. He was almost too eager to kill something threatening you."

Lyn blinked. Closed her mouth on what she'd been about to say.

"You were nervous. He responded to protect you with deadly force." David shoved his hands into his pockets. "It's excellent in terms of his engagement and the progress you're making with him. It was almost dangerous for my friend while you weren't used to controlling what Atlas could do."

True. The protective suit was more than sufficient in most cases but if a dog really wanted to kill the man inside, it could eventually happen.

"I figured a day off from the more intense training would be good for both of you." David brought her attention back to him by tapping a finger on the big calendar he had on his desk. "You can come back later today and spend some quiet time walking the grounds but let's give him some time to unwind and you some time to get more comfortable with his capabilities."

"Okay." She hesitated. "I thought you might..."

"You're doing great." He cut her off before she could voice the self-doubt. It was one of the only times he did interrupt her. "Seriously, we couldn't have made this much progress with Atlas without you."

"We're doing great," she countered, happiness filling her as he smiled at her assertion. "I couldn't do this without your expertise either."

"So go take a day and hang out with Sophie. New Hope's a nice town to walk around."

She gave him a bright smile and walked out of the office. The idea of a day out to clear her head and be around another woman was suddenly a fantastic change of pace.

Sophie was still in the kitchen with Brandon and Alex, chatting about the various dogs. When Lyn re-entered, Sophie stopped. "So. Conference complete. Are you allowed to come out to play or do you still have homework to do?"

"My schedule looks open for the day." Lyn snagged an extra piece of bacon from the plate on the breakfast counter. "But I'm looking for a more adult kind of fun day."

Brandon choked on his coffee.

Alex cracked up laughing.

David stopped in his tracks behind her.

Lyn kept her gaze on Sophie, refusing to look back to see David's expression.

Sophie's smile broadened into a crazy grin. "Oh, New Hope is the *perfect* place. Wear comfortable shoes."

*   *   *

"That tea set was amazing. Why didn't you buy it?" Lyn asked as they waited to be seated.

"No place to display it right now." Sophie sighed. "I love tea sets and I've got an everyday set at home to use, but a set like that one? It needs to be displayed and used. Too gorgeous to tuck away in a cabinet."

"That wasn't the first time you've gone to look at it, either." The shop owner had recognized Sophie.

Sophie grinned. "The goldfish set is my favorite, but I always stop in to see the new pieces she has on display. The designer has a catalog and comes out with new themed pieces every year. The new Phoenician bird design is incredible. Oh, and there's this older ladybug themed set of teapot, cups, and platter."

The way Sophie chattered on about tea sets and good afternoon tea services made Lyn's stomach growl.

Sophie laughed. "We'll have to go someplace for afternoon tea sometime, or maybe I'll put together one at the kennels and Boom can join us."

"Sounds good to me, especially if you're baking again." Lyn hoped she'd be around long enough, but then, her project with Atlas was open-ended based on his progress, so it was a possibility.

"Question for now is, what will you have here?"

"You haven't led me wrong yet today." Lyn settled into the seat and set her shopping bags at the side of the little table. "What do I absolutely have to try?"

Sophie had been a fantastic shopping companion for the morning, whisking Lyn off to New Hope to explore quaint shops up and down a historic main street. They'd browsed and chatted, exploring locally made clothing and art. With Sophie as a guide, Lyn had learned more history about the area than she'd ever thought possible.

"Hmm." Sophie pondered for less than half a second. "The boys have been feeding you mostly hot subs and pizza, I'm guessing. Maybe some Chinese takeout."

Lyn groaned. "Yes. Do any of them cook? Ever? I've had more General Tso's this week than I've had in the last two years combined."

She hadn't wanted to insist on fresh salads or grocery runs when she was only a guest.

"This one, then." Sophie reached across the table to point out a sandwich. "It's roast turkey and cornbread stuffing and cranberry, all on toasted white bread. So good."

It sounded delicious. "Perpetual Thanksgiving."

Sophie nodded. "Not a bad thing, as far as I'm concerned. But feel free to pick anything that looks good. With this restaurant, you can't go wrong with anything on the menu. Plus, it's a fun place."

It was obviously popular. Every table was taken and the servers bustled between seated customers. The atmosphere was warm and the servers were good-natured. Friendly in the way only people who enjoyed where they worked could be.

Their orders were taken by a cheerful girl who looked to be high school age, maybe first year of college.

"What's the story here?" Lyn had no doubt Sophie would know. The morning had been a fun, quirky litany of stories.

"Hah. This place has an incredibly young owner, who is also the chef." Sophie nodded toward the back. "Came up with the concept when he was...fourteen, maybe? It's the nation's first restaurant completely run by young people."

"Really?" Lyn raised her eyebrows. The menu was well put together with some complex flavors in those items. "That's young. Very young to be starting a business."

She wasn't familiar with labor laws for minors in this state but it seemed far-fetched.

Sophie nodded. "It's an inspiring story and they had the support of friends and family. Dinner is all fixed price style, European influence now. It's a definite romantic hot spot."

"And have you been here for a particularly good date or two?" Despite chatting about shopping preferences and art, they hadn't touched much on personal life. Lyn wasn't sure if it was off-limits but she figured it couldn't hurt to ask.

"Nah." Sophie sipped water. "I'm too busy with work to deal with the insanity of dating. Every few months I try to go out with a guy or two. There's a couple of awkward dates with inane conversation and I swear off men until I forget just how painful dating can be."

"Ah well, I can completely understand." Lyn played with her straw. "It gets worse when you travel all the time. Most guys don't want to wait a couple of weeks for a second date. So even if I find someone remotely interesting, he's moved on by the time I'm back in town. Or he's decided I wasn't interested because I keep telling him I'm out of town."

Sophie nodded in understanding. "Tough situation. But then again, you've been here about a week now. You usually in one place for this amount of time?"

Lyn shook her head. "Most times, a client consultation is just a few hours. Training sessions are the same. I try to schedule clients in the same area together to make a trip out cost-efficient. Depending on how the dog and the owner are doing, I might come out every week for a month then switch over to once a month for a while to make sure the training stuck."

Sophie gave her a knowing smile. "Stuck with the dog or the owner?"

Lyn laughed. "It's almost always the owner who needs training. Once the dog figures out what a command means and which command a particular human is trying to give them, they're generally good if there's consistent practice. It's more about figuring out the right routine for the whole household so the dog is behaving the way the owner wants. Not always as easy."

"Brandon says most of the time dogs aren't bad, they're just bored." Sophie glanced out the window as if the man would materialize.

Lyn didn't blame her. Her own thoughts had been drifting back to the kennels, too. Wondering what David was doing with her out of his hair and how Atlas was doing.

"Yeah. A bored dog gets destructive," Lyn confirmed.

"So your specialty is more dog psychology than actual training, isn't it?" Sophie's face lit up as their food arrived.

Lyn took a minute to try her sandwich. "Mmm. Good call."

"Mmm." No words from Sophie either.

After enjoying their first bites—because good food deserved proper attention—Lyn pulled her brain back to the last question. "It seems like psychology, but getting where a dog comes from and how he or she is thinking makes training exponentially more effective. Besides, dogs are some of the most honest creatures you can work with anywhere."

Sophie nodded, more knowledge in her eyes than Lyn had anticipated. Lyn shifted in her seat.

"The boys work with dogs for a lot of the same reasons, you know." Sophie's tone had become softer, more somber.

"Not sure I get what you mean." And Lyn wasn't sure she wanted to.

Sophie popped a French fry in her mouth. "Brandon grew up in this area. Did any of them mention it to you? He left for the military right out of high school and didn't come home to stay until he was ready to retire from active duty. He started Hope's Crossing Kennels as soon as he got back."

"Okay. Guessing you grew up with him?" Lyn leaned her chin on her hand, interested. The kennels looked fairly new, with all up-to-date equipment, so she'd guessed they'd been established recently.

"Yup. I was his next-door neighbor growing up. Once he bought the land for the kennels, I made sure his finances were all in line to keep him in the black." Sophie's expression grew distant and maybe a hint obstinate as she continued, "He wanted to make a place for himself because no place felt right when he got back. It's hard to find a comfort zone when they return from overseas. The contrast, the change from deliberately stepping into danger every single day to being surrounded by people running from place to place completely unaware of what could happen... there aren't words for it."

Lyn nodded. Her stepfather hadn't ever stayed for long. And it'd made her bitter. But this was the first time someone had given her this perspective.

"Alex and David arrived as soon as the main building and kennels were built. They all had experience as handlers. They put together their business model to provide basic and obedience training for the community and to train working dogs for military and police units." Sophie seemed to have forgotten the rest of her sandwich, working her way through the French fries instead. "It didn't take long. Brandon was a hometown hero and they're all gorgeous."

Lyn chuckled. "I hadn't noticed."

"The basic and obedience classes are packed with single women who've suddenly decided having the protection of a dog at home is a good idea." Disgust colored her words but Sophie waved it away. "They eventually settled into business and now people come from hours away to work with them. And their dogs are the best. They provide working dogs to police units all over the country and to the military, too."

"David's training techniques are incredibly effective." Lyn admired him for his work with any of the dogs on site, especially Atlas. It took a rare person to put pride aside to work in the situation they had. Lyn was lucky Atlas was responding to her and thankful David was coordinating with her in Atlas's best interest.

"To hear some of the ladies talk, David is incredibly effective in a lot of ways." Sophie studied her.

Lyn hoped her face was completely blank, fighting the heat rushing up to her cheeks. "I wouldn't know and I don't think it'd be appropriate if I did."

Sophie raised a single, perfectly groomed eyebrow in a high arch. "No?"

"It's not professional." Saying so had sounded perfectly logical when she'd had the conversation with David at the beginning of the week. Here, with Sophie, not so much. Lyn didn't want to be so short—not when Sophie had been so nice all morning—but Lyn wasn't sure how to turn this into an easier-going chat.

"Weak." Sophie shook her head. "I like you. And I'm straightforward with people I like. So I'm going to say this: this isn't a corporate environment. Plenty of people can work together plus engage in extracurricular activities."

Oh, and Lyn had been imagining them. Working with David every day was an exercise in self-control and mental focus. Every time he bent over to pick up a tennis ball, she was presented with the most grope-able ass she'd ever seen. And the other day he'd taken off his shirt in the afternoon for a few minutes to switch out to a clean one. The sight of all those wonderful muscles rippling underneath his skin had left her drooling, just a little. Luckily he hadn't noticed.

"We're both focused on Atlas as a priority." Might be the truth, but also another dodge.

"True. And he's important. I get it." Sophie nodded. "It's not easy under all the scrutiny either. Since Atlas was in the papers, people are coming out of the woodwork, aren't they?"

"There's a lot of oversight." As personable as Sophie

was, Lyn kept her stepfather's interest to herself. Not that she wanted to hide it. But it'd just complicate things and be a whole lot more history to share than she was ready to do in one sitting.

"Which means a lot of stress, maybe some anxiety." Sophie pinned her with a direct look. "And there is very obviously tension between you."

"Maybe." Okay, a lot. But Sophie had already laid it out there and Lyn wasn't ready to say it out loud. "Why do you have an opinion about it?"

Sophie had said she liked Lyn. And Lyn hadn't been this close to another woman in years. Sophie could be a real friend someday if things here worked out. Lyn didn't want to mess it up with a fight over David.

"David is one of my best friends. He's become a big brother to me. If you hurt him, I'd have to come after you." One French fry was popped into Sophie's mouth and another was waved in the air between them. "But if you might be good for him, it's my duty as a little sister to get involved and get things moving since the two of you are obviously being obtuse about it."

CHAPTER SEVEN

Cruz stood on the main street people-watching, basically.

Tourists were walking by and giving him a healthy amount of space on the sidewalk. Considering the sheer number of visitors on a Saturday afternoon, he was more than happy to be free of the crowds of people. Of course, part of the reason why he'd been given so much space was probably because he was in a shit mood and wasn't bothering to keep it from showing on his face. He wasn't going to check out his reflection in a storefront window to confirm.

He'd spent an entire morning up at McGuire, accessing SIPER Net to view the report on Calhoun's death, and he didn't have answers. Only more questions. He'd have preferred to bring the report back to his office where he could read and re-read and brainstorm, but those kinds of documents were secure and accessible only via SIPER Net. Which meant if he wanted to refresh his memory on the report, he had to drive up to McGuire and sign in to a secure location to gain access. No taking anything out with him.

All he wanted now was to sit down, have lunch, and brain dump the questions he had so he could compare them with his other notes at home later. Why he'd stopped in New Hope on the way home was a question he wouldn't answer to Forte or Rojas, but he'd be honest with himself.

Lyn and Sophie had come up to New Hope.

And knowing Sophie, there was no way the ladies had finished their shopping yet. Add the knowledge of how hungry Lyn got around lunchtime—she basically had an internal lunch bell inside her belly—and he was pretty sure they'd be seated in one of the trendy places along the streets eating their way through a menu.

What he didn't know was what he was going to say when he found them. Joining them would probably happen. He wasn't the type to give bullshit excuses for why he was around town either. He had promised Lyn they were good when she'd turned him down for a dinner date. And he'd been careful to keep things professional and easygoing through the week as they focused on Atlas's rehabilitation. But this was their first day away from each other. He'd wanted to check in on her and hadn't thought twice about stopping.

Now that he was here, though, he wasn't sure if she'd think it was creepy.

He'd consider himself creepy.

Maybe he should go home and pick up fast food on the way.

As he turned to head back to his car, he caught sight

of a man across the street. The guy was doing a good job blending in with the wall of tourists checking out the old railroad station. Only he'd been there for as long as Cruz had been standing around debating whether to continue finding Lyn and Sophie or leaving. No other visitor had been hanging out for as long. There was only so much time a person could spend staring at an old building. Photographers and artists were the only exceptions that came to mind.

This man had neither a fancy camera nor tripod. No art supplies either. He was dressed like a tourist but wasn't. Fit beneath the t-shirt and jeans; wearing work boots, not sneakers or loafers. Plus, the way the man stood kept the wall at his back and all approaches in easy view.

Definitely not the usual person out to enjoy the sights and shopping.

"David!" Sophie's voice erupted about a block down the street as she and Lyn emerged from a restaurant.

His person of interest didn't flinch. Despite remaining in his relaxed position leaning against the wall, the man's balance shifted easily to a more ready-for-action position. Interesting.

"Didn't you hear us?" Sophie arrived at his side and gave him a friendly punch in the arm.

"I heard *you*. Entire street did, too." Cruz tore his gaze from the other man to focus on Sophie and Lyn before Sophie made a bigger scene. "It's never good to reinforce bad behavior."

Sophie gasped in mock outrage and Lyn choked on a laugh.

"You two just finished lunch?" He'd might as well chat with them and make sure all was well.

"Oh, actually, I think I forgot something at the shop down the street." Sophie made a big show of fishing through her shopping bags. "I better go try to find it."

Obvious. So incredibly, painfully obvious.

Lyn leaned over to look in the bags, too. "I'll..."

"No, no." Sophie waved a hand. "Stay here and chat with David. I'll only be a minute."

Before Lyn could say anything else, Sophie was walking at a fast clip down the street expertly dodging other shoppers on the sidewalk.

Damn. He was pretty sure a grenade had just fallen into his foxhole. If he stayed, it was likely to be a mess. If he made a run for it, Sophie would shoot him down in his tracks.

Lyn cursed under her breath.

He studied her. "You don't have to wait with me if you don't want to."

What? He didn't see any reason to pretend politeness if either of them was uncomfortable.

She looked up at him with wide eyes, her lips parted in surprise. Her very kissable...Shit. He should go.

"I don't mind waiting with you." The words came out quick, with a weird note of panic.

Oh, even better. Creepy might not be a strong enough word for the reaction he was inciting in her.

He did not want to be the cause of it. "It really is okay. It's your day off. You should get to relax."

He took a step away, then suddenly stopped. Because her hand had shot out to snag his wrist.

"I really don't mind." Her grip on his wrist was firm, not hesitant.

Interesting. He turned his wrist in her hold until she

released him and he caught her hand in his instead. "No?"

Her fair skin turned a pale pink over her cheeks. He wondered if other parts of her flushed when she was embarrassed.

She left her hand in his, relaxed and warm. "Feels weird being out and about instead of working with you and Atlas."

"It's been an intense week." So was this... moment. Or whatever it was. He rubbed his thumb over the back of her hand, enjoying the softness of her skin. Hanging around was becoming a better and better idea.

She nodded. "He's coming along very well. And I've enjoyed the opportunity to learn from you."

Very well was an understatement. Atlas's transformation over the last several days was continuing. His responses to commands had become quicker, more enthusiastic. The dog was starting to actually pay attention to his surroundings and listen for commands. His desire to *work* was coming back. And that drive was key in a military working dog.

"There's a lot more to this concept of balance you've been talking about than I'd initially given credit to." Cruz had been skeptical at first. The whole dog-whisperer technique of head shrinking a dog had been tough to keep an open mind to at the beginning. Most of his training had to do with understanding the natural drivers of a dog and making sure training coincided with those instinctive impulses. "It's good to see him engaged."

Of course, Cruz had some reservations. The rehabilitation they were doing with Atlas was good now. But in the future, the question would be whether Atlas had become too attached to a single handler again. They'd have to cross that bridge when they came to it.

Lyn, though, had lit up thinking about Atlas. "Seeing him in action is exhilarating. I knew the military service dogs could do amazing things, but seeing it in person is a whole new level of wow."

She'd said "wow" several times through the week. And every time, Cruz had pondered how he could make her say it in bed. Completely inappropriate, but hell, as long as the thoughts stayed locked inside his brain they couldn't hurt. And they were definitely entertaining.

Cruz grinned. "Atlas is capable of more. Maybe we should take you out and rig you up for some of the more adventurous training exercises. A little rappelling, maybe even take you to one of the bases and arrange for a jump out of a helicopter."

Could be a lot of fun. Though it'd depend on how she faced the challenge. Atlas had done it plenty of times, but back then his handler had been practiced in the action first. If Lyn was nervous or afraid when she tried, Atlas would react to her anxiety.

"Really?" Lyn's eager expression and her genuine smile made Cruz rethink. She'd come through some crazy shit already. A little hop out of a helicopter wasn't likely to daunt her.

"We'd need to get you trained first." He wanted to take her out on those new experiences himself. Savored the idea. And if he imagined a few other naughty experiences, too, who could blame him? Adrenaline was a great aphrodisiac.

She probably looked fantastic in rappelling gear. All those nifty straps.

Probably unaware of his line of thought, Lyn shrugged. "Training is usually for the human half of the pair anyway. The canine just needs clear leadership."

He snorted. Once in a while—okay, more than sometimes—she sounded like a textbook waiting to be written. If it'd been anyone else, Cruz would've probably rolled his eyes. But from her, he'd kind of gotten to enjoy listening. It wasn't as if she was wrong.

Occasionally. But not always.

A movement at the edge of his peripheral vision drew his attention. "Why don't we talk about it more after you get back to the kennels? You and Sophie must have more shopping planned."

As much as he hated to cut this conversation short, there was something not right out here.

Lyn's smile faded a fraction. "Oh. Yeah."

On one hand, he hated to dim her happiness even a little bit. On the other, if she was somewhat disappointed to have him suggest she go do other things—especially after a week of working side by side with him from dawn to dusk—maybe she'd reconsider her decision to keep things just professional between them.

Something to file away for later. For now, he wanted to send her and Sophie safely on their way so he could satisfy curiosity.

"I'm glad I ran into you today, though." He made sure to catch her gaze and hold it until the blush came back into her cheeks. He might be pushing his luck but hopefully it didn't harm his chances to let her know he was still interested.

"I am too." She ran the tip of her tongue over her lower lip.

Instant hard-on. Even more because it'd been a self-conscious reaction on her part and not a purposeful invitation. Lyn didn't do coy as far as he could tell.

He watched her head on down the street and disappear into the same store Sophie had gone back into. He'd bet money Sophie had been in there watching them the whole time. Childhood friend of Forte's or not, she'd become a little sister to all of them. Complete with the nosy tendencies.

With both of them occupied, he started his own easy walk down the street toward his car.

His friend, the tourist who was not a tourist, finally left his perch by the wall and meandered off on his own. Only the man's path took him toward the stores.

Cruz let a group of passing tourists obscure his line of sight for a minute and cut down one of the small alleys. Two minutes later he was back on the main street a couple of blocks up from where he'd been with a clear view of the stores where Sophie and Lyn were shopping.

The other man's target might not be anyone Cruz knew. But he was too close to the ladies.

A minute later, Cruz was on another one of those little side streets coming up behind his not-a-tourist leaning against the wall pretending to wait for someone inside a store.

Cruz advanced at a leisurely pace so his footsteps wouldn't cue his target in and deliberately shoulder-bumped the guy as he passed.

"Oh, sorry." He turned to face the guy, looking him straight in the eye.

The man stood straight, balanced forward over his toes, definitely ready for action. "No worries, man."

Cruz studied him. "You sure about that?"

A pause. The man's eyes narrowed. "Just out for a little sightseeing."

"This small town is good for that." Cruz was absolutely sure the guy couldn't care less about small-town atmosphere and historic points of interest.

The man smiled, the kind that left a greasy sort of residue impressed in the mind. "Ex-military, right? You've got the look. What service?"

Yeah, the other man had the look, too, despite the unkempt facial hair and generally sloppy way he dressed. Far away, he'd appeared fine, but up close his t-shirt was stained and left partially untucked. His jeans were torn in places no fashion designer would've planned.

"Air Force." Cruz left it at that.

"Navy SEAL." The other man jabbed his own chest with a thumb.

Well, said a lot about a man when he felt the need to specify Special Forces. Cruz was willing to bet the other man wasn't active duty anymore. Wouldn't be hard to find out.

Either way, even a man who could reach the level of skill to be Special Forces could decline, lose his edge. Combat shaped soldiers in a variety of ways and as much as people wanted to think it was for the good, sometimes men got twisted. Or they already were and service had brought out the jagged edges in them. This man was not a shining example of a military hero by anyone's definition.

"What brings you to New Hope?" Cruz genuinely wondered.

"Ah, let's be real. I'm following your girl." The other man shrugged. "You'd already figured it out or you wouldn't have dropped by for this...discussion."

He'd guessed. Had been hoping not. Cruz was glad they weren't going to pretend coincidence. But then again, the guy being forthright was its own kind of message.

"Why?" Cruz was getting tired of the chitchat.

"She's working with a dog and that dog is carrying a whole lot of trouble along with it." The man spat on the sidewalk without ever taking his gaze off Cruz. "Anyone with a brain should stay far away from that shit."

Charming. Message received.

"What's it got to do with you?"

The man tilted his head. "Look, I'm just keeping an eye on things here, making sure no one gets too nosey. It's what guys like us do, right? Guys like you and me, we keep an eye out for trouble to ourselves and our own. Nothing wrong with that."

He paused.

"You understand, don't you? You'd have a brother's back, wouldn't you?"

Cruz considered. There was a whole lot of meaning in those questions. Overseas, deployed out in the middle of nowhere, a serviceman had to rely on his fellows to keep him safe. No man could survive in the middle of that chaos alone for an extended period of time without *someone* to watch his back.

Normally, it went unspoken. If someone had to ask the question, it was a threat.

From then on, the soldier had to wonder if the people around him really had his back. Or if they'd let him take a bullet and become just another casualty of war.

"Look, I'm just watching." The other man held up his hands. "I won't bother you, you don't get in my way. Agreed?"

"Look but don't touch." Cruz kept his tone pleasant. "Always happy to meet another serviceman."

The guy smiled again. "I owe you a drink sometime. You have a nice day."

Cruz turned on his heel and walked away.

Pulling out his phone, he texted Sophie.

Shopping trip is over. Need you two to head back to the kennels. STAT.

In less than a minute, Sophie responded.

???

Irritated, he typed faster.

There's something wrong here. I need you to go home now. I need to know you are both safe.

Sophie was strong-willed but she also knew when to listen.

Headed to the car.

That taken care of, Cruz circled around yet again. He wanted to know if his newfound friend had a partner in town. It shouldn't have been as easy as it was to sneak up on this guy. If he was a Navy SEAL, he wasn't the best of the best. Cruz had worked with a few teams in his time deployed and guys like this one made it into the Special Forces teams but they didn't last. If Cruz could figure out who this guy was—and he intended to—he was willing to bet the man had a dishonorable discharge. There were bad apples even in the most elite parts of the service. Sad reality. And obviously, the man had either thought Cruz wasn't worth the effort of even trying to mislead or he'd been sent to give Cruz the threat in addition to keeping an eye on Lyn.

Finding a good vantage point, Cruz pulled out his phone.

"Yeah."

"Beckhorn, you know if there are any parties particularly interested in Atlas's case?" Cruz asked the question quietly. The line could be tapped but he doubted it. At least not yet. This would let Beckhorn know that there were indeed interested parties.

"Can't imagine why," Beckhorn responded in an uninterested drawl.

"He's been in the papers and all." Cruz watched Sophie and Lyn emerge from another store, chattering as normal as you please. They headed straight for the parking lot and got in Sophie's car.

A small amount of tension unwound as they headed home toward safety.

"I get the occasional inquiry about him. Nothing outside the standard check-in." Beckhorn snorted. "Come to think of it, you owe me a progress report."

Perfect opening.

"I'll get it to you this afternoon." And Cruz would send along a couple of encrypted pictures of his new friend, too.

"I'll look forward to it."

"Yup." Cruz ended the call.

Now all he had to do was be prepared for Sophie and Lyn when they caught up with him later. They'd be expecting answers once he got back.

CHAPTER EIGHT

I'm glad I ran into you today.

Every time she remembered those words—and the look in David's steel blue eyes when he'd uttered them—Lyn's cheeks burned and other parts of her did things she didn't ever talk about to anyone.

Maybe she should feel uncomfortable. Or intimidated.

Nope. What she wanted to do was rewind back to the day she'd asked him for professional space and take back what she'd said. Or better yet, go back to the moment he'd almost kissed her and take things into her own hands.

Because every day she got to know David Cruz, she wanted him more.

If he'd been the least bit bitter or defensive or even indignant about her turning him down, she could dismiss her attraction to him and convince herself he was just another guy. Instead, he'd not only honored her request for professionalism but he'd gone on without any of the distance any normal person would create after the rejection. He'd made it easy for her to continue working with him. And she'd learned so much about him because of it.

And now she was pacing in the cabin again—his cabin—because he'd been concerned for her safety. For Sophie, too.

Sophie hadn't argued, only driven straight back to the kennels. When they'd returned and Sophie had explained to the guys, Brandon had insisted on seeing Sophie home—in a different car. All Sophie had told Lyn was that the men of Hope's Crossing Kennels didn't make requests like that unless there was a real issue.

Great. So now what? She'd have to wait until David returned to find out.

'Course, considering his military background and habits and...everything, he'd probably only tell her what he thought she needed to know. Which was next to nothing. As generous as her thoughts had been toward him a second ago, now she was thinking about him from this perspective and *everything* about David Cruz shouted military for all that he was honorably discharged.

Military equaled distance. Military meant you were never equals. Military meant you were forever shut out of a part of his life.

She'd spent her childhood watching her mom wait for her stepfather to come home. And when he was home, he wasn't. Not really.

Gah. Frustrating. So much of what she respected about David had roots in the deeply ingrained military honor he embodied. He wasn't just a man who used to wear a uniform. He was a man who made a uniform what it was. She couldn't help admiring the qualities. And she couldn't help being wary of what it'd mean to get involved with a man like that.

She'd hated it in a stepfather and sure as hell wasn't looking for it in a relationship of her own.

Her phone rang and she rushed to answer it without even checking the caller ID, hoping it was David. Impulse now. Logic later. "Hello?"

"Miss Evelyn Jones?" An unfamiliar voice was on the other end of the line.

Her heart dropped into the bottom of her belly. Why was she so disappointed? "Yes?"

"I'm Officer Hanley." The man cleared his voice. "I was responsible for taking your report from the night of the attack."

"Ah." She vaguely remembered the man. Sandy blue hair. Light-colored eyes. It'd been a difficult night, one she'd been actively trying not to dwell on. "Hello, Officer."

It wasn't her intention to sound flat. All the warmth got sucked out of her voice. Her mouth had gone dry. Maybe he needed to ask her a few more questions about the night at the hotel.

He went on when she didn't say more. "It's not normally our practice to call, and you seem to be with good friends, but in a situation like this I felt you would want to know..."

She waited as he trailed off. After a long, drawn-out second she grew impatient. "Yes?"

"The man who was taken into custody the next morning made bail today." The words came out in a rush, like ripping off a Band-Aid.

Stunned, Lyn almost dropped the phone. Cold fear twisted her gut and her heart rate kicked up until she heard it beating in her ears.

It's really too bad you came back.

She did a slow turn, frantically scanning the room. Alone. But the curtains were all open and the night was dark beyond the windowpanes. Any minute his face could appear, peering through the glass. The hunger in his eyes. She remembered...

"Miss Jones?" Officer Hanley sounded concerned, maybe regretful. He hadn't wanted to give the news to her.

"I'm here." She yanked her thoughts into place, tried to pitch her tone to calm and grateful. "Thank you for letting me know."

"Like I said, miss, it's not something we usually do but all things considered..." He cleared his throat again. Maybe it was a nervous habit. "Anyway, the guys at Hope's Crossing are good men. Stick close to them and you'll be fine. The man will see his day in court."

Of course. Officer Hanley couldn't refer to him directly as the man who'd attacked her. Innocent until proven guilty and all that. "I understand. Thank you again."

He blurted out a few more reassurances then ended the call.

Lyn clutched her phone to her chest. After a moment she shook her head, pocketed the phone, and rubbed her hands together. Nervous. Scared.

This entire trip had spun her world around. She traveled alone all the time! Now, she was jumpy in a cabin on private property with better security than any hotel had. She wanted to be mad at somebody. The men who'd attacked her—there'd been two, not just the one—and whoever had sent them. Thugs like that had to have some sort of boss to tell them what to look for.

Only she didn't know what she could possibly have. None of her clients gave her anything of value in print. They arranged for direct deposits to her bank accounts for her training and rehabilitation services. She never had access codes to their property or to any sorts of diagrams of their estates.

There was no reason for those men to have been looking through her things that night. And now, they were both out there. Loose. And angry with her.

Stars shot through her vision and she realized she'd been holding her breath. She let it out in a whoosh, then deliberately took air back in slowly. Hiding in the cabin like a mouse was a bad idea. They wouldn't need to come find her. She'd terrify the life out of herself.

She snagged a jacket and a small flashlight David had left for her before heading for the front door. Her hand on the doorknob, she froze. Maybe he'd known. That would explain why he'd sent her and Sophie back from New Hope earlier.

It didn't make sense, though. Telling her and Sophie would've precluded any hesitation. Not that they'd been slow to follow his request. There just wasn't any reason she could think of for him not to tell her. Unless he hadn't wanted to frighten her.

But he'd been so serious, with so much conviction in his statement about her safety. His expression alone had been enough to unsettle both her and Sophie. The actual reason couldn't be much more of a leap. Could it?

No way to know while she was still in the cabin. It might be dark outside but all the paths between the buildings were well-lit and the dog kennels and main house were in clear line of sight. Anyone on the paths would be seen by the people in the main house and most of the dogs on the property. She'd walk quickly and get from point A to point B. Calling one of the guys to come get her seemed like overkill.

As she stepped out into the night, the dark didn't close in on her. Solar lights lined the walkways and there were overhead lights at intervals along the paths, too. She headed directly to the main house but paused as she heard the low tones of David's voice over by the kennels.

Instantly calmer, she turned toward the sound and followed the covered walkway along the side of the main house. David was within shouting distance. The others probably were inside or similarly close by. Everything was a lot calmer. All she needed to do was not be alone.

"You can't be mad because we left you alone all day."

She stopped in her tracks. It hadn't been all day. Then she realized he was talking to Atlas.

Leaning against the dog's kennel with his broad back to her, David looked as relaxed as she'd ever seen him. Was there a single t-shirt he owned that didn't fit him like a second skin? If there was, she'd hide it or give it to Atlas to sleep on. Fitted clothing suited her just fine.

"Everyone needs a day off, including you." David carried on his conversation with Atlas. "Definitely her. She works hard as any person I've ever met, in or out of the service."

She couldn't help a smile. Funny, but the casual talk probably got Atlas used to the sound and cadence of

David's voice. After all, she did the same thing. Dogs were good listeners.

"Besides, she took you for a walk before she left. It's not like you didn't get time with her." He might've sounded jealous. Maybe.

Or wishful thinking on her part. Hard to tell.

"At least she likes you." Definitely some chagrin there. "I might've broke the camel's back today. Situation came up and no time for an explanation. She's the kind of lady who likes to be informed when things are happening. So I'm betting she is not too happy with me now."

Well, she hadn't been a while ago. Then there'd been a phone call and panic and she'd been reserving real anger until she found out if he knew what was going on and hadn't told her. But this, this didn't sound like the same thing.

David pushed off from the kennel and squatted, resting his elbows on his knees and balancing easily on the balls of his feet. "You and me, Atlas, we know what it is to be sent out into unsecured territory. Overseas, we went in ahead of anyone else. Drop zone, airfield, absolute middle of fucking nowhere. We went in to pull others out. And we're okay with it. It's what we signed up to do."

There was a pause. Lyn thought hard about what David was saying. Years ago, other military wives would talk to her mother about safe, well-established Air Force bases well within American territory. They'd made it sound like there was minimal risk. Of course it was awful when husbands had to deploy, but there'd never been a hint of the kind of danger David was talking about to Atlas. What he and Atlas had survived—it was something she'd known some select few had to do, far removed from anyone she knew or cared for. Only, it wasn't so far removed anymore.

"But she should be able to enjoy a safe afternoon shopping. That town is a freaking tourist attraction. It's the small, historic place to go around here to walk around and have a relaxing day." Anger was seeping into David's voice and an answering low growl issued from Atlas in response. The rapport between the two of them was getting stronger. "Instead, I see a man who shouldn't be there. Bad news. And my gut tells me she wouldn't have to worry about any of it if it weren't for us."

Why? Who? And what did they have to do with any of it?

Too many questions. She put her hand over her mouth to keep from blurting them out. If she walked up now, it'd stop him and she was *not* about to pretend she hadn't overheard.

David sighed. "She looked like she had a good time today. Hated to cut it short."

It took every ounce of will she had not to lean forward and listen harder. The breeze was blowing toward her, away from Atlas. But if she made any noise now or if the wind changed, Atlas would let David know she was near. And David was one of the best trainers she'd ever worked with. He'd be able to read Atlas clearer than printed text.

"Not sure how to proceed at this point, Old Man."

She scowled. Atlas wasn't old!

But then she took a breath and counted down slowly,

letting the air back out silently. She'd heard her step-father call his war buddies "Old Man" the few times she'd been around them. It was a thing, she supposed, and even the passing point of similarity to her stepfather knocked her feelings about Cruz back into a jumbled mess.

"If it were Calhoun or any other soldier, I'd brief her. Give her the details and let her decide. But she's not a soldier. And she shouldn't have to worry about these things." A pause. "She's a solid trainer. And she's done you a lot of good. She deserves better than being sucked into whatever shit storm we're about to go into next. Something is about to break, somewhere. I feel it in my gut and you've been on edge all day. We both know it's coming, whatever it is. And I want her clear before it does."

"Oh no. You are *not* sending me away." She slapped her hands over her mouth. Then wondered how the hell they'd moved while she'd been listening in the first place. Fantastic the way she didn't even pay attention to what she was doing when she heard epic statements of idiocy.

David and Atlas were both on their feet.

Since there was no sense lurking around the corner, she walked the rest of the way to them, trailing her hand against the chain-link of the kennel so Atlas could snuffle her fingertips.

"Listening long?" David didn't back away from Atlas's kennel and she decided she didn't have any issues with stepping into his personal space.

Being near Atlas was only a partial excuse.

"Well, I still have questions so maybe I didn't listen

long enough." She lifted her gaze to his.

Steel blue eyes, the color of storm clouds. Wow, but she liked looking into them. At the moment, his brows were drawn over them, giving him a severe expression. She ought to be at least somewhat intimidated by it but maybe she was building up a tolerance. Besides, being here with him was so much better than a couple of alternatives.

He came to a decision while she was pondering those. It crossed his face and then he seemed resigned. "What do you want to know?"

She swallowed. "Everything. Whatever there is. Whatever is going on. Because I'm already all sorts of caught up in it and I think you worry about what it means."

His lips pressed together in a thin line.

She nodded. "Yeah. You do. And I do too."

"There's a certain safety to not knowing the details." He wasn't just standing there anymore. He was looming.

And it wasn't going to scare her. Not anything he'd do. Because there were two men out there who'd already taken her sense of safety and ripped it to shreds. "Only when you're sitting, waiting, hoping the bad things won't come to find you. You sent me back here today and I followed your lead because it was the right thing to do at the time. But I won't be staying here forever. I need to know what I'm facing when I step off this property."

He opened his mouth.

But she wasn't done yet. "The man who attacked me already set foot here, so even this place isn't perfect. Now he's made bail and he's walking around free as you please. While you and Brandon and Alex are here with the dogs, there's a line of defense. Isn't that the way you put it? But no place all on its own is safe. The dogs are kenneled and you all have to sleep sometime."

"Never at the *same* time," David muttered.

She blinked, caught by surprise. The idea of the men each taking a turn in sleep and being awake was unsettling. Whether it was because they never let go of their military habits or because they were actively expecting trouble, it wasn't something normal people did. The realization settled over her that Hope's Crossing Kennels had never been a simple kennel.

This place had always been more, from the first day she'd walked into the office. It and the men who ran it were more than simple civilians with a shared love for dogs. They were men who'd survived hell and come to live with the rest of them again. And their survival skills had never been forgotten or even set aside, only concealed for the peace of mind of the community.

"He won't get to you. I'll be here for you." David's voice came to her—soft, serious, and sincere. A promise.

When she refocused on him, it was with a new awareness.

"You can't be everywhere." She looked down at Atlas standing pressed against the chain-link next to her. The big dog was as close as he could physically be with the fence between them. "No one can. We all live with the chance something will happen."

Her stepfather had explained his reasons for being away from home to her and her mother over and over again. He was away so she and her mother could sleep safe at night. Every time he'd said it, the words had come by rote, a quote or a mantra, rather than words said with sincerity. She'd always said the same to him in reply. There was always a chance something would happen while he was away.

Back when she'd started, it'd been with a whole lot of teenage angst. In her mind, she or her mother could get hit by a bus and her stepfather would've been too far away to do anything about it.

"Maybe you're right. The more information you have, the more prepared you can be." David leaned in closer, until his heat whispered along her skin. Not looming anymore. Definitely not looming. "Seems fair enough."

"I want the knowledge I need to protect myself." The way she'd gone out on her own to learn how to shoot a gun the minute she'd reached adulthood.

"What will you do armed with information? Go hunting?" His words whispered against her hair.

"No." She shivered.

"Good. Going hunting would be stupid. Will you run?"

She shook her head. "I'm not sure. Running sounds futile if someone with any kind of skills or obsession is after me. It depends on what is actually going on. But once I have the full picture I can make an informed decision. Something that makes sense."

"Okay." But he didn't wax eloquent with the things she needed to know. "Why did you come out here, Lyn?"

Frustration sparked and she clenched her jaw. Changing gears wasn't going to help her.

"I got the call from the police." Seemed like a long time ago. Being out here with David and Atlas always made time pass faster. But hold still, too. Like they were all in their own little bubble. "They said I should stay near friends."

Of course, these two were the closest she had to friends anywhere. Not just nearby. Sophie might become a friend if they kept in touch. But the side effect of traveling all the time tended to be a whole lot of acquaintances and virtually no close friends. Even the town she had on her driver's license as home wasn't anything more than a place to send junk mail.

"Are you worried he'll come after you again?" David's hand came up toward her face slowly, his index finger extending and exerting gentle pressure under her chin to get her to look up at him.

When she met his gaze, she was drawn in closer without ever moving. They were in the eye of a storm and the air directly around them had gone still.

"Yes." It took effort to get the affirmative out. Frustrated, she pushed forward with the conversation. "Doing nothing but waiting was going to drive me crazy. I was getting cabin fever."

His nod was almost imperceptible. Still, something settled inside her. He got it.

"Whatever is going on, you know more about it than I do." She licked her lips; her mouth had gone dry.

His gaze dipped, focusing on her mouth. "I might. I know something. I'm not sure it's related. But this next question is important."

Can I kiss you?

She was doubtful that was the question he was going to ask. But the moment was drawing out and she very much wanted for him to ask it. "Okay."

"Do you think I would hurt you?"

"No!" It popped out before she had time to think about it. Anger burned up from her chest and spread outward. She scowled. "Of course n—"

He kissed her.

CHAPTER NINE

His kiss wasn't light or gentle or teasing. His lips came down on hers with heat and firm pressure. His hand moved from her chin to cup the back of her head, urging her to tilt for him. She did, opening her mouth and giving him access, too. His tongue swept in, hot and searching. She answered in kind and they explored each other.

This was ... *wow*. More than wow. Heat swept through her and she reveled in the sensation he sent coursing throughout her body with his kissing.

It was a long time before he let her up for air and when he did, she realized she was clutching the front of his shirt with both hands. Oh hey. How about that?

"You need to get over this."

What?

Shocked, she started to step back but David's hand was still on the back of her head and his other arm came around her waist. Tucked against him, she looked up to see him glaring at Atlas through the chain-link fence.

The big dog had reared up and put his front paws on the fence.

"You can deal," David said to Atlas. "Don't even tell me you gave Calhoun this kind of interference when he was with somebody."

Butterflies tickled her and she buried her face in David's chest as she giggled.

"What? That's seventy-five pounds of canine jumping up on me if it weren't for this fence." Despite his words, amusement colored his tone and his arm remained firmly around her waist.

"With the two of you, there isn't anything that can keep me worried." She smiled up at him, enjoying the fit of their bodies against each other.

David gave her a lopsided grin. "Good. I'd like to say we make a solid team but Atlas here is working for you but not with me, if you get what I mean."

"Ah well, he's a free agent for the time being." She didn't want to ruin the mood. But it'd be stupid to pretend Atlas wouldn't be returned to duty once they'd gotten him back to one hundred percent responsiveness. The big dog was too good to retire yet.

"True." David pressed a kiss to her temple.

"So." She could barely believe her own audacity but the last few days, the last few minutes in particular, were all about personal evolution, apparently. "Where were we before Atlas expressed his opinion?"

Because she'd like to get back to that. And explore. In detail.

Okay, maybe she wasn't as daring as she could be. Yet.

"Here." David caught her mouth for another hot, fantastically mind-blowing kiss. "But I think we should all head someplace more private."

"All?" Catching her breath was a challenge.

He tapped her nose. "Don't go thinking too hard because it's not anything too exotic."

Keeping one arm around her waist, he snagged Atlas's leash and gave Atlas the command to sit. There it was again: the half-second of consideration before Atlas made the decision to follow the command. David didn't comment, but he didn't have to. They both recognized it. He simply opened Atlas's kennel.

More rehabilitation required before Atlas would be ready for duty.

"Since you feel safest with both of us," David commented as he hooked Atlas's leash onto his collar, "then both of us will see you back to your cabin and stay there with you through the night."

He'd just invited himself to her cabin. For the night. Yep, she'd heard the key points there.

A thrill rushed through her. It might've been better if she'd invited him but she was definitely not opposed to the idea. Especially considering how nice it was to be tucked against his side as they all started walking back to her cabin. The lighted paths had less contrast and the dark beyond them wasn't as sinister. She didn't jump at every sound. It was a world of difference in company she trusted.

Her heart just about burst out of her chest once they got there, though. The idea of going back inside, where she couldn't see anyone coming... "You're definitely both going to be here. All night?"

It took everything she had to suppress the shiver when

her mind went into overdrive and images of a man's face peering into her windows flashed across her vision.

His arm tightened around her waist, grounding her and bringing her back to reality. "We'll keep watch."

"Just tonight?" And that was the issue, wasn't it? She'd forgotten momentarily about the danger out there. His kiss had blown it right out of her mind but it was still there.

He didn't push her inside the cabin, or even nudge her. She swallowed hard and walked in on her own. The attack hadn't happened here, after all. But at the hotel, she'd been shoved inside. And next, they'd hurt her. They'd been about to do worse.

A whine cut through her thoughts and Atlas shoved his head under her hand. His cool nose pressed against the inside of her arm as he wriggled his head, demanding her attention.

"We'll be here and we'll take each night as it comes." David was still outside. He'd stayed back and given her space with her fear.

She was grateful for it. Every door—every time she'd walked through one—she'd shoved this far back into the corner of her mind. Mostly, it'd worked. But not tonight. Too many thoughts were crowding her head and she wasn't able to compartmentalize the way she normally would. Maybe David had seen it all this week when she hadn't been completely aware.

Even knowing he was with her and wanting him there, she wasn't sure she wouldn't have panicked a little in that moment if he'd been right behind her. "I'm sorry."

He shook his head slowly. "No apologies. Not ever."

She opened her eyes wide against sudden, unexpected tears. "I'm kind of embarrassed. But I really appreciate...this."

He was being incredibly considerate, and thoughtful, and patient. She couldn't say the words without the emotions spilling over, and tears weren't sexy. She wanted to recover the excited moment earlier, not be stuck in this echoing fear now.

David only gave her his smile, the one that had never failed to tempt a return smile from her over the last week. "I can stay out here. Atlas can keep watch inside."

"No!" Her response was immediate and maybe a little horrified. "Please don't stay out there. Come inside."

The last ended on a whisper. Even if it was him, someone outside would freak her out even more.

"Okay." He stepped inside slowly and shut the door behind him.

Immediately, the imaginary vice around her lungs eased. She rubbed Atlas's head absently, taking comfort from his weight as he leaned against her leg. Her embarrassment was evolving rapidly into something else and her cheeks burned with shame.

"Hey." David's voice was quiet, coaxing. "You don't need to be embarrassed. And this is all about what will make you comfortable. You're safe with us and everyone here would go the extra mile to see to it that you feel that way. Nothing you say or do is wrong."

She laughed then, but even to her ears she sounded like she was on the verge of tears. Maybe this was what hysteria felt like. This unhinged, out-of-control feeling. Like she could lose it at any minute. "I'd really like to forget what made me come out in the first place and what made me lose my mind when I came back in here."

"Would you feel better staying someplace else?" Another completely rational, patient question.

He was a good guy.

She shook her head. "Honestly?"

"Honestly."

She lifted her gaze to his face, taking in the solid lines of his jaw and his serious countenance. His expressive eyes and those lips that'd completely scattered every rational thought from her mind not too long ago. "I'd like to go back to how I felt when you kissed me, because that's the best I've got in my short-term memory currently and it was way better than any kiss I remember ever."

Too much information. Definitely. And embarrassment was taking on whole new levels.

David's eyebrows rose during her comment and the bastard started to look *smug*. "There's a high bar set there. I'm going to need to try to outdo myself now."

She opened her mouth to yell at him. What she'd say, she wasn't sure, but she'd come up with something witty on the fly because he was going to be impossible to work with if she let—

He closed the distance between them and bent to capture her mouth. She hadn't dodged. Her mind had been too preoccupied with generating witty commentary. Which was a lost cause because his lips burned into hers until she gasped and he deepened the kiss until she was drowning. His tongue teased and coaxed her until she responded in kind.

"*Foei.*"

She was breathless and off balance, leaning into David and blinking to clear her vision. David had an arm around her and the other out, holding Atlas at arm's length. The big dog had tried to jump on David again but this time David had caught him and held him back, balanced on his hind legs.

"*Foei*," David repeated. "That'll be enough of that."

There was a long pause as man and dog stared each other down. Atlas finally settled back on all fours, then sat. Lyn had never been caught in the middle of a pissing match between men before, but somehow she imagined it'd be something like this. Probably.

"He'll be all right sleeping out here," she whispered. Maybe she was being disloyal to Atlas. All things considered, she'd make it up to him tomorrow with extra-long walks and a whole lot of belly scratches.

Tomorrow.

David nuzzled just behind her ear and caught her earlobe between his teeth in a gentle nibble. Then he brushed his lips over her ear. "Both of us can make do out here while you get some rest."

"What?" She jerked her head back, almost catching his chin as she did.

He kept hold of her and brushed her cheek with his thumb. "You've got a lot going on inside your head right now and you are the definition of vulnerable. I'd be a complete ass to take advantage of you."

Please. Take advantage.

"I want to re-establish your sense of safety first." He just had to sound incredibly reasonable. "And then, take you out on a real date."

"A date." She repeated the words slowly, rolling the idea over and over in her head. Now that he mentioned it, she'd hated saying no the first time he'd asked. Still, he was being incredibly stubborn at the moment and part of her didn't enjoy the way he was holding out. Mixed messages.

"I figure I should at least buy you dinner before I try taking advantage of you." He winked, and there was enough heat in his voice to make it clear he was interested.

Her resistance evaporated. "You are incorrigible."

He screwed up his face in mock dismay. "Sorry. Can you use a smaller word?"

"Impossible." She balled her hand into a fist and thumped him on the chest.

"That's only one syllable shorter."

"Bad!" She thumped him again. "You are a bad, bad man."

He laughed and snuck a kiss, which she gave him. And she nipped his lower lip for good measure. "I plan to be."

"Good." She was pouting and smiling at the same time and she didn't even know how he'd managed it.

He grinned. "See? Bad. Good. I can handle the easy vocabulary."

"Tease." She threw it out there as an accusation.

"I'll add it to the plans." He grinned. "Limited vocabulary. Excellent memory."

"Fine." She blew out a breath. "I guess we'll be calling it a night then."

A very frustrating, probably restless night. His kisses alone had her melty and tingly and wound up in all sorts of ways. God, how would it be when they did get all tangled up?

He nodded solemnly. "It would be a good idea."

"But not together." She might've sounded disappointed. And it served him right if he heard it and felt guilty.

He kissed her. Kissed her until she melted for him, all the rigid outrage gone as she pressed up against him trying to fit herself against the entire length of him. She wanted to touch everywhere. When he let her up for air, he gave her a smile that meant bad, bad things. "Not yet."

* * *

"David? Are you hungry?"

Define hungry, he thought, because first thing in the morning his appetite was focused on something much more satisfying than pancakes.

He didn't open his eyes. Instead he considered his surroundings, how close Lyn might be, and most important, whether he had his pants on. He shifted a leg, took note of the loose slide of something too soft to be denim across the top of his thigh.

Nope.

He did have a light blanket across his lower half. The thin fabric protected him from the chill in the cabin but it definitely wasn't enough to hide him from the light of day. While he was mostly certain Lyn found him attractive, she might not appreciate the part of him most awake first thing in the morning. At least not yet.

Lyn sighed. "Different question. Bacon? Yes or—?"

"Yes." There wasn't ever another answer. Ever. He opened his eyes and sat up. It'd been a long night and he hadn't gone to sleep until a few hours ago.

Lyn was already headed back to the kitchen area so he couldn't get a look at her expression yet. Her hips swayed as she walked, though, which could've been a torturous tease if he hadn't already spent a week or so appreciating her walk. So she wasn't throwing anything special into how she was getting around for his benefit. Biggest issue at the moment was her not giving him any clues as to whether she was upset with him for the way last night had played out.

He'd been trying to be a good guy. Do the right thing. His balls were blue enough to torture him without her being angry with him this morning.

"Did you sleep well?" Safe question. He hoped.

Her gaze shot up and pinned him to the couch. "Did you?"

Not quite mad, but definitely touchy. He'd have to proceed with caution.

"Well…" He drew out the response to give himself time to think. "I stayed on watch until Forte texted me a few hours ago to let me know we've got an eye on the grounds. Then I was up for a while longer, thinking of you."

God, he enjoyed the way pink spread across her cheeks. He planned to tease her more often. This was also a good sign. He'd take whatever he could get.

From the middle of the floor, Atlas snorted and rolled on his side.

No opinions from the peanut gallery, thanks.

Not that he had any delusions of the dog being a mind-reader, but there was no doubt Atlas was aware of the pheromones floating all over the place. Dog probably had a better idea of Lyn's mood than David did.

"If you were so…interested, maybe you shouldn't have insisted on sleeping out here last night." She turned to the stove and a second later, the sizzling of bacon filled the room with mouth-watering aroma.

He took the opportunity to snag his jeans from where they were hanging over the end of the couch. "Seemed like we were on the same page, but you did get some up-setting news yesterday. Wanted to give you time to ease into things."

Plus, he'd still been on edge after the run-in with the other ex-soldier earlier in the day. He didn't trust himself to keep things light and easy. Her first encounter with him should be at his best for her, not when his old issues were so close to the surface. She'd seemed to appreciate his reasoning last night.

Of course, she'd given him a look that could kill a man when she'd closed the bedroom door.

As she set a plate on the table, it landed with a loud *thunk*. He winced. Maybe she'd reconsidered overnight.

Enough.

He stood and got himself into his pants while she was still being stubborn giving him her back. Then he stepped over Atlas and came up behind her in the kitchen, putting a steadying hand around hers on the skillet to keep her from whacking him across the head with it. Other hand on her hip, he ground his own into her backside so there was no way she could ignore the raging hard-on he still had even zipped up inside his pants.

"Believe me, I wanted to join you in your room last night." He leaned his head close to the side of hers and nipped her ear. "But same reasoning applies this morning even if we both lost some sleep from frustration."

She didn't try to step away but her back was straight as a board and her shoulders squared.

"You're being very considerate. And I should appreciate it. I thought about it a lot last evening. I don't like the mixed messages and I don't like running hot only to be put into a forced cool down. You had me incredibly wound up last night and then you decided it was all about the chivalrous thing to do."

He swallowed hard. Okay. He backed up a fraction and gave her room. "I'm sorry."

After a moment, she sighed, turned off the heat on the stove and placed the skillet down safely. Then she turned into his arms. Rising up on her toes, she pressed a kiss against his jaw. "But you had good intentions. I'm hoping talking about this will prevent a repeat and that you'll make it up to me."

No sane man would ignore that hint.

He kissed her, enjoying the sweet honey taste of her mouth. He also gave thanks she'd changed her mind about keeping professional distance because even the minimal space between them due to the clothes they were wearing was too much. He sincerely hoped she'd be as interested in pursuing this thing between them after he clued her in to all the other shit going on around them.

And the thought effectively chilled him. A man didn't need cold showers when he had this much insanity to deal with inside his own head. His mood was grim by the time they'd finished breakfast and gathered up Atlas to head back to the main house.

"It's a vet visit for you, Atlas." David noticed Atlas had been much more amenable to commands this morning. Small battle won there. He expected to have a few more instances like last night's contest of wills before Atlas made the decision to listen a hundred percent of the time. It was a turning point between every dog and handler. The trick with Atlas was to get him to a point where he would accept a new handler at all.

Lyn held Atlas for Doctor Medicci while she checked on the healing scrape along his side. Atlas stood still under examination, amazingly responsive to Lyn's encouragements. David stood back and let the ladies work.

"He's healing well, not showing any signs of pain." Medicci murmured as she ran her hands along Atlas's back and legs. "You kept him on light exercise, right?"

"Easy training and daily walks. No running for any real distance," Lyn answered. She paused then added, "Mostly. He's an active dog."

"Mmm." Medicci sounded noncommittal but not angry. Atlas was looking good and they all knew it. "On principal, he should be kept to light exercise a while longer but as long as the area around the wound is free of redness or swelling, he should be fine. Sutures will dissolve on their own."

"Got it." David figured he'd keep the training review at the current pace. No need to rush Atlas, and Lyn was working wonders with the dog in general.

"While I'm here, I'll do his basic exam and take samples for the standard tests." Medicci took out her stethoscope and pressed it to either side of Atlas's chest.

Things looked to be fine until Medicci took out the big scanner and passed it over Atlas's back. She frowned, checked the device, then passed it over him again more slowly. "He's chipped, isn't he?"

"All military working dogs are." David pushed away from the wall and came to stand at Lyn's side. He ran his fingers through Atlas's coat along the dog's right shoulder, seeking the small bump under the skin he'd encountered grooming. "It's right here."

"Whatever that is, it's not a functioning microchip." Medicci shook her head. "I just used this before I got here on two other dogs. It's in working order. His chip must've malfunctioned or been damaged."

It wasn't likely, as small as the chips tended to be, but anything was possible.

"I'll remove it now and we'll re-chip him to be safe." Medicci reached for her sterile implements.

"Remove it." David cleared his throat. "But we'll take him on base to get a new one in."

Two feminine gazes pinned him with questioning looks. It was not the most comfortable he'd ever been. "The microchips for MWDs are more robust than the average pet chips linking a bar code to an owner's name, address, and phone number. All military working dogs have GPS too."

Medicci nodded. "We're going to need to restrain him. This won't cause major pain but it will be more than a pinch."

"You don't need to put him out, do you?" Lyn sounded concerned.

He didn't blame her. Anesthesia wasn't something to do lightly. He'd never seen Medicci do it, wasn't sure she could on an on-site visit like this.

Medicci shook her head. "Normally, it'd be something I'd recommend an office visit for. These chips are intended to be permanent and even though they're inserted to sit below the skin, they can sort of migrate over time. If they do, I'd need to make a bigger incision and maybe even tease apart the tissues to get a good hold of it. "

She spread the fur to expose the bump David had pointed out. "This one is easy to locate, obviously. It'll be a pinch. Just enough of an incision to retrieve the chip. Should be fine to restrain and muzzle him. But you two should probably leave the room so he doesn't associate any negative experience with either of you."

CHAPTER TEN

"Come in." David closed out a few spreadsheets and directed his attention to Medicci as she walked into his office.

"All done. Lyn is with Atlas now, fussing over him." Medicci smiled. "Good to see a softer touch for these dogs sometimes. You all do a great job with them; don't get me wrong. But the battle weary deserve a dose of spoiling here and there."

David didn't plan to argue since he agreed. "Small doses. Anything I should know about aside from what we talked about before?"

The amusement fled from Medicci's face, her gaze darkening and the corners of her mouth turning downward. "A couple of things. First, once I shaved away the fur around the area, it looked to me as if the chip had been placed fairly recently. The skin had newly healed from an incision. It definitely hadn't been there for several years. Which was odd because I thought the size of the bump was indicative of scar tissue forming around the chip. There *should've* been more scar tissue around it under the skin, developing a sort of sheathe. That wasn't the case."

Medicci placed a wax-covered object on his desk. Her expression was completely blank. "This is not the microchip any vet anywhere implanted. Military or otherwise."

David touched the wax. The right length, but flat and rectangular instead of cylindrical. It was a micro SD card, for shit's sake. What was it doing in Atlas?

Of course, he'd seen something like this before in animals and in humans. Hell, people had been known to bury the damn things in open sores on their own bodies, letting the wound scab over. It was scary what a person would do in the face of necessity . . . or desperation.

He had no idea what to say but Medicci definitely didn't need to know everything. "This is—"

Medicci held up her hands. "It's out. As long as there is no threat to any animal's health under my care, I don't need to know. It's best if I don't, isn't it?"

David nodded, grateful. He'd lie if he had to. But the best lie was one he didn't have to tell. Or truth. That worked well, too, in the proper dosage.

"Keep the incision clean and he'll heal just as fast if not faster than the other injury. If you think there's more, we could do an X-ray at my office to locate any other potential implants. I didn't detect any more bumps under his skin, though." Medicci headed for the door but paused. "He's a good dog."

"He is," David agreed.

And all this time, he'd really been carrying the weight of Calhoun's last message on his shoulders.

He pocketed the micro SD and headed down the hall, finding Lyn with Atlas in the examination room. "How's our guy?"

"Acting like nothing happened." Lyn laughed, giving Atlas a hearty rub around the shoulders.

Atlas deigned to give David a doggie grin, tongue lolling out. When Lyn's rubbing migrated over his back to his rump, the dog's eyes practically rolled back into his head as if to say, *Oh yeah, that was the spot.*

Atlas had to really trust Lyn to allow her behind him that way and in a dominant position. Even for butt rubs. Usually military work dogs were too dominant and aggressive to let anyone but their handlers such privilege. In Lyn's hands, Atlas could almost be a normal dog.

"Let's keep things easy for him today. You feel comfortable going for a walk around the property? Forte's still on watch this morning and he's got your mobile in case he sees anything on the perimeter cameras."

Lyn straightened, her expression momentarily somber. "Didn't realize you had video surveillance all around the property."

"Had it on the entrances before and added more to cover the entire perimeter since last week." David and the others had considered it previously and cursed themselves for not already having it installed. No matter how quiet the town was where they were located, forewarned was forearmed and they'd corrected the mistake immediately, each of them contributing to the cost from their own private funds. "We'll all have notice if anyone is even snooping around the fences, much less tries to step onto the property again."

She nodded slowly. "All right."

Atlas had settled down, sensitive to her change in mood. He'd be hypervigilant with her this agitated. Which was even better. The big dog wouldn't be tempted by random distractions like squirrels or rabbits while Lyn was agitated. No running off chasing furry things or coaxing her to play fetch. He'd stay with her and ensure her safety. He shouldn't be running today anyway.

"Okay. Take a long walk then, and I'll get some administrative work done here. Check back in with you both at lunchtime."

Lyn nodded. A minute later she had Atlas on a leash and they were out the door.

Back in his office, David dug into one of his drawers. After way longer than he'd like, he came up with a small toolkit. Armed with those tools, a soft cloth, a firm bristled toothbrush and isopropyl alcohol, he went to work. Removing wax from a micro SD card wasn't fun but it wasn't hard either. He'd done it with fewer tools to hand. This time, though, he wanted to do it right in one shot with minimal chance of further complications.

Once the wax was completely removed and he was sure the contacts on the micro SD were perfectly cleaned, he loaded it into his memory card reader. A few minutes to scan for viruses and he had two files, both video. The first was tagged as highlights and the second was significantly bigger, compressed, and encrypted.

Calhoun had intended for David to find these first. David was going to make a guess that he was supposed to view the highlights to get a clearer idea of the issue at hand, then take the time to absorb the other video over more time. First things first. He made copies and backed them to his secure storage, then made secondary backups to his cloud storage. Encrypted.

Then he took his computer offline and double-clicked the video file to watch it.

"What's Calhoun's status?" a voice offscreen asked.

"Stable, sir. He'll live. Unconscious for now." Only the legs and torso of this speaker were visible.

The camera was low—around waist height or lower. Meaning it was likely a camera attached to a canine tactical assault suit. Probably Atlas's specifically. Normally those cameras were used to give human handlers and the rest of the team knowledge of what lay ahead as the canine took point. In this case, it looked like Calhoun had been injured and Atlas was still in use. Not recommended, but there was usually a backup on the team able to take over the working dog if something should happen to the handler.

"Just as well," the offscreen speaker said. "Not sure our teammate has the stomach for what we need to do here."

Not likely. Calhoun had had the balls for anything that needed doing.

The unseen man continued, "We'll use the dog to terrorize the prisoner. Damage to extremities is acceptable but try to keep it limited. We want to be able to patch him up if we need him alive past this evening."

David set his jaw. It went against his morals to use a dog this way. But war wasn't noble. He'd done things he'd have nightmares about for the rest of his life. He was only sorry Atlas had been commanded to do similar.

The video skipped. Highlights reel, after all.

A man was secured to a chair. He'd been worked over already and there were several more men in the room. Once in a while, a face came into frame and David paused to capture the image of the face. Only a couple; the camera hadn't captured all of them. But he was going to need those for later, especially since the SEALs had covered the name tags on their uniforms for the interrogation.

"Wait! Wait! You want this man? I can give you his location. We can do business."

English. Fairly well-spoken and with the kind of accent that indicated a higher level of education. David listened more carefully.

"You want him. I want him dead. Kill him for me and I will make sure you and your future company have exclusive business once you are established."

David stopped the video and replayed. If he'd heard correctly, this wasn't an interrogation anymore. It was evolving into something uglier: a conspiracy.

"It's what you do, isn't it? Once your career is complete with the US military, you go private. Establish a private military company. Mercenaries." The man was sweating, could barely see out one swollen eye, but no one was stopping him or redirecting his discussion to more pertinent information. They were all listening. "Mercenaries need work. The best work is here. Will be here, for decades to come."

True. Even once the war was officially over and troops were brought home, the area would be ruled by unrest. Mercenaries had job security in those sorts of hot spots all over the Middle East and surrounding regions.

"I will be the head of my organization. Not some middleman. Don't just capture and interrogate the man you are looking for. Kill your target for me. We will do business for a long time to come."

An unseen man—probably the commanding officer based on the authority in his tone and the way the men in camera view deferred to him—spoke. "You make a very interesting proposition. We can make a deal."

Son of a bitch.

* * *

A sunny morning with blue skies and a light breeze went a long way toward banishing her worries. Lyn didn't want to live a paranoid life. Walking with Atlas had been a lot easier than she expected, relaxing even. She babbled about random things like the trees around them and the squirrels she spotted. He listened. He was good like that, being a dog and all.

People made things way the hell too complicated.

This trip, she'd spent far more time than usual pondering her childhood. Contrasting and comparing her experience to what she was learning about David specifically, and Brandon and Alex by virtue of their work at the kennels. They were so very different from the wealthy clients she normally worked with in terms of their knowledge of dogs and the way military life had influenced their life after. They were complex men with simple desires: build a good life, train good dogs.

And they were all single. It hadn't required a morning shopping with Sophie to figure out why, though the woman had provided some interesting insight. Every one of the men, including David, had serious issues to work through.

Lyn's parents had lived walking on eggshells. Too many secrets between them, unresolved misunderstandings, and unaired grievances. They'd remained married but they'd fallen out of love. Lyn had trouble believing maintaining the appearance of propriety had been worth the misery in a loveless marriage. But then, her mother had been married once before and probably preferred the security marriage afforded her.

Lyn's stepfather could've been worse. He could've been abusive, for example, but he hadn't been. He'd just never had a use for Lyn's mother or for Lyn. There'd been so much more important away than there was to pay attention to at home.

She should steer clear of David for those telltales. He preferred to work on a need-to-know basis, and he was the person to decide what she needed to know. It was something she could work through on a professional level but in a personal relationship they were going to slowly deteriorate. She wouldn't be able to stop herself from resenting it over time.

The memory of his kiss stirred up fluttering sensations in her chest and brought heat to her cheeks. He was good. Really good. And the chemistry between them was more intense than anything she'd experienced with anyone else. No way was she going to regret the kisses last night. But what she needed to decide was whether she wanted more.

"Lyn." David came striding across the grounds.

David standing still was a striking figure. The man in motion was enough to make her stop in her tracks and stare. He had an economy of motion, neat and efficient, but covered distance faster than she imagined a man could just walking. She wondered what he was like running an obstacle course. Actually, she'd pay to watch him traverse one of those. Maybe there was one of those traveling challenges coming through the region in the near future. Sophie would help her enter him.

Plans for another day.

"Change in plans." David came to a halt a few yards short of them. His jaw was set and he wore a decidedly grim expression.

"For the day?" She considered him. "Or in general?"

"This project with Atlas could be closed out a lot sooner than we planned." He frowned. "It's not the way I want it to work out, but it might be for the best. You don't want to be involved in what's probably coming next."

"I'm capable of deciding what I want, given the full picture." Oh, he was not going to toss her to the curb.

"It'd be safer for you."

She held up her free hand. "I was attacked in my own hotel room the night I arrived. One of those attackers showed up here the next morning. Now that man is on bail and no one ever found the other guy. Last night you told me I could feel safe here. And now you're telling me it's safer for me to go out there. Make up your damned mind."

Anger and frustration welled up inside and this time he was not going to dispel it with a kiss. He'd dismissed it, distracted her from it, and done everything to take her attention away from the cause but now he was trying to push her away and this was the limit.

"Why don't we go inside and—" Not a single sign of his truly comprehending showed in his face. He was still focused on getting her to do what he wanted.

"No." She widened her stance, figuring he couldn't possibly make her move. Atlas came to heel at her side, watching the exchange between her and David intently. "We can talk about this right here. Give me good reasons, supported with real information, and I will make a decision based on those."

David sighed. "It's better if you—"

"This is not a military operation." She cut him off. "If we are truly partners working for Atlas's best interest then we share information. Nothing less."

She shut her mouth then. Interrupting him twice was already beyond rude. She wanted to resolve this, not antagonize him into throwing her off the property for real.

David worked his jaw, obviously reining in his own temper. "Anything to do with Atlas is looking to be complicated."

The dog in question glanced over at the sound of his name but stayed where he was.

"His previous handler wasn't only lost in the line of duty." It sounded like a struggle for David to share even that much and he looked all around them.

They were yards from the perimeter fence and even farther from the main house. No one was near enough to overhear.

David continued, scowling. "Atlas's previous handler's name was Calhoun and we served together when I was still active. We were friends. So receiving texts from him wasn't unusual."

She wasn't sure where this was going so she waited.

"Any communication from deployed military is monitored." David shoved his hands into the front pockets of his jeans. "His last text was out of character for him. Odd. But what I read into Calhoun's last text to me could be discounted as paranoia."

He looked at her, braced. Waiting for a reaction.

She considered it. Considered David. He wouldn't be worried over something that wasn't an actual threat. "Just because a person is paranoid doesn't mean they're delusional."

That won her a ghost of a smile. Nodding, he continued. "Text was weird as hell. Typically any bar on base would only issue two drinks in a night over there. But we drink so infrequently, two is more than enough. I figured he was in between missions, low on tolerance and sleep, and drunk texting me."

Lyn snorted. "Better than texting an ex."

"But a drunk text still has a purpose behind it." David pulled his hand out of a pocket and rubbed his face. "Dramatic, I know. But he was going on about Atlas and carrying the answers on his shoulders."

Lyn raised her eyebrows. "So he could've been referencing a book I read in college or mythology."

David snorted. "We do a lot of reading deployed, believe it or not. But Calhoun wasn't into that kind of fiction as much as mythology, especially as it applied to strategy and the art of war."

"So we're thinking the Titan Atlas, then. I remember he was supposed to carry the celestial spheres on his shoulders but that's all I've got." She'd had a phase as a kid reading up on Roman and Greek mythology. Atlas was one of the only Titans she remembered at all. If they got into Nordic gods, she was going to have to start running Internet searches.

David held up both hands. "The message meant exactly what it said: Atlas carries the answers on his shoulders. There was a micro SD card in his shoulder instead of a locater chip."

"Oh." Well, her overactive imagination could take a break, then.

"I've got some of the data running through a decryption now but I'm not sure which encryption he used. It's going to take a couple of days." He gestured back toward the main house and his office. "But Calhoun left me a highlights reel to give me an overview of the issue. It's bad."

"Is this where the conspiracy theory starts?" She wanted to laugh it off but she was afraid it was real.

Lyn studied David. He was agitated, tiny muscles in his jaw jumping beneath the skin as he clenched and unclenched his teeth. As fantastic as this story sounded, it was serious.

David tilted his head to the side briefly. "It's contained and involves plans of a small group of people for after they leave active duty, at least as far as I know."

Relief swept through her and her knees wobbled a bit. She'd worried it was one of those impossible, reaching-up-through-the-ranks kinds of things they showed in action hero movies. "But it's not the peaceful, quiet life sort of retirement, I'm guessing."

"Nope. Some men come home and want to build a life." David looked out over the kennels. "Others want to find a way to go back and keep doing what they did, for more pay and less red tape. The problem is, this is someone's golden parachute, a way for them to make insane amounts of money after they retire from the military and go private. It means deals and contracts and connections that have nothing to do with protecting our country anymore, and everything to do with making profit off of other people's chaos. Anyone planning to go this route has no issues taking out anyone who might get in their way."

She wasn't sure if she understood the latter but she did the former. It was what Brandon, Alex, and David had done here. They were putting their lives back together. Finding their way back from whoever they'd become overseas.

"You need to find these men, don't you?" For his friend, Calhoun. For Atlas.

"They're responsible for Calhoun's death." The one statement held so much conviction. "I need to know why and how. And I need to see them held accountable."

"Do you know where to start looking for them?" She wasn't sure how she could help, but she wanted to. Because David needed to do this for his friend, but she wanted to do this for David.

"I saw one, yesterday. Shouldn't be hard to find him again," David commented. "He's keeping a close eye on Atlas."

And her by association.

"He was in New Hope yesterday. That's why you told us to come back here." Her anger had been settling but it sparked back up. "You could've told me."

David held up his hands again. "I knew he was following but I didn't have the connection until we found the micro SD today. I don't have the full picture yet, just a bunch of pieces to the puzzle, and I'm going to have to dig for the connections to assemble everything."

It was her turn to rub her face with her hands. "What about the men who attacked me?"

"Not military. Hired thugs, most likely. But they've got to be connected." David drew in a deep breath and let it out. "I'm going to find that connection, too, and see them held accountable for what they did to you."

"You sound like a man about to turn into a caped crusader." She regretted the words as they came out. It was the wrong thing to say and she didn't mean to make little of what he planned to do.

He shook his head. "I'm not a superhero. But there's something wrong here and it's got a cascading effect. Hurting people like you and probably others. This is about doing the right thing, and seeing to it Calhoun didn't die for nothing."

She'd always thought of honor as a word on a plaque or written under a crest. David was teaching her about the meaning of it.

"I'd like to help, however I can." She put every ounce of sincerity she had into it, to make up for her previous statement. "It'd bring a lot of attention on if you took me off Atlas's case. I can work with you still, and help track down the rest of the information you need."

"You don't have the training for this." But he didn't sound adamant.

"Any time you leave the kennels, you're going to be watched, aren't you?" She tried to think as quickly as possible. "Just like me. They're less likely to think something is off if we're together and working with Atlas. It could just be another approach to his rehabilitation. Without me and Atlas, it'd be obvious you're up to something."

"You have a point." He wasn't happy about it. His shoulders sagged.

"I said it last night and I still mean it; there's nowhere I feel safer than with you and Atlas." Truth again.

His gaze locked on hers, searching. After a long moment he sighed. "Okay. We work on this together, but anything starts to go sideways and you listen to me. No arguments in the midst of shit going down. Understand?"

She bit her lip. Not a small thing to ask and he'd hold her to it. "Agreed, so long as I can ask my questions once we're someplace safe again and you promise to give me the full, unedited answers."

"Agreed."

CHAPTER ELEVEN

I s it horrible to ask for a rest stop?"

Cruz glanced at the digital display on the dashboard. Only an hour and a half into their road trip. Granted, they'd been caught in some traffic getting past Philadelphia but they hadn't even made it through Delaware. Traveling through it on I-95 was almost literally a blink-and-you-miss-it sort of thing.

Atlas chose that moment to let out a brief whine from the back seat. Dog probably sensed her discomfort but damn, it seemed like Atlas was always going to take her side in awkward situations.

He sighed. Well, he'd decided to bring the two of them along. If this was an indicator for the rest of the trip, he should be glad there were rest stops at regular intervals the whole way there and back. "There's a big rest stop just up here."

"Thank you." She fidgeted. "Have we gotten at least close to halfway there?"

Nope. "Is this your way of asking if we're there yet?"

"No!" She huffed. "It's been a while since I've been on a road trip instead of a flight. I guess I've been spoiled by the availability of a restroom en route."

"You don't ever get stuck in a window seat with someone sleeping?" The image of her squirming in a coach seat, too polite to wake somebody up, amused him.

"It happens, but usually people want to get up at least once during a flight and stretch their legs, too." She shifted in her seat again. He increased his speed some to get them to the rest stop faster. Entertaining as it might be, he didn't actually want her uncomfortable if he could do something about it. "The longest I've ever had to wait is the twenty minutes or so during takeoff or landing."

"And you've never been caught having to go then?" The rest stop came up on the left-hand side and he slowed as he took the exit.

"Murphy's Law kicks in once in a while and I have to go just because we're not allowed to leave our seats." Lyn laughed—a self-conscious, sort of embarrassed sound. "I try to always time it so I go right before we board and right before we land so I don't have the issue."

He could see her milling around at the airport, timing her visit to the rest room perfectly to boarding. "What do you do if the flight has a delay after you've boarded?"

"Hope I can make it." She sounded serious, grim even.

He went over a speed bump nice and slow. No need to aggravate the full bladders in the car. A parking spot opened up right up front near the entrance to the welcome center building. He pulled in smooth and dropped the car into park.

"Thanks!" She popped out of the car.

He got out and called after her. "I'm going to take Atlas a ways down so he can do his business. When you're done, come down this way and meet us."

She waved in acknowledgment, hurrying into the large building.

Cruz chuckled. She really had to go.

Honestly, he didn't mind. It was a long way down to Richmond, Virginia, and the Navy SEAL he'd located. Sheer luck the guy was stationed close enough to seek out with a casual day trip. A long one, but doable in a day and a night.

The man had been one of the soldiers in the highlights video and it'd taken some creative digging to figure out who he was. Cruz was still waiting on the decryption for the full-length video, hoping to get better face shots of the others in the room for identification. In the meantime, Cruz was on a mission to get information from the one he'd located but doing this with Lyn and Atlas put a different spin on the trip. He was willing to take some time and go at an easy pace for this ride. Serious as things were, he couldn't help but smile with her around.

Maybe it was her way of enjoying things all around her. The outlook was contagious. She'd been looking out the window the entire trip and commenting on the greenery or buildings or whatever she saw. The world hadn't gone to crap when you looked at it through her eyes. Not that she was naïve, because a person blinded to the bad all around them would irritate the hell out of him. No.

She was aware of the awful things in life. But she took them, dealt with them, and still came through with a positive outlook. It took a different kind of strength than the obvious and he admired her for it.

Atlas walked beside him on the lead, relaxed and mildly interested in the people around them. The big dog had watched Lyn go until he couldn't see her anymore but had come along with Cruz without resistance. He was alert as he should be, but relaxed in his own way. He even stopped to sniff a weed.

They both had it bad.

And Lyn? She didn't even know the power she had over them.

* * *

David had no idea how attractive he was.

Lyn paused to take in the scene. David and Atlas had reached the end of the long walkway leading away from the welcome center building. Maybe they'd even made it to the plot of grass marked for dog walking and come back. But currently, they were surrounded by a pack of teenage cheerleaders and a smattering of moms. No doubt the moms were every bit as interested in catching the surly man's eye as the teens were.

And David had on his best grouch face, scowling and generally attempting to brush off any attempts at conversation.

Only when it came to questions about Atlas, his armor had chinks. His answers might be curt but he still answered. And the teens peppered him with more questions. She could see the girls pointing to the big dog.

From a distance, Lyn couldn't make out what David was saying but his dark, growly voice sent delicious shivers across her skin.

The man gave good voice.

Of course, the moms weren't in a hurry to lead their girls away either. They added their own comments and laughed, tossing their hair salon-perfect hair. Lyn tugged at a loose lock of her own hair self-consciously. She'd caught a look at herself in the mirror in the bathroom. Tidy but not exactly looking like a supermodel. Every one of those women was made up, done up, and looking fabulous. How did women manage it on road trips and *why* would they bother chaperoning a bunch of cheerleaders?

Because leave a man like David out on his own within five hundred yards of those teenage girls and they'd flock to him. It was hot-guy radar. Had to be.

Lyn hung back, unwilling to break it up. Insecurity was an ugly beast and she readily admitted she was succumbing to it. Rather than show it to David, it'd be better to wait at a distance. Instead, she observed Atlas—which was her job, after all. Atlas was standing at heel, trying to keep all of those waving hands in sight. Generally, dogs didn't like all those grasping hands coming at their face. So far, though, Atlas had managed not to get defensive. He was wary but not upset. Under control. David was doing his part as handler, keeping the girls at a minimum distance to allow Atlas to feel safe.

They weren't rehabilitating him to be friendly.

Social, yes. Able to pass calmly through anything and still follow commands, absolutely. But he wasn't a pet and he wasn't expected to play with random people. He wasn't a PR dog.

He could play, if he wanted. He did play with her and with David. Most of his games revolved around a much-loved tennis ball and fetch. She loved seeing Atlas happy. And once in a while, the perpetual tension left David's shoulders. His face relaxed and the worry lines fell away. David was even more handsome when he was happy, too.

But neither of them was the domesticated male those women and girls expected. It was unfair of them to demand either David or Atlas be safe, perfectly behaved, even submissive to poking and prodding and unwanted attention. But if they made one move to try to shoulder their way out of there, they would go from military hot to scary dangerous. If David even tried to be more assertive about insisting they leave Atlas be as a service dog, they'd decide David was mean rather than respecting Atlas's space.

Not fair.

Suddenly, Lyn started walking. Neither David nor Atlas could be rude to get away. They were essentially trapped. And it'd reflect badly on them if they snapped to be free of the twittering attention showered on them. Fine. She could be a bitch on their behalf.

"I bought us coffee for the road." She plastered a broad smile on her face as she shouldered her way right through the other women and girls.

Passive–aggressive whispers and mean girl giggles surrounded them. Ugh. She didn't miss high school. And really, what was it about people losing all respect for personal space or someone working? Lyn remembered similar gaggles forming around hot police officers or firemen when she'd been on school field trips, more years ago than she cared to count.

The center of attention—be they a man or a woman—always had an awkward time extracting themselves while leaving a positive impression.

David looked like he'd seen salvation. Atlas's ears swiveled forward and his tail even moved side to side once. *Tock, tock.*

One of the girls said something. Lyn ignored it. "Hope you weren't waiting too long. Ready to go?"

"Yup." David wrapped an arm around her shoulders like she was a lifesaver and he was drowning. They headed back to the car as the girls made sad pouty faces. The grown women shot looks that could put Lyn six feet under. David dropped a kiss on Lyn's hair.

No blushing. None. Nope.

Damn it.

Delighted warmth ran through her. Even if it was for show, he filled her with a happy glow.

Once they all got in the car, David let out a long sigh. So did Atlas.

A person would think they'd been through days of combat instead of surviving minutes with hungry ladies. Well, the latter might've been worse. Depended on the type of guy and his preferences.

David started up the car. "Let's go."

Lyn smiled at him—a genuine, happy smile.

* * *

"It should be the next right and up the street on our left." Lyn hoped the GPS was correct. Otherwise, it'd be an incredibly awkward conversation when they knocked on the door.

Actually, it was going to be awkward no matter what. At this point, how awkward was more an order of magnitude.

"We're going to drive around the block first," David said, passing the right-hand turn and continuing onward. "Never hurts to get a good look at what cars are parked on the street and nearby."

"Did you get a look at the car the man was driving in New Hope?" She wondered if she should've been keeping an eye out for it this whole drive.

Of course, they'd seen a lot of cars on the drive down from Pennsylvania to Virginia. It'd been a solid road trip. Atlas had settled into the back like a champ with very few issues. Come to think of it, Atlas probably had more experience than she did with road travel. The military working dog had also been trained in para-jumping and rappelling, so he was a lot more experienced in traversing distances in every direction. Officially, the purpose of this trip was to socialize Atlas in a variety of environments and record his reactions. She wondered what sort of other environments they were going to take him into today.

"I did get a look at his car." David scanned the street as he drove, parking around the corner from the house they wanted to visit. "But the man used to be a Navy SEAL. He'll have switched cars by now. Either gotten a rental or maybe a cheap used car from a local dealership. Something easy to acquire and even easier to get rid of."

Lyn shifted in her seat. The man could be anywhere, still following her. "Why didn't we call the police?"

David hesitated. "No solid proof he was following you. It would've been my word against his. At most, they'd be able to bring him in for questioning but would've released him again. And he'd have gotten more careful."

"Oh." The word sounded quiet, timid, to her ears.

"This way, he's still confident and hopefully underestimates me." He reached out to brush her cheek with his knuckles briefly. "Which gives me an advantage in keeping the bastard away from you."

His touch gave her more reassurance than she thought possible and she tucked his words away to think about later. There'd been a lot of information to process in a short period of time.

He gave Atlas the order to stay and left the car windows cracked for airflow. It was cool outside so Atlas would be safe in the car waiting for them. As they walked toward the house, they kept a casual pace.

"Do you think he's home?" It was late afternoon on a weekday. The entire neighborhood was quiet, though.

"I think he will be home. He works day shift right now, based on my intel. Should've gotten home about twenty minutes ago so long as he didn't get caught up on base." David didn't seem concerned and he didn't elaborate on his sources of intelligence either. "If his family is home, he's less likely to get overexcited."

She didn't like causing trouble for the man's family. It was one thing to search out a bunch of soldiers in her mind but now that they were here—about to talk to one—the ramifications were widening in scope. By a lot. "We're just here to ask questions though, right?"

David was silent for a second as they turned and

walked up the driveway. "For right now, yes. But we all make choices and the reasons behind them get complicated."

She didn't have a chance to pursue the topic because they'd reached the front door and David knocked.

The sound of small feet stampeded toward the door before a feminine voice called out, "Let your father answer the door."

The man who answered the door was lean and dark, and intimidating. Lyn wondered what it was like living with a father like him, but then the man gave them a ready smile and laugh lines creased the corners of his eyes. "Can I help you?"

"Sean Harris?" David asked, extending his hand. "I'm David Cruz. I'm reaching out to some of the teams who worked in co-op with the Air Force military working dog teams. Wanted to get some feedback if you can spare a couple of minutes."

The man's smile quickly disappeared. Perhaps David's approach was too transparent. Which unsettled Lyn because she'd considered his introduction pretty circumspect.

"Seems unusual." Harris's voice maintained a neutral and significantly colder tone.

David spread his hands out at his sides. "I'm retired from active duty, working on consult with the three-forty-first training squadron. Doing some informal research on how we can improve interactions with co-operative teams. Particularly the SEAL teams since you do have dogs of your own."

"Not every unit, as I'm sure you're aware." The ice melted a fraction but Harris didn't step back to invite them inside. Beyond him, Lyn caught sight of three curious children. None of them could've been older than maybe ten years old. "My team has worked with several Air Force pairs."

David nodded. "Did any of them stick out to you as particularly difficult to work with? Any of the dogs have behaviors incompatible with the primary objectives of your team?"

"Not that I remember." Harris wasn't buying it. Lyn noticed he hadn't done more than glance at her the entire conversation but she got the sense he was keeping an eye on both of them.

"Any of the teams memorable at all?" David asked.

"I don't know what you think you're doing digging into things no one should know about." Harris was done with pretending. "But you both need to walk away. Now."

David dropped the pretense, too. "There's a man dead and no one knows the real reason why either."

Harris's gaze swept the street to the right and left before filling the door even more, blocking Lyn's view of his children. "I can't talk to you. You should know this."

Which meant there was something to talk about. Lyn couldn't believe they were in the middle of something so dire that a man as tough as this one obviously was could be frightened into silence.

"I'm trying to do right by my friend," David said quietly.

Harris didn't even flinch. "I have a *family*."

Then he closed the door in their faces.

CHAPTER TWELVE

It's hard to hold it against him." Lyn climbed back into the car.

Atlas sat up from the back seat and touched her cheek with his cool nose. She reached up to give him a scratch on the side of his head and he leaned into her hand.

David finished buckling himself in and started up the car. "You think so?"

He'd been silent on the walk back to the car. His jaw set but otherwise his features were neutral. Blank, almost. Only to her, he could never be a blank, forgettable face.

"Well, family is a reason a lot of people do a lot of things, even things that aren't exactly the right thing." If someone had asked her a few years ago if she'd ever request a favor of her stepfather, she'd have ripped their head off and told them where they could shove it and the very thought of asking. She'd been determined to show him she had the intellect, talent, and determination to make it on her own in a field he'd dismissed as unimportant. But here she was, because she'd swallowed her pride and decided the chance to work with Atlas was worth her stepfather's patronizing oversight. It'd been a compromise of her principles. She wasn't sure what David would've thought of her choice but chances were he'd made difficult choices of his own.

David didn't respond to her statement, though. Instead, he was looking straight ahead and guiding the car onto the road.

She sighed. So did Atlas. It would be a really long drive back up to Pennsylvania if David stayed withdrawn. On the other hand, she could understand his wanting to be left to his own thoughts. She could imagine—and it wouldn't be even close to the reality—what he might be thinking about the dangers his friend had faced without the very men he was supposed to call his teammates guarding his back. If everything around you was likely to kill you, having the team you're with willing to leave you exposed had to have been terrifying.

Only some didn't show fear, not in the way she or other people might be expecting to see it. Everything they presented to the world was very possibly different from what was actually going on inside their heads. David was hard to read in general and in this instance completely shut down. He might be angry or upset, sad or scared. But there wasn't much body language for her to go by. All she had was Atlas and the big dog didn't seem concerned by David at all as the dog leaned into her. She rubbed her forehead with her right hand since Atlas still had a monopoly on her left.

Humans were complicated. It was why she preferred working with dogs.

"Atlas, *af*." David gave the command as he pulled onto the main highway. Atlas looked at him for a long moment, then turned and settled down to lay across the back seat. The delay in obeying commands was still there, but it was getting shorter. At least in response to David.

She turned her head as she mentally did a little happy dance. Baby steps with Atlas. Every improvement, however subtle, was worth celebrating.

Lyn continued to look out the windows and watch the world zip by. No need to reinforce the command for Atlas since the dog had obeyed. In fact, if she'd tried it would've undermined David's authority anyway. Besides, she agreed Atlas shouldn't be standing up between them on the higher speed roadways. If something happened, the big dog would fly right up into the front seat with them or even possibly through the windshield. Technically, they should have him secured in the back and not just free to lay back there.

"I should consider getting an SUV with one of those cargo nets to partition off the back for dog transportation." Thinking out loud wasn't a bad thing. Hopefully.

"Huh?" David didn't turn to look at her but his response was louder than expected.

"Well, this probably won't be the last time I need to transport a dog in my career. I should provide a good example. Maybe be ready to make recommendations to dog owners." Made sense to her. It'd take more saving, though, and a couple of good clients.

"Oh." David nodded. "I was worried there for a minute."

She blinked. "Why?"

There was a hesitation. "Well, you know Atlas needs to go back to Lackland. Even if he's retiring, there's a process for adoption and applicants are considered in a specific order."

"Oh." She'd read about it in her research. "Yeah, I know. Usually handlers or their families have priority, right?"

Another nod.

"But..." She bit down on what she was going to say next.

"Calhoun doesn't have family. At least no one in a position to take Atlas." David addressed the difficult topic anyway. She admired his ability to take things head on. 'Course, she liked a lot of things about him. Too many.

"So who would be next in line?"

"Other military or families. There are several variables under consideration."

"I figured." She didn't look back at Atlas but she was tempted to pull down the vanity mirror so she could see him in the reflection. "Things have been moving so fast with him. I hadn't thought about where he'd go next. Hard to imagine what it'll be like to see him go."

She felt a sinking feeling in her belly. She wouldn't just be saying good-bye to Atlas.

"You might be able to visit him," David offered. "Depends on who gets him. I plan to try to stay in touch."

With her, too? She didn't ask. Maybe later, but things were too...new. She wasn't sure where they stood yet.

"Maybe. I think he'd like a new forever home with a family. It might be awkward for me to pop in, though." She struggled to put the empty feeling into words then gave up and tried for a different direction. "Did you ever want one?"

"Want what? A dog? I have all the dogs I can fit into my life back at Hope's Crossing." There was happiness in his voice. Pride. It made her smile.

"I meant a family." Now that she'd said it, she sort of wanted to take it back. The good humor left his face.

Damn. Just when he'd started to come back to a cheerful mood.

"No. Not in a conventional sense." He said it slowly. Carefully. "While I was active duty, I had my own demons. Every deployment was another chance to work through them. Only I picked up new ones every time I went out there. I figured it'd be the worst idea in the world to have a wife and kids waiting for me at home, wondering and never knowing if I was going to make it back. And depending on the wife, my kids might never understand why I was always away. She might not understand it either. I've seen too many marriages filled with constant fighting over that. I didn't want that for anyone."

Had her stepfather? She tried to remember. But her perception of him from her childhood had been of a stoic man. Stern. Immovable. She'd spent a long time thinking he hadn't cared at all.

This was the first time David had said so much about his past, though, and she wanted to know more about him. "What did you do in between deployments? Go home?"

He snorted. "Nah. Not because it was bad or anything. I just didn't fit in."

"Oh." She didn't know what to say. "That's hard."

"Well, my parents divorced while I was a teenager.

High school angst doesn't get much worse than what I had. I was angry. At my dad. My mom. Myself. Just always angry." He opened and closed his hands on the steering wheel. "Mom left. Dad remarried. I got angrier."

She reached out, touched his thigh with her fingertips. Not sure if it'd be welcome but it seemed more than trying to come up with words. He dropped his right hand from the steering wheel and took hers in his. Warmth enveloped her hand and tingles ran up her arms and along her skin.

Wow, it didn't take much. His touch had her so finely tuned to him. Aware.

"I enlisted right out of high school. Basically took my diploma in hand and went straight into the Air Force. Some of my other friends went Army or Navy, but I knew what I wanted to be."

She cocked her head to the side. "And you've always gone to do what you set out to do?"

He squeezed her hand. "Basically. It took a while, but becoming a PJ was worth every second of hell to get there."

"A PJ?" Her favorite pajamas popped into her mind. And then she wondered what he tended to wear to bed.

Bad Lyn. Bad.

"Para rescue jumper."

That made more sense. "Ah. Must've taken a while."

He lifted one shoulder and dropped it in a half-shrug. "Longer than I wanted, not as long as most."

Not too prideful, not too humble either. She smiled.

"Any time I did go home, the house was full of half-brothers and -sisters. All way younger than me. Dad had rebooted his family life. He didn't make me feel unwanted, but it was awkward." He paused. "His new wife was nice enough but we never clicked."

"I'm sorry."

"It's not even a thing." He lifted her hand and kissed the back before placing it back down on top of his thigh. "Mostly, the kids like me just fine while I'm buying them video games or whatever is on their online wish lists for birthdays and Christmas."

But he didn't have a home to go back to. "Didn't they even think about it, though? Sure, you made it comfortable, easy for them. But they left you outside their world."

That made her furious.

"My choice to leave," he reminded her. "And I don't need to be angry with them. Plenty of other things to work through all on my own."

"You mentioned demons." She said it quietly. Not sure he wanted to talk about it. Her father had always sent her to her room if she asked about his deployments, what he did.

"Yeah." David fell silent for a while. His hand was a comforting weight on hers, though. A sign he wasn't pushing her away. "It's a weird thing, being over there. You become . . . institutionalized. And when you come home, you feel out of step. Hard to back down from the level of hyperawareness you need to maintain overseas. People want you to be a hero. But they want you to be the perfect citizen, too. The problem is, to be out there and survive, you become a rough man . . . ready to do violence."

It was a part of a saying. It swam up from her memory as one of the things her stepfather had repeated often at the dinner table.

People sleep peaceably in their beds at night only because rough men stand ready to do violence on their behalf.

The line was attributed to George Orwell. Her mind brought up the source she'd researched. The words had always stuck with her but some of her Internet research had said it wasn't a direct quote, more an interpretation of what the man had said. She'd looked it up in the hopes of impressing her stepfather. But he'd pinned her with a stare and asked her if she truly appreciated what the words meant or the men who stood ready to defend her sleep.

Until now, listening to David, she hadn't.

"It's not fair to expect you to switch gears when you come back." It was hard to know what to say so she went with what she thought, felt. Honest.

He barked out a laugh. "True. I try not to think about fair. Life's generally not."

"But some people try to make it that way." She would, moving forward. No matter where tomorrow took them. Mostly because she'd always been told life wasn't. And seriously, it wouldn't ever be if no one ever tried.

"Yeah." David shook his head. "I thought Forte was crazy when he said he was going back to his hometown to open up a kennel. But he'd saved every penny from the day he enlisted. And it added up. Then he got me and Rojas to come out to look at the place. It was huge. Right in the middle of a decent-sized town and close to a couple of different cities, but still private."

"Perfect?" She could imagine. All the different environments to fit a wandering soul. They could go to whatever surroundings their mood needed in a day trip. Or night.

"Absolutely."

"I can see the draw." They'd even come several states away and were still going to make it back in one day. She wondered if he'd even considered stopping for the night.

"Besides. Working with the dogs helped." David lifted his chin to indicate the rearview mirror. Looking up, she could see Atlas in the mirror too. "Look at him. He loved unconditionally."

Hearing the word come from David, easily, tugged at her. Too many men wouldn't say the word even about somebody else. Like the word was somehow a worse curse than any other four-letter word in existence.

"Dogs do." And she loved them back. Every one she'd ever met. Because they were so worth it.

"A dog like him—one with a heart that big—he loves without question once he decides to give it," David continued. "He laid his life on the line for his handler, because to him, it was worth it. But sometimes half the team doesn't make it back."

David paused.

"It wasn't his fault." Never. Not even knowing what had truly happened, she wouldn't believe Atlas had failed his handler.

Sometimes, no matter how hard anyone tries, lives are lost.

"No. And I thought maybe he'd pine away. Some of them do. And it would've hurt Calhoun worse than dying all over again if his dog had died of heartbreak.

Calhoun would've wanted somebody to help Atlas through this. And someday, maybe Atlas will choose somebody new to look to." David glanced over at Lyn.

Her heart leaped. And then she squashed the happy dance. Atlas wasn't hers. None of the dogs she worked with were actually hers.

Atlas stirred in the back, having heard his name. He gave a quiet whine.

Her own bladder decided to alert her to the amount of time they'd been moving. Glancing at the clock, she couldn't believe how much time had already gone by over the course of their conversation. "So how close is the next rest stop?"

"Not far." David released her hand and picked up his phone. A quiet command and the phone's GPS kicked in. "There're stops all up and down this highway. If not actual rest stops, then exits to get food or gas."

No sooner had he said so than a sign came up for a rest stop in a couple of miles. They sat in companionable silence as they approached and he pulled into a parking spot to one side, closer to a patch of grass and some trees.

"You go on ahead and I'll let Atlas take care of his business." David gathered up Atlas's leash from the console between them.

"Okay." She popped out of the car, the call of nature too urgent to even care about dignity. Atlas, apparently, was feeling the same way, considering how fast he hopped out of the back of the car and sat to have the leash attached to his collar.

She hurried to the building and took care of business. On the way out, she bought three bottles of water and some beef jerky.

David and Atlas were standing next to the car as she returned, both looking in her direction but not actually watching her. Or at least it didn't seem like it, because David didn't return her smile or even react to the bag of beef jerky she waved at him.

As she approached, David put a hand to the small of her back and rushed her back to her side of the car. "See anything odd inside?"

"No." She got in quickly and didn't protest when Atlas hopped in after her and scrambled over her lap to get in the back seat.

As David closed her door, headlights turned on suddenly from the row ahead of them and blinded her. Tires screeched. David rolled across the top of the car's hood. She got the impression of a dark car screeching past them, so close they clipped the side-view mirror.

Atlas let out a deep bark, lunging back up to the front seat. Lyn turned and grabbed his collar as David yanked the car door open and dove in, slamming the car door shut as he turned on the car. "Seat belt!"

"*Af.*" Lyn gave the big dog a nudge and Atlas returned to the back seat as she reached for her seat belt.

David didn't wait, throwing the car into reverse. Her head almost hit the dashboard but they turned sharply and she was slammed back into her seat as they went into drive. Desperately, she fumbled the seat belt until she got it buckled as David sped back out onto the highway.

"Sit tight." Whether the grim order was for her or for Atlas, she didn't know. But she was guessing it was for her since he hadn't said Atlas's name.

More screeching as a car came up on their right and cut in front of them. David decelerated sharply to keep from running off the road and then poured on the speed, getting ahead of the other driver again.

"Is this a good idea?" The bottles of water were rolling around by her feet.

"Sure it is." He sounded *cheerful*.

They barreled down the highway in the left lane and she watched the streetlights flash by as streaks across the windows. Somebody had tried to run him down and force them off the road. Maybe even were trying to kill them. Her heart pounded through her chest and in her ears. There wasn't anything she could do.

"Reach into the glove compartment." David's instruction was urgent but calm. "There's a flashlight in there. Point it back over your shoulder before turning it on. Do *not* look into it. Do *not* point it in Atlas's face. It's way more intense than your average flashlight."

She did as instructed.

"Handy high-powered flashlight for heavy weather conditions," David explained. "It might as well be a hand-held spotlight. If we're lucky, it'll shine in the bastard's eyes and blind him some. At minimum, it'll be a distraction. Just hold on to it and turn it to the left and right a couple of degrees."

The small, black cylinder fit into her hand, heavier than she expected, and the power button was easy to find. Making sure Atlas was laying down low, she followed David's directions. A veritable spotlight poured out the back of the car.

David nodded. "Good."

Suddenly, David turned right, barely making an exit and slamming the breaks to slow down enough not to flip them over on the curving ramp.

"Turn off the light." The words came through gritted teeth as he picked up speed again.

She did.

They twisted through several smaller roads until they were in a nondescript neighborhood, parked among a few other cars in an equally nondescript apartment complex.

He shut everything down and made sure all the lights were out, even on the dash.

"All right?" His voice came low and calm as his hand touched her shoulder in the darkness.

She nodded, hoping he could see her because words weren't coming at the moment.

"Hang in there for a few minutes until we know for sure we've lost whoever that was."

She swallowed hard. "Okay."

"Atlas." There was a stirring from the back seat, low in the foot wells.

David released his seat belt and turned in the seat to check on Atlas. "Keep an eye out the windows. Tell me if you see anything."

She peered out into the dark but there was nothing. No cars. No people. It was really dark in this parking lot. "Apartment complexes should have better lighting in their parking lots."

The thought popped out of her mouth.

David chuckled, returning to his seat. "They should. Most don't."

"Good for us in this case?" She clutched the flashlight

as if it was a weapon. And maybe it could be. If someone came up, maybe she could blind them until they could get away. She should get one for herself.

"Very good for us." David paused. "Change of plans for the evening. Best thing for us to do is be unpredictable."

"Which means we're sleeping here tonight?" Outside. Exposed. She shivered even though the car was still warm. With Atlas and David, she could do it if it was necessary. She might not actually sleep, though.

"No." David was silent until she turned to look at him. Her eyes had adjusted so she could make out his face and his gaze caught her, reassured her. He wouldn't let anything happen to her. "Let's get you someplace safe tonight. Then we'll head out again in the morning."

CHAPTER THIRTEEN

T his... was not what I expected."

Cruz turned to grin at Lyn, happy to see some color returning to her previously pale face. Her tone was more of hesitant surprise than dismay, which was good. "Exactly."

"And you just happened to know about this place tucked away in a little town off the highway?" She sounded dubious.

Okay, he'd be asking questions too if he were in her place.

He chuckled. Her mind was always working as she studied every conceivable angle of a situation. Kept him on his toes and made messing with her fun. "In fact, yes."

She planted her feet at the end of the walkway and crossed her arms. Next to her, Atlas came to heel, then sat. "Seriously."

Cruz kept walking, unhurried, until he reached the

top of the walk and tapped a discreet, stylized sign. It had the silhouette of a German shepherd and a concise warning—not enough to scare away potential guests but enough to assure likely thieves that the property was guarded. "Not every puppy is suited for military or police service. We try to be sure to find good homes for the youngsters who don't make it all the way through training. We've got clients all up and down the East Coast."

The shadows cleared from her expression and curiosity sparked in her eyes. Easy as that. For all of her wariness, she believed too quickly. Somebody, someday was going to take advantage of her. The thought tightened his chest. It wasn't fair of him to want a person to be both wary and trusting.

But then his expectations of people hadn't ever been fair. It was why he worked better with dogs.

"I guess they'll have no problem with Atlas coming inside with us, then." The big dog, sitting next to her, looked up at her then at Cruz and voiced a short bark.

Dog was getting more talkative than Cruz ever remembered him being, even with Calhoun. As a rule, the military working dogs were trained to be silent most of the time. Her habit of conversing with him was changing Atlas more than Cruz had initially considered. The question would be whether Atlas reverted to a more stoic behavior pattern once he was working with another military handler.

He should if he was going back overseas.

Time spent with Lyn was nothing to regret but Cruz was more than a little worried about the impact her moving on would have . . . on both of them. Lyn's caring heart had softened them. If times were peaceful, it might not be as much of a worry but they'd just been given a taste of combat conditions in a place where there shouldn't be any. Now, more so than ever, they needed to be vigilant. "Shouldn't be a problem." He waited until they'd joined him before climbing the few steps to the landing of the historic bed and breakfast. "And I should be able to handle any introductions to their dogs to avoid any potential issues."

Her gaze settled on him, one eyebrow raised in an eloquent expression.

He nodded to her. "Not saying you couldn't, but since these bruisers know me it'll go faster if I do it."

Subtle tension went out of her shoulders and the corners of her lips turned up in a rueful smile. "You have a point there."

Any animal was more responsive with a familiar person. No matter how skilled the trainer, familiarity helped things go along more quickly. He'd met a lot of people with too much pride to acknowledge this simple practicality. As if admitting it made their skill less somehow. Or because they had to prove their abilities could overcome the advantage.

Lyn could be competitive. He had no doubts there. But she'd worked alongside him, burying her pride for the common goal. It'd made it easier for him to set his own emotional baggage aside and focus on Atlas.

Tonight, though—he was going to start taking more of a lead in the situation.

Almost getting run down did that to a man.

"Hopefully, they've got a room open for us." He reached out and knocked on the door.

"Will they hear that? There's a doorbell." She pointed.

He shrugged. "Don't want to wake up any other guests. There's rooms on the ground floor. The dogs will hear the knock and alert them to someone on the property."

Sure enough, Atlas stood. His big ears swiveled forward and nose twitched as he watched the door. The big dog stood ready and alert, every line the perfect balance of tension and listening. He was waiting for the barest whisper of a command.

Lyn huffed out a soft breath. "That'll work."

Quiet footsteps came to the door and paused. An older man peered out the tall thin window beside the door. A moment later, the deadbolt turned and the door opened. "David Cruz? What brings you to our door tonight?"

Cruz held his hands to his sides, palms open. More for the benefit of the big dog behind the older man than the man himself. Unarmed. Nonthreatening. The breeze at his back would carry his scent inside for the German shepherd. "How are you, Thomas? We were driving up north and got tired. Thought we'd stop in for the night if you've got the room."

"Always room for you or any of the boys from the kennel." The older man nodded to Lyn. "Hello, miss. Welcome."

Lyn gave him a shy smile. "Hello. This is Atlas."

Atlas had eyes only for the German shepherd. Until they were introduced, neither of them would relax. David planned to get it done as soon as possible. For the meantime, he shifted enough to block direct eye contact between the two dogs.

"Don't think I've ever seen David here in the com-

pany of a lady when he's working with his dogs."
Thomas gave Cruz a significant look as the older man
stepped back and opened the door wider, giving his dog
a quiet command to stand down. "You remember old
Brutus."

"He's looking good." David stepped inside and ran
his hand down Brutus's back as the dog's tail waved side
to side once in greeting. Gray around his muzzle and
eyes showed his age. He had a couple of good years in
him yet, though. "You mind if I put on his lead and take
him outside? I've got another dog to introduce him to
and it's best to do these things out on neutral territory,
off your property."

Thomas nodded, reaching for one of two leather leads
hanging from a hook on the wall. "Not at all. I'll go get
Caesar. We'll introduce 'em all at once. Kathryn will get
your room ready. You're lucky tonight. Master suite is
the only room empty."

Cruz shrugged. "Ah. Any room would be fine."

"Maybe for you. We give hospitality to ladies here."
Thomas tipped an imaginary hat toward Lyn.

Lyn laughed. "And it's appreciated."

Cruz opted out of the conversation and instead spoke
quietly to Brutus. Immediately responsive, the dog sat
for him and turned his head to make it easy to clip the
leash to his collar. "You've been keeping up on their
training."

"More like they've been keeping us up on ours."
Thomas chuckled as he stepped away. "It's the way you
and the boys changed our lives by helping us with Brutus
and Caesar. Couldn't have done it without you."

Cruz smiled, suddenly awkward and embarrassed. It

was what he did, training dogs. A job well done meant a happy owner and a content dog. It meant a dog was more likely to have a home for the rest of his days. Comfortable. Belonging.

Lyn called to him quietly. "Let's get them all introduced and then head up for some rest. It's been a weird night."

Yeah. Tomorrow wasn't going to get any more normal.

* * *

Lyn wandered around the room—suite, really—and took a moment to simply enjoy. She stayed in hotels all the time and they were most definitely *not* all made equal. In fact, even hotels in the same chain varied to a certain extent, depending on location. She hadn't spent much time in bed and breakfasts or inns or even boutique hotels but seeing this place, she might need to do research to start including these in her accommodations for the future.

This room was decorated with Old World charm, overlooking a garden with a formal fountain elegantly lit for nighttime viewing. As Lyn wandered past the queen-sized bed, she ran her hands over the sheets and pillowcases. Cotton woven so fine to the touch, she couldn't wait to get into bed. Okay, and she was a sucker for a thick down comforter, too.

Peeking into the bathroom, she bit her lip. "Hey, David?"

"Yeah." She heard David walk into the suite and shut the door. He must've unleashed Atlas, too, because she heard the sound of the big dog shaking himself.

"Mind if I take a bath?" Who knew what he'd think but damn it, there was a real Jacuzzi in there. "A real bath."

David chuckled. "As opposed to a pretend one?"

She tore her gaze from the Jacuzzi, and shot him a pointed look. "It's been an interesting road trip. I'd be stiff from the hours in the car alone. But then we had some insanity." She held up her hand when he was about to say something. "A lot crazier than I think I can process all at once. I'd like a long soak because I don't know how anyone is supposed to stay loose during that kind of driving and I will be sore tomorrow. This'll at least help it from being worse."

A long moment of silence. "It would be good. Go for it."

Lyn started into the bathroom and halted. Leaning back out of the bathroom she studied David. "We are safe for the night, aren't we?"

David tipped his head to the side. "Like I told you before, I don't have all the answers. But yeah, we should be safe tonight."

Should be? It was one thing to go searching for pieces of a puzzle. This had all gotten exponentially more real. David's reserved personality was somewhat frustrating all on its own but the way he hadn't talked to her more about what had just happened or any precautions he might be taking wasn't helping her relax any either. She *did* have faith that he was taking them, but she'd appreciate being part of the decision making. Which wasn't exactly fair because she didn't have the knowledge or the skills to be able to help in any sort of planning for this kind of thing. It was only for her pride, really.

She should be on equal footing with him. She should be actively a part of deciding their next move. Instead, she was asking if he minded if she took a bath. Her hard-fought independent nature had evaporated at the sight of a Jacuzzi tub.

She sighed, consciously relaxing her jaw and wondering if he'd been aware of her grinding her teeth. It wasn't good for her to think in circles and wouldn't be constructive to talk to him about it because he'd be damned one way or the other with the way her current thought process was stuck in a loop.

She just... needed to be away from all the strong personalities for a while.

"Okay." She looked at Atlas. "You, stay out here and be his wingman."

Atlas dropped his jaw open and let his tongue loll out.

She stepped inside and closed the door.

David's voice called to her. "Better lock it; he can open doors."

She turned and responded through the closed door. "You know, this is like a scene where a velociraptor looks down at the doorknob and..."

"He can do it a couple of ways. Use a paw, use his nose. He can even spring himself from most crates on his own." David didn't sound serious.

Nah. None of the dogs she'd worked with had ever turned a round doorknob. Maybe if it were a handle, something for him to get a paw on and pull down—like the velociraptor did in the movie—but this wasn't likely. She left it unlocked and turned the hot water taps to start filling the tub. It wasn't as if David was going to come peeping.

She trusted him not to. And to be honest with herself, the thought of locking herself away from the only other friends she had in a strange place triggered a tightness in her chest. Probably a reaction to the freaky car chase. She wanted some distance from them but not actual isolation.

All the more reason to soak in a nice tub and relax, work through some of these weird nerves, and get back to steady ground.

There was a lovely wooden tray on a small table next to the tub, maybe teak? A few packets of bath salts were arranged in a glass jar, labeled with ingredients. A small handwritten card warned to read ingredients carefully in case of allergic reactions.

"Wonder how many times that's happened," she muttered.

"You need something?" David's voice came through the door.

She straightened and studied the door thoughtfully. How close was he to the door if he heard her? "No. Just reading a few labels out loud."

"Okay. Holler if you need anything."

"Thanks." She was guessing she wouldn't need to raise her voice by much. He must be sitting right next to the door. Odd . . .

A snuffling sound came from under the door. Atlas.

She paused and thought that through. No. David wasn't lurking by the door listening and damn, she should know better. Atlas must be by the door waiting for her and had reacted to hearing her mutter. David was a very perceptive trainer. He must've been watching Atlas and seen the cue.

Mystery solved and significantly less creepy. But then, David wasn't the type of guy to do such things.

Sighing, she picked out lavender bath salts and poured the contents of the little packet into the water. Definitely not thinking straight and a good thing she hadn't lingered out in the bedroom to talk with David like this. She felt bad enough about the way she was jumping to conclusions inside her own head. It'd be horrible if he heard her.

Turning off the water, she tested the heat before getting in. About right. And when she turned off the main light switch, the little porcelain night-light on the wall above the vanity provided just enough to see by. She undressed, leaving her clothes in a heap on the floor and stepped in carefully. She'd gather her clothes up later and hang them up to air out. Right now, she wanted to soak. Desperately.

Lowering herself into the tub slowly, she smiled. Really hard to find mid-range, reasonably priced hotels with a tub deep enough to enjoy a truly good soak. Most tubs, you could sit about waist deep or bend your knees and neck. Not exactly optimal. But here, she was settled comfortably in the deep tub with the water line right up to her shoulders. The heat immediately started to seep into her limbs. Oh, this was so good.

Inhaling the lavender-scented steam, she started to systematically tense and relax her body a part at a time. First her toes, then her feet, then her calves... and on up. Tension released in areas she hadn't realized had been seized up. It didn't take more than ten minutes, but the relaxation exercise helped immensely, more so in combination with the hot soak.

She'd probably still be sore tomorrow but not as bad as she might've been.

Come to think of it, the whole night had turned out better than what could've been.

She'd reached for her car door handle when the other car had almost run down David. Stupid. Even if she'd have managed to get the door open it would've probably been too late to do any good or she might've hit him with it and slowed his escape. She hadn't been thinking so much as horrified. Actually, if she'd opened her door and the car had collided with it, it could've hurt her pretty badly, too.

Swallowing hard, she wrapped her arms around herself.

David had been quick and avoided the danger far better than she could have. And then the drive...

At those speeds, would any of them have walked away from a crash? Atlas hadn't been secured. He'd have bounced around the car like a ping-pong ball. Even with the seat belts, she and David could've been seriously hurt.

Visions of the car running off the road, flipping over and rolling, flashed through her mind. There was a chattering noise and it took her several seconds to identify the sound as her own teeth. The water around her was still warm but she was shaking all over. She'd drawn her knees up without noticing and she sat in a semi-fetal position in the tub trying to hold herself together.

But it was too late. The panic attack was in full swing. More images streamed through her mind of the dark, the bright headlights. The sounds of engines and screeching tires echoed in her ears. Her heart beat harder and she couldn't catch her breath.

Then the sounds changed to words.

...*she won't see our faces.*

There was a sharp bark.

"Lyn? You okay in there?"

But we can show her a couple other things before we leave.

She held her breasts, trying to protect them from the painful pinch. Squeezed her eyes shut and tried not to see his face. *No. No. No.*

Another bark, deeper, and a scratching sound.

There was a soft creak as the door was opened and Atlas was there, leaning over the tub, licking her face.

"Lyn! I'm coming in."

She didn't protest, glad for Atlas and relieved as she realized David was there.

David reached in and lifted her out of the tub, cradling her against his chest. "It's okay. You're okay."

"S-sorry. S-sorry!" She couldn't stop shaking, couldn't stop her teeth from chattering.

"It's okay. We're here." David carried her out of the dimly lit bathroom into the warm light of the bedroom and set her on the bed.

She wanted to cling to him, ask him not to let her go. But he was back in seconds and wrapped a soft blanket around her.

David sat next to her then, his arm open in invitation. She tipped right into his chest, burying her face in the hollow of his shoulder. He stilled for a minute. "Just this once. *Over.*"

She looked up in time to see Atlas jump onto the bed and give her a quiet, concerned whine. The big dog stared into her eyes for a long moment, then lay down pressed up against her other side. His heavy weight against her hip helped settle her jangling nerves.

"I love baths. I don't know why I'm like this. I hate this." She was babbling and she had no idea why.

His hands rubbed up and down her upper arms, warming her through the comforter. "Could be a lot of factors. These things sneak up on you."

He was matter-of-fact about it, accepting. None of it was weird to him. She was so glad he wasn't calling her crazy. She was a little worried that she was, in fact, losing it.

"I don't understand what's wrong with me."

He kissed her forehead. "None of this is wrong. You've been through awful things. They'll come back and bite you once in a while."

She considered his words. "You get these...moments. Panic attacks?"

"Yeah. Not often. More nightmares than these, but I've seen it enough." His voice turned rough. "It's nothing to be ashamed of."

Leaning into him, she breathed in the scent of him. He smelled like clean air and woods. "How do you make it stop?"

"You don't." Simple. Matter of fact. Gruff but not callous. "You figure out how to work your way through it each time it happens, but don't try to avoid it and don't convince yourself it won't happen, because that's when it'll catch you with your pants down. Accept it. Work through it."

It was what he did. She considered his words. Short, to the point. But not without caring. His understanding helped more than lots of talking. He'd gotten through these kinds of things. Nightmares? He woke up every day and walked out into the world and she couldn't ever remember a moment she'd thought he was anything but capable and confident and on top of it all.

He'd shared a weakness with her and somehow, it made her ridiculously relieved to know she wasn't alone.

David's arm had closed around her and he used his free hand to clear strands of wet hair from her face. "Take your time and get your bearings. Look. Listen. Smell. Everything is different. You're safe here. It's all good."

It was his face she looked at. His chiseled features and dark hair, his steel blue eyes. She etched it into her memory and drove away the other man's disgusting leer with the warmth and concern of David's expression. Here was safety, strength. This was what she wanted to remember.

She leaned up and pressed her lips against his. He held still for a long moment, not pulling away but not reciprocating. Then his lips parted and he returned her kiss gently.

But it wasn't enough.

"More," she whispered against his lips.

David lifted his head and tucked her against his shoulder again, resting his chin on her head. "You're really upset right now. It'd be better to tuck you in and let you get some rest."

No. No sleeping. She didn't want nightmares.

"There's too many things crashing inside my head. Too many bad memories." She needed him to understand. "I'm terrified and I don't want these things to keep ambushing me in the dark."

His arms tightened around her. "It takes a while to

work through these, sometimes a long while. When they happen, you've got to find your way through. Breathe. Look around you." He paused. "Maybe see a professional to talk through it. You've been through a lot in less than two weeks."

She shook her head. "A shrink isn't what I need right now."

"Well, I'm not sure of one who's got office hours at this time of night anyway but soon. Everybody handles these things their own way. You'll find your way."

She huffed out a laugh. Maybe. Probably. So far, she liked his method of dealing. The panic had receded to a faint jangle in the back of her head and she was grateful. It'd be even better to replace it with something positive.

"To be honest, I want better memories." She pulled away from him just far enough to look up into his eyes, catch his gaze. It was important for him to know she meant every word she was about to say. "Make love to me? Not because I'm upset. But because you're wonderful and I'm insanely attracted to you. Because I want to make memories with you. Good ones. Can we do that?"

CHAPTER FOURTEEN

Oh boy, did he want to. Cruz struggled with his raging libido.

"This isn't right, Lyn." He needed to get off this bed and out of this room. Stat. What she was offering would test the self-control of a saint and he wasn't one. Not even close.

"You've already insisted we do the right thing once." She reached out of the cocoon of the comforter he'd wrapped around her and snagged a handful of his t-shirt.

He could break away easily, but because it was her holding him, he wouldn't. Did she even know?

"I'm completely awake and in full control of my mental faculties." Her gaze held his with a steady, smoldering burn.

Every part of him was waking up in response to her. Woman knew what she wanted. "You are extremely upset and vulnerable."

Part of him wanted to pounce on her, press his

lips against every delicate part and run his tongue along her body until he found sensitive places even she didn't know about herself. Curled up as she was, completely naked under that comforter, she was definitely vulnerable.

His damsel in distress narrowed her eyes at him and pressed her lips together. "There's a whole lot of life going on and it doesn't make sense to me to wait for happier times or calmer days."

She had a point there. She was also shrugging out of the comforter some and the smooth skin across her exposed shoulder was insanely enticing.

"Besides, there's a certain excitement about the last twenty-four hours at least." Her cheeks warmed to a rose flush. "I've never felt more alive than now."

He could understand her reaction. Extreme danger, potentially life-threatening. One of the ways people could deal with coming through those kinds of situations intact was to celebrate life. And hell, as far as he was concerned, enjoying it with another person was even better.

Buying himself some time to clear his head, he straightened and looked Atlas in the eye. "Let's get you settled for the night."

Lyn leveled a smoldering stare on him, letting him know she definitely didn't plan to cool off while he was stepping away, and caressed the big dog's head. "Good night, Atlas."

Of course she'd sound happy, all sorts of sweet and innocent. None of them was fooled, though. Atlas was probably more than aware of the pheromones floating around the room.

Atlas reluctantly followed him off the bed and out of the bedroom into the sitting room. There was a large crate for guest dogs set up, complete with water and food bowls, freshly laundered blankets.

"*Hok*." Cruz motioned to the crate.

Atlas studied it, then Cruz, for a long moment before entering. He sniffed around for a few seconds, then lay down with an audible huff.

"Sorry, bud." Cruz had a small amount of brotherly sympathy for the big dog. Besides, depending on how he answered Lyn, he might end up out here bedding down next to the big dog. "We've both slept in strange places. At least this is comfortable."

Besides, if circumstances were reversed out in the field, Cruz wouldn't have begrudged Atlas. Well, things were different for dogs.

Moving on.

Lyn was still curled up at the top of the bed with the comforter gathered around her when he returned. He strode across the small room and paused. The lights were all on but in their vintage fixtures, the glow they cast was soft.

* * *

"Stay with me, David." She rose up out of her comforter when he came within reach, pressed a kiss on his jaw.

His control frayed and dissolved. Heat rushed up through his body and up into his head despite the few moments of clarity he'd gained earlier. Nope, he hadn't had a chance.

As her lips found his, he angled his head to give her

better access and opened for her. Their tongues danced and explored. He drank in her sweetness, her lips touched with a hint of salt from the bath. He wondered if he'd get the same complex flavors when he ran his tongue over other parts of her.

When, not if.

Oh, he was going to hell.

"Are you sure?" He wanted to give her every opportunity.

Her gaze was steady, though, and her smile was warm, intimate—a visual caress just for him. "What's taking you so long?"

He chuckled. "Oh, you have no idea what you are getting yourself into."

He climbed onto the high bed and stalked up to her on hands and knees.

"I have high hopes." She reached out to him, caressing the sides of his face.

Her lips were soft, welcoming. He kept the kisses light for the moment, playful. "Do you want the lights out?"

She froze for a moment and he drew back so he could catch her gaze. Shadows and fear flickered in her eyes.

He made a soft hushing noise. "I like the lights, if they're okay with you. I like seeing you."

The tension eased throughout her body and he let his weight settle over her as she gave him kisses as her answer. Her body was pliant under his, her curves pressing against him and tempting his control. He'd burned out most of it trying to resist her at all.

He ran a hand along her side, enjoying the silky smoothness of her skin and the curve of her hip under his hand.

She nipped at the corner of his mouth and tugged at his t-shirt. "No fair."

He sat up long enough to pull the t-shirt over his head, enjoying her touch as she sat up with him to run her hands over his chest. "I haven't had a chance to shower yet. I could—"

She shook her head, tugging at his belt. "Uh-uh, I've waited long enough."

Okay then. He helped her with undoing his pants and both of them chuckled as he got out of them without leaving the bed, mostly because she wouldn't let him. Once he was naked, she ran her hands over him, hungry and greedy in the best of ways.

This was another aspect of Lyn he enjoyed, the way she met him in every activity. She didn't just sit back and let him do all the work or always take the lead. She met him head on.

As her fingers wrapped around the length of him, he shuddered. "Careful."

"I'm done being careful."

The heat of her mouth closed over him and he almost lost his balance, his control, and everything right then and there.

He buried his hand in her gold hair. God, she was doing things to him and he'd have all sorts of catching up to do. And he would.

She sucked and licked the head of his shaft as her fingertips teased the tender skin under his balls. He groaned under the onslaught of sensations, almost blinded by how good it felt. He gritted his teeth and reached for whatever willpower he had left not to thrust or rush her in any way.

A moment later, she released him, looking up the length of him with wet lips and a very saucy expression. Growling, he pushed her back on the bed. He settled himself between her legs and ground his hips into her, rubbing his erection along her slit. She was already wet, ready for him.

"There's so much I want to do for you," he groaned. Then he kissed her neck, tasted the slight salt left behind by her bath mixed with the natural sweetness of her skin. "But I want to be inside you now. Right now."

"Please." Her whisper tickled his ear and her hands gripped at his hips.

He drew back and reached to one side, pulling open the drawer of the nightstand and fishing out a condom from the box thoughtfully hidden there. It'd been Kathryn, not Thomas, who'd pulled David aside before settling them into the room to tell David she kept the master suite well stocked with amenities for all sorts of needs. He sent the saucy old proprietress silent thanks.

After unwrapping the condom and rolling it on, he was back to Lyn as fast as he could be. He nuzzled her breasts until she giggled, her arms wrapping around his shoulders. Capturing one taut nipple in his mouth, he suckled until her breath caught.

"Tease." Her voice was husky now with a tinge of impatience.

Good. That made two of them. He took one of her hands and guided it south, placing her hand on his rigid shaft and letting her guide him in. He watched her, kept her gaze locked with his. Any moment, any fear, any doubt, and he'd stop. But he didn't want to miss this. Wanted to enjoy every bit of it with her.

As she positioned him at her opening, he pressed inside her, hot and slick. Tight. Her eyes fluttered shut and her neck arched as he filled her. He fisted the comforter on either side of her as he pulled back out and slid in, rocking against her in a slow rhythm.

Her breath changed to heavier panting and he drank in the sight of her gorgeous breasts rising and falling as he continued to move inside her. She groaned and grasped his forearms, trying to angle her pelvis for even better penetration.

He bent his head low to catch her mouth for a hot kiss. "More?"

"Oh, yes." Her face was flushed and her hair spread out all across the bed under her. She was beautiful.

And he planned to give her everything she wanted.

He coaxed one of her knees higher against his side, then hooked his arm underneath. The new position allowed him to go deeper. She called out brokenly and her inner muscles convulsed around him.

She was close. He was closer. And damn it, he was going to hold on until she got there.

He dragged in breath after breath, slowing his pace and savoring every slide in and out of her. She clutched at his shoulders then shifted her grip to his hips, urging him deeper and faster. Every time he rocked into her, she made fantastic sounds of pleasure. Her breasts bounced beneath him and he couldn't deny her what she wanted.

Increasing his rhythm, he drew out and plunged back into her faster.

"David! Yes! Harder!"

Yes. Pleasure gathered low and tight, his balls even

tightened, until every other thought left his brain and his focus was only on the feel of being inside Lyn.

Her thighs tightened and her hips thrust upward as she gasped, then she came apart beneath him. He pulled out and slid himself back in tortuously slow as her inner muscles convulsed around him and she came, hard.

They held on to each other in the aftermath, both breathing hard. Every few moments one or the other of them twitched, sending a cascade of sensations through both of them. Hypersensitive, it was agony to leave her and clean up in the bathroom. But when he came back, she'd moved over on the bed and pulled down the sheets to tuck them both in.

He climbed into the bed next to her and tucked her up against his side. "Is it okay with you if we wake up early tomorrow?"

She snuggled into his shoulder. "Mmm. Sure."

There was a beat of silence as he pondered turning off the lights in the room. It wouldn't hurt to leave them on, for tonight at least. Given time, she'd work through her triggers.

"Fair warning," Lyn whispered, her lips brushing his lower jaw. "I'm very partial to morning ambushes so we might be waking up a little earlier than you planned."

His lips stretched into a real smile. "Yes, ma'am."

CHAPTER FIFTEEN

Cruz didn't enter the neighborhood this time until buses had gone through for just about every age group. People in suburban areas like this took notice of a lone stranger walking through when children were headed to bus stops. He didn't want the attention and he wasn't interested in the kids.

What he wanted was to catch Sean Harris at home, alone. Or at least without his children around, amping up his need to protect his family.

Lyn and Atlas were back at a small coffee shop with the car parked outside. He'd tucked them in the back corner of the place away from windows and in direct line of sight of a security camera. Safe as he could make them without being there. Then he'd headed back to Harris's home on foot. He didn't want the possibly familiar car tipping Harris off to this visit before he could confront the man face to face. And he didn't want Lyn involved in case things got ugly. Besides, the less she knew about all this, the better.

It'd been one thing to bring her along the first time. She'd added to the impression of a friendly visit. Just a few questions. No danger to anyone.

This wasn't likely to be a friendly visit.

Harris was home. His car was in the driveway. The minivan wasn't. Good. Likely his kids and his wife were out of the house.

Cruz wasted no time heading straight for the front door and ringing the doorbell.

It took no more than a minute for Harris to answer. "I already talked to you. We're done."

Before Harris could close the door, Cruz shoved his booted foot in the doorjamb. "Someone tried to run me down last night. Then they tried to run me and my friend off the road. You know anything about that?"

Surprise flashed across Harris's face, then his mouth pressed in a grim line. "I told you I can't talk to you."

"Considering someone knew where to find me to make a go at me, I'd say they know I was here yesterday." Cruz tipped his head. "They might even know I'm here again. Could be they're planning on asking you what I wanted to talk to you about but I'm guessing they haven't yet. Either way, they're going to be making some assumptions. How much you want to bet they'll err on the cautious side and assume you talked to me anyway?"

"How stupid are you, threatening me?" Harris's face had turned a ruddy red.

"I'm not. I'm making some educated guesses." Cruz kept one hand on the doorjamb and the other loose at his side. Nonthreatening, but ready to bring up to guard if Harris decided to throw a punch. Harris was probably in good shape. It'd be a challenge, but Cruz had been keeping up his conditioning, too. "And I'm going out on a limb figuring you're a decent man who didn't try to turn me into roadkill last night."

The other man was definitely angry, but he wasn't homicidal.

"Look. I was home all night. It wasn't me." Harris worked his jaw and then shook his head. "Why did you come back here? You don't have enough evidence to convince you to stay out of this?"

Cruz shook his head slow. "Just getting started. Whatever this is, my friend died because of it."

"It's not espionage or a threat to the country or any of that shit." Harris was loosening up, eyes darting past Cruz up and down the street.

Cruz was keeping an eye out himself, using the reflections in the small windows to either side of the door.

"This was just a business deal." Despite his claim, Harris sounded like he was swallowing glass talking about it. "The kind of business that takes years to complete. We all needed to keep our mouths shut. Some of us didn't."

"Calhoun knew about this...deal?" No way. Calhoun had been a man of honor and he wouldn't have gotten caught up in any shady dealings. He'd wanted to come home with nothing on his conscience, no guilt and no regrets.

Not likely to happen for any of them. A person had to make choices out there. Some of them weren't black and white, right or wrong. But if a soldier could make the best decisions possible, then it made coming home easier.

Harris shook his head. "Nah. Your friend took a hit to the head from a stray piece of wall in a rundown building we were entering. He made it through the initial incursion but was down and unconscious while we were mopping up the site."

"You call interrogating someone mopping up?" Cruz raised an eyebrow.

It might not be wise to let on how much Cruz did know about what was in those videos, but obviously Harris was still playing it safe. Cruz needed him sharing more. Give a little to get to what mattered.

Air rushed out of Harris in a whoosh, as if Cruz had sucker-punched him. "How much do you know? Forget it. Look. Your friend wasn't awake when we interrogated that son of a bitch and didn't make a deal. The rest of us, what the fuck were we supposed to do? Once some of us were in, we all had to be. None of us was willing to risk being the only man standing back from it."

And now they were getting somewhere.

"What was it?" Cruz asked.

Harris held up his hands. "Doesn't matter."

"My friend thought it mattered enough to keep evidence," Cruz growled. "Hiding it was a gamble with his life and he lost. I want to know why."

"Evidence got your friend killed. Knowing too much gets a lot of people killed," Harris shot back. He worked his jaw for a moment and then sighed. "But you know too much already. Look, it was a trade of services. Okay? We were asked to kill our target instead of taking him into custody. In exchange, our new business partner would take over the insurgent cell and after official military units were pulled out of the area, there'd be a need for private contracts. Those choice contracts would be offered to us first, once we'd retired from active duty and went private ourselves."

Cruz raised his eyebrows. "Going for a long-term retirement plan."

"If you call going private retirement." Harris's voice was grim. "I don't. What matters is after we were done and came back from that mission, we were split. Our unit was reorganized and each of us was reassigned."

Not good. Someone high up was involved then. And whoever it was wanted these men alone and constantly on edge. Even if their new units weren't a part of it, there'd be no way to know who could be trusted. Who was involved, who wasn't, and who would stand aside and let a hostile sniper take you out just to make life simpler for the rest of them.

"One of us wanted to talk anyway—and maybe he talked to your friend, Calhoun—but he took a shot to the back on an easy search-and-retrieval mission a few weeks later. Message came across to the rest of us loud and clear. Back out or talk about the deal and we wouldn't know when a hostile bullet would take us out. Our own team wouldn't have our backs. Or worse— we'd take out some poor innocent bastard who'd have no idea why one of us was being left to die." Harris swallowed hard. "I'm not willing to have that kind of blood on my hands. You don't need to know more details. I wish I didn't know. But I'm going to see this through to the end or until I can see my way clear without harm to my family."

"Could take years." Cruz understood. The position this man was in was a waking nightmare. Any mission could be the one: the time when a teammate stood aside when they should cover him. No way to know, and no man could be completely vigilant a hundred percent of the time.

"This was always going to take years." Bitterness flavored every word from Harris's mouth. "And for people who believe honor is an outdated concept, it isn't a problem. But some of us are still burdened with a sense of things gone to shit."

"Calhoun was going to blow this open; I get it." Cruz fished for more. "But who was he going to tell? How?"

"I don't know." Harris shrugged. "Does it matter? This needs to be zipped up tight. No way to know how news of this could impact the future. For now it's a business deal."

"Later, it could be a political skeleton." Cruz continued the thought. Never knew when a military veteran was going to run for office. This kind of thing could play havoc with a campaign for senator or the presidency, or however high the main person wanted to go. "How was the other SEAL going to opt out?"

Silence. Harris obviously didn't want to continue. But Cruz's foot was still in the doorjamb and the man had already spoken more than intended. In for an inch, in for a mile and all that.

"He reached out to all of us first and said he didn't want to be a part of it. Swore he wouldn't tell a soul, just didn't want to be involved any longer." Harris sighed. "E-mail went out encrypted."

Not easy to intercept then. And not as likely to have been read by just anyone.

Cruz nodded. "So one of you either eliminated him or passed on the information to make it happen."

Harris didn't respond. His face was grim. The anger simmering behind his eyes wasn't for Cruz anymore. Otherwise, Harris would've shoved Cruz off his front doorstep already. No. The anger was directed someplace else, toward the people responsible for holding all of this over Harris's head.

Good. Talk more. Give up a way to get to the real people responsible for Calhoun's death.

"When you're out there, you have to make the best choice out of the options you've got. And they're not good. Ever." Harris glared at Cruz. "Who do you have out there in the world to worry about? Who will be hurt based on the choice you make today? Who could pay the price if you make the wrong one?"

Cold washed over Cruz. He pushed words through gritted teeth. "No one."

Harris raised his eyebrows. "You and I both know better. There's a certain kind of person that's alone with no one to care if they live or die. You might've been one of them in the past, but it's been a good while since. You've got people who will get caught in the blast radius if this explodes in your face. Family isn't just by birth."

It was Cruz's turn not to respond. Lying would only insult both of them. He had shown up with Lyn at his side. And he could pretend hers was a friendship but their connection was something more even if he hadn't admitted it to her directly. Didn't surprise him to have Harris hint at it. Man wasn't stupid. He was just a man caught in a foxhole with no way out.

"Think hard about how much further you want to take this." Harris wasn't threatening. Hell, there was some sympathy in his voice. "We all want to do the right thing by our brothers and sisters in combat. But our first priority is to look to the living. Don't bring down the kind of shit storm that'll hurt the people you care about. Calhoun wouldn't want that."

Anger burned away the hesitation. "What do you know about what Calhoun would've wanted?"

Harris's expression turned sad. "He was a good guy. Didn't have long to get to know him when he and his dog were attached to our unit. But you know how it is. You get a feel of a person pretty quick out there. He tried to do the right thing."

"Then it shouldn't be a surprise I'm out here, trying to do right by him." Cruz couldn't help the rumble in his tone.

"Maybe." Harris drew the word out slowly. "But then you have to think about what the right thing is for the living first."

And Harris had family. Cruz got it. He did. But someone needed to answer for Calhoun's death and the others'.

"At least give me names of the other soldiers in your unit. Give me something to go on." Cruz tried again. He'd find a way through this mess to see Calhoun didn't die for nothing.

Harris shook his head. "I've already said too much. I could be a dead man already. Maybe. No more."

Cruz ground his teeth but didn't press harder. Harris was right. It'd already been too much.

"Thanks for this, at least." Cruz figured any additional words were over the top so he walked away.

It was time to get Lyn and Atlas back home and for him to find another angle to go at this entire issue.

CHAPTER SIXTEEN

Lyn walked in and dropped her travel bag on the bed. She'd need to do laundry. Soon. Like in a couple of minutes, before she forgot and tried to go do something else. Like maybe flop down onto the bed and take an impromptu nap. The cabin was starting to feel like home, complete with cozy nap-inducing temptations. Blankets. Pillows. Bed.

Of course, her thoughts were scattered. Had been since she'd gotten out of the car.

"That is one potent male," she said out loud to the empty cabin.

And she wasn't talking about Atlas.

Memories of last night had kept popping back into her head in the car, making her blush. Damn her fair complexion. It was such a giveaway.

And David, the bastard, had noticed every single time and given her a knowing smile so sexy, the rest of her heated up, too. She'd even been tempted to instigate a make-out session at one of the rest stops, if a car full of kids with a puppy hadn't pulled up right next to them. Probably a good thing she hadn't. It would've been downright mean to Atlas.

At least they'd made it the entire way up from Virginia to Pennsylvania without further . . . adventures. This whole case had been one crazy occurrence after another. Even without the insanity, she hadn't caught her balance in regard to David Cruz since she'd arrived. Working side by side with him—seeing him every day—and the more she learned about him, the more she wanted to know. He'd taught her a few things about herself, too. And she was all for continuing education.

But a tiny worry niggled at her, now that she was away from him and truly alone for a few minutes. This warm, happy sensation was a temporary high. It had to be. This sort of thing wasn't sustainable, and she knew this from witnessing it in her mother and dozens of military wives growing up. This was either going to fade or end abruptly. In fact, it'd be just like any of her other dating experiences since she'd become a training consultant. Wouldn't it?

Temporary.

Eventually, she was going to move on to the next client and the next dog. Maybe they'd keep in touch. Or perhaps they'd cut it clean when she left. The latter was actually the more practical so she could easily see David opting for that.

"Ouch." She sat on the edge of the bed abruptly.

The thought burst her bubble of happy effectively. In

fact, she was quickly dropping into a serious need for fudge brownies. David hadn't even said a single word about the future or end of one, when it came to them. Her own brain had decided to take the trip on its own. He wasn't to blame at all.

Maybe she still had a bag of those dried cherries dipped in chocolate she'd bought in New Hope with Sophie.

She stood and walked back out into the main living area. Movement was good when she was thinking too hard even if she didn't find her remembered snack. Truly, this was her problem. Too much worrying, too much dwelling on things out of her control, and too much agonizing over things that hadn't happened yet. This was a project with real exposure and Atlas was a great dog. This thing she had with David was chemistry like *whoa* and better than she'd imagined even when she'd been daydreaming about it and him, specifically. Neither was over yet.

Maybe both were a chance for her to live in the now. Focus on the project and do better than she'd ever done in the past, for Atlas. And enjoy her time with David. At the very least, there'd be memories to savor for a long time to come. And if she stopped worrying for a few minutes, even, maybe something would surprise her.

Maybe.

There were a lot of uncertainties and most of them weren't under her control. She'd never been good at handling such situations in the past and she didn't want those frustrations or disappointments to ruin what she had now. Been there, done that. Regretted it.

This. Here. Now. She'd shoot for no regrets.

Her phone rang. It was her stepfather.

Of course. Because he had a sixth sense for when she was implementing positive changes in her life. And would call—not to support or encourage either.

"Jones speaking."

"You have caller ID. You know it's me." Her stepfather sounded irritated.

"Our last phone conversation didn't start off on the best of notes so I thought I'd try answering the call in a different way." There. Perfectly reasonable. And she thought she'd managed a positive tone too. Sort of.

Okay, at least neutral. She didn't do fake cheer and he'd have recognized it for what it was anyway.

"You are late on your status reports." He sounded distracted.

At least he hadn't insisted she call him "Father" before he'd gotten to his point.

"We took Atlas on an extended behavioral training trip, socializing him in multiple public environments with varying crowd types." Truth was always the best way to start these things, but it was so much easier to leave out the bits she didn't want to share via an e-mailed status report as opposed to phone conversation. Spoken out loud, she lost some of her confidence with her stepfather, always.

"An extended trip takes more than a day?" And there it was, the doubt and inevitable censure in his voice.

"Multiple." She would not waver on this. "We stopped at various places both with suburban surroundings and crowded city areas. Indoor and outdoor. It's good to see what he's still sensitive to and what kinds of crowds he'll need further exposure to in order to get him back to his former level of training."

There was a long silence.

"I see." And the hesitation this time—if she could believe it—was doubt on his part. "I'll admit I haven't paid this close attention to the military service dog training program in the past. I've only recently become responsible for public perception on high-profile veterans within the last several years. The majority have been of the human persuasion."

Somehow she was surprised, actually. Her stepfather was detail-oriented if nothing else, and she assumed he'd keep himself thoroughly informed on the particulars of any project. Most especially one in which her performance, or that of any other contractor, could and would reflect on him. After all, he'd provided the extra support she'd needed to get this contract in the first place. Otherwise, David Cruz and his partners made much more sense in working with a high-profile military service dog regardless of background.

Of course she'd made her arguments but to be honest, she'd understood her chances were slim initially. It'd been why she'd swallowed her pride and coordinated with her stepfather in the first place. She'd completely expected to be in the red with her stepfather for something close to forever for this particular support from him. His hesitation was unexpected.

She pushed her advantage. "Atlas is a multi-purpose trained dog. He's not just explosives detection or search or drug detection. He's got to be flexible and adaptable to step up to anything the team needs him to do. His missions could take him through crowded populaces as much as remote locations so he needs to be able to move through those and anything in between while still being able to focus on the task he's been given. I want to be thorough about his rehabilitation."

"Of course." Her stepfather had recovered apparently and managed to get irritable in the bargain. "I'm aware of the value this asset represents. The steps required to return him to full working status, however, seem to be unorthodox."

She counted to five, figuring she didn't have until ten to get back on firm footing with him. "An unusual approach has proved effective, as my previous status reports demonstrated. Wouldn't you agree?"

"He's made progress." Not complete, but he'd allow at least that much.

"Rehabilitation has renewed Atlas's drive in a way simple retraining wouldn't. He's eager to work again and almost one hundred percent responsive." Her pride for Atlas's progress seeped into her tone. "David Cruz has also been very generous in sharing his expertise in training technique. I've found the information he's shared valuable as well."

In a whole lot of ways.

"According to his records, David Cruz is a creditable trainer. He wasn't directly assigned to a military service dog while he was on active duty, though. I find it interesting that he's chosen this profession now." Her stepfather would have access to David's service record. Somehow that was downright predictable.

Come to think of it, though, she didn't know exactly why David had come to Hope's Crossing Kennels. Funny. Each time he'd shared with her, she'd thought she'd learned so much about him. And then a moment like this demonstrated how much of his background was completely undiscovered.

She'd ask, though. Because it was something she did want to know.

"Cruz was a para rescue jumper." Her stepfather must've opened David's service record right there, on the spot, based on the pensive note in his commentary. "Air Force. Obviously not much ambition for himself, since he left the service without advancing as far as his records indicate he had the potential to achieve."

Of course it was always about potential. What her stepfather never understood was that people measured success in different ways. Their goals weren't the same as what he'd expect. What satisfied a person—made them feel whole—wasn't something quantifiable or repeatable in each individual the way following a recipe to bake a cake would be.

"Self-worth isn't always measured by promotions or advancements." She should've kept her mouth shut but nope, the words had slipped out dry and disapproving as you please.

"Your opinion in this case may be biased," her stepfather snapped. He had no tolerance for her opinions, especially when they were expressed with "attitude," as he'd made a point to tell her back when she was younger.

He couldn't know, though. Not about her and David. Her stomach twisted. "How so?"

"You're working side by side with the man. Obviously you're pleased with the cooperative arrangement." Her stepfather huffed. "Any partnership introduces bias. You're too close. You can't see the forest for the trees.

This is why I insisted you give me *timely* status reports so I can ensure you have the objective perspective this requires. That asset is too valuable to ruin with sentimentality."

This, she could address. The idea of him knowing about her and David was too many levels of complicated. No way was she going there until she absolutely had to.

"I've demonstrated repeatedly my ability to accurately assess and rehabilitate dogs of a wide variety of breeds and temperaments." And her record demonstrated it in glowing personal recommendations from her clients. "No matter how cute the tiny toy breed or how intimidating the larger breed, I approach each case with objectivity. As soft as some might consider the psychological foundation to the rehabilitation approach, it is by no means compromised by sentimentality."

It also turned out this way. Conversation ramped up until the big words drowned out the practical meaning of the discussion. It was a contest to see who could speak with greater formality and not get caught at a loss for words. It wasn't about the original topic anymore.

"In this case, it's not you I have concerns over."

Oh. Lyn rocked back on her heels. Almost uttered the gut response and ruined the whole conversation. "I see."

"David Cruz is obviously working with Atlas in honor of the memory of his deceased friend. They served together." Her stepfather cleared his throat. "I can sympathize to a certain extent. It's not easy to lose the men you've fought beside. But at least it was overseas and in combat, as opposed to some sort of overdose or home and asleep in bed."

Because passing away at peace in bed was the most horrible way for a person to die.

Some people were willing to put away their uniforms. Maybe not her stepfather, and she could respect him or the choice, but she also wondered if he ever gave any sort of consideration to the alternative choices people made.

"I want your status reports expanded to give me insight into how Cruz is reacting to Atlas's progress." Captain Jones made a clicking noise with his tongue. "My concern is that he is chasing ghosts better laid to rest instead of focusing on the task at hand. I do not want this asset put at risk because a man couldn't leave well enough alone."

There was an interesting way to put it.

"What would he be looking into?" Because now she wanted to know why her stepfather was coincidentally concerned with David's investigation of Calhoun's death. It wasn't a secret as far as she could tell. David had mentioned openly going to the nearby military base to look over the reports.

"Every friend is convinced there are suspect circumstances around the way a man has died in service. They're looking for a reason. Call it a form of grieving. My concern is that Cruz could become delusional, depending on how much he's indulging in other bad habits veterans occasionally pick up once they leave the service. While you are the contractor I've engaged to work with this asset, he is also involved in the project and could reflect on it negatively."

Ugh. And it was always about how things could reflect back on his reputation.

Anger had been slowly building through this latter part of the discussion. "Why single out David Cruz? There are several trainers here on site and there've been handlers involved with Atlas since he returned to the US. Did you keep close tabs on every one of them?"

"Once this asset came under my sphere of influence, everyone involved with it was scrutinized, yes." Captain Jones huffed. She could almost picture him tugging the front of his uniform straight in his annoyance. "Cruz is of particular concern both because of his service record and his direct involvement with the asset."

She bit back an ugly retort.

Her stepfather was judging a man he'd never met and assuming the worst about him based on the unfortunate outcomes of other people's lives. She wouldn't deny things happened like this. Truly. It happened a lot. And she understood that.

But the men of Hope's Crossing Kennels had built something so much better here with their energy after they'd left active duty. To suspect any of them of having succumbed to delusions or alcoholism or drug usage— any of the things her stepfather was alluding to—was so completely wrong, she couldn't ignore it.

"These are good men here." She said it slowly and clearly. All pretenses of friendly conversation dropped. "I would stake my reputation on the quality of their training and the kennels they've established. They build a safe haven and are continuing to give to the community in their own way. It's not the Service, but it is still incredibly admirable."

Silence. Then her stepfather cleared his throat again. "All the same, I would like reports on his approach and activities while he's working with you and the dog. All influences on the asset are of interest to me at this time."

"He has a name. Atlas is doing well." He could acknowledge David as a good man and Atlas as a living soul, not a simple thing to be inventoried.

"He has a designation number and responds to the name 'Atlas's." Her stepfather made the clarification. "If you want to work with more military working dogs, you should ensure you refer to them as both their designation and their name."

She didn't know how to respond to that. He was right. And it killed her to admit it so she kept silent.

"This could be the first of many contracts for you and you would do well to look at it as a key objective to come out as the lead trainer in this." There he went, setting goals for somebody other than himself. Maybe it worked for the people under his command. It didn't suit her. "I didn't mention this at the beginning because you have a stubborn tendency to go in exact opposition to my suggestions in order to spite me. However, I hope you've matured enough to realize this is counterproductive to your career development and I would like to think you wouldn't jeopardize the career you've worked hard to establish against my better judgment in order to spite me again."

Of course not. He'd trapped her in logic. Go against his recommendation and she hurt her own career. Follow his suggestion and she'd be following his lead, doing exactly what he wanted her to do. He won either way.

"Working independently is admirable, Evelyn." And there was her full first name.

She gritted her teeth.

"What it doesn't give you experience in is leadership." His voice took on a distinctively patronizing tone. "Only by working with people—actual humans—and earning their respect, can you learn leadership."

"Not everyone respects you." As soon as she said it, she snapped her mouth shut. Now she sounded petulant even to herself.

He remained unperturbed. "No. You are correct. Let's clarify then and say you become a true leader when people follow you even if they don't respect you because they have no choice but to acknowledge yours is the better judgment."

Like this particular situation.

"I'm sorry you don't like this." He paused. "And I would like to remind you that life isn't about getting people to like you. It's about ensuring that what needs to be done, is. They can hate you and it wouldn't matter so long as they do what needs doing."

She sighed. "I'm not in the military."

It wasn't so much the status reports. She gave those to her clients regularly as a standard practice. Being able to see the progress of their relationship with their dog over time positively reinforced the hard work involved and illustrated the value of her services. But she didn't work with people or dogs who didn't like her. If she wasn't able to build a rapport, she refunded the money and dissolved the contract.

"No, but this would be true in any corporate environment." She didn't hear it but she could picture him shrugging.

A key reason she'd chosen a profession with the flexibility and freedom she had now. It hadn't been the easy path by any means. But it had been truer to the way she wanted to spend her time.

"All of this complexity is only conjecture and words." She'd had enough of both. "For me, it boils down to a simple truth. I like dogs better than I like people. I will continue to work with Atlas because I want to see him happy."

"A working dog is happy working. Not so different from a worthwhile human being." Her stepfather continued with his inexorable logic.

God, was he never wrong?

"I think we've beat this conversation into the ground." She was definitely worn out from it. He always did this to her. Give him another ten minutes and she'd have a raging migraine.

"Fine. I want your agreement, though, that you will update your status reports in accordance with my request."

She sighed. Anything. Anything at all to end this. "You did not make a request. You instructed me. Understood. I'll have a report ready tomorrow."

"Tonight."

She'd accuse him of needing to have the final word but he hadn't terminated the call. He was waiting for her to acknowledge him. Damn it. Forget time in the Service. Her stepfather alone was enough to drive her to heavy drinking.

A brisk knock scared her right out of her thoughts.

"Lyn?" David's voice came through the door.

"Fine. Tonight." She ended the call before her stepfather could hear anything more or say anything to put her in an even worse frame of mind.

CHAPTER SEVENTEEN

David let himself into the cabin, scanning the room more out of habit than any suspicion of someone in there with Lyn. She'd have found a way to warn him. His girl had a good head on her shoulders, after all. The last couple of days had proved it.

Something was off, though. Lyn had a deer-in-headlights look on her face and while it was adorable, he didn't think she intended for him to read her so easily. She was used to reading the dogs and people around her, not the other way around. Her ability to detect bullshit seemed as fine-tuned as any delicate instrument, but he'd developed his perception around some of the most closed-off personalities a person could come into contact with and remain sane.

So to him, her expressions and body language were an open book. One he enjoyed reading as he ran his hands over her, kissed her into quiet desperation.

Her current tension wasn't anticipation and nothing

about her posture was an invitation. He was a little disappointed actually, but more immediately he was concerned.

"What's wrong?" And whatever it was, he wanted to eliminate it.

She blinked. Panic flashed in those big blue eyes for a second before she got hold of herself. "Oh. Nothing."

Uh huh. Try again, darling. "I could guess, but we both know this would go a lot faster if you told me so I could help you."

She laughed, a short huff of dry humor. "If it's all the same, I'd like to avoid introducing you to even the concept of my stepfather."

His stomach dropped. Guess introducing him to the family wasn't high on her list of priorities. Funny, the idea of introducing her to his hadn't occurred to him but the idea of not hit him in the gut. Hard.

Her gaze was on him now and she took a step toward him. "I'd love for you to meet my mother someday. If the idea of it doesn't make you want to pack your bags and head someplace far, far away. It's just introducing you to my stepfather would mean I'd have to *see* my stepfather and I try to avoid him pretty much all the time."

The sucker-punched sensation eased up a bit and he took a slow breath. "Okay. I take it you talk to your stepfather on the phone, though."

Had to be who he'd heard her talking to if the man was at the forefront of her mind. He'd not wanted to eavesdrop though. It'd been why he knocked and waited for her to tell him it was okay to enter. Suddenly, he was more careful of her personal space than he'd be with normal people. He honestly couldn't care less if he got other people upset but her—well, things had evolved.

"Yeah." She drew out the confirmation as she looked away, out the window. Obviously she had a lot on her mind when it came to her stepfather. "Recently more so than the last several years."

And not in a good way, apparently.

"Yeah?" In his experience, family had a way of coming in and out of life, sort of the way comets were gone for years then back in the night sky. Signs of the Apocalypse, too. "Any family trouble?"

Lyn shook her head. "More of a disagreement."

She scrunched up her face, the tip of her tongue showing.

Damn, she was adorable and sexy simultaneously. He had no idea how she managed it but he liked it. A lot.

"Most of my discussions with him are disagreements, really. So it's not a surprise. It's just frustrating."

David didn't know what to say. He waited and when her weight shifted forward as if she was about to walk toward him, he opened his arms in invitation.

She came to him without hesitation and snuggled deep as he closed his arms around her. Warmth spread through him and he dropped a kiss on her hair. She might never understand how much it meant to him, the way she'd come to him. No hesitation. No fear. No reservations. Every time she did it, he came unhinged. "Family always seems to know the exact buttons to push."

She nodded, her face pressed against his chest. "Mmm hmm."

After a moment, her arms slipped around his waist. He was pretty happy to stand there and enjoy.

But Lyn wasn't the type to be silent for long. He grinned when her head popped up, almost catching him in the chin. "What buttons does your family push?"

Oh, hell. "There's a heavy answer to what you probably meant to be a light question."

She leaned back in his embrace so she could gaze up at him, her expression somber. "I'll take the heavy with the fun. I'm guessing it requires a lot to get under your skin when it's people who matter. You're incredibly patient once you've decided someone is worth your time."

He grunted in response and she giggled and rose up in his arms to press a soft kiss against his jaw. Embarrassed, he tucked her back against him and thought hard. He wasn't sure what to do with her.

If he wanted to keep her, he owed her answers to her questions. And the intent might not have been clearly thought out before, but he did. He wanted to keep her near, like this.

"I enlisted pretty young and I didn't have a handle on how much it'd changed me my first time out. When I got home, I wasn't good at compartmentalizing yet, or pretending to be . . . normal."

He remembered the change in their expressions, the moment when real smiles froze into polite horrified masks.

"They expected you to be normal? What was normal in their eyes?" Lyn's questions were murmured against his shirt and her arms remained around him. No hint of her pulling away.

He tightened his arms around her anyway, because she wasn't trying to get away.

"I was rough around the edges, rude." He shrugged.

"It was embarrassing to them. They felt I'd developed bad habits, and I had. I smoked. I drank. I cursed at everyone, even the kids, without meaning to."

Lyn nodded and he absorbed her acceptance like a balm on his memories. Funny how they were still raw. He'd thought he'd made his peace with the reality of it.

"It wasn't the habits that were the problem, though. Those were ... manifestations. I needed, craved a change in my state of mind. Whatever could do it for me, I went after it. It was all to take me out of the numb and help me feel something different than the shit place I was in most of the time." He cleared his throat, suddenly thick with emotion. "Next time I came home, my father quietly said they didn't feel comfortable leaving the kids home alone with me. Never been so ashamed in my life. I'd never hurt those kids. Never."

But his being near them was a bad influence and maybe even a danger. He'd accepted it. Taken accountability.

Lyn's arms tightened around his waist. "You respected their wishes."

"'Course."

"But did they ever come to you, try to understand you?" There was a thread of anger there in her voice. For him. And he found himself holding onto it like a man drowning. No one had ever been angry on his behalf, not a civilian. Not someone outside the service. Not someone who hadn't lived it. Lyn was, though, for him. "They were concerned about the kids and themselves. Fine. But did they make any effort at all to be there for you?"

"I was a grown man. Fighting for my country. I could take care of myself."

It's what he'd told himself over and over. He'd never had this part of the conversation with his family.

"They had expectations of you but didn't stop, did they, to ask you if they were fair?" Lyn was working up a temper now. Her hands had fisted the back of his shirt.

"Life isn't fair, darling. I'm okay with that." He'd felt he deserved it.

"I'm not!" Her head popped up this time and he captured her mouth in a kiss.

He was more than hungry for her. He wanted to drown in her sweetness, the way she made him feel whole and cared for. As he kissed her, he continued to hold her close and urged her body to meld against his. A needy whimper escaped her lips and he nipped the corner of her mouth before settling his over hers for another deep kiss.

Bitterness, disappointment—it had all sat ignored and festering for a long time and finally it had washed away in the wake of this tidal wave of... whatever the hell she made him feel.

God, she made him happy.

He finally let them both up for air and she was clutching at him for balance. Which was all good as far as he was concerned. "Let it go. It's okay now."

"How is it in any way okay?" She was a little breathless. He'd have to work on making her more so. But she was still riled up.

She was hot when she was mad. Sexy hot.

"Because it's past and gone now and wouldn't do anyone any good. It'd hurt them to know but not be able to go back and fix it." The truth of it settled in his bones as he spoke it out loud. "I don't want to cause them any hurt or regret. I just want to find happy on my own."

He smiled down at her, his happy, and wondered if she'd understand. She could be dense about the impact she had on the people around her.

She was still hung up on the issue, though—had it between her teeth and wouldn't give it up.

"Let it go," he said again, putting more force behind his words. "I want to so I need you to as well. Deal?"

Defiance was still there, a fire in her eyes. But she sighed and relaxed in his arms. "Okay. But only because you've built so much here for yourself now. This place is good for you."

"You're good for me." There, he'd said it. Out loud, directly to her. Not to the air or to Atlas; to her.

She bit her lip. "You mean that?"

He'd said it, hadn't he? He could say the obvious but he'd rather kiss her instead. So he did. And when he pulled back, he brushed his lips over hers, teasing, until she rose up on her tiptoes and claimed his mouth with her own insistence.

She did get demanding when he teased her enough. He should tease her more often.

* * *

Lyn couldn't get enough of David. Really, she couldn't.

Kissing him was everything she could ever want and not enough all at the same time. She loved the feel of his mouth on hers, the taste of him, and the way his hands roamed over her body. He let her pull back and brush her lips against his, playing, and nip at his lower lip. He bit her back gently in kind and then settled his mouth over hers in a deeper kiss to steal her breath away.

He caught her by surprise, dipping low and hoisting her up in his arms, and she squealed. Embarrassed, she buried her face in his shoulder but he only chuckled as he strode into the bedroom.

"I like the sounds you make." His voice was rough, deepened with a need she'd only recently started to get to know.

She clung to him as he lowered her onto the bed, coming down on top of her. "I like the things you do to me."

"Yeah?" He smiled against her lips and pressed his pelvis into hers.

"Mmm." She nuzzled his neck and then set her teeth against his skin.

He paused, his hands tightening on her body. "Do that again."

She did, this time sucking a little as she bit him.

He groaned and kneed her legs apart. When he pushed his thigh higher between her legs, she let her eyes flutter shut and her head fall backward. "Tease."

He chuckled. "Oh, this? Not this."

His weight lifted off her then and her eyes flew open as she looked for him. But David hadn't left, only rolled off the bed to chuck his clothes off. He gave her a challenging look, his eyebrow arched, and she smiled and pulled off her own shirt. She was wriggling out of her jeans when he rejoined her on the bed and helped pull them down her legs.

Fun. Lighthearted. She couldn't help smiling. This

was different from her other experiences with men. Those had been short, to the point, and just about the sex. With David, there was give and take, fun and moments of passion to steal her breath away. She learned about him when they were together like this, in ways that didn't involve conversation. And she learned new things about herself, too, parts of her personality he brought out in her.

He caressed and kissed his way up her legs, bringing her thoughts back to exactly what he was doing. When he reached her panties, he ran a finger under the edge until she squirmed. Grasping both sides, he pulled those down and tossed them over the edge of the bed to join her pants.

"Pretty." His gaze ran over her from her toes, up her legs, and lingered over her sex before traveling up her belly to her breasts and finally finding her gaze, holding steady there. "So incredibly pretty."

Heat filled her everywhere his gaze had gone, and that was all over. She bit her lip.

His gaze still holding hers, he cupped her sex in one hand and reached up to caress one of her breasts. His touch was so intimate, comforting and compelling at the same time. When his fingers parted her, exploring and teasing her entrance, she let her eyes flutter closed and arched her back.

One of his fingers entered her and she bucked, the pleasure of his touch already driving her crazy. Then his other hand, caressing her breast as it was, shifted just enough for him to brush her nipple with his thumb. She cried out.

"Wet and hot." He slid his finger in and out of her

in a slow rhythm. "Is this the way you like me to touch you?"

She panted. If he wanted her to use words, he was a cruel man.

Then he pushed two fingers into her and she arched for him again, fisting the sheets.

He chuckled. "I'll take that as a yes."

Oh good. She'd keep breathing and words could come later. Because the way he continued to touch her, play with her, was sending pleasure coursing through her body until it coiled low in her abdomen. When he found her clitoris with his thumb, adding pressure in time with the slide of his fingers inside her, she lost ability to think at all.

He petted her through the orgasm, prolonging it with gentle strokes. And when she opened her eyes again, he climbed over her, putting on the condom as she watched. Then he leaned forward until his forehead touched hers. "May I?"

She loved the way he asked, didn't presume, each time. In answer, she twined her legs with his and looked deep into his eyes, then nodded.

He reached down with one hand and positioned himself, then entered her in a smooth slide. She gasped as he filled her, her muscles stretching to accommodate him. This was another way they fit, so, so well.

Once he was buried to the hilt inside her, he paused, his breath hot in her ear. Then he began to move, firm and steady, pulling out and sliding back into her in a deep steady rhythm.

She groaned, her already sensitized body rising to a crest again. "David, please."

Not even sure what she was asking for, she clutched at his shoulders, tried to encourage him. He drove into her faster, harder, his hands reaching around her to cup her behind and angle her for an even better fit. Every stroke pushed her closer to the edge until she arched under him helplessly, gasping.

He buried his face into her shoulder and growled as he came too, shuddering with the power of his release.

Lyn kept her arms wrapped around him as he slowly relaxed, lowering his weight onto her. His breath was hot against her skin and after a few moments, he rolled to one side and rose up to give her a quick kiss on the bridge of her nose.

"Be right back." He went into the bathroom and returned a few moments later with a cool, damp washcloth to help wipe her down.

This was a gesture she appreciated, too. His care, and the way he wanted to see to her comfort, took their time together beyond sex to something much more intimate. She wanted this.

Once he settled back onto the bed with her, she snuggled up against his side, content.

"What's on the agenda for Atlas's training later today?"

He froze next to her.

Unsettled, she rose up on one arm so she could see his face. "I didn't mean to break the mood. No work talk in bed?"

She'd said it in a semi-teasing tone, but lost even that as his brows drew together.

He sat up. "I'd wanted to talk to you about this, but I didn't plan for us to get distracted."

She raised her eyebrows. "Us sleeping together is getting distracted?"

He reached out and ran his hand up her arm. "You are absolutely a distraction, in really good ways. Please don't take this wrong."

She drew in a slow breath. "Okay. I'll try not to, but let's get back to what you got distracted from."

"This is going to be bad timing." He eyed her with trepidation.

Oh, great. "Better bad timing than not talking to me at all."

He nodded, ran a hand through his hair, then got started. "I was coming over here to talk to you about how we were going to move forward with Atlas's training schedule."

She nodded. So far, nothing to be worried about.

"You've done incredible things with his rehabilitation. His socialization is up to par based on the last couple of days of travel." He paused and she waited. His words came out faster. "I wanted to suggest we adjust your participation in his training to intermittent sessions while I focus more on his specialized skill sets for explosives detection and human search."

It was her turn to raise an eyebrow. Dogs like Atlas searched out humans for other reasons than the search-and-rescue dogs trained in the United States. There were other reactions built into Atlas's training, other behaviors expected. He was expected to act more independently in the search and respond differently on locating said human. She could understand how she didn't have the experience in the training technique to work with Atlas for those behaviors.

Still, this was more than two trainers talking about techniques. She gathered the sheets up around her, suddenly vulnerable.

"Intermittent." She said the word slowly. "What sort of intervals?"

"Well, maybe twice this coming week, then we could move to once a week or even once every other week. You could go check on your other clients and come back for his sessions." David's voice had gone neutral, the way he did when he wanted to distance himself from a situation. Compartmentalizing.

"You want me to leave." Oh God, and they'd just slept together. "This was good-bye sex?"

"No!" He tried to reach for her but stopped when she flinched back.

"Sounds like it is." Embarrassment and anger burned through her.

"I don't want to say good-bye, Lyn, but I want you safe." David didn't sound neutral anymore. In fact, the urgency in his tone drew her gaze back to his. "Atlas and me, we're in this. We're going to find out exactly what happened to Calhoun and we're going to make sure this video doesn't get buried. The deeper we get into this, the more likely shit is going to rain down around my head. I want you clear of it all."

She couldn't argue with the danger. The car chase the other night had frightened the hell out of her.

"When this is over, I'd like to come to you." David leaned toward her. "Or you can come back here, whichever you want. I'd like for us to see where this thing between us goes."

"But you want me to give up my work with Atlas. Just

leave." She gritted her teeth. "I think you need to grab your clothes and step out."

"Lyn—"

She shook her head. "You want me to think about this with a cool head, you need to take yourself out of here."

He studied her for a minute, then did as she asked.

CHAPTER EIGHTEEN

What's wrong?"

Cruz scowled at Rojas where he sat at the breakfast bar playing some game on his smartphone. "Who says anything's wrong?"

"You've been glued to Lyn's side since she got here." Forte pulled open the fridge and peered inside. "If you're not with her, you're with the dogs or in your office at your computer. Since you walked in here and sat your ass down in a chair, I figure Rojas's got a point. Something's wrong."

"True." Cruz took the beer Forte offered him and took a swig as he thought about how to fix the mess he'd made. He didn't hide anything from Forte or Rojas. It was part of the reason they were able to live with each other. Trust.

In fact, he'd sought them out. Staying inside your own head for too long resulted in spinning wheels. He needed their perspectives to see his way clear.

"So where's Lyn?" Forte asked, leaning against the counter.

The three of them lingered like this sometimes. It wasn't as if they were lifelong friends. They'd served together and in a lot of ways they knew more about each other, because of that intense period of time, than most people ever found out in a lifetime. It'd been Forte who'd told Cruz and Rojas to come to Pennsylvania. And hell, Cruz hadn't had anyplace in particular he'd wanted to go right out of the service. Neither had Rojas. The man had only had one prerequisite: a safe place to raise his daughter. Hope's Crossing Kennels had been a place to start, and if Cruz hadn't been a fit he'd have moved on. Only, Forte had made it the right place to be for all of them. Expectations were straightforward. Life was pretty simple. And it was a life.

Cruz hadn't realized he'd been missing anything until Lyn came along, and now he'd told her to leave.

"Packing." Cruz sounded sullen and he didn't want to. It'd been a solid decision. Logical.

The other two men froze.

After a moment, Rojas started playing his game again. "You get into a fight or decide things were getting too complicated?"

Of course the other two had noticed. They'd spent their military careers taking cues from body posture, subtle signals, and the smallest gestures. Either of them could've noticed the new intimacy in the way Lyn responded to him from the moment they'd returned. Maybe even as soon as they'd stepped out of the car. He'd have noticed if it'd been one of them.

"Complicated." Cruz scowled at the beer. It was

cold but not cold enough. Or he was too irritated to enjoy it. "This thing with the video Calhoun sent me. There's too much shit involved. She'd be in the line of fire."

Cruz glanced around. Rojas's daughter was likely over at the cottage they shared but he should've checked before shooting off his mouth. They all tried to keep the cursing to a minimum around the Boom. Unfortunately, the kid walked around quiet as a cat and hell, they all cursed worse than sailors.

Rojas shook his head without taking his eyes off his game. "Woman's already been attacked twice. At the hotel and right here on this property."

Forte growled.

"Not a one of us is happy about how that happened and it won't happen again," Rojas continued. They all had reasons to ensure the security of this place. It'd become a haven. It needed to stay that way. "But what I'm saying is this: she's already been yanked directly into the middle of whatever is going on. You're not going to save her any issues by sending her away."

Forte nodded. "Whoever tossed her hotel room thought she had information and it was before we even knew what Calhoun had left with Atlas. They think she's a part of it and she is at risk no matter how far away you send her."

Cruz scowled. "I can keep focus on me. I've got lines on at least one more of the SEALs on that team. One of them is going to give away more than they intend to. We're all good, but over enough time we all develop cracks in our stories."

He hadn't been a SEAL but he'd been Special Forces.

And he'd been a man with secrets to keep. The trouble with need-to-know information was if you knew, you didn't want to. Secrets lived with you forever and eventually you were desperate for a way to purge them. One of these guys wished he was out but he had family to protect. There had to be at least one or two more who wanted out.

"Maybe so." Forte spoke slowly. He had a tendency to think as he spoke and random brilliance occasionally fell out of his mouth. Most of the time, though, it was bullshit. Still, the rare jewels of wisdom were worth it. "I'm thinking anyone with enough influence to have SEALs afraid on domestic soil, not just on a mission, has a far enough reach to cause her harm the minute she leaves this property."

So this time was one of those one in a million moments where Forte's point was so true, it should've been obvious to David from the beginning.

Cruz cursed again.

"It's too dangerous here. They've got eyes on her already." Cruz couldn't see a way to get Lyn out of this mess. "She's got clients on the West Coast, a business to run after all this is over."

"And she planned to be here until this project was complete, right?" Rojas asked.

"Yeah. It was open-ended, though. No idea when Atlas is going to be declared recovered." Beckhorn had Cruz's back on that. It was the way any of them worked. They took as long as the dog needed to be ready for the work it had to do. And every dog was different.

"I'm guessing she didn't have clients scheduled any time soon because of that." Rojas could be so damned reasonable. "She's not going to have an immediate job to pick up where this one lets off."

Great. More guilt to add to the weight in Cruz's chest.

He shook his head. "You've both got good thoughts. No disrespect here, but I've got a gut feeling. She needs to get out of here. I've got no logic to go up against the reasoning you've put out there. It's just a feeling."

And even as he admitted it, he hated it. Because it wasn't a logical decision. He didn't have good reasons even if he'd convinced himself he did. And Lyn was a smart woman. She'd have refuted his reasons every bit as effectively as Forte and Rojas had just done if Cruz had given her a chance. Only he hadn't. And he'd probably damaged whatever it was between them in the process.

She was very mad at him. And when she had time to cool off and really think it through, she was going to be over here to tell him exactly what his two best friends already had.

He raised his gaze and looked each of them directly in the eyes. "Something isn't right. She needs to get someplace safe."

They got it. He could see it in their expressions. Sometimes it wasn't about logic. They'd all learned to follow their instincts when everything else in the world told them to do different. Following those gut feelings had seen them through hell and back, through multiple deployments each. Sometimes the world didn't make sense.

"You could lose her if you push her out of here." Rojas's warning was almost inaudible. He would know. He'd lost a wife by pushing her away. "If she decides to move on before you catch back up with her, are you ready to deal with that?"

No.

Cruz swallowed. "I'm going to have to."

This was the right thing to do. And if nothing else, each one of them did his damned best to do the right thing.

* * *

When Lyn came through the door, both Forte and Rojas made a break for it.

"Good luck, man." Forte gave him a parting slap on the back.

Great thing about brotherhood: they were willing to leave a man to the inevitable without any witnesses to see him ripped to shreds. Cruz appreciated it.

Lyn strode into the kitchen and came to a stop outside of arm's reach. The distance she left between them hit him like a brick wall. She'd changed into a fresh pair of jeans and a soft knit top. Its fabric clung to her curves and he wanted nothing more than to run his hands over her. Her hair was gathered up in a knot, looking suspiciously wet. She must've taken a shower. He should've stayed and joined her.

But no. He'd gone and pushed her away, so he needed to clear his head of things he shouldn't be caught up in thinking and focus on what she had to say. Thing was, she muddied up his brain process without even trying.

She lifted her chin. "I've been thinking about what you said. Not one of your reasons holds up against good, solid reasoning."

Here we go.

He was hoping she'd listen to him once he let her blow off her steam. Maybe she'd understand if he explained. He was willing to give it a try. She was the most instinctual trainer he'd ever met and if anyone could understand what was driving him to risk this thing they had, it'd be her. He hoped.

"I'm listening." He turned toward her in his seat, giving her his full attention because she deserved it.

Maybe she wasn't used to it, because she hesitated. It took her a full minute to recover, visibly gather her thoughts and open her mouth to speak.

"Sorry to interrupt." Forte was back. "Beckhorn has been trying to get ahold of you and you haven't been answering your phone. We've got company waiting at the main gate and neither of you is going to be happy with what they're here for."

Atlas.

He'd gotten pretty good at reading her expressions. Same thought crossed her mind and there was a hint of fear, too. They'd both been ready for a scuffle but neither of them had been prepared to let Atlas go. He'd brought them together.

They moved for the front door in unison.

* * *

Lyn nabbed her laptop bag on the way out the front door, letting David get a step ahead of her. He'd outdistance her regardless, with his ground-eating stride and longer legs. When he didn't, she was silently grateful. The partnership between them wasn't gone, despite his telling her to leave earlier.

Please don't let this be over yet.

They'd barely started to explore what was between them and had only made partial progress with Atlas. She wasn't ready to leave either of those unfinished.

The two men at the front gate were standing next to a blocky SUV, bare to the point of utilitarian. But then, she was used to the rental SUVs with frills and extra features. It wasn't obviously a military vehicle as far as she knew but it didn't look like the usual thing an average person would buy, either.

Add to it their stance and general attitude and Lyn figured they had to be military. Spending time around David, Brandon, and Alex had gotten her used to the body language. Neither appeared to be particularly intimidating and, in fact, wore such neutral expressions she studied them even more closely.

David probably saw more than she did. Whatever this situation was, and she had her suspicions, she was glad she was side by side with him. Standing up to these men alone would've been a lot more of a challenge.

The men waited for them to approach rather than coming to meet them. When David came to a stop, so did she, at a distance slightly farther away than would normally allow for comfortable conversation. Already there were irritating undercurrents being exchanged between David and the strangers. Glances and minute frowns. Dogs and cats weren't the only ones that got into pissing contests.

"David Cruz and Evelyn Jones?" the older man asked, but it sounded more like a statement than a question. He knew he had the right people. "Sergeant Zuccolin. I have orders to retrieve the military asset known as Atlas. Came through early this morning. Captain Beckhorn has been notified."

Lyn preferred straightforward souls like David, Alex, and Brandon. This man talked more like a politician despite his brevity. His tone was too pleasant. He spoke as if they were all good friends and this wouldn't be met with any protest of any kind.

"I'd like to see a copy of those orders, Sergeant Zuccolin." David's tone was flat.

The older man clenched his jaw. "I'm sure Captain Beckhorn has forwarded them to you electronically."

"To be honest, there may have been a lag in communication." David made it sound as if that sort of thing happened all the time. "He only called as we were informed of your arrival. I had to choose between coming out to greet you and speaking to him. If you men wouldn't mind waiting a few minutes, I'd be happy to call him back to hear what he has to say."

"There's coffee up at the main house." Lyn regretted mentioning it immediately. Both strangers gave her the once-over and dismissed her from consideration. The look was so incredibly familiar from her childhood and the occasions when her father had brought guests to the house. She cursed herself for not choosing something with more impact to say first.

A person has seconds to establish an impression. In terms of appearance, she was slight and definitely a civilian. On opening her mouth, she hadn't had any great contribution to the conversation. Anything she said from here on out would barely be heard.

Damn it. She had better social skills than this.

The only reason she could think of for being this off-balance was the discussion with her stepfather directly followed by her aborted faceoff with David. Too many thoughts were churning inside her head and she hadn't had a chance to resolve anything. She'd need to shove all that aside and quickly.

"Waiting won't be necessary." Sergeant Zuccolin glanced at his companion, who stepped over to their car and retrieved a folder from the passenger side. "We brought a hard copy."

"Appreciated." No irritation in David's comment or expression. These men were all going on minimal auditory or body language cues. Poker would be torture with any of them.

David read through the orders. It took a few minutes and they all waited. She cheered inwardly as he took the time to look for the loophole. There had to be one.

Then as he looked up and met her gaze, she realized it was because he couldn't find one. The men had come here and could afford to wait because there wasn't anything David could do. She stared at him. Opened her mouth.

He shook his head once. Brief. Barely a movement. He was giving up.

Well, she didn't plan to.

She lifted her chin and stared directly into the sergeant's eyes. "You know who I am, I assume, other than my name."

Throwing around her identity—actually her stepfather's—irked her to no end, but in this case it was the only card she had in her hand. She'd use it.

Practicality.

Sergeant Zuccolin nodded with reluctance.

She didn't blink or turn her head. She kept her gaze steady on his. "Good. Then you'll see the wisdom of sending your colleague there over to the guest cabin to gather my belongings and place them in the vehicle. I'll see to Atlas and prepare him for the trip."

"Wait a minute." Anger was starting to show in David's demeanor and she didn't dare make eye contact with him. "I want to know what business you have accompanying our dog off this premises. We are supposed to be working on his retraining together."

"Atlas is the property of the military, as I have been reminded multiple times, even by you, Mr. Cruz." It hurt to use his formal name this way. She wondered if he'd ever forgive her. Considering what was going to come to light next, probably not. "My contract is to *rehabilitate* him, not work with you. I go where he goes."

This would be for the best. It was becoming very clear whatever was going on around Atlas, her stepfather hadn't been keeping tabs on her for his reputation's sake. He'd been using her to keep up to date on David and how much he was learning about the circumstances around Calhoun's death. If she went with Atlas, David could be free to continue investigating without her stepfather's scrutiny.

Sergeant Zuccolin didn't step in. Man must be wiser than she'd initially given him credit for. Instead, he leaned over to his fellow soldier and murmured a few words.

The man nodded sharply and approached Lyn. "Ma'am, if you'd show me where to go, I'll accompany you to gather both your belongings and the asset."

She nodded.

David wasn't finished, though. "Enlighten me. Who are you that you can amend their orders to go with them?"

"It's not about who I am." It never was. She'd struggled for years to build her own identity and it still boiled down to this. "It's about who my father is. Captain Francis Jones of the US Navy. I get the impression he's a few pay grades higher than your Air Force Captain friend in San Antonio. He sponsored my request to be allowed to work with Atlas. I'm sure he'll confirm upon request."

And she was sure she hadn't made any friends for making the comparison in ranks between Air Force and Navy.

But it was worth it. David's jaw tightened and his eyes narrowed slightly. There might've been a vein popping across his forehead but she might've imagined it. Either way, he was angry, not hurt. And his anger was much more preferable to leaving him visibly hurt in front of these men.

"Jones is a common name." David had his calm well in hand. In fact, his tone had gone cold. "I'd thought it was a coincidence. I stand corrected."

"Well, then, there's just a few things left to do then." Lyn was at a loss for anything else to say so she walked past David and headed for the cabin.

It took moments, since she was packed anyway. The soldier who'd accompanied her didn't comment. Good, because she didn't owe *him* any explanations. She was too busy hoping someday David would give her the chance.

Atlas was on his feet and happy to see her when she approached the kennel. She almost cried when he eagerly sat and turned his head so she could attach the leash to his collar. He must've picked up her mood, though, because on the walk back, he remained at a precise heel position. He took notice of the man walking with them and Sergeant Zuccolin when they approached. They were unknown and Atlas regarded both of them as threats in relation to her.

"Load him in the crate." Sergeant Zuccolin gave the order to the man next to her.

"I'll take care of securing him." Lyn made her statement firm and didn't give anyone time to argue with her.

She led Atlas around to the back of the SUV. The soldier hurried after her with her bags and juggled them for a minute in order to open the door for her.

"Atlas, *over*." On her command, Atlas jumped easily up into the back of the SUV. "*Hok*."

Atlas obeyed her immediately, entering the crate and turning to face her as he lay down. His ears were cocked backward, though, and his head tilted to one side as he regarded her. This wasn't like the previous road trip and he had to be sensing her stress. It was a good thing these men weren't watching him and probably didn't care to use him to guess at what was going through her mind.

David, on the other hand, had moved around to a vantage point where he could see both her and Atlas. Carefully keeping her eyes on Atlas, she leaned in and gave the big dog a caress on the cheek. "Hopefully you'll understand one day soon."

Words for David, not Atlas.

"Miss Jones, we'd like to get going." Sergeant Zuccolin had lost whatever patience he had initially.

"Will there be stops along the way? I didn't have a

chance to take Atlas to relieve himself before sending him into the crate." She didn't want to leave. Everything about this was rushed, off, and for once she desperately wished she could call her stepfather.

It wasn't likely he'd ordered this. Maybe he hadn't even known. His last instructions to her indicated he'd expected her to be around David for a while longer at least. This didn't fit.

"I assure you, we'll be stopping before you know it." An odd quirk popped in the sergeant's voice as he spoke. Or maybe she'd imagined it.

She nodded and closed Atlas's crate door. No bungee cords or anything to secure the latch so she left it. Atlas was well-behaved now so she doubted it'd be an issue.

"Good-bye, Mr. Cruz. It was a pleasure to work with you." She met David's gaze this time but it was still frigid.

He only nodded. "Miss Jones."

And that was it. She turned back toward the SUV. The other soldier had the front passenger seat door open for her and she climbed in without looking back. As they drove away, she tried to unobtrusively watch David in the side-view mirror.

He never moved.

Then they turned onto the main road and trees hid him from view.

CHAPTER NINETEEN

It didn't take a genius to catch the hint that she wasn't wanted. Her two military companions were stoic and noncommunicative as they pulled onto the main road headed for the highway.

Oh, she hadn't expected them to be friendly and chatty or even make small talk, but they could at least answer her questions. So far, they'd been mute and possibly pretending to be deaf. She'd figured it was because they were concentrating on getting on the road so she'd subsided.

Now that they were picking up speed and headed on a major road, it could be worth another try.

"What's the next step for Atlas?" She tried to sound friendly, positive, yet professional.

Nothing. If anything, the only response from the man driving was a deepening scowl. Maybe he'd been hoping she'd be quiet the whole ride. Not that this SUV was particularly quiet. It was utilitarian, absent of the padding and console treatments she was used to seeing in vehicles. As a result, there seemed to be something rattling in the center console, the doors, pretty much everywhere.

There was a radio but no one had turned it on and she wasn't ballsy enough to reach out and start fiddling with it. She didn't know the local radio stations anyway since she and David had alternated playlists on their phones for their road trip. David and Atlas had been much better driving companions.

But that adventure was over. In a whole lot of ways, most likely.

She tried communicating with her current travel companions again. Simple question. Perfectly reasonable. "Which base are we headed to?"

Zilch.

In the back, Sergeant Zuccolin might have shifted in his seat a bit. Maybe.

There was an awful cold creeping across her skin and through her insides as the situation forced introspection. She probably wasn't wanted back at Hope's Crossing Kennels either. Maybe David was moving back into his cabin at that very moment.

It might be a while before she could work up the courage to call him. Try to explain. He might not even take her call. And if he didn't, would an e-mail be opened or immediately deleted? What about a text?

There were so many ways for her to reach out to him and he could ignore each and every one of them.

There was no telling how long she'd manage to stay attached to Atlas once they got to whatever military base they were heading to. She'd most definitely be going through some challenging conversations. Ideally, she wouldn't have to reach out to her stepfather directly to keep herself a part of the project. Maybe she could apply what she'd learned from working with David, Brandon, and Alex to her approach for reasoning with the military men she'd be encountering once they reached their destination. Get started on a more positive note with a better impression.

Sergeant Zuccolin had most definitely formed an opinion of her already. It might be good, but probably the best she could hope for was neutral. Possibly bad. He'd been a direct witness to the surprise she'd sprung on David and it hadn't been a nice one.

Betrayal came to mind. *Stabbed in the back* might be a good way to describe it, too. David had looked like he'd been smacked.

She owed David an apology no matter what. It hadn't been something she'd set out to do to him, but she should've talked to him about it sometime earlier. The unsettling feeling had snuck up on her and she truly hadn't recognized it as keeping a secret from him until the moment she told him. Maybe he'd understand. Things had happened so quickly, she'd spent very little time thinking about any role her stepfather played in all of this or why he might want reports on Atlas.

Stupid.

But it was the truth. And if there was anything David valued beyond excuses and apologies, it was honesty. Simple, bare, sometimes brutal. He gave it and appreciated it in return. She should tell him. Whether he believed her or not was up to him but at least she could give it to him to do with as he chose.

The scenery was passing by as a blur outside the window. She barely took notice. They'd be getting on Interstate 95 soon if they took a similar route to the one David had on their road trip. At least, if she remembered it correctly. If this was a long ride, she was likely to lose her mind wondering about what she should do. To be honest, there was no time like the present. Later she might be too busy to keep her thoughts clear and it'd also be too easy to push it off repeatedly until she never reached out to him. Now was better.

She took out her smartphone and swiped the screen to unlock it. Tapping the message icon, she started to text David.

"Time to end this farce." Sergeant Zuccolin's hand shot over her shoulder and grabbed her phone out of her hands.

"Hey!"

She didn't have time for more as the sergeant grabbed for her hands, starting to wrap duct tape around her wrists.

Panic blinded her and she thrashed.

"Fuck!" The SUV swerved as her flailing hands contacted with the man's shoulder. The hell was his name? She should know both of their names so she could report this.

If she survived.

Atlas was barking and growling. The metal crate crashed in the back.

Her brain had gone into overdrive as she struggled against the sergeant. He was too strong, though. In seconds, he'd captured her hands and wrapped the duct tape around her wrists. Once. Twice.

Metal screeched and clanged. The sergeant shouted as Atlas came flying into the back seat.

"Shit! How did he get loose?" The enlisted man started to pull over.

"No!" Sergeant Zuccolin shouted even as he struggled with Atlas. "Keep driving, you idiot. I've got this."

Not likely. Another minute and Atlas was going to get through the sergeant's defense with a kill bite. It would be bad. Atlas killing a US soldier would be bad. He wasn't on duty. He could be put down.

And he was doing it for her.

She needed to get him out—safe, away.

Desperation pushed Lyn to wrench the door handle. The door opened and the ground shot by as they started to accelerate again. Quick. Had to be quicker. She jammed her foot against the door to keep it open as wide as she could.

"Shut that door!" the driver shouted.

She ignored him. "Atlas! *Hier*!"

Atlas left off the sergeant in the back and jumped into the front seat, into her lap.

"No you don't!" The sergeant grabbed her by the shoulder, his forearms bloody and ripped up from fending off Atlas.

Not what she had in mind anyway. "Atlas! *Over! Over! Zoek* David!"

Atlas whined but obeyed. He launched out of the SUV, clearing the dangerous pavement to hit and roll in the grass past the road's edge. A normal dog might've been hurt, but Atlas had jumped out of planes and helicopters in his career. She'd had no doubts he could make the jump and get to David.

The sergeant yanked her shoulder painfully and she let her leg off the door. It slammed shut and she desperately searched for Atlas in the rearview mirror.

Her heart leaped when she saw his rapidly shrinking form get to its feet.

The vehicle slowed. "Do we go back for the fucker?"

"We got gloves? Any gear to keep him from ripping us up?" The sound of rummaging came from the back of the car.

"No sir."

"Bitch doesn't have any in her crap either." Sergeant Zuccolin let out a long string of curses. "No. We'll never catch the bastard out in the open like this and even if we did he'd rip chunks out of our hides. Let him disappear. Long as he's not with anyone who can connect him to us, he should just end up in a shelter. He's been erased from the system so they'll come up with jack if they scan for his chip and that bastard will scare any shelter into destroying him instead of holding on to him for adoption."

Never. Lyn was sure Atlas had understood her. She'd told him to jump, to track David. Atlas hadn't ever misunderstood her since the day they'd met. He'd have understood her this time.

"You sure? Orders were to secure the dog."

Zuccolin paused. "Could use the girl to tempt him back."

Lyn kept her expression as blank as she could. She didn't think Atlas would come back if she didn't call him. But if they got ahead of him, into his line of sight, and tried to do something to her . . . she wasn't sure what decision Atlas would make.

"Fuck that. Dragging her out to bait the dog would

take too long, catch too much attention and we'd still have to restrain him." Obviously Zuccolin didn't want another encounter with Atlas any time soon. "I'm going to need stitches everywhere. Goddamned lucky he didn't break my forearm. Call Evans and have him intercept in case the mutt makes it back to those kennels."

So many people involved. David needed to know. Atlas would get to him and then David would know something was wrong. She twisted her wrists, trying to work at the duct tape around her wrists.

Pain exploded on the left side of her head, blinding her. As she sucked in air, her vision cleared slowly.

"The fuck did you think you were doing, bitch? Think I didn't see you? Something must've tipped you off." Sergeant Zuccolin was screaming. "Did you think you could message your boyfriend? Jump out of the car? We'd have run you down in minutes. Around here, by the time anyone called that in—if they saw it at all— we'd have been long gone. And trust me, it's no issue ditching this vehicle."

Lyn swallowed hard against the fear churning in her stomach. Bad, this was so incredibly bad. She'd figured she couldn't get away. But Atlas? He was fast, too fast for them to go after even in a car. He'd find his way back to the kennels and to David. He would.

"What did you say to the mutt?" Obviously her new favorite sergeant wasn't an actual dog handler. "Waste of time. You're not military and not his real handler. Soon as he gets clear he's going to go do whatever the hell he damned well pleases. This isn't the movies. He's not fucking going to go find help."

Yes, he was.

Though he wasn't a Collie with a little boy for a best friend; he was a Belgian Malinois and one of the US military's best. He'd track the man she'd named because Atlas knew him, trained with him, knew she'd worked with him. Atlas would track his way back to him and bring David back to her.

CHAPTER TWENTY

Cruz tossed the hose to the side and stomped over to the spigot to cut the flow of water. He should've brought the damned thing with him, but instead he let the metal nozzle drag across the concrete floor of the kennels screeching and setting his teeth on edge.

Great. He was making his own temper worse. Next thing, he'd head into Philly and look for a good, wholesome brawl.

Because that would be such an incredibly constructive use of his time.

Cleaning out Atlas's kennel was supposed to have been constructive, actually. It only made him miss the big dog, and by association, the woman who'd helped work with him.

It was easier to focus on the dog.

Cruz had to admit Atlas had been one in a million. An optimal combination of the kind of intelligence, drive—

and yes, aggression—a trainer looked for in a military working dog intended to support special forces units in the worst hellholes humankind could create.

There'd been a quiet air about Atlas that demanded respect. His pining for Calhoun had been a final expression of a kind of loyalty rarely found anywhere, in man or beast. It'd been honorable, simple in its expression and enough to tug at the toughest heart strings. And it'd taken a wisp of a blonde with a heart just as big as Atlas's to bring him out of it.

Lyn had coaxed Atlas—and Cruz, too—to live again. Not merely exist.

Maybe Cruz had been mourning the loss of a good friend, but he hadn't been struck as hard as Atlas. Nothing so noble. Because he'd never let anyone in that way. He'd been coasting along, trying to find a place to fit in again. Lyn had caught him up with her conviction and her good intentions and wound Cruz around her finger every bit as much as Atlas.

And now they were both gone.

Finally finished pulling in the hose and looping it on its hook, Cruz left Atlas's empty kennel to dry and went into the shed where they kept grooming tools and the various dogs' gear. Lyn hadn't taken Atlas's gear. But then, they hadn't practiced much with it in their training sessions to date. Most of what they'd covered had been leash work. Cruz had been planning to take the lead with Atlas more before getting Atlas into his harness for some of the more specialized training.

Might be just as well. Who knew what Lyn would've done with the knowledge? Whatever information she'd been passing along all this time had to have been fragmented. Cruz cursed himself for sharing anything with her at all.

He picked up the harness, working over the chest strap and other parts, searching by feel for something out of place. He'd done it a hundred times before and after they'd found the micro SD card under Atlas's skin. Too obvious for Calhoun to have hidden something in Atlas's gear and others must've searched the same way. But until the bigger video finished going through Cruz's decryption program, there was nothing else to go on.

Harris had ended up being a dead end, confirming what Cruz already knew but providing no further leads. The other man was probably subject to dangerous scrutiny for his trouble, too. A pang of guilt hit Cruz at the thought. The man *did* have a family—one that wanted him—and he seemed to be a genuinely decent guy.

Doing the right thing wasn't as straightforward as it'd seemed before going down there.

Nothing was, actually. And it'd started getting cloudy from the minute Lyn walked onto the kennel property. He should've dug further into her story when she'd first shown up. Should've followed up with Beckhorn to find out who had approved of her assignment to a military project. Hell, he should've paid closer attention. Because she'd played him and he had only himself to blame. Idiot. Jackass. Stupid. A few of the possible ways he could describe himself at the moment.

He'd fallen hard for Evelyn Jones and all along, she'd been reporting back to Daddy on his progress with Atlas. He didn't know which hit his pride worse: that he hadn't even suspected her or that it'd always been about the dog.

Not fair to Atlas. Everything came back to him and none of it was his fault. Atlas was the catalyst in all of this, in so many ways it made Cruz's head hurt.

Cruz placed Atlas's harness back in its storage crate. He'd pack it up for shipment tomorrow. Today, he didn't have it in him. He needed to get outside and do something more constructive.

Rojas was outside, working with one of the big German shepherds they'd rescued recently from a shelter. Three of them had been abandoned after their wealthy owners decided to divorce and leave, too concerned with their own affairs to worry about the futures of the very expensive dogs they'd ditched. Purebred, none of them older than six months, and all of them solid with basic obedience and the beginning of Schutzhund training in them. Not a one of them socialized for human interaction, unless you counted chasing intruders off private property.

The shelter hadn't had the resources to rehabilitate the dogs for normal family homes. The aggression they were already showing, their training, and lack of socialization resulted in the shelter labeling them unadoptable. If Rojas hadn't pulled them, they'd have been destroyed. Instead, he was working to see if they could be directed to a better life.

Cruz came to a stop and watched the dog watch him. Intelligence there, and suspicion. "How's it going with this new batch?"

"Promising." Rojas had a good hold on the leash, relaxed but ready to get control if the big GSD lunged unexpectedly. "This guy definitely has potential but he's got trust issues."

"I can see that." Cruz noted the way the dog let loose a whisper of a growl as he took a step closer.

"*Fooey*." Rojas gave the correction and deliberately continued to talk with Cruz in a pleasant tone. "These boys were all trained in German."

Point was to demonstrate to the dog that Rojas would indicate when aggressive behavior was okay and when it was not. Trick was a dog had to trust his handler to let him know. This one, not so big on the faith yet.

"Huh." Cruz kept his posture loose and nonthreatening, his gaze locked with Alex's. "Not unusual for guard dogs. Track down the breeder yet?"

"Sent them an e-mail. They may not have the resources to place these guys, as old as they are." Rojas shook his head. "But any breeder worth anything is going to want to know where their dogs went."

And if they didn't care, Hope's Crossing Kennels would take note of it, too. They worked with breeders across the country to get the best dogs to train for military, police work, and rescue. No way did they want to support a breeder who didn't care about where their dogs went. Said a lot about those sorts of establishments and none of it good.

"Any of the three likely for multi-purpose work?" Cruz figured this particular dog wasn't likely. Not yet. Maybe after a couple weeks' rehabilitation.

There he went thinking with Lyn's line of thought.

Rojas shrugged. "Maybe one of the other two. This guy's got a chip on his shoulder. I'm trying to work through it but he responds to Boom better than me."

Cruz raised his eyebrows. "Is it a gender thing?"

"Maybe." Rojas scowled. "But he's too rough. Nipped at her hair and ears, shoved her around a little. She can hold her own most times but he's got to learn better manners across the board."

"Ah." Cruz paused. "Maybe I'll start an assessment on one of the other two."

"Sure. Check them out. I'm figuring they'd be solid for police work but one of them might have the knack for multi-purpose." Rojas led the GSD away. The big dog kept craning his neck to keep Cruz in his line of sight for as long as possible. Definitely not looking to Rojas as a handler yet.

Atlas had begun to look to Cruz. Definitely looked to Lyn. It'd been an important step in his retraining. A dog needed to look at his handler to receive a command. But more than the literal meaning, a dog well-bonded to his or her handler was aware of the human on multiple levels. It was the establishment of a strong rapport that made a team effective.

If he wanted to poke at a sore spot some more, he could admit it'd been Atlas's willingness to acknowledge Lyn—trust her—that'd made Cruz relax. In Cruz's experience, dogs had better judgment than humans when it came to character.

Made it doubly shitty the way she'd betrayed them both. Now she was riding along with Atlas back to a military base to continue preaching her rehabilitation philosophy to someone who might not give her two seconds' notice. It'd serve her right, but it wouldn't be in Atlas's best interest.

He needed to stop thinking about Lyn. He still had to

track down the people responsible for Calhoun's death and see to it they paid for what they'd done in the way it'd hurt them most.

The real question he should be asking was whether Lyn's father was involved. Seemed likely. Maybe that was the lead Cruz needed to follow. He headed for his office.

"*Fooey!*" Not a quiet correction this time. Rojas was yards away and straining to hold an eighty-five-pound GSD on a leash.

Growling low and throwing all of his weight against Rojas, something had set the dog off. Cruz followed the dog's line of sight to the front gate and saw a sleek Belgian Malinois running at top speed up the driveway.

What the . . . ?

"Atlas! *Hier!*" Cruz called, reaching for a leash—any leash—off the wall.

Atlas didn't need to change course. He was already headed directly for Cruz. Then a lean figure cleared the tree line in obvious pursuit, weapon up and aimed at Atlas.

CHAPTER TWENTY-ONE

Cruz yanked out his smartphone and activated voice recognition.

"Incoming. Single gunman. Opening fire on Atlas."

The text went to Forte and Rojas as a pre-set group.

Something was wrong. Very wrong. If Atlas was here, where the hell was Lyn? And what could happen to make Atlas leave her? Cruz could imagine several scenarios, none of them good.

Cruz bent to retrieve his gun from the hidden holster at his ankle. Staying close to the main house for cover, he moved to meet up with Atlas.

The intruder opened fire on Atlas as the dog approached, but the man had taken the shot on the move. Dumbass. It went wide, kicking up dirt to one side of the dog's path. Not a surprise.

Thank God the only people at the kennels currently were Cruz, Forte, and Rojas. Gunfire wasn't new to them. But shit, Rojas and Forte would be irritated as hell if any of them caught a bullet. Cruz was already pissed. Worse, any of the dogs on the property were at risk.

Gunshot or no, Atlas wasn't deterred or distracted. True to his training, he headed straight for his objective: Cruz.

Another shot fired. Cruz cursed and took aim. He didn't want to put a bullet in a person if he didn't have to, even if he was on Hope's Crossing Kennels property, but the asshole was shooting at *his* dog.

Suddenly he heard the sound of other dogs barking on approach and he grinned. Atlas reached him as three German shepherds streaked past them toward the intruder. Rojas must have set them loose. Perfect distraction and with three of them, the gunman wasn't likely to have time to single out a target and hit any one of them.

Handy to have rescued Schutzhund-trained guard dogs on hand. Socialization was not a primary concern at the moment. They had the experience and training to do exactly what was needed—intimidate the hell out of the intruder and potentially neutralize the threat.

The man stopped in his tracks and even from this distance, Cruz could see him go pale at the sight. Hell, Cruz wouldn't be thrilled in the face of the oncoming canines either. He'd be looking for a tree or wall to climb. Fences weren't a safe bet because most German shepherds and Belgian Malinois could climb those even without specialized training.

Backpedaling, the man tripped and fell on his ass, his baseball cap falling off to expose more of his face. And he looked incredibly familiar.

Cruz put a leash on Atlas as Rojas and Forte arrived, armed and looking grim. The three men advanced on the man cowering in the center of three GSDs. Now that they had him at bay, if he so much as moved, they'd be on him ripping and tearing. Two of them were holding position—barking and snarling—making one hell of a racket. The third and largest was bristling and baring his teeth, but he was silent.

Dangerous, that one. He was the likeliest to break and attack the man physically.

Rojas must've shared the assessment, striding around to leash the biggest dog first. Forte took a position between the other two and leashed them.

"I wouldn't relax if I were you." Cruz figured it was only fair to warn the man. "There's enough slack in all these leashes to let these dogs ruin your day."

Possibly his life. It all depended on how far things went. The three GSDs were trained to rip and tear, possibly break bone. Atlas was trained to go for a kill bite.

Speaking of Atlas, now that the intruder was essentially neutralized, Cruz turned his attention to the big dog. Panting heavily, Atlas must have run a decent distance at high speed. If he'd known his way, he might've gone as fast as he could. No telling where he'd been freed and how familiar he'd been with the area. Lyn and Cruz had taken Atlas for long walks as far as five to eight miles away in both directions along the main road next to the kennel. So chances were, Atlas had been close to home when he'd gotten loose.

Taking a knee, Cruz ran his hands over Atlas checking for injuries. No blood, no bullet holes or grazes.

"Any damage?" Forte made the question curt, expressionless. No need to give the prisoner any impressions to go on.

Cruz shook his head. "No. He's run hard though. He'll need to be cooled down."

Not an immediate need but soon. There was a higher priority and Atlas would agree.

Forte nodded sharply, then focused on the intruder. "You want to tell me why you are on my land, opening fire on a dog under our care?"

"Dog's not yours." The other man's answer was sullen, belligerent.

"And you would know, wouldn't you?" Cruz jerked his chin at the man. "This is the guy who was following our lady friends in New Hope."

The man knew Lyn's name for sure but he might not know Sophie's. No need to give him information.

Still, at the mention of Sophie, Forte's grim expression darkened and chilled. Not a good combination for the intruder. "I think we're going to have a little chat while we wait for the police to arrive then."

"Get up." Rojas barked out the words.

"Fuck that. Damned dogs will eat me." The intruder grimaced, but didn't move a muscle. He was staring at Atlas.

Seemed the man had seen what a working dog could do. Maybe he'd witnessed what Atlas specifically could do.

"Stay where you are and we'll let them loose." Forte sounded almost cheerful and let up on the leashes of the two smaller GSDs just enough to let them loom closer. "Do as we say, you have a better chance of walking away with your skin intact."

The man swore and scrambled to his feet, holding out his hands palms open. His gun lay forgotten a few feet away where Rojas had discreetly shoved it with a foot.

"Not fond of dogs?" Forte didn't even bother sounding nice about the question. "Maybe you should get to know these a little better since you tried to shoot one of them."

* * *

"Sit the fuck down and don't make a sound or I'll gag you 'til you choke." Zuccolin's mood had only gotten worse during the drive.

They'd broken speed limits getting here but seemed like everyone did on the main highway. Their car had only gone with the flow of traffic and there'd been no lucky police stop to give her the chance to scream for help.

Lyn stumbled to the chair and sat. When the other man grabbed her arm, she jerked free and pain blinded her again as Zuccolin struck her across the face.

"Don't hit her again." The voice echoed inside her skull as she blinked to clear her vision.

"Sir, she's caused a shit-ton of trouble." Zuccolin's tone had changed abruptly. Being around a commanding officer would do that to a man.

"She was not your objective. Her presence is going to be a serious issue and you will answer for this problem." The tone was flat, cold, and horrifyingly familiar. "Do not ever hit her again, for any reason. Is that understood?"

"Yes, sir." Zuccolin stepped away as the other man finished duct-taping her elbows to the arms of the chair. Her wrists were still bound.

But she wasn't gagged yet and she craned her neck to get a look at the officer. "Captain Jones."

Her stepfather sighed and stepped farther into her peripheral vision. "Insisting you use family titles at this moment would be useless. You should not be here at all."

She knew that tone. Her stepfather was in a cold, quiet rage. The kind that snuck up on the cause and exploded in ways a person never forgot. What made it scarier was not knowing when he'd actually snap and lash out.

Had he thought she wouldn't get tangled up in this mess? "You backed me. Made sure I got on this project."

"You were to do what you do best: rehabilitate the dog. Get close. Report back to me." Her stepfather clasped his hands behind his back and shook his head. "If you stumbled across the video, I took steps to ensure you didn't have time to understand what it was you had. I could assure my business partner that you didn't know enough to be a danger to our business interests. If you'd have followed your instructions you'd have moved forward in your career none the wiser of this situation and the better for it."

"Well, good to know your reasoning was logical." Lyn let the derision creep up in her voice, not caring about antagonizing the person currently keeping her safe. She was tired of letting him hold her well-being over her head. "And here I was worried I might owe you when really, I was doing you a favor. I was spying for you."

"Yes." He didn't even have the grace to express guilt over it.

But for her, it washed over her and drowned her. She provided her clients with status reports as a standard practice. Fine. And providing them to her stepfather had been an irritation because he'd turned them from a professional courtesy into a way for him to control her. But somewhere in there, she should have recognized when they hadn't felt right anymore. When she'd started avoiding telling David about them. That was when she'd stopped being naïve and started betraying him.

"What are you going to do with me now?" She wiggled in the chair and raised an eyebrow at him. There was a certain level of ridiculous to her current position but she also wasn't delusional. He wasn't going to let her go. Not now.

Silence.

"Sergeant Zuccolin."

The sergeant snapped to attention. "Yes, sir."

"Where is the animal?"

Well, at least she wasn't in the current spotlight. She listened as Zuccolin gave a halting report of what had transpired from his arrival at Hope's Crossing Kennels to the warehouse. And she was going to hell in a hand basket because she took some pleasure out of listening to the bitterness in Zuccolin's words as he had to describe how an itty bitty lady civilian let loose their target.

"I see." If anything, her stepfather's tone became more monotone. He was not pleased.

"Sir, Evans set out to intercept. He'll bring back the dog." Zuccolin definitely had lost his confidence.

"Evans is as likely to kill the animal as anything else." Her stepfather began pacing. "This has escalated into a complete clusterfuck and I'm holding you directly responsible."

Apparently, Zuccolin had some experience with her

stepfather's arctic anger, too, because the man had gone pale.

It took a minute for Lyn to realize she was the one laughing. Okay, maybe she was going into shock or sliding into hysteria. Neither was good because she needed to use her brain. She focused on her stepfather. "Whatever this is, did you actually expect it to stay all neat and tidy the way you planned it?"

His jaw tightened as he studied her. "If it had been my plan in the first place, it would have been executed efficiently and without complications. Unfortunately, I joined this particular project in later stages, once the dog was already back on domestic soil."

Well, it was good to know her stepfather hadn't been a part of David's friend's death. A tiny relief in the midst of this insanity. She wasn't even sure why, but she was glad.

"But you're not on the right side of lawful, either, are you?" Maybe she was hoping.

Her stepfather only held her gaze, a sadness in his eyes she'd never seen before.

Nope. He wasn't going to suddenly neutralize these two men and rescue her. He really was a part of all this.

"I don't even want to know why." And her voice sounded empty in her own ears.

"I'd have been disappointed if you approved." Her stepfather walked toward her. When he moved to touch her face, she turned away but he grabbed her chin. "Even if we get ice on this, it's going to be bad."

"Why bother?" She was tempted to ask if he was going to kill her but she really didn't want to die, and why tempt fate. She'd learned a long time ago not to ask her stepfather questions if she didn't want to know the answers. And she was pretty sure she didn't want to know yet.

He huffed this time. "You are never going to grow out of this pig-headed stubbornness. It's not a phase. It's a character trait."

"I prefer to consider it perseverance. Maybe tenacity." Talking seemed to be a good idea. Keep everyone talking.

Give David as much time as possible to come find her.

CHAPTER TWENTY-TWO

Cruz stood with his back to the wall in the room they used for on-site veterinary needs, Atlas sitting at his side. The old dog was seeing the inside of this room more often than most of their canines did. All things considered, though, Atlas was in good shape and practically trembling to go into action.

So was Cruz, but they needed to know where they were going and what they were getting into first.

"How do you want to handle this?" Forte leaned against the examination table, currently not in use. Might be before all this was over but thankfully, it wasn't yet. If that ex-SEAL had stopped to take a steadier shot, Atlas might've been hit.

Heat coursed through Cruz's veins, pushing at his already frayed control. Thinking on the possibilities didn't help his temper. Wherever Lyn was, she probably wasn't out of reach yet but every minute could be taking her farther away.

"We can't take much time before we really do notify the local authorities." Rojas threw in his two cents from his seat on the one stool in the room. "We need to stay clean from a lawful point of view if we want to look at this guy through bars and us on the right side of 'em."

"We need to know where Lyn is, what kind of head count we're dealing with at the location, anything useful for safe extraction, and anything additional the shithead knows about Calhoun." Cruz paused. "In that order. Lyn takes priority."

They all nodded in agreement.

"Every minute counts for Lyn." Cruz wasn't just pointing out the obvious in a kidnapping situation. Every second ticking by wound him up tighter and tighter with the need to go out and do something to help her, to get her back. Atlas was no different, taking in all the actions around him, watching with an air of impatience. Cruz got the impression the big dog was evaluating how every action was taken. Right now, they were moving too slowly.

But they needed to approach with a strategy in mind; otherwise they could do more harm than good to Lyn and to themselves and the people who'd miss them. Like Boom and Sophie.

"Question goes back to you." Forte faced Cruz.

Cruz thought hard. Lyn was his and Forte would take his lead on this. What he was about to do was for Lyn and she wouldn't thank him, or forgive him, for becoming a monster to save her from monsters. If he could find a better way, one that would leave their consciences clean—or at least not scar them any more than they already were—it'd be best to try.

"We mess with his head first." Cruz put some force behind his words, as if sounding confident about it would make it the right choice. Sometimes it did. "He's not the brightest light bulb out there for sure. Say the right thing and he'll sing."

"You sure?" Forte's gaze had gone cold, flat. "Mind games are the way you want to go?"

Uglier, more direct options hung in the air between them.

"We'll get the most accurate information out of him this way, not just what he thinks we want to hear." Truth. Plus there was the question of Cruz's temper. This course of action gave Cruz the best control over the situation. "We try to soften him up any and I might be tempted to go too far."

His anger simmered right now, coiled and waiting, familiar. The stranger he'd locked away within himself had been coming closer to the surface of his mind through this whole ordeal. Compartmentalization bullshit. The driving need to go find Lyn was all that saved the man they had in custody from being beaten to within an inch of his life, or worse. Cruz had done it before and even if he already hated himself for it back then, he would do it now if it weren't for Lyn. Everything he was doing and *how* he was going to do it was because he had her in his life now.

Because without her, there wasn't a good enough reason to keep trying to be someone other than the stranger he used to be.

"Beckhorn found the man's service record and sent it over." Cruz owed Beckhorn big for the favor, too. It'd be worth it. "There's a few things in there to leverage."

"That was fast. Beckhorn hasn't lost his touch." Rojas snagged the printout off the examination folder. His eyebrows raised after only a few seconds of skimming. "Yeah, this asshole is easy."

"This isn't just about Lyn." Forte crossed his arms. "The shithead tailed Sophie, too. And we have Boom to worry about. Whatever we do to get the info we need, this guy goes away where he can't hurt any of them anymore. That means we call the police. We can't delay any longer without opening ourselves up to scrutiny and giving this guy loopholes when he has his day in court. If you think you can do this, do it now while I put in the call. We'll be on a countdown."

Last time they'd had to call in the police, it'd taken half an hour or so to respond. Not a lot of time.

Cruz blew out a breath. "It'll be enough. Any more than that and you two will have to stop me from getting physical anyway."

To say he had a short fuse was probably a message from Captain Obvious.

Forte straightened and headed for the door leading to the main house. "Let's get to it then."

* * *

Cruz strolled into the kennel where they'd tied up their man with Atlas on a short leash at his side. The streaming video from cameras on this side of the run would show a cut-off time coinciding with shots fired. Completely believable to say a stray bullet had taken out the security feed.

The guy was covered in sweat and obviously frustrated by his inability to get free of the binding keeping him in the metal chair. All he'd managed to do was tip himself over on the concrete floor. For once, Cruz regretted how clean they kept their kennels. He wouldn't have minded if the guy managed to roll himself in some crap.

They'd all suffered worse.

"Neal Evans. You've really lost your edge, man." Cruz decided to start out conversational but he didn't have to be nice. "You're ex-Navy SEAL. Maybe it's been too long since you got through SERE training."

Survival, Evasion, Resistance, and Escape. Any special tactics personnel would have been required to go through some level of SERE training prior to selection.

"Fuck you." The answer carried a whole lot of ire.

Good. Forte, Rojas, and Cruz were all special tactics, too. Every one of them had pitched in to make sure Evans wasn't getting loose before they were ready. Cruz personally wasn't sure he could even get out of those bindings on his own. Well, not in the short time they'd taken to converse and decide on a course of action.

Give a man enough time and anything was possible.

"Ah well, we could've given you more time, Evans, but we're running low on patience." Cruz strode over and yanked the chair back to an upright position. If the guy's head snapped up at the sudden movement, not a big deal.

"I'm not telling you anything." Evans was sucking air through his mouth, his breathing labored.

Cruz took a good look at the guy's face. Evans might've tipped the chair over and used his nose to break his fall. Maybe. It didn't appear to be broken. "I think you will. It'd be your best shot at getting clear of all this with a chance at a live."

"Ha!" The bark of laughter made Atlas lift his lips in an answering snarl. The man's gaze darted from Atlas to Cruz back to Atlas and he sobered up quick. "I've got a sweet retirement parachute set up for me. Golden. You can't touch me."

Cruz tipped his head toward the man. "Thing about golden parachutes, they're not actually good for saving your life. In the last few minutes, you've managed to make yourself a very visible inconvenience."

Evans gritted his teeth and kept his mouth shut.

Ah, but not for long. "Police are on their way. See, my partner's kid lives here and with the trespass just last week the police aren't likely to think this is unrelated. There'll be a lot of questions. I don't think it'll be easy to convince a judge to allow bail. All things considered, I'm pretty certain your employers will consider you expendable."

"No fucking way."

Yup. Barely any poking and the man was already back to responding. Even if Evans planned to keep his mouth shut, he was one of those guys who couldn't.

"You've demonstrated you're sloppy enough to be made tailing a target. Or didn't you mention our little meeting in New Hope to them?" Cruz shook his head. "Never keep things from Big Brother. You never know who he's got watching you while you watch someone else."

Beady eyes widened a fraction then narrowed. "You're trying to mess with my head."

Yes. But why lie when the truth was so handy?

"You've also trespassed on private property in broad daylight with a weapon in hand, opening fire. All captured on security feed. How much do we want to bet your employers are going to consider you too stupid to live?"

"I know too much for them to just leave me out here." Too stupid just gave an excellent reason for why he wasn't likely to live much longer.

Cruz nodded. "Yeah. And your face is nice and clear in the video I've recovered, too. You know, the one you've been convinced Evelyn Jones was going to find eventually."

"Bitch will give up the video. Probably already has." Evans sneered.

Cruz clenched Atlas's leash in his fist. "She doesn't know anything, doesn't have the video. But I do and I'm here. I also know what to do with it, whereas she wouldn't."

"Trade then." Evans rolled his head in a stretch. "Give me the video and let me loose, I'll make sure you get the girl back."

This time, it was Cruz's turn to laugh. And he did, "There you go overestimating your value again. I already spelled it out to you. You're expendable. I could trade the video alone for Evelyn Jones, no issue. Don't even need to mention your name."

Actually, it'd be best for Evans if Cruz didn't but he doubted Evans would see it that way.

"You need to let me go. I can contact the people who have your girl. Faster than you can track them down. I can arrange for the trade." The desperation was growing in Evans's tone as he started to believe Cruz.

"There's a lot of men featured in this video. You all decided to bring Atlas here into the interrogation, use him to terrorize your prisoner. None of you thought to check to see if the camera on his harness was still capturing video feed. The camera caught your faces." Cruz shook his head. "Unfortunate."

For Calhoun it had been, once he'd found the feed. The entire SEAL team had been in on the interrogation, listened to a man beg for his life and offer something none of them could resist in the moment.

And Calhoun had never made it home to get the video to the right people. It could mean the end of careers for several of them. Some of them deserved it, like this dirt bag. For others, it wasn't so clear, like Harris. Cruz was beginning to understand how alone Calhoun must've felt trying to decide what to do.

In the end, Calhoun had tried to do the right thing and they'd let him die for it.

"Look. We cut a deal, okay? Prisoner wanted the same man dead as we did. It coincided with orders. We did nothing wrong. We just secured a side agreement with the prisoner. It'll make us all rich in another couple of years. The new company's going to get started soon. The prisoner we set loose is the leader of his group and he's giving us exclusive contracts as soon as we're all out and ready to go private." Evans lifted his chin. "You're out now. You ever consider going into the private sector? There's going to be big money contracts with this outfit. Immediate money to be making."

And have this snake at his back? Pass. "I'm not thinking too far in the future right now. I'm just interested in a trade and I'm still not convinced you even know where to find my girl."

"I do!" Evans leaned forward. "We've been using some warehouses down on the Philly waterfront as a base of operations. They were only supposed to retrieve the dog but when she got in the car, too, our guys took her along. When the dog got loose, I was sent to clean up the loose end."

And what would they do with Lyn?

"But you don't have the dog. I do." Cruz didn't dare let his concern for Lyn show on his face.

Evans didn't seem to notice. "Yeah. But they can't have gotten all the way to the warehouse yet. I can call them."

"Or you could give me the number and I can call them."

Evans scowled. "No fucking way."

Well, Evans was caught up in the possibilities of a trade but he wasn't quite out of his mind.

Cruz kept the pressure going. "How many times do I need to explain to you how very expendable you are?"

"Look. You give me the video and whatever the hell it was stored on, then I'll give you everything you need to know about your girl. Where to find her, who's there. Everything." Evans coaxed. "If you give me the video, I can take it back to my bosses and everything will be right again. You can even keep the dog."

Cruz hadn't planned to structure another course of action on the fly, but he hadn't anticipated Evans being stupid enough to think Evans was going to remain valuable to this group either. They'd already been using Evans as their fetch and carry man. Somehow, the man still thought he was going to be in on the full deal whenever it came to fruition. This was an opportunity to make a trade for information that'd be way more accurate than what might come out of coercion.

Time was short. And if Cruz managed things correctly, the video would still end up in the hands of the authorities. If he worked this right, he could get to Lyn, too—hopefully in time. Calhoun would agree Lyn's life came first.

"Deal. You tell me everything I need to know first, then I'll give you the video. Start with the exact location of where they took Evelyn Jones and how many men are there."

CHAPTER TWENTY-THREE

Approaching the warehouse in question hadn't been as much of a challenge as Cruz had initially thought it'd be. Once he'd gotten the location from Evans, it'd been a matter of driving close enough to park his car out of sight and approach on foot.

Pedestrian traffic in the area had been easy to blend into and there were plenty of tiny side streets to duck into as they'd gotten closer. Now, there were just old crates stacked up in a maze between them and the warehouse itself.

He'd waited in the shadows to observe as long as he dared, figuring a man and a dog caught the eye much more readily among normal pedestrians. Taking a moment now to be sure they hadn't been watched on approach could make the difference between bringing Lyn home and none of them getting out of there at all.

Atlas had settled down to wait next to Cruz, the big dog's shoulder barely touching Cruz's left leg in a heel position to keep Cruz's strong-side clear. Atlas's behavior was sliding more into the working attitude he'd been trained to adopt when out on a mission. No suspicious movement in or around the warehouse and no sign of anyone coming to investigate either of them.

Both of them were embracing old habits better suited to action than to civilian life.

In situations like this, Cruz wasn't going to regret it. Of course, he hadn't missed the hurry-up-and-wait aspect. Moving at the right moment was key. But recognizing the difference between patience and paranoia became better with practice and got rusty with disuse. His timing had to be on point today.

He proceeded forward, keeping to cover as much as possible and taking calculated glimpses of the warehouse and its surroundings. The more he was able to see of it, the more likely someone was going to be able to spot him. Taking a full circuit around the building from a distance gave him a chance to choose his entrance and determine whether there were eyes on it.

Atlas paused suddenly—rigid stance, his head up and weight forward—the dog's attention directly ahead of them. His big ears had swiveled forward, catching sound too faint for Cruz to hear yet. Atlas had detected another human approaching, blocks away from normal foot traffic. The only people wandering this area were the ones he was looking for or predators of the streets. Based on information from Evans, accurate thus far, it was more likely to be one of a couple of guards on the perimeter of the warehouse area.

Taking on a guard alone would be a challenge. If the other man spotted him approaching, an alarm could be sounded before Cruz could subdue him. A one-on-one, straight fight would take too long and potentially leave Cruz damaged. He couldn't afford to take every guard head on, by himself.

But Atlas was too fresh from overseas, the dog's rehabilitation incomplete. Atlas hadn't yet been retrained to bite to break instead of his fiercer combat training, bite to kill. Here, on US soil, Cruz didn't want to risk Atlas killing a man.

Torn, Cruz looked down at the dog, considering. Atlas gazed back up at him, waiting for a command. What he saw in the dog's eyes wasn't the ready eagerness of 100 percent obedience. Here, now, Atlas was waiting to see what he would do.

Lyn's safety, possibly her life, hung in the balance and trust had to begin with trust. There wasn't time to wait for human backup and he had a partner right here with him, if he could time things right. Take the lead in this partnership and make himself understood.

Dropping Atlas's leash, Cruz crouched low and murmured a command he'd never taught Lyn to use with Atlas. "*Reviere.*"

Atlas sprang forward and streaked around the corner. Cruz darted to the left and around stacked crates, listening as he did. Moving as quickly and safely as possible to circle around, Cruz pied the next corner in order to give himself a chance to bring his weapon to bear and got his eyes on the target as Atlas came around on the other side.

It was the perfect opening and critical moment. Cruz charged forward as the other man began to lift his weapon to take aim on Atlas, oblivious to the danger from behind. Before the man could fire, Cruz threw his left arm around the man's neck in a choke hold and brought up his right arm to throw off the man's aim.

Atlas streaked across the remaining distance and leaped up, taking the man's right arm in his jaws. The man dropped his weapon as the dog's momentum took them all to the ground in a nearly silent struggle. But Cruz's choke hold was tight and in moments the other man's struggles weakened as his air supply was cut off.

A dog like Atlas could exert something close to triple the bite strength of a human. Once the other man began to go slack, it was time to stop the dog before he broke the man's forearm.

"*Los*." Cruz scowled when Atlas didn't release the man. The dog wasn't throwing his head back and forth to rip and tear, but Atlas wasn't letting go either. Cruz stared into Atlas's eyes, refusing to let go of the man between them.

Atlas stared back.

Cruz set his jaw and it wasn't anger but determination that filled him. Drove him. There wasn't time for this. Lyn didn't have time for this. "*Los*."

Something changed in Atlas's stare. The challenge in his eyes flickered out, a decision made, and the big dog released the man.

Laying the poor bastard down on the pavement, Cruz reached into his back pocket and pulled out a few zip ties to bind and some duct tape to cover the man's mouth. Securing any guards as he took them out was better than having them come after him again if they came to. And he didn't plan to kill if he didn't have to.

Picking up Atlas's lead, Cruz straightened and ran his hand along Atlas's flank. *"Braafy."*

Good dog.

With one man down, he needed to move even more quickly. It'd be just him and Atlas. Both Forte and Rojas were holding down the fort back at the kennels—Forte handling the police report and their intruder, Rojas seeing to his daughter as she came home from school. Both would be following to provide backup as soon as he could but it was a toss-up as to which of them could get free first.

He couldn't afford to wait. The situation wasn't optimal but he and Atlas needed to move quickly.

Cruz studied the warehouse and a door tucked away in an alcove set in the side of the building. Security camera was hanging by a hinge and obviously not operational. Could be the best entry point.

He headed for the entrance, pausing to hug the wall and study a large ventilation grate in the same alcove. Cover was rusted almost completely off. The ventilation shaft behind it was big enough to accommodate a full-grown man. But hell, he was heavy. Atlas might be lighter than his German shepherd counterparts but the dog wasn't tiny either. The two of them in a rusted-out metal shaft were not going to get far without making a shit-ton of noise. They were not ninjas.

But he didn't have to pass it by completely. Taking out his pocketknife, he pried the cover the rest of the way off and set it on the ground against the opening to the ventilation shaft.

Then he and Atlas stepped over to the door.

They stayed to one side and listened. Atlas sniffed

along the bottom edge. No sign of danger around or on the other side. No indicators from Atlas that there was either person or improvised explosive device waiting to surprise them.

And Atlas would've scented either.

It took more precious minutes to quietly pick the lock. Not his favorite activity but luckily it was a simple one, old and not particularly secure. This entrance had definitely been overlooked while the hostiles were securing the location.

Once inside, Cruz eased the door closed behind them and immediately took them to one side to crouch under the cover of a set of stairs. He drew in a breath, deliberate and slow. The air was musty, thick with dust and stale. No one had opened any windows or doors on this level for a sufficient length of time to ventilate the place.

What he could see of the warehouse's ground level was covered in more dust. It was a wide open space with random clutter along the outer walls. No places to hide and no places for hostiles to pop out and surprise him.

Atlas turned his nose upward, sniffing, and his big ears swiveled as the big dog studied the ceiling. Cruz strained hard to identify whatever Atlas was hearing in the quiet stillness.

It wasn't complete silence, though. Now that he knew to listen more closely, there was a faint murmur coming from above. Not loud enough to identify voices or what was being said, only enough to recognize the rhythm of conversation.

Up they would go.

Cruz unhooked Atlas's leash. Inside the warehouse with all the crap scattered everywhere, the leash could snag and it'd be best to let Atlas go ahead to react as necessary. In the meantime, letting the big dog loose freed up both of Cruz's hands.

The two of them proceeded out from under the cover of the stairs and along the near edge of the room. Atlas was ranging forward, the way he'd been trained, nose to the ground and weaving back and forth in a snakelike path. Every few steps, the big dog would lift his head to catch any target odors in the air before returning his focus to the floor.

For his part, Cruz scanned the room and listened hard as he followed Atlas. Once they reached the far wall, Cruz put his back to the wall and considered their options for going up to the next level: stairs or a freight elevator.

Thus far, they'd managed not to pause in hallways, doorways, or windows. Riding up in an elevator was asking for attention and unless they both could climb out quickly, it was a kill box. Stairs weren't easy either. In his experience, stairs were where men died.

Cruz approached the foot of the stairs and listened hard, peering up into the darkness. Atlas wasn't any more enthusiastic but both of them could hear the murmurs of conversation more clearly.

Atlas gave a low, eager whine with an upward lilt, his head slightly tilted.

Up was where Lyn was.

A trickle of relief flooded through Cruz. Atlas must've recognized Lyn's voice among the murmurs. The eagerness would only be for her. She was still alive and able to talk then. Which meant she was conscious. Hopefully, she wasn't hurt.

Hang on, Lyn. We're on our way.

They were halfway up the stairs when Atlas froze again, his posture tense. A low, almost inaudible growl rumbled in the big dog's chest. Another guard approaching.

For the second time, Cruz gave Atlas the command to search out a human target.

* * *

"I'm guessing you're not going to share the full scope of your nefarious plans with me." Actually, she was torn between wanting to know what could possibly have possessed her stepfather and being too disgusted with his involvement to listen.

He shook his head. "The more you know, the less likely it'll be possible to convince my business partner to let you move on with your life."

"Promises to forget everything I've seen so far aren't believable either, huh?" Rolling her eyes might be too much attitude.

Talking was good. Drawing things out. Buying time. And well, this was probably the longest conversation she'd ever had with her stepfather.

Her stepfather sighed. At least that was familiar. "Don't insult either of us by playing stupid. Sarcasm will only shorten what patience I have."

Zuccolin snorted.

Jones slanted an irritated look at the other soldier. "Isn't it about time for you to check in with the rest of your team, Sergeant?"

Zuccolin stiffened but walked away, his footsteps

striking the floor in measured cadence. Only marginally comparable to a toddler sulking and stomping his way out of the room.

"America's finest?" She raised her eyebrow at her stepfather.

No. She hadn't caught the faintest twitch at the corner of his mouth. Had she? Nah. "All this for a choppy video hidden on a dog?"

"The problem with any shred of evidence is that it is still evidence." Her stepfather strode over to a window and gazed out. "However, the canine is not the only reason we are here or even the primary objective. I placed what should have been sufficient resources on surveillance in order to ensure the dog would present no threat to our plans."

"Sufficient might not be the correct term." She bit her lip.

He turned and glared at her. "Over the years, you have made antagonizing me an art form. I assure you, it's not as effective a tactic as you might believe."

"Force of habit." Keeping her responses shorter might be wise but she was running out of conversational cues.

He huffed. Then he continued to talk, surprisingly. "I've had interviews with several local candidates. There's a land-bound military ship just over the bridge in New Jersey used as a training and testing facility. Many IT contractors with appropriate security clearances have gained relevant communications experience there but are dissatisfied with the temporary nature of their contract work. They're looking for more exciting projects with better pay. Not a single one of them displayed the nimble intelligence you exercise just to deliver a witty comeback."

A compliment. Sort of. "I'm guessing social interaction wasn't exactly a part of any of their skill sets either."

Her stepfather tipped his head to one side, considering. "Enough to communicate in a professional capacity, but you make a valid point. Cultural fit isn't a high priority in our search but perhaps it should be. The teams we're assembling will be isolated on occasion."

"And you have to be able to trust the men who are supposed to have your back." David had taught her that.

Jones frowned.

Oh, had she said that last bit out loud? Maybe. Though Captain Jones had always seemed to read her mind as a teenager. She'd like to think her adult mind was less transparent but around him, the temptation to succumb to petty immaturity was about as irresistible as a chocolate cupcake with fudge frosting and salted caramel.

"Building the right teams takes patience and time." Her stepfather clasped his hands behind his back. "Sometimes you need to make do with what's available and cherry pick when opportunity arises."

Whatever he was getting at, they'd gone so far into the abstract she was wondering if maybe she had a concussion because she wasn't tracking anymore.

A shout cut through her sluggish thoughts. A dog's growl followed, loud and deep. It sounded familiar and she was hoping she wasn't going crazy.

Atlas.

Hope shot through her—or adrenaline—she'd take either. She continued to wiggle in her duct tape bindings while her stepfather and the one remaining soldier focused their attention on the approaching chaos.

Sergeant Zuccolin was backpedaling, crossing past the doorway and back out of view in the hallway. A black and tan blur streaked past and a shot rang out.

A dog yelped in pain.

"No!" she screamed, jerking in her chair and tipping over. Her shoulder crashed into the floor. Lifting her head, she craned her neck to see the doorway. "Atlas! Atlas?"

CHAPTER TWENTY-FOUR

Cruz advanced through the doorway, his handgun at the ready, focusing on the armed threat and relying on his peripherals to catch any other threats in the room. Farthest from the ideal situation, but based on conversation he'd identified Lyn and someone she knew. She was smart to keep up the conversation and distract her captors. Her discussion had covered the majority of their approach and the exchange let him get a basic idea of location, at least for the two speakers.

Only the asshole, Zuccolin, had the timing to encounter them when there'd been no cover. Only choice had been to engage without the advantage of surprise or any chance of stealth. Atlas had stayed true to his training and taken point.

But Cruz couldn't think about that now. The primary objective was Lyn. Locate. Extract.

He'd worry about the rest after.

The solider who'd accompanied Zuccolin was drawing his weapon.

"*Stop* moving," Cruz growled. He immediately stepped to one side of the door, away from the hinges, to have his back to the near wall plus a foot or two of extra buffer space. There were a few crates in case he needed to dive for cover. "You're going to want to get the safety back on that and put it on the ground. Now."

A procedure they were both familiar with and in the other soldier's place, Cruz would be fighting a nasty internal battle. But the other soldier valued his life and complied quickly.

Lyn was tied to a chair overturned in the middle of the room, and to the other side of her had to be the person he'd heard her talking with earlier. An older man and an officer, with his hands out to his sides. No immediate threat.

Still, Cruz was only one man and he had two potential hostiles in the room with a completely immobilized Lyn.

"Lyn?" He kept his gaze on the nameless soldier with the officer at the edge of his periphery.

"Hi."

Relief flooded through him and he blinked quickly to keep his sight clear. "Good to hear your voice."

"I'm pretty happy to see you, too." Her words were wobbly but she was talking and making a good attempt at upbeat.

"Can you get up on your own?"

There was a creak as she wiggled on her side. "No."

Her frustration was much better than the possible alternatives. If she'd been hysterical or panicking, or even devoid of hope, he might not be able to get them moving. But his girl had fight in her and he could work with that.

He skirted the room, keeping the wall to his back and getting closer to her. "Hang out for another second."

The nameless soldier's eyes gave away his intent. Cruz charged and crashed into the man shoulder to shoulder as the other man tried to reach down for his gun. The other man stumbled and Cruz followed through with a knee to the head. His opponent fell to the floor unconscious.

Cruz let his momentum carry him forward and gathered his feet under him for a smooth controlled turn, expecting the old man to have taken advantage of his back being turned.

"Son, why didn't you just shoot him?"

Cruz trained his handgun on the officer, the last man standing.

The officer held his hands up, still empty. "Well, don't start shooting now."

"Who are you?"

"Captain Jones…"

"Her father…"

Both the officer and Lyn spoke at the same time.

Well, shit.

"My *step*-father," Lyn clarified. "Which doesn't matter considering the circumstances."

"You are not in a position to fully understand the current situation." The other man's voice definitely sounded patronizing in a familiar way.

"Trust me, I'd be very happy to survey things from a higher viewpoint. All I've got now without craning my neck is a bunch of shoes and an unconscious man. At least, I think he's unconscious. Hard to tell from here." For her part, she obviously wasn't letting on whether her stepfather was a threat or not.

When in doubt, everyone is a threat. Cruz did not lower his weapon.

Despite his exchange with Lyn, her stepfather was watching Cruz.

Cruz tipped his head in her direction. "Help her up."

Her stepfather complied with slow, deliberate movements. The man could've yanked her chair up or followed the order in a number of ways that could hurt her. It was a calculated risk to let the man touch her at all.

But Cruz was going on a hunch.

Her stepfather cradled her head as he helped set her upright and broke the duct tape binding her to the chair. Odd gentleness for a kidnapper.

"She wasn't supposed to end up here." Her stepfather stepped away from her again to a safe distance. "Only the canine was supposed to have been retrieved."

"Is Atlas hurt badly?" Lyn was yanking off the remainder of the duct tape and rubbing her arms. It'd probably been tight enough to cut off some circulation.

Cruz ignored her question. "And what were you going to do once she showed up?"

Captain Jones pressed his lips together. "To be honest, I was weighing my options. However, you arrived. All the others are . . . unconscious?"

"Indisposed." Cruz had managed to take out any of the other guards with Atlas's help, leaving them zip tied and unconscious.

"How many men?"

Interesting question. Still, Cruz had a feeling Lyn's

stepfather was a man of many layers. Time to give him the chance to peel back a few. "One outside. Two at the top of the stairs. The sergeant outside the door and our friend here."

A sharp bark and a growl had Cruz down on one knee, turning his weapon to the door. A man stumbled through the doorframe with seventy-five pounds of Belgian Malinois on his back.

Cruz charged forward a second time, engaging with the newcomer. The other man had no chance and was shortly on the floor, unconscious.

"Atlas!" Lyn sounded so happy. God, he was glad she could still be happy.

Atlas stood panting, his left shoulder laid open by a bullet graze and trickling blood down his foreleg. But the big dog was looking at Cruz, waiting to be released from his last command given out in the hallway. *Bewaken*. Guard.

Cruz jerked his head in Lyn's direction. "Okay."

Atlas broke his stance immediately and bounded over to Lyn, licking tears off her face. She flinched and Atlas whined softly.

Cruz got a good look at the side of her face and anger burned through him until the edges of his peripheral vision started to darken. There was a horribly spectacular bruise developing across her cheekbone up to her temple. It had to be painful if even Atlas's gentle touch hurt her.

"I'll be making sure the man who hit her will never do it again," Captain Jones said quietly, calm, cold. Very cold.

"You want to tell us what you're doing here, Captain?" Cruz asked. He still hadn't holstered his weapon. The captain hadn't asked him to, either. That made Cruz more certain there was a lot more going on here.

Captain Jones nodded. "I'll be making a phone call shortly to have them taken into custody. The two of you should leave."

"Not the question I asked."

"As I said to Lyn earlier, the less you know, the better," Captain Jones countered.

Cruz shook his head.

The two of them glared at each other.

Captain Jones sighed. "This is a covert investigation. I became aware of this group a short while ago when I was approached with the opportunity to join as a business partner. However, my concern was the recruitment plan. Several soldiers seemed to be a part of the planning process under duress."

"You could say that." Cruz didn't bother keeping the growl out of his voice. He wasn't active duty anymore; insubordination wasn't an issue.

"Your friend, Calhoun, had put in for a transfer. It was denied. When he died and his dog was sent back here, I was asked to intercept. Instead, I made sure the dog got to where Calhoun wanted him to go." Captain Jones shrugged. "It's easier to flush out the true intents of people if you let them act on their plans for a certain amount of time. I sent Lyn so I'd know when you were getting too involved. I've needed time to identify all the people involved, not just those most directly visible. If you forced my partner to move too quickly, it would have been unfortunate."

"For you?" Lyn was on her knees, her arms wrapped

loosely around Atlas's shoulders. Her bravado was good but she needed the comfort of Atlas's strength to hold on to for the moment.

Cruz desperately wanted to go to her, hold her, and check every inch of her for any other hurt.

"Organizations like this are like patches of weeds." Captain Jones's voice took on a patronizing tone. The man really let Lyn get under his skin. "It takes time to determine how far the roots have spread and determine the best way to cut them out. Otherwise, they just pop back up someplace else. When I conduct an investigation of this magnitude, I don't just pull up the visible weeds. I root up every runner and eliminate the issue."

Bastards like these people would always be around. Cruz didn't envy the Captain a job like that.

"I still need to learn more about my...business partner and his potential investors." Captain Jones took out his phone.

"You mean you're still working with this man, whoever he is." Lyn didn't bother to hide her disgust.

"His business plan has serious ethical issues." Captain Jones raised an eyebrow at her. "Currently, there's no proof tying him to all of this besides my word. The best I would be able to manage with any accusation at this time would be a dishonorable discharge. He'd still be free to move forward with his plans, albeit under a certain amount of scrutiny from the US government. That, however, is insufficient."

"There are people being hurt—dying—while you gather your evidence to make sure this guy has no loopholes to slither through." Cruz thought about Calhoun.

A sad look flashed past Captain Jones's eyes and was

gone. "Some are surviving because of my intervention as well. The video your dog had implicates many men who only agreed under duress. It would be unfortunate to catch them in the same net we use to snare my business partner."

Harris had a family. How many others did? How many wives, kids, relatives would be hurt if men like Harris were caught up in legal action?

"I see what you mean." Cruz paused, then tossed a bit of information out. "We have a mutual acquaintance, Evans. He's got a copy of the highlights right now. Probably plans to bring it back to you or your partner in exchange for bailing him out."

Captain Jones nodded. "His ability to identify the entire group here puts this portion of the operation at risk. A good reason to cut losses here and leave."

Cruz had been planning to give Evans enough rope to hang himself. This wasn't exactly what he'd had in mind, but it'd do. The investigation Captain Jones was conducting was serious business, every bit as dangerous as the situations Calhoun and the other men were facing. And then some. If Jones's business partner suspected him, Lyn's stepfather was a dead man.

Captain Jones regarded Cruz with a steady gaze. Cruz gave the man a nod in grudging admiration. This undertaking wasn't easy. And he might never be sure he had every person involved.

"Take her out of here, Mr. Cruz. Do a better job of keeping her safe." Captain Jones's voice cracked. "I will continue my mission. It won't be much longer and then the men who didn't want to be part of this in the first place will be able to breathe. You've done me a favor with the group here. It will be fairly easy to see to it these men face charges while I go back to my business partner and tell him how unfortunate it was that they were incompetent enough to be compromised."

Cruz nodded. What else was there to say? He needed to get Lyn safely out of here and then he could absorb the new information.

"Lyn knows nothing. I'm sure my business partner will keep an eye on her and agree. Especially when he's told the asset was killed here."

"You are not touching Atlas." Lyn shot to her feet.

"Sergeant Zuccolin shot the dog dead. We both saw it." Captain Jones stared at Cruz.

Cruz nodded. "I run a kennel. I could've brought more than one dog."

The other man nodded.

Lyn held her peace.

It would be better for all of them if no one was looking for Atlas anymore. And now that Atlas had chosen his handlers, easier for him, too.

"Take the dog with you." Captain Jones's tone was definitely gentler. "He's seen enough and based on your reports, it's likely his rehabilitation will require further work. It would be best for everyone if he disappeared."

Lyn bit her lip, obviously caught without words.

Well, that was a first.

Captain Jones looked at Cruz. "My condolences for the loss of your friend. This is the best I can offer you in his memory, for now."

It would have to be enough.

CHAPTER TWENTY-FIVE

Minor concussion, if that. Some bad bruising." Forte packed up his med kit. "Pretty sure you'll be all right with some real rest. You sure you two don't want to go to the emergency room?"

Cruz looked at Lyn, who shook her head.

"I just want to stay here." Lyn had curled up on the couch with Atlas, sitting as close as the big dog could manage on the floor.

"Whatever you need." Cruz turned to Forte. "Thanks, man."

"Okay, but if she develops a headache or nausea or starts acting odd at all, she really does need to see a doctor. Call up to the main house if you need anything." Forte left.

Cruz sighed. "Are you sure you don't want to go to the emergency room? Forte is EMT certified but he's not a doctor."

Lyn shook her head slowly. She was in obvious discomfort and the bruise on the side of her face was blooming into an even more impressive sight as the hours went by. Anger burned Cruz every time he looked at her face.

It was a good thing the man who'd hit her would be in prison.

"It feels a hundred percent better just being here." She gave him a smile. "And no headache, just some throbbing when I turn my head too fast."

"Then quit shaking your head." He gave her a kiss to take the sting away from his retort. She was a trooper, no doubt about it. "You hungry at all?"

She wrinkled her nose.

"I'm not saying I'm going to put a full cheesesteak in front of you piled with fried mushrooms and onions." David chuckled. He could go for one of those himself, though. "I was thinking maybe I'd exercise my actual cooking skills and make you a cup of soup."

She stared at him and then blinked slowly. "You mean put powder into a mug and add hot water."

The idea of grilling for her, though—of putting a whole meal he'd made in front of her—that bore some consideration. He'd never thought it'd be worth the effort before, but for her it'd be more than fun. It'd be fantastic.

He grinned. Best to start simple and try not to burn anything on the property to ash. "Boiling water is cooking 101. We all learn to do it."

She huffed out a laugh. "I can't argue with that and some soup does sound pretty good. But do we have any of it here?"

Simple question but there was a tremor beneath her

words. She wasn't quite ready to be left alone yet. Even with Atlas lying on his very own dog bed here in the main living room, she wasn't ready.

Totally reasonable and he didn't plan to let her out of his sight. In addition to her comfort, he'd been looking her over from head to toe every few minutes, reassuring himself she was hale and whole and safely with him. "I'll call and see if Forte can find it in the kitchen. I planned to ask him to include me in the late night order for cheesesteaks anyway."

The look she gave him was skeptical. "You could've told him that before he left."

He shrugged. "I wasn't sure what you were eating yet."

She swatted him on the shoulder. It did his heart good to get her feisty.

It took less than a minute to text Forte with what he wanted.

"I thought you were going to call." Lyn crawled over from her nest in the pillows and blankets on the couch.

He gathered her into his lap while he waited for Forte to respond. "Sometimes I call up to the main house, but generally I don't like to blow up someone's phone with ringing. Heck, when we need to get Rojas late at night we always text anyway because it's past Boom's bedtime. Mostly, it's Forte who calls everyone."

"Hmm." She snuggled against him.

He wrapped his arms around her and finally let himself relax. This. This kind of time spent with her meant so much and he'd almost lost her. And he was possibly going to ruin it by sending her away anyway. But she had to go; she had her life, the one she'd built for herself.

After all that'd happened, she'd be wanting to get back to it and he didn't know if there would be room for him once she took up her old life again.

Chickenshit that he was, he couldn't make himself ask her.

"Penny for your thoughts."

He realized she'd been watching him as he'd run around in circles in his own head.

"You scared me today." First thing he could think to say. And it was the truth, too, because looking at her, all he could do was hold her closer.

She bit her lip. "I hurt you first, then we both ended up scared out of our minds." She paused, swallowed. "I'm sorry."

At some point in the past, it might have bothered him for someone to read him so well, to have seen far enough into him to the vulnerability of fear. But this was Lyn.

He shook his head. "No apologies. You have a good head on your shoulders and you did so many things right today."

"Hello? I got myself kidnapped and dented in the face."

He tightened his jaw and relaxed it deliberately. Good thing Zuccolin had been taken into custody and would be held accountable for what he'd done to her. Her stepfather had assured them both that all of the men involved, including her two initial attackers and Evans, had been arrested by military police and would be awaiting court-martial. Jones's mysterious business partner had withdrawn his considerable influence so there would be no easy breaks for those men.

Leaning close, he pressed his lips gently to her good temple. "You foiled the bad guys and saved Atlas."

"So he could go get you to come save me." A pause, then her tone turned bitter. "As far as my stepfather is concerned, I am still the clumsy idiot blundering around messing up his well-laid plans."

All of the history between her and her stepfather was not going to be healed in one day. "I'm glad he was doing the right thing back there. At first, I was thinking the worst."

She let out a slow breath. "So was I."

Her shoulders slumped with what had to be guilt and she dipped her chin low until it almost rested on her chest.

"Hey." Cruz freed up one of his hands to slip a finger under her chin and tip her face up so he could see her expressions. "You know the truth now and you can act accordingly."

"It's not like I can call him up and say, 'Sorry for almost screwing up your sting operation.' I think that'd expose him in all sorts of bad ways." She rolled her eyes.

Cruz couldn't help a grin at her sarcastic tone. "I'm sure he's glad you are intelligent and perceptive enough to know that's not the way to go."

It was part of the reason why she attracted him. Things made sense to her without effort or arduous explanation or fighting. She got it. All of it. Or at least as much as he'd managed to share with her so far. It could take a lifetime to open up all there was for her to see.

"So what then? I'm not even sure. There'll be future military contracts based on what he said. And we'll have to see how his office manages the press with Atlas disappearing, go along with it. Until then, it's business as usual, I guess?" There were a couple of questions left unspoken as she waited for his response.

He kissed her, because he didn't want to hold off on the things they both enjoyed and because he wasn't sure how she'd feel after he gave her his response. Tasting her, exploring her, enjoying the play of their tongues, he savored every moment. Her hands came up around his face and tangled in his hair.

He wanted this. Working with her, talking, maybe arguing a little, and definitely playing. Filling his days with a mix of these things would be more than he'd ever hoped for in terms of happiness. Fulfillment. All those words he'd taken out of his expectations for himself somewhere in the middle of his time in service.

But if you love something...

* * *

Lyn almost forgot her own question in the midst of their kissing. His hands had wandered too, sliding down her thigh to cup her behind and squeeze. She was wondering if she could coax him into some very gentle intercourse maybe, since she only had a mild concussion.

It'd take her mind off her aches and pains. Medicinal. Really.

But when he drew back, his expression changed from the soft look he only wore for her to a more serious, intense expression.

He hadn't gone neutral, hadn't compartmentalized. This was new.

"Here's the thing." He ran his hand through her hair

and she closed her eyes, enjoying the feel. She relaxed with his touch, listening to the timbre of his voice. As long as it stayed warm like this, didn't go flat or distant, it'd be okay. "Your life has been turned upside down since day one of you getting here. If we think back on it, a whole lot has happened in almost no time."

She opened her eyes, sought his gaze. "It happened, we happened."

Fear pricked at her despite her earlier thoughts. What was he trying to say?

He nodded and kissed her forehead. "We did. I really like us as a thing and I want us to last."

"Good." She settled, relaxing back into his embrace. *Us.* She liked the sound of it.

But he leaned back and tapped her nose with a fingertip. "You might have a different perspective once all the excitement settles down, though. Believe it or not, it gets boring around here. The whole reason Forte chose this location was for the peace and quiet."

Something she had yet to experience. But the location was tucked away and if you didn't drive twenty minutes in either direction on the main road, you wouldn't realize how close it was to the rest of the world.

"With ready access to two major metropolises and several major airports," she countered. "From what I understand, you all took advantage of the city nightlife on a pretty regular basis. This is not exactly a remote small town hidden away in the middle of nowhere and you get a fair amount of business-related traffic coming on site."

Not to mention any number of canine personalities running rampant. When they'd arrived back on site, the three new GSDs had been wandering loose from their kennels. Apparently their intellects combined resulted in Houdini-level escape skills. Alex had been about to rip his hair out getting them back on leads. Their recall was good but not 100 percent, so it'd taken a little effort on Alex's part to get them back into their kennels.

"Point." He gave her a wry grin. "What I'm trying to say is you've been basing all your impressions so far on some high-stress experiences."

She opened her mouth to argue, but he kissed her. And for a minute—okay, maybe several—she was lost. But she pulled herself together as soon as he let her up for air. "Trying to distract me is futile."

He raised an eyebrow. "I like a challenge."

She opened her mouth, closed it, then swatted his shoulder. He only grinned.

"I want you to stay with me, Evelyn Jones," he whispered. "Here, with me. But I want you to leave first. Get some distance and clear your head. Process all the things that happened to you. You might decide you want to leave it all far away. I will understand, no matter what you decide. But I want you to take the time."

Her breath left her and it took a long second for her to pull together her first thought. "You're asking me to go away again."

Her heart twisted in agony at the thought. She struggled to listen as he continued.

"This isn't exactly the same. Before I was trying to protect you, and taking away your work was the wrong thing to do." His arms tightened around her briefly before easing up enough for her to get up out of his lap if she wanted. But he continued, "This, I want for you because what happened to you isn't easy. You were attacked, shot at, kidnapped, and beaten. Not any one of those things is something you'll process overnight. Not tomorrow. Not a week from now. Believe me. And staying here might let you hide from it more than deal with it. A big part of your career has you traveling places by yourself."

Biting her lip, she held her initial retort. He'd been through these things, seen friends go through them. The look in his eyes, the earnest sincerity in his voice, the way he held her against him spoke of how much he cared about her.

"If you give life a chance to get back on track, you'll have perspective. See clearly. And then when you decide what you want, we'll both know it's because it's the right thing for you." He nuzzled her ear. "And you'd be welcome back here if that's what you want. I'll stay by you and work with you through every one of your nightmares. But you'll at least have had a chance to think it all through. Your choice."

Hers. He always made sure to let her know it was her choice. And it meant everything. The biggest difference between him and her stepfather was the way David respected her right to choose. The confidence he had in her ability to make the right decision.

"Don't say anything now." He tucked her head under his chin. "I want you to take your time, go out on a couple of client trips, get back into the rhythm of your career, and then decide. Is that fair?"

Lyn stared at him as her temper simmered. "No."

He blinked, stilled.

Oh, everything he said made sense, especially the consideration of her traveling alone. She'd already had issues glancing out the windows of the cabin into the falling darkness. Reflections on the windowpanes startled her, like strangers staring in for the first few moments before she really looked at what was there. Tonight was not going to be an easy night and she was glad to have the secure warmth of his arms around her with Atlas nearby.

That was her point, though. She didn't need time alone or distance from him to process.

"I don't leave things unfinished." Rising out of his embrace momentarily, she turned and straddled his lap. Resting her hands on his chest, she looked deep into his gaze.

He waited, silent. Listening.

Listening was something her stepfather had never done. At least, it'd never felt like he had. But David always did. He'd taken the time to hear her out every time she'd had something to say while they worked together. And here he was now.

"You're right about there being a lot of things to process. But"—she tipped her head to the side—"I don't need solitude to think straight or see my way clearly and I definitely don't need to go back to my old life to figure out how I want to live my days. If there's one thing I learned from you here, it's that you can't ever go back and being too stuck in the past doesn't work."

A muscle twitched along the side of his jaw. She'd hit a nerve. But that was okay. She leaned forward, her hands flat against his chest, and kissed the spot on his jaw. When she straightened, his lips had softened from the hard line and he settled his hands on her hips.

"I was so caught up in proving to my stepfather that

I could be out on my own, I didn't even realize I'd established myself already. I was just...running, charging forward to prove a point." She gave him a smile and warmth spread through her chest when he smiled in return. "Working with you and Atlas gave me perspective. And maybe I needed some chaos to knock me off my train tracks and really think about what I'm doing, where I'm headed."

She paused and he held his peace, patient. It was never a race to get a word in edgewise with him and for that, she was grateful.

He gave her so many things. Time, consideration, caring.

"What happened is going to give me issues for a good while." She smoothed her hands over his chest, taking comfort from the hard muscles under her palms. "But whatever steps I'm going to take toward recovering from this won't be backward to resuming my old life. I'm moving forward and I want to do that with you."

She held her breath.

His hands tightened on her hips. "You sure?"

"I love you, David Cruz." She kept her gaze steady on his. "And you remember I was first to say it."

He laughed. "I'd have said it first if you needed me to."

"Well, now's a good time." Because she did need to hear it.

He sat up straighter and kissed her first, his mouth sliding over hers in a dizzying, intense kiss. Heat seared through her and she clutched at his shoulders as his arms tightened around her waist, pulling her in snug against him. And still he kissed her, drowning them until they were both breathless. "I love you, Evelyn Jones. Since

I don't even know when. I want you in my life and I'll wait forever if you need me to."

She pressed her forehead to his and closed her eyes. "No more waiting. I'm done waiting for my choices to feel like mine."

His arms tightened around her in a fierce hug, then loosened enough to relax again. "So what's next, Miss Jones?"

His teasing tone made her smile wider. Wow, had she ever been this happy? It bubbled up inside her and she barely knew what to do with it all. "Well, we've got some administrative stuff to work through here with wrapping up the contract paperwork and submitting any reports they'll need."

He nodded, running his hands up and down her thighs. There was a naughty gleam in his eyes and she narrowed hers as she put in the extra effort to remember what she was saying.

"And you were right about my having other clients. I've got people who need me to work with them and their dogs."

Atlas barked.

She glanced over at him, sitting close, his tail sweeping the floor in a happy wag. Reaching over, she gave him an affectionate scratch behind one ear.

"I think he's going to have to accept it's a part of your job." David chuckled. "He's got to learn to share you."

"Mmm." She looked back to David. "I'll still be traveling some and next time I leave, there should be texts. Texts from you, pictures of Atlas, maybe we should create accounts on a couple of social media apps. Whatever it takes to feel connected."

"But you could use this as a home base." He made the offer quietly.

Her words caught in her throat for a moment and she bit her lip as she nodded. It seemed impossible in such a short time, but this cabin and Hope's Crossing Kennels had come to feel like a home in ways her actual apartment way back on the West Coast never did.

He grinned. "I'm on board with that. Maybe we'll travel together, too, go to a few training conferences together and learn some new techniques."

Or he could kiss her some more and remind her of a few of his techniques. She lost time in his kisses, enjoying the taste of him and teasing him back in turn with nips at his lower lip.

Happy. She was so happy with him.

She opened her eyes, met his gaze. He wasn't her stepfather. Hell, her stepfather wasn't even who she'd thought he was. David was everything she hadn't even known she needed and now that she was back in his arms, she didn't intend to give him up.

Lyn took a deep breath. This was it. And if she could let go of everything she believed she knew, quit comparing, she wouldn't mess this up. "No matter where my job takes me, I think I could find my way back here. This is home." She met David's gaze, steady, loving. "*You* are home."

David folded her in close against his chest. "I'll be here for you. Count on it."

Look for more in the True Heroes series:

Ultimate Courage
Absolute Trust
Total Bravery
Fierce Justice
Forever Strong

ABOUT THE AUTHOR

Piper J. Drake is a bestselling author of romantic suspense and edgy contemporary romance, a frequent flyer, and day job road warrior. She is often distracted by dogs, cupcakes, and random shenanigans.

Play Find the Piper around the internet for insight into her frequent travels and inspiration for her stories.

You can learn more at:
PiperJDrake.com
Facebook.com/AuthorPiperJDrake
Twitter @PiperJDrake
Instagram @PiperJDrake
YouTube.com/PiperJDrake